Praise for Thomas Olde Heuvelt's *HEX*

The Lineup: 13 Scariest Books of 2016
B&N Editor's Pick: Best Horror Books of 2016

"Creepy and gripping and original, sure to be one of the top horror novels of 2016."
—George R. R. Martin

"Thomas is a great writer, the next genre superstar."   —Paul Cornell

"Reminiscent of vintage Stephen King, and I can think of no higher praise. Chilling, moving, and . . . profound."   —John Connolly

"Sets ancient magic against contemporary technology to create a kind of dark fairy tale that seems ultimately believable in today's world. A terrific debut novel."   —Jeffrey Ford

"A thoughtful horror story, and one that is all the more chilling for its uncompromising view of humanity."   —Robin Hobb

"Takes the horror/thriller genre to a whole new level. It's deeply unsettling, wholly original, brilliantly written, and contains scenes that will haunt you for a long time to come. I dare you to read it."
—Sarah Lotz

"A treat for all fans of dark fiction . . . A modern spin on the witch's curse story that forces us to take a closer look at ourselves. Who is really evil after all? It may not be who you think. This is just the beginning and I can't wait to read his next one."   —Ann VanderMeer

"Hidden tensions and human weakness trigger a witch hunt that boils over into persecution, scapegoating, and a shocking denouement. A powerfully spooky piece of writing."   —*Financial Times*

HEX

THOMAS OLDE HEUVELT

TRANSLATED BY
NANCY FOREST-FLIER

TOR

A TOM DOHERTY ASSOCIATES BOOK
NEW YORK

HEX

Copyright © 2013 by Thomas Olde Heuvelt

English translation copyright © 2016 by Nancy Forest-Flier

The publisher gratefully acknowledges the support of the Dutch Foundation for Literature.

Nederlands
letterenfonds
dutch foundation
for literature

A Tor Book
Published by Tom Doherty Associates
175 Fifth Avenue
New York, NY 10010

www.tor-forge.com

Tor® is a registered trademark of Macmillan Publishing Group, LLC.

The Library of Congress has cataloged the hardcover as follows:

Olde Heuvelt, Thomas, 1983– author.
    Hex / Thomas Olde Heuvelt ; translated by Nancy Forest-Flier.—1st U.S. ed.
        p. cm.
    "A Tom Doherty Associates book."
    ISBN 978-0-7653-7880-4 (hardcover)
    ISBN 978-1-4668-6458-0 (e-book)
1. Haunted places—Fiction. 2. Witches—Fiction. 3. Dutch fiction—Translations into English.
4. Black Rock Forest (N.Y.)—Fiction. I. Title. II. Forest-Flier, Nancy, translator.
    PT5882.25.L38 H4913 2016
    839.317—dc23

                                                                    2016287124

ISBN 978-0-7653-7881-1 (trade paperback)

Our books may be purchased in bulk for promotional, educational, or business use. Please contact your local bookseller or the Macmillan Corporate and Premium Sales Department at 1-800-221-7945, extension 5442, or by e-mail at MacmillanSpecialMarkets@macmillan.com.

Originally published in the Netherlands by Luitingh-Sijthoff

First U.S. Edition: April 2016
First U.S. Trade Paperback Edition: April 2017

Printed in the United States of America

0   9   8   7   6   5   4   3   2   1

To Jacques Post,
my literary shaman

PART 1

-|-|-•-|-|-|-•-|-•-|-|-|-|-|-|-|-

2DAY? #stoning

ONE

STEVE GRANT ROUNDED the corner of the parking lot behind
Black Spring Market & Deli just in time to see Katherine van Wyler
get run over by an antique Dutch barrel organ. For a minute he thought
it was an optical illusion, because instead of being thrown back onto the
street the woman melted into the wooden curlicues, feathered angel
wings, and chrome-colored organ pipes. It was Marty Keller who
pushed the organ backward by its trailer hitch and, following Lucy
Everett's instructions, brought it to a halt. Although there wasn't a bump
to be heard or a trickle of blood to be seen when Katherine was struck,
people began rushing in from all sides with the urgency that townsfolk
always seem to exhibit when an accident occurs. Yet no one dropped
their shopping bag to help her up . . . for if there was one thing the
residents of Black Spring valued more highly than urgency, it was a
cautious insistence on never getting too involved in Katherine's affairs.

"Not too close!" Marty shouted, stretching out his hand toward a
little girl who had been approaching with faltering steps, drawn not by
the bizarre accident but by the magnificence of the colossal machine.
At once Steve realized that it hadn't been an accident at all. In the
shadow beneath the barrel organ he saw two grubby feet and the
mud-stained hem of Katherine's dress. He smiled indulgently: So it
was an illusion. Two seconds later, the strains of the "Radetzky March"
blared across the parking lot.

He slowed his pace, tired but quite satisfied with himself, almost at
the end of his big circuit: fifteen miles along the edge of Bear Mountain
State Park to Fort Montgomery and right up along the Hudson to West

Point Military Academy—which folks around here called The Point—where he veered off toward home. Back into the forest, the hills. It made him feel good, not only because running was the ideal way to rid his body of the tension it accumulated after a long day of teaching at New York Med in Valhalla. It was mainly the delightful autumn breeze *outside* Black Spring that put him in such an excellent mood, swirling through his lungs and carrying the smell of his sweat to more westerly regions. It was all psychological, of course. There was nothing wrong with the air in Black Spring . . . at least, nothing that could be proven by analysis.

The music had lured the cook at Ruby's Ribs to come out from behind his grill. Joining the other spectators, he gazed suspiciously at the barrel organ. Steve walked around them, wiping his forehead dry with his arm. When he saw that the beautifully lacquered side of the organ was actually a swinging door, and that the door was ajar, he could no longer suppress a smile. The organ was completely hollow inside, all the way to the axle. Katherine was standing motionless in the dark as Lucy shut the door and hid her from view. Now the organ was an organ again. And boy, did it play.

"So," he said, still panting, his hands high on his hips. "Mulder and Scully been lining the coffers again?"

Marty walked up to him and grinned. "Says you. You know how much those fuckers cost? And I'm telling you, they're pinching pennies till they holler." He jerked his head at the barrel organ. "It's a total fake. A replica of the organ from the Old Dutch Museum in Peekskill. Pretty good, huh? It's just an ordinary trailer underneath."

Steve was impressed. Now that he had a better look, he could see that, sure enough, the façade was nothing but a hodgepodge of mawkish porcelain figures and carelessly glued geegaws—and badly painted, too. The organ pipes weren't even real chrome, but gold-lacquered PVC. Even the "Radetzky March" fell flat: an illusion, without the delightful sighing of the valves or the slapping of the perforated music cards that you would expect from an instrument of yesteryear.

Marty read his mind and said, "An iPod with a big-ass speaker. Pick the wrong playlist and you get heavy metal."

"Sounds like one of Grim's ideas," Steve laughed.

"Uh-huh."

"I thought the whole idea was to divert attention *away* from her?"

Marty shrugged. "You know the master's style."

"It's for public events," Lucy said. "For the fair, or during the festival if there are lots of Outsiders."

"Well, good luck." Steve grinned, getting ready to continue on his way. "Maybe you'll collect some money while you're at it."

He took it easy on the last mile, heading home down Deep Hollow Road. As soon as he was beyond earshot he stopped thinking about the woman in the dark, the woman in the belly of the barrel organ, though the "Radetzky March" kept playing in his head to the rhythm of his footsteps.

-+-|-|-|-

AFTER A SHOWER, Steve went downstairs and found Jocelyn at the dining room table. She shut her laptop. With the subtle smile on her lips that he had fallen in love with twenty-three years before and that she'd probably have until the day she died, despite growing wrinkles and bags under her eyes (forty-plus pockets, she called them), she said, "There, enough time for my boyfriends. Now it's my husband's turn."

Steve grinned. "What was his name again? Rafael?"

"Yup. And Roger. I ditched Novak." She stood up and slid her arms around his waist. "How was your day?"

"Exhausting. Five straight hours of lectures with one twenty-minute break. I'm going to ask Ulmann to change my grid, or mount a battery behind the stand."

"You're pathetic," she said, kissing him on the mouth. "I ought to warn you that we have a voyeur, Mr. Eager Beaver."

Steve drew back and raised his eyebrows.

"Gramma," she said.

"Gramma?"

Pulling him closer, she turned around and nodded over her shoulder. Steve followed her glance through the open French doors and into the living room. Sure enough, standing in the odd corner between the couch and the fireplace, right next to the stereo—Jocelyn always called it her Limbo because she couldn't figure out what to do with it—was a small, shrunken woman, skinny as a rail and utterly motionless. She looked like something that didn't belong in the clear golden light of the afternoon: dark, dirty, nocturnal. Jocelyn had hung an old dishcloth over her head so you couldn't see her face.

"Gramma," said Steve meditatively. Then he started to laugh. He couldn't help it: With that dishcloth, she made an awkward, ridiculous spectacle.

Jocelyn blushed. "You know I get all creeped out when she looks at us that way. I know she's blind, but sometimes I get the feeling it doesn't make any difference."

"How long has she been standing there? Because I just saw her in town."

"Less than twenty minutes. She showed up just before you came home."

"Go figure. I saw her in the parking lot at the Market and Deli. They had put one of their new toys right on top of her, a friggin' barrel organ. I guess she didn't like the music very much."

Jocelyn smiled and pursed her lips. "Well, I hope she likes Johnny Cash, because that's what was in the CD player, and reaching past her to press play once is enough for me, thank you."

"Brave move, madam." Steve stuck his fingers in the hair along the back of her neck and kissed her again.

The screen door flew open and Tyler came in with a large plastic bag that smelled of Chinese takeout. "Hey, no hanky-panky, okay?" he said. "I'm underage until March fifteenth, and until then my tender soul can't bear to be corrupted. Least of all within my own gene pool."

Steve winked at Jocelyn and said, "Does that go for you and Laurie, too?"

"I'm supposed to experiment," said Tyler as he put the bag on the table and wriggled out of his jacket. "It's age appropriate. Wikipedia says so."

"And what does Wikipedia say we should do at *our* age?"

"Work . . . cook . . . raise allowances."

Jocelyn opened her eyes wide and burst out laughing. Behind Tyler, Fletcher had wormed his way in through the screen door and was pattering around the dining room table with his ears cocked.

"Oh Christ, Tyler, grab him . . ." Steve said as soon as he heard the border collie growl, but it was too late: Fletcher had caught sight of the woman in Jocelyn's Limbo. He broke into a deafening bark, which shifted into such a shrill, high whine that all three of them jumped out of their skin. The dog flew through the room but slid across the dark tiles; Tyler was just able to grab him by the collar. Barking wildly and pawing the air with his front legs, Fletcher came to a halt between the French doors.

"Fletcher, down!" Tyler shouted, jerking the leash sharply. Fletcher stopped barking. Wagging his tail nervously, he began to growl deep in the back of his throat at the woman in Jocelyn's Limbo . . . who hadn't moved a muscle. "Jesus, couldn't you guys, like, tell me she was here?"

"Sorry," Steve said, taking the leash out of Tyler's hands. "We didn't see Fletcher come in."

A wry expression spread across Tyler's face. "Suits her well, that cloth." He threw his jacket over a chair and ran upstairs without further comment. Not to do his homework, Steve assumed, because when it came to homework Tyler was never in a rush. The only thing that made him hurry was the girl he was dating (a pert little cutie from Newburgh who unfortunately couldn't visit very often due to the Emergency Decree), or the video blog on his YouTube channel, which he had probably been working on when Jocelyn sent him to Emperor's Choice Takeout. Wednesday was her day off and she liked to keep it simple, even though everything from the town's Chinese takeout place tasted pretty much the same.

Steve led the growling Fletcher to the backyard and locked him in his kennel, where he jumped up against the wire mesh and started pacing restlessly. "Cut it out," Steve snarled, more sharply than the situation perhaps called for. But the dog got on his nerves, and he knew Fletcher wouldn't calm down for the next half hour. It had been quite some time since Gramma had dropped in on them, but no matter how often she came, Fletcher never seemed to get used to her.

Back inside, they set the table. Steve was unfolding paper containers of chicken chow mein and General Tso's tofu when the kitchen door flew open again. In came Matt's riding boots, rolling over the floor, as Fletcher continued barking nonstop. "Fletcher, Jesus!" he heard his youngest yell. "What's wrong with you?"

Matt entered the dining room with his cap askew and his riding breeches crumpled up in his arms. "Ooh, yummy. Chinese," he said, hugging both parents as he passed. "I'll be right down!" And, like Tyler, he ran upstairs.

Steve regarded the dining room at around this hour as the epicenter of the Grant family, the place where the engaging lives of individual family members slid over each other like tectonic plates and came to rest. It wasn't just that they honored the tradition of eating together whenever possible, it had to do with the room itself: a trusted place in the house, framed with railroad ties and a million-dollar view of the stable and the horse pen at the back of the yard, with the steeply rising wilderness of Philosopher's Deep right behind it.

He was serving up sesame noodles when Tyler entered the dining room with the GoPro sports cam he'd been given for his seventeenth birthday. Its red REC light was now on.

"Turn that thing off," Steve said firmly. "You know the rules when Gramma's here."

"I'm not filming her," Tyler said, pulling up a chair at the other end of the table. "Look, you can't even get her in the picture from here.

And you know she hardly ever walks when she's inside." He gave his dad an innocent smile and switched on his typical YouTube voice (music 1.2, flair 2.0): "And now it's time to ask you a question for my *très important* statistics report, O Worthy Progenitor."

"Tyler!" Jocelyn shouted.

"Sorry, O Twice Worthy Childbearer."

Jocelyn looked at him with friendly resolve. "You're going to edit that out," she said. "And get that camera out of my face. I look awful."

"Freedom of the press." Tyler grinned.

"Freedom of privacy," Jocelyn shot back.

"Suspension of household duties."

"Cutting allowances."

Tyler turned the GoPro on himself and assumed a tormented face. "Aww, I get this kind of crap all the time. I've said it before and I'll say it again, my friends: I'm living in a dictatorship. Freedom of speech is seriously jeopardized in the hands of the older generation."

"Thus spake the Messiah," said Steve as he served up the General Tso's, knowing that Tyler would edit most of it out anyway. Tyler made clever cuts of his opinions, absurdities, and street footage, which he dubbed with catchy pop and fast-paced video effects. He was good at it. And with impressive results: The last time Steve looked at his son's YouTube channel, TylerFlow95, it had 340 subscribers and more than 270,000 hits. Tyler even earned some pocket money (absurdly little, he admitted) from advertising income.

"What did you want to ask?" Steve said, and the cam swept over to him immediately.

"If you had to let someone die, who would it be: your own child or an entire village in the Sudan?"

"What an irrelevant question."

"My own child," Jocelyn said.

"Oh!" Tyler cried with great sense of drama, and out in his kennel, Fletcher perked up his ears and began barking restlessly again. "Did you hear that? My very own mother would mercilessly sacrifice me for some nonexistent village in Africa. Is this an indication of her third-world compassion, or a sign of dysfunction within our family?"

"Both, darling," said Jocelyn, and then called upstairs, "Matt! We're eating!"

"But, seriously, Dad. Say you had two buttons in front of you, and if you push one your own child dies—*moi*, that is—and if you push the other a whole village in the Sudan dies, and if you don't make a choice before the count of ten they both get pushed automatically. Who would you save?"

"It's an absurd situation," said Steve. "Who would ever force me to make such a choice?"

"Humor me."

"And even then, there's no right answer. If I save you, you'll accuse me of letting an entire village die."

"But otherwise we all die," Tyler insisted.

"Of course I'd let the village die and not you. How could I sacrifice my own son?"

"Really?" Tyler whistled in admiration. "Even if it's a village full of severely undernourished child soldiers with bulging little bellies and flies buzzing around their eyes and poor abused AIDS mothers?"

"Even then. Those mothers would do the same for their children. Where's Matt? I'm hungry."

"And if you had to choose between letting me die or all of the Sudan?"

"Tyler, you shouldn't ask such questions," said Jocelyn, but without much conviction; she knew perfectly well that once her husband and oldest son were on a roll, intervention stood as little chance of success as . . . well, as any intervention in the larger political arena.

"Well, Dad?"

"The Sudan," said Steve. "What's this report about, anyway? Our involvement in Africa?"

"Honesty," said Tyler. "Anybody who says he would save Sudan is lying. And anybody who doesn't want to answer is just being politically correct. We asked all the teachers and only Ms. Redfearn in philosophy was honest. And you." He heard his younger brother come rumbling down the stairs, and called out, "If you had to let someone die, Matt, who would you choose: all of the Sudan, or our parents?"

"Sudan," came the immediate reply. Outside the camera frame, Tyler nodded at the living room and ran his finger over his lips, miming the closing of a zipper. Steve shot a reluctant look at Jocelyn, but he saw from the way she was biting her lip that she was willing to play along. One second later the door opened, and in came Matt with only a towel around his waist, apparently straight from the bathroom.

"Awright, you just got me an extra thousand hits," Tyler said. Matt pulled a clownish face at the GoPro and wiggled his hips back and forth.

"Tyler, he's thirteen!" Jocelyn said.

"Seriously. That clip with Lawrence, Burak, and me doing a shirtless lip-synch of The Pussycat Dolls got over thirty-five thousand hits."

"That was close to porn," Matt said, pulling up a chair next to him with his back to the living room—and to the woman in Jocelyn's Limbo. Steve and Tyler exchanged an amused glance.

"Can't you wear some clothes at the table?" Jocelyn sighed.

"You wanted me to come down and eat! My clothes smell like horse, and I haven't even had a shower. By the way, I liked your album, Mom."

"What?"

"On Facebook." With a mouth full of noodles he pushed himself from the edge of the table and tottered on the hind legs of his chair. "You're so cool, Mom."

"I saw it, darling. Four on the floor, okay? Or you'll fall again."

Ignoring her, Matt turned his attention to Tyler's lens. "I bet you don't want to know what *I* think."

"No, I do not, brother-who-smells-like-horse. I'd rather you took a shower."

"It's sweat, not horse," Matt said imperturbably. "I think your question is too easy. I think it's much more interesting to ask: If you had to let somebody die, who would it be: your own kid or all of Black Spring?"

Fletcher started up a low growl. Steve looked out into the backyard and saw the dog pressing his head low to the ground behind the wire mesh and baring his teeth like a wild animal.

"Jesus, what's wrong with that dog?" Matt asked. "Apart from being a total nutcake."

"Gramma wouldn't happen to be around, would she?" Steve asked innocently.

Jocelyn dropped her shoulders and looked around the room. "I haven't seen her at all today." With feigned urgency, she glanced from the backyard to the split red oak at the end of their property, where the path led up the hill: the red oak with the three security cams mounted to the trunk, peering into various corners of Philosopher's Deep.

"*Gramma wouldn't happen to be around.*" Matt grinned with his mouth full. "What'll Tyler's followers make of that?" Jocelyn's mother, a long-term Alzheimer's patient, had died of a lung infection a year and a half before; Steve's had been dead eight years. Not that YouTube knew, but Matt was having fun.

Steve turned to his oldest son and said, with a severity that was not at all like him, "Tyler, you're cutting this out, right?"

"Sure, Dad." He switched voices to TylerFlow95. "Let's bring the question closer to home. If you had to let somebody die, *o padre mio*, who would it be: your own kid or the rest of our town?"

"Would that include my wife and my other child?" Steve asked.

"Yes, Dad," Matt said with a condescending laugh. "Who would you save, Tyler or me?"

"Matthew!" Jocelyn cried. "That's enough of that."

"I'd save you both," Steve said solemnly.

Tyler grinned. "That's politically correct, Dad."

Just then, Matt leaned back too far on his chair legs. He flapped his arms wildly in an attempt to regain his balance, red sauce flying off his spoon, but the chair fell backward with a crash and Matt rolled onto the floor. Jocelyn jumped up, startling Tyler and causing the Go-Pro to slip out of his hands and fall into his plate of chicken chow mein. Steve saw that Matt, still with the flexibility of a child, had caught his fall with an outstretched elbow and was giggling hysterically, lying on his back and trying to hold the towel around his waist with one hand.

"Little bro overboard!" Tyler whooped. He aimed the GoPro down to get a good shot, wiping off the chow mein.

As if he'd received an electric shock, Matt began shaking: The expression on his face turned into a grimace of horror, he knocked his shin against the table leg, and he uttered a loud cry.

+-+-+-+-

FIRST: NO ONE will ever see the images that Tyler's GoPro is shooting at that moment. That's unfortunate, because if anyone were to study them they'd be witness to something very odd, perhaps even unsettling—to put it mildly. The images are crystal clear, and images don't lie. Even though it's a small camera, the GoPro captures reality at an astonishing sixty frames per second, producing spectacular clips taken from Tyler's mountain bike racing down Mount Misery, or when he goes snorkeling with his friends in Popolopen Lake, even when the water's cloudy.

The images show Jocelyn and Steve staring with bewilderment past their youngest son, still on the floor, and into the living room. In the middle of the image is a spot of congealed noodles and egg yolk. The camera jerks the other way and Matt is no longer lying on the floor; he rights himself with a spastic twist of his body and shrinks back, bumping into the table. Somehow he has managed to keep the towel around his waist. For a moment it feels as though we're standing on the undulating deck of a ship, for everything we see is slanted, as if the whole dining room has come apart at the seams. Then the picture straightens up, and although the splotch of noodle hides most of our view, we see a gaunt woman making her way through the living room toward the open French doors to the kitchen. Until then, she has stood motionless in Jocelyn's Limbo, but suddenly she's right there, as if she has taken pity on the fallen Matt. The dishcloth has slid off her face, and in a fraction of a second—maybe it's only a couple of frames—we see that her eyes are sewn shut, and so is her mouth. It all happens so fast that it's over before we know it, but it's the kind of image that burns itself into your brain, not just long enough to pull us out of our comfort zone but to completely disrupt it.

Then Steve rushes forward and slides the French doors to the living room shut. Behind the half-translucent stained glass we see the gaunt woman come to a halt. We even hear the slight vibration of the glass as she bumps up against the pane.

Steve's good humor has vanished. "Turn that thing off," he says. "Now." He's deadly serious, and although his face is hidden from view (all we can see is his T-shirt and jeans, and the finger of his free hand stabbing at the lens), we can all imagine what it must look like. Then everything goes black.

-+-+-+-+-

"SHE CAME RIGHT for me!" Matt shouted. "She's never done that before!" He was still standing next to the fallen chair, holding the towel around his waist to keep it from sliding down.

Tyler started laughing—mostly from relief, Steve thought. "Maybe she's got the hots for you."

"Ew, gross, are you kidding me? She's ancient!"

Jocelyn burst out laughing, too. She took a mouthful of noodles but didn't notice how much hot sauce she had put on her spoon. Tears sprang from her eyes. "Sorry, darling. We just wanted to shake you up a little, but I think you shook *her* up. It really was strange how she came walking up to you. She never does that."

"How long was she standing there?" Matt asked indignantly.

"The whole time." Tyler grinned.

Matt's jaw dropped. "Now she's seen me naked!"

Tyler looked at him with a mixture of absolute amazement and the kind of disgust that borders on a sympathetic sort of love, reserved only for big brothers toward their younger, dim-witted siblings. "She can't see, you idiot," he said. He wiped off the lens of his GoPro and looked at the blind woman behind the stained glass.

"Sit down, Matt," Steve said, his face stiffening. "Dinner's getting cold." Sulkily, Matt did what he was told. "And I want you to erase those images now, Tyler."

"Aw, come on! I can just cut her out. . . ."

"*Now*, and I want to see you do it. You know the rules."

"What is this, Pyongyang?"

"Don't make me say it again."

"But there was some kick-ass material in there," Tyler muttered without much hope. He knew when his father meant it. And he did indeed know the rules. Reluctantly, he held up the display at an angle toward Steve, selected the video file, and clicked ERASE, then OK.

"Good boy."

"Tyler, report her in the app, would you?" Jocelyn asked. "I wanted to do it earlier, but you know I'm hopeless at these things."

Cautiously, Steve walked around to the living room via the hallway. The woman hadn't budged. There she stood, right in front of the French doors with her face pressed against the glass, like something that had been put there as a macabre joke, to replace a floor lamp or a houseplant. Her lank hair hung motionless and dirty under her headscarf. If she knew there was someone else in the room, she didn't let on. Steve came closer but deliberately avoided looking at her, sensing her shape from the corner of his eye. It felt better not to look at her up close like this. He could smell her now, though: the stench of another era, of mud and cattle in the streets, of disease. She swayed gently, so that the wrought-iron chain shackling her arms tightly to her shrunken body tapped against the varnished doorpost with a dull clank.

"She was last seen at five twenty-four p.m. by the cameras behind the Market and Deli," he heard Tyler's muffled voice say from the other room. Steve could also hear that the woman was whispering. He knew that not listening to her whispering was a matter of life and death, so he concentrated on the voice of his son, and on Johnny Cash. "There are four reports from people who saw her, but nothing after that. Something about a barrel organ. Dad . . . are you okay?"

His heart pounding, Steve knelt down next to the woman with the stitched-up eyes and picked up the dishcloth. Then he stood up. As his elbow brushed against the woman's chain, she turned her maimed face toward him. Steve dropped the dishcloth over her head and scrambled away from her and back to the dining room, his forehead drenched in sweat, as Fletcher's fierce, alarmed barking came from the backyard.

"Dishcloth," he said to Jocelyn. "Good idea."

The family continued eating, and all during dinner the woman with the stitched-up eyes stood motionless behind the stained glass.

She only moved once: When Matt's high-pitched laugh sounded through the dining room, she tilted her head.

As if she were listening.

After dinner, Tyler loaded the dishwasher and Steve cleaned the table. "Show me what you sent them."

Tyler held up his iPhone with the HEXApp logbook on display. The last entry read as follows:

> Wed. 09.19.12, 7:03 P.M., 16M ago
> Tyler Grant @gps 41.22890 N, 73.61831 W
> #K @ living room, 188 Deep Hollow Road
> omg i think she digs my little bro

-+-|-|-|-

LATER THAT EVENING, Steve and Jocelyn were both sprawled in the living room—not in their regular spot on the couch but on the divan on the other side of the room—watching *The Late Show* on CBS. Matt was in bed; Tyler was upstairs working on his laptop. The pale TV light flickered on the metal chains around the blind woman's body—or at least on the links that weren't rusted. Beneath the dishcloth, the dead flesh at the open corner of her mouth twitched, barely visible. It pulled on the jagged black stitches that sewed her mouth tight, except for that one loose stitch in the corner that stuck out like a bent piece of wire. Jocelyn yawned and stretched herself against Steve. He guessed it wouldn't be long before she dropped off to sleep.

When they went upstairs half an hour later, the blind woman was still there, something of the night that the night had now recovered.

TWO

ROBERT GRIM WATCHED the screen with distress as movers lugged furniture, wrapped in canvas and plastic, out of the moving van, and carried it into the residence on Upper Reservoir Road, following instructions of the harebrained yuppie bitch. It was camera D19-063—the late Mrs. Barphwell's plot—although he didn't need the camera number to tell him that. The image occupied the greater part of the western wall in the HEX control center as well as the greater part of Grim's tormented night's sleep. He shut his eyes and, with a huge amount of willpower, conjured up a new image, a sublime image: Robert Grim saw barbed wire.

Apartheid is an underrated system, Grim thought. He was no supporter of racial segregation in South Africa, or of the strict purdah that separated men from women in Saudi Arabia, but a revolutionary and disturbingly altruistic part of him saw the world as divided into people *from* Black Spring and people *outside* Black Spring. Preferably with lots of rusty barbed wire in between. Under ten thousand volts, if possible. Colton Mathers, head of the Council, denounced that attitude and, in accordance with The Point's demands, called for a controlled integration project—because without new growth, Black Spring would either die out or evolve into some inbred commune that would make Amishville, Pennsylvania, look like a hippie Mecca. But Colton Mathers's expansionism was no match for damn near three hundred fifty years of cover-up policy, which was a relief for everyone. Robert Grim pictured the councilman's ego as a particularly fat head. He hated it.

Grim sighed and rolled his chair along the edge of the desk in order to glance at the statistics, tables, and measurements on the monitor in front of Warren Castillo, who was drinking coffee and reading the *Wall Street Journal,* feet up on the desk.

"Neurotic," Warren said, without looking up.

Grim's hands tightened into a cramp. He stared at the moving van once again.

Last month things had looked so promising. The real estate agent had taken the yuppie couple to visit the house, and Grim had prepared for the operation down to every last detail, referring to it as "Operation Barphwell" out of respect for the elderly former occupant. Operation Barphwell consisted of a provisional fence right behind the property, a truck full of sand, a few concrete slabs, a large contractor sign with PO-POLOPEN NIGHT BAZAAR & CLUB, READY MID–2015 written on it, and hidden concert speakers with subwoofers playing pile-driver sounds from the iTunes New Age & Mindfulness section. And, indeed, after the security cams showed the Realtor's car approaching the town on Route 293 and Grim gave the signal to start the sound track, the pounding was hard to ignore. Together with Butch Heller's hammer drill, which the tile setter haphazardly drilled into the concrete slabs, it suggested the construction of castles in the air.

Delarosa was their name and New York City was their game. According to information Grim had received from The Point, the husband had won a seat on the Newburgh City Council and the wife was a communications advisor and heiress to a men's clothing fortune. They would wax lyrical to their Upper East Side buddies about their rediscovery of country life, excrete two point three bloated babies, and decide to return to the city in about six years.

But that's where things got sticky. Once they had settled in Black Spring, there was no going back.

It was essential that they be *kept* from coming to Black Spring.

The effectiveness of the fake construction site should have been beyond question, but just to make sure, Grim had stationed three local kids on Upper Reservoir Road. There were always teens in Black

Spring willing to take on a job for some cigarettes or a crate of Bud. This time it was Justin Walker, Burak Şayer, and Jaydon Holst, the butcher's son. The real estate agent watched his commission go up in smoke when the local youths accused Bammy Delarosa of working the night shift as soon as she got out of the car, and invited her for a circle jerk to the hydraulic stomp of the pile driver.

That should have ended the matter. When Grim contentedly settled into his bed that night, he congratulated himself on his ingenuity and quickly fell asleep. He caught himself dreaming about Bammy Delarosa, who in his dream had a humpback. The humpback had a mouth that tried to open and scream, but it couldn't, as it was stitched shut with barbed wire.

"Brace yourself," Claire Hammer said the following morning when Grim entered the control center. She held up a piece of paper. "You're not going to believe this."

Grim did not brace himself. He read the mail. Colton Mathers was furious. He accused HEX of a serious error of judgment. The real estate agent had started asking questions about the sign reading POPOLEN NIGHT BAZAAR & CLUB, READY MID–2015. Grim cursed Mrs. Barphwell's death, but her next of kin had called in a real estate agent from Newburgh instead of Donna Ross Hometown Realty from Black Spring, who was paid by Grim to pursue a policy of discouraging people rather than attracting them. *One way or the other, you're dealing with Outsiders here,* Mathers wrote. *And once again, you're being far too creative in the execution of your duties. How in heaven's name am I supposed to get out of this mess?*

That was the councilman's worry. Grim's worry was that the Delarosas had fallen in love with the property and had made an offer. Grim immediately made a counteroffer using a false identity. Delarosa bid again. So did Grim. Wasting time until buyers lost interest was crucial in these matters—Black Spring fared well in the real-estate bubble.

A week later, Warren Castillo called him at lunchtime from the control center just as he was about to start in on a mutton sandwich from Griselda's Butchery & Delicacies. The Delarosas' Mercedes had been spotted in town. Claire was already on her way. The risk of a Code Red—a sighting by Outsiders—was next to zero, and Warren already had two people on alert. Moving as fast as he could and fuming about his unfinished mutton sandwich, Grim raced up the hill. He was out of breath by the time he ran into Claire near the Memorial Footbridge on Upper Reservoir Road.

"You want *what*?" the New Yorker asked in disbelief after they had accosted him and his unnaturally tanned wife in front of Mrs. Barphwell's bungalow. The Delarosas had come without their real estate agent, probably to convince themselves one more time of the extraordinary character of the house and its surroundings.

"I want you to terminate the purchase of this house," Grim repeated. "You're not making any more offers, here or on any other property in Black Spring. The town is prepared to compensate you for the inconvenience by paying you five thousand dollars toward the purchase of any other plot, at any other location—as long as it isn't in Black Spring."

The Delarosas looked at the two HEX officers with frank incredulity. It was a hot day, and even here in the shelter of the Black Rock Forest, Grim felt a drop of sweat run down his balding temple. His baldness set him apart somehow, he thought. A bald head inspired yuppies and women. Robert Grim, despite being in his mid-fifties, was an intimidating presence due to his height, his horn-rimmed glasses, and his natty tie, and Claire Hammer was an intimidatingly beautiful woman, except for a rather high forehead that she shouldn't emphasize so much.

On the way to the property they had talked about how to tackle the situation. Claire preferred an emotional approach and some sissy story about family ties and childhood memories. Grim was convinced that when dealing with these kinds of career geeks it was best to shoot straight from the hip, and he didn't listen to her. It was because of her forehead. It distracted him. There was something expendable about a woman with an overly high forehead—especially if she emphasized it like that.

"But . . . why?" Mr. Delarosa asked after finally recovering his voice.

"We have our reasons," Grim said impassively. "It's for your own good that you leave right now and forget all about it. We can lay out the details of the agreement in a contract. . . ."

"What authority do you represent, anyway?"

"Irrelevant. I want you to terminate the purchase, and you'll be given five thousand dollars for it. There are some things money can't buy. For everything else, you got us."

Delarosa looked as if Grim had just suggested that he was going to publicly execute his wife on the town scaffold. "Do you think I'm crazy?" he raged. "Who do you think you're dealing with?"

Grim closed his eyes and hunkered down. "Think about the money." He himself was thinking about cyanide. "And take it as a business proposition."

"I'm not going to let myself be bribed by the first neighborhood watchdog who comes along! My wife and I love this house and we're signing the contract tomorrow. You should be glad I'm not pressing charges."

"Listen. Mrs. Barphwell had a leaky roof every fall. Last year it did considerable water damage to her floors. This," Grim said, gesturing with two hands, "is a shitty house. There are beautiful properties in Highland Falls—just as rustic but right on the Hudson, and the house prices there are lower."

"You're wrong if you think I can be fobbed off for five thousand dollars," Delarosa said. Then something occurred to him. "Are you those jokers from the Night Bazaar? Why the hell are you doing this?"

Grim opened his mouth, but Claire beat him to it. "We don't like you," she snapped, hating her role, but in top form as usual. "We don't care for city slickers like yourselves. They pollute the air."

"It's a healthy dose of inbred humor," Grim added confidentially. He knew they had just lost their case.

Bammy Delarosa looked at him stupidly, turned to her husband, and asked, "What exactly are they saying, dear?" Robert Grim imagined her brains as something burned to a crisp under a sunbed and now encrusted on the inner wall of her skull.

"Shush, hon," Delarosa said, and he drew her up close. "Get out of here, before I call the police!"

"You're going to regret this," Claire said, but Grim pulled her away.

"Never mind, Claire. It's useless."

That night he called Delarosa on his cell phone and begged him to give up on the purchase. When the man asked him why he was going to so much trouble, Grim told him that Black Spring suffered from a three-hundred-year-old curse, and that it would infect them, too, if they decided to settle in town, and that they'd be doomed until their death, and that there was a wicked witch living in Black Spring. Delarosa hung up.

"Damn you!" Grim shouted now, staring at the movers. He threw his pen at the big screen and the twenty monitors around it jumped to new camera angles, offering views of people loafing around in town. "I was doing you a fucking favor!"

"Relax," Warren said. He folded up his newspaper and laid it on the desk. "We did everything we could. He may be an intellectual, cocksuckin' asshole, but at least he's *our* intellectual, cocksuckin' asshole. And she looks like a juicy little piece."

"Pig," said Claire.

Grim stabbed at the screen with his finger. "In the Council, they're rubbing their hands together. But when these folks raise hell, who's going in to clean up the mess?"

"We are," Warren said, "and we're good at it. Dude, let off some steam. Be happy we've got something new to bet on. Fifty bucks on a home encounter."

"Fifty bucks?" Claire was shocked. "You're crazy. Statistically speaking, home encounters never come first."

"I feel it in my fingers, baby," Warren said, and he began drumming on the desk. "If I were her, I'd go over and check out the new meat, if you know what I'm saying." He raised his eyebrows. "Who's in?"

"Fifty dollars—you're on," Claire said. "I say they see her on the street."

"The security cams," chimed in Marty Keller, their online data analyst, from the other side of the control center. "And I raise the stakes to seventy-five."

The others stared at him as if he had lost his mind. "Nobody ever sees those things if they don't know they're there," Warren said.

"He will." Marty nodded at the monitor. "He's just the type. They see the security cams and start asking questions. Seventy-five."

"Count me in," Claire said promptly.

"Me too," Warren said, "and first drink's on me."

Marty tapped Lucy Everett, who was in the chair beside him listening in on phone calls. She took off her headphones. "Say what?"

"Are you in on the bet? Seventy-five bucks."

"Sure. Home encounter."

"Get the fuck out of here; that's my bet!" Warren shouted.

"Then you have to share the winnings with Warren," Marty said. Lucy turned around and blew Warren a kiss. Warren wiped it off and dropped into his chair.

"What about you, Robert? You in?" Claire asked.

Grim sighed. "You guys are more disgusting than I thought. Okay, they'll hear about it in town. There's always someone who can't keep their mouth shut."

Marty jotted it down on the whiteboard with a dry-erase marker. "That leaves Liz and Eric. I'll send them both e-mails. If they join, we'll have a kitty of . . . five hundred twenty-five dollars. That's still two seventy-five for you, Warren."

"Two sixty-two fifty, darling," Claire said.

"Silence, dragon woman," sulked Warren.

Robert Grim slipped into his coat to get some pecan pie in town.

His mood was spoiled for the rest of the day, but at least he'd be able to enjoy some state-subsidized pecan pie. Even though he had no official authority without the Council's mandate, and even though everything had to be reported to his contact at The Point on a quarterly basis, Grim did hold the executive power in Black Spring, and one of his talents was to pry up subsidies from what he called the Bottomless Pit. The annual salaries of the seven HEX employees were paid out of this pit, as were the four-hundred-something surveillance cams and their operating system, the filtered server with Internet access for the entire town, a couple of very successful parties (with excellent wine) following Council meetings, and free iPhones for everyone under the compulsory reporting regulation who preferred to use the HEXApp instead of the 800 number. This last had made Robert Grim the most celebrated man in Black Spring among the younger population, and he could often be found daydreaming about some random young (and usually long-legged) brunette from town coming to the control center to explore the legendary proportions of his cult status amid the piling props still reeking of seventeenth-century decay.

Robert Grim had always remained single.

"By the way, we got an e-mail from John Blanchard," Marty said as Grim was getting ready to leave. "You know, that sheep farmer in the woods, from Ackerman's Corner."

"Oh, God, him," Warren said. He raised his eyes to heaven.

"He says his sheep Jackie gave birth to a two-headed lamb. Stillborn."

"Two-headed?" Grim asked incredulously. "That's horrible! That hasn't happened since Henrietta Russo's baby in '91."

"His e-mail kind of freaked me out. He went on about prophecies and omens and something about a ninth circle or whatever."

"Ignore him," Warren said. "At the last Council meeting he said he had seen strange lights in the sky. He said that 'the ignorant and the sodomites will be punished for their pride and greed.' The guy is nuts. He sees omens in morning wood."

Marty turned toward Grim. "I mean, should we keep it? Here's the photo he attached." He clicked on his touch pad, and a photo of an ugly, fleshy, dead thing in the dirt appeared on the big screen—and, sure enough, you could easily discern two deformed lamb's heads. Jackie hadn't even wanted to lick off the membrane. Half cut out of the photo and somewhat out of focus, she could be seen eating hay and refusing to give the fetal monster the time of day.

"Ugh, what a freak," said Grim, and he turned away. "Yes, have Dr. Stanton take a look, and put it in formaldehyde along with the other specimens in the archive. Anybody else up for pecan pie?"

A unanimous "yuck" came from all the staff members, so at first Grim didn't hear that Claire was the only one who didn't say "yuck," but "fuck." He had already grabbed the doorknob when she repeated it: "No, seriously, Robert. Fuck. Marty, give me the Barphwell parcel on full screen."

Marty dragged the photo of the dead lamb away and the movers came back into view.

"No, do the cam *at* her parcel, D19 . . . 064."

Grim went visibly pale.

The security camera was located on the lamppost in front of the Delarosa bungalow plot and offered a view of Upper Reservoir Road that sloped down through the edges of Black Rock Forest. The moving van was parked on the right, and you could see the workers picking up boxes and disappearing from the bottom of the image. The rest of the street was empty, except for about twenty yards farther up, on the left. Standing on the lawn of a low-lying house across the street was a woman. She wasn't looking at the movers but was staring down the hill, motionless. But Robert Grim didn't need to see her up close to know that she wasn't staring at all. Panic struck him.

"Oh, dammit!" he shouted. His right hand went up to his mouth and covered it. "Dammit, how the hell is that possible . . ." He ran back to the desk and his eyes flew across the screen.

The enormous truck was obstructing the view for the yuppie couple and their movers, but it would only take one fool to walk around the loading ramp and they'd see her. Code Fucking Red quadrupled. They'd call 911: a seriously mutilated, underfed woman—*yes, she looks disheveled; send an ambulance and the police.* Or, worse: They'd try to help her themselves. Then the consequences would be vast.

"What's she doing there, for Christ's sake? Wasn't she supposed to be with the Grant family?"

"Yes, until . . ." Claire looked in her log. "At least until eight thirty-seven this morning, when the kid apped that he had to go to school. After that the house was empty."

"How does the old bag figure it out?"

"Relax," Warren said. "Be happy she's not in their living room. She's standing on a lawn; we'll put the old umbrella clothesline on her, with sheets. You and Marty can be there in five minutes. I'll call the folks from that property or one of their neighbors and ask them to cover her with a blanket till we get there."

Grim ran to the exit and pushed Marty down the corridor. "What a clusterfuck."

"If they see her, we'll say she's part of the festival," Warren said. He flashed Grim a smile that was more appropriate for a mojito at a salsa party than a situation where people could die, and failed abysmally in his goal to calm Grim down. "A joke from the locals to welcome the newbies. *Ooo-ooo-ooo,* what a little suggestion can do. It's only a witch."

Robert Grim spun around in the doorway. "This is *not* fucking Hansel and Gretel!"

THREE

THE LAST WARM day of the year came and went. The semester was weeks under way and Steve Grant had begun to adjust to the rhythm of alternating between classes at New York Med and his job as project leader at the scientific research center. Jocelyn was working three and a half days a week at the Hudson Highlands Nature Museum in Cornwall and the boys had begun to settle into their new school year at O'Neill High School in Highland Falls, albeit with the usual reluctance. Tyler had made it through junior year by the skin of his teeth and was now taking extra math classes to keep on track for his finals. It made him irritable. Tyler was a man of words, not of numbers, and if he passed this year—a big "if," if you asked Steve—he wanted to work with words. Journalism, preferably at NYU in the city, although that would mean commuting back and forth every day. A dorm room on campus, at such a distance from Black Spring, would be too dangerous. It would creep up on him slowly, almost imperceptibly . . . but in the end it would hit home, and possibly too unexpectedly for him to see it coming.

Matt had waltzed through his first year of junior high and begun his second with the hyperactive mood swings of puberty. He surrounded himself with girls from school and seemed to share their endless giggling fits as well as their PMS rages, and would go into a funk at the drop of a hat. Jocelyn had expressed her concern that Matt might come out of the closet this year or the next, and although Steve had raised his eyebrows at the idea he suspected Jocelyn was right. The idea alarmed him, not because either of them held conservative views but because he still saw Matt as what he always had been: a sweet, vulnerable child.

They're really growing up, he thought, not without a touch of wistfulness. *And we're growing old. No one's making an exception for us. We're all going to get old . . . and it will be in Black Spring.*

Plunged into a grave mood by this thought, he walked down the path along the horse pen to the end of the yard. Although it was almost eleven, it was still quite warm. A typical late-summer evening with no hint of fall in the air, though WAMC had predicted rain for the following day. The woods rose up high before him, silent and pitch-black. Steve whistled for Fletcher, who was hiding somewhere out there.

On the other side of the fence, Pete VanderMeer's cigarette glowed in the dark. Steve raised his hand and Pete sympathetically tapped two fingers to his temple. A sociologist to the core, Pete often sat in his backyard smoking far into the wee hours. He had taken early retirement a couple of years ago on account of rheumatoid arthritis. His wife, Mary, brought home the bacon ever since. Pete was fifteen years Steve's senior, but his son, Lawrence, was the same age as Tyler, and the families had become close over the years.

"Hey, Steve. Trying to squeeze the last little bit out of summer?"

He smiled. "As much as I can."

"Enjoy it while it lasts. There's a storm coming."

Steve raised his eyebrows.

"Haven't you heard?" Pete exhaled a cloud of smoke. "We've got fresh meat."

"Oh, shit," Steve said. "What kind of people are they?"

"A couple from the city, still pretty young. He's been offered a job in Newburgh. Put me in mind of you guys." One of the horses in the stable whinnied softly. "Ain't that a bitch? It's easier if you're born here, like me. They'll make it, if their marriage is strong enough. Most of them do. But I don't need to tell you that."

Steve smiled resignedly. He and Jocelyn weren't originally from the area, either. They had moved into their renovated colonial hideaway eighteen years before, when Jocelyn was pregnant with Tyler and Steve had accepted an appointment with the GP group practice at New York Med. There had already been problems with the sale before they left Atlanta—a surly real estate agent, unexpected difficulty obtaining a mortgage—but it was an ideal place to raise children, the Hudson Valley woods all around and within commuting distance of the campus.

"I hope for their sake that the wife had a say in this, too," Steve said. "I still thank the boulders from the bottom of my heart every day."

Pete threw back his head and laughed. Jocelyn had been working on her Ph.D. in geology at the time and had fallen in love with the boulders left behind by the glaciers that ran the whole length of Deep Hollow Road, from their property to the center of town. Steve had never dared tell her out loud, but he suspected that the boulders had saved their marriage. If the move to Black Spring had been all on his account, he didn't know whether Jocelyn would ever have been able to forgive him. She may have wanted to, but the grudge she would have held against him simply would have been too strong.

"Oh, it'll blow over in the end," Pete said. "They'll never fully own this place . . . but Black Spring will own *them,* all right." He gave him a quick wink, as if they were two boys sharing a secret. "Anyway, I should be heading to bed. We're going to have some work to do one of these days."

They said good night and Steve walked out to the back of the property, looking for Fletcher. From the barn came the sound of one of the horses—either Paladin or Nuala—sniffing, a restless sound, yet intimate at the same time. Oddly enough, Steve loved life in Black Spring despite its restrictions. Here in the dark he felt a strong sense of belonging—something that, like so many aspects of the human psyche, couldn't be rationally explained, yet existed nonetheless. Steve was too scientifically minded to believe in something spiritual such as the power of place, but even so, there was a more primitive, intuitive part of him that knew his neighbor was right. This place owned them. And even now, in the lee of the late summer night, you could feel that the place itself belonged to something older. Their house was on the edge of the Black Rock Forest nature reserve, at the foot of Mount Misery. The chain of hills, pushed up by the glaciers in past ice ages and cut out by meltwater, had been exerting an attraction on the people who settled there ever since ancient times. Anyone who dug there would find the remains of settlements and burial grounds from the Munsee and Mohican tribes. Later, when the Dutch and English colonists moved in and drove the River Indians away from this area, the cultivated wilderness retained its character and the hills were used by heathen and pagan cults for their rituals. Steve knew the history . . . but the connection that historians failed to make was the influence of the place itself. That connection was irrational and only existed if you lived here . . . and it took hold of you.

Admittedly, it hadn't been easy, those early years.

First came denial, then came anger. The denial ended abruptly when, after seven weeks of disbelief and bewilderment, they booked a monthlong vacation in a splendid Thai bamboo beach bungalow. Steve had thought it might be a good idea for Jocelyn to get away from all the fuss for a while during her pregnancy. Halfway through their first week in Asia they both became depressed, as if an intense, invisible sadness had washed over them from the Gulf of Thailand and was now devouring them from the inside out. It had no origin or direction, yet it was there and it spread like an ink blot. Steve absolutely refused to admit that it could have anything to do with the Council's warning that the length of their vacation was foolish—life threatening, even—until, after less than a week and a half away from home, he began playing with the idea of hanging himself from the bamboo ceiling using the bungalow's bedsheets.

Christ, how long was I standing here? he had asked himself when he woke from the daydream with a shock. Despite the tropical heat, Steve had goose bumps all over his arms and back. He had been standing there with the linens in his hands. He didn't know what could possibly have possessed him, but the image from behind his own bulging eyes as the sheet cut off the oxygen supply to his brain and the hydrostatic pressure of his cerebrospinal fluid increased had imprinted itself in his mind, vivid and horribly tempting. In the vision, he had still been alive. Looking down, Steve had seen his own dangling feet, and upward, the sea, and behind that—death. *What in God's name was that?* he thought, splashing water on his face. *I wanted to do it. I really wanted to do it.*

Jocelyn had also had a vision. Not of killing herself. She had mated with a donkey, then stuck a carving knife into her belly to cut out the baby.

That same evening they had packed their bags, rebooked their flight, and returned home headlong. As soon as they were back in Black Spring, the profound sadness had slid away from them like a veil of tears, and the world had seemed manageable again.

Never again had it been as bad as it was then. They had carried on intense conversations with Robert Grim and a small group of volunteers from town who had been appointed by the Council, among them Pete VanderMeer. "You'll get used to it," Pete had said. "I used to think Black Spring was like death row, but now I see it more like a little stable, with a cage door. You're allowed to stick your finger through the bars every now and then, but only to show that you're fattening up nicely."

When Steve and Jocelyn had realized there was no point in denying the truth, the powerless feeling had slowly turned into depression and a smoldering sense of guilt, which exacerbated the tension in their marriage. But the baby's arrival had brought healing. When Tyler was six months old, Steve let go of his desire to not only understand the situation but also to *change* it, and decided that his move to Black Spring had been a gesture of love. He found a way to move on, but in his heart he bore the scars: Tyler would never grow to become a war correspondent, just as Jocelyn had had to suspend her field research on the Greenland ice caps. Their love was for the desolate and the remote, not for the Hudson Valley sediment. It had broken their hearts, just as every unfulfilled dream breaks the human heart, but that was life. Jocelyn and Matt had learned to love the horses—Matt especially enjoyed riding, and now was in his fifth year of competition—and Tyler had his GoPro and YouTube channel. You adapted, and you made sacrifices. You did it for your children or for love. You did it because of illness or because of an accident. You did it because you had new dreams . . . and sometimes you did it because of Black Spring.

Sometimes you did it because of Black Spring.

A tawny owl screeched in the woods, startled itself, and fell silent. Steve whistled for the dog once again. He began to feel ill at ease. Superstition, of course, even ludicrous, but on a night like this, when he could feel the power of this place in the dark, it was present nonetheless. He didn't think back on those first years very often. It was all somewhat blurred in his memory; it had that structure of melting snow that dissolves as soon as you squeeze it. He remembered that they had asked themselves whether it was ethical to bring a child into the world in a place like this. Jocelyn had snapped, somewhat caustically, that in times of war and famine children were born under far more difficult circumstances.

After that, they had lived relatively happily for the most part . . . but the guilt had never entirely gone away.

"Fletcher, come here!" he hissed. Finally Fletcher came pattering out of the darkness and walked up to Steve, not directly, but in an arc, to show that he really hadn't done anything wrong. Steve locked up the stable and followed the dog along the crazy-paved path to the back door.

Silence reigned in the house, quiet with the sounds of sleep. The only light came from Tyler's open bedroom door upstairs. The boy was just coming out of the bathroom when Steve got to the top step. Steve hunkered down like a boxer and Tyler parried deftly, their typical Steve-and-Tyler greeting.

"You ready for tomorrow?"

"Will we ever be?"

Steve smiled. "A regular philosopher. Don't stay up too late, okay?"

"No, I'm about to turn in. G'night, Dad."

But when Steve went to the bathroom half an hour later there was still light shining through the transom above Tyler's door—the pale radiation from his laptop. He considered saying something, but thought better of it and decided to allow the boy his privacy.

Just before going to sleep he rose from his side of the bed and looked out the window. Jocelyn didn't stir. Their room was at the back of the house and it was too dark outside to distinguish shapes, but somewhere in the night Steve thought he could see the red dot of light from the surveillance cam in the oak at the back of their property. Then it was gone. Perhaps a branch had blown in front of it. It made him think of the burning tip of Pete VanderMeer's cigarette. The screeching tawny owl. The restless sniffing of the horses. Even the light coming from Tyler's room. *They're standing watch*, he thought. *They're all standing watch. Why?*

To guard what's theirs. It was an incoherent thought, but it was followed by another that was much more lucid, a thought that slipped into his weary mind and trickled through with a cold fluidity: *Sometimes you did it because of Black Spring.*

He dismissed it and fell asleep.

FOUR

THE ENTRY POSTED the next morning on the website *Open Your Eyes: Preachings from the Witch's Nest* read as follows:

> tonight we're gonna do it!! #awesome
> #mainstream #omfg #lampposttest
> *Posted 10:23 a.m. by: Tyler Grant*

Obviously, no one in Black Spring read the entry that day. The five people who were aware of the website's existence and who knew the password were all between sixteen and nineteen years of age, and would not in a million years think of visiting the *OYE* website via the town providers.

The website's welcome pop-up read as follows:

> OK, here's a warning that you're totally thinking you won't read, just like the I-am-18-or-older bs you click away when you jack off. But this is different: this is a disclaimer you have to memorize word for word, better than the O'Neill Raiders fight song (for the heroes among us) or the Gettysburg Address (for the neonihilists). This warning is **COMPLETE SECRECY** and **NEVER FUCKING EVER LOG IN IN BLACK SPRING**, not even on your iPhone or tablet. Big-time 404 message if you do it anyway, but they can still trace the URL with their keylogger. Only discuss content IRL, not via Skype, not even if there's a cow standing on the cable somewhere between you and HEX. To be clear: we have an Emergency Decree here in BS in which 1) keeping

or distributing illegal images of Gramma K. will result in a one-way
ticket to Doodletown and 2) leaks are regarded as "a serious threat to
municipal public order" and have been dealt with since, like, the Middle
Ages with total corporal punishment ("we-have-not-administered-
such-punishment-since-1932," LICGAS*). Take the hint: **WHAT
WE'RE DOING IS DANGEROUS**. The only good thing about a town
that gets off on indoctrinating the young is that you all know how to
keep a secret. I'm trusting you guys. I don't wanna bitch about it, but I
check the statcounter every other day so I can see exactly who's
logging in and from where. Anyone who breaks the rules will get a
lifetime ban from *OYE* without prior warning. And that's before Colton
& Co. start their freak show. **STICK TO THE RULES**. That's our
ultimate fuck-you to the system!

 * like I could give a shit

They stuck to the rules, all right. *OYE* was probably the one online
guerrilla movement that only operated in the full light of day: All its
users lived in Black Spring and slept in their own beds at night.

But not that night. That night they sneaked out of their rooms,
climbing down drainpipes and gutters like warriors in occupied territory, and set off with shovels, rope, a black cloth, and a pair of wire
cutters. They weren't what you'd call close friends, not all of them. Of
the five who went out that night, Tyler considered only Lawrence
VanderMeer from next door and Burak Şayer his real friends—not just
the kind you held textathons with until silly o'clock in the morning,
but the kind you told stuff to, private stuff. Yet that wasn't the whole
story, not if you had no one else to depend on. Born in Black Spring, you
knew each other from early on and feared the adults, not your allies.

It was the first night that fall that it rained. Not a summer shower,
but a real autumn rain, the kind that seems drowsy and endless. By the
time they had completed their mission forty minutes later, they were
soaked to the skin. They took each other's hands and Tyler solemnly
said, "For science, guys."

"For science," Lawrence echoed.

"For science," Justin Walker and Burak said in chorus.

Jaydon Holst shot them a glance dipped in liquid acid and said, "Up yours, faggots."

The next morning, with bags under their eyes that hung to their feet, they gathered on the patio of Sue's Highland Diner on the town square—although "square" was probably giving it too much credit. It was more like a gathering of shops and restaurants on Lower Reservoir and Deep Hollow Road surrounding the Little Methodist Church—which they all called Crystal Meth Church on account of the shape of its windows—and the old, sloping Temple Hill Cemetery. There were even those who found "gathering" too strong a word for the feeble excuse for eateries and retail establishments there at the intersection. Among those skeptics were the five boys on the patio at Sue's, lethargically sipping their cappuccinos and lattes, too worn-out to get overly excited about what was coming.

"Don't you kids have to be at school?" Sue asked when she brought them their order. It had stopped raining, but it was chilly, and Sue had had to remove pools of water from the plastic tables and chairs.

"No, the first two periods were cancelled, so they let us out," said Burak. The others nodded in agreement or squeezed their eyes shut in the pallid sunlight. Burak held a job as a dishwasher at Sue's, which earned them a free first round. After that they usually moved on to Griselda's Butchery & Delicacies on the other side of the square (Griselda was Jaydon's mom), which meant another free first round.

Burak wasn't lying, not entirely. The first two periods really had been cancelled—but no one had let them out.

"We've had an alert, boys," Sue said.

"I know, ma'am," Jaydon said amiably, a sure sign for everyone who knew Jaydon Holst to start seeing the word "BEWARE" in huge blinking neon letters. In fact, as Tyler had once remarked to Lawrence, Jaydon was the reason why the word "beware" existed at all, as well as the words "involuntary commitment" and "disaster waiting to happen."

But they all knew his background, so they tried to be sympathetic. "We figured we'd just sit here, so we can help out in case something happens."

"You're an angel, Jaydon. I'll tell your mom that when I go pick up the bacon this afternoon." Burak tried his best not to laugh as Sue put an ashtray down in front of him. "Can I get you boys anything else?"

"No, thank you, ma'am," Jaydon said with a smile that rose up like a cloud of carbon monoxide.

She was about to take the open menu away from the table when Tyler quickly put his hand on it, more forcefully than he had intended. "Can I hold on to this? I might want to order something else later on."

"Sure, Tyler," Sue said. "You just holler, all right? And I'll let you know if I get any messages. It probably won't be necessary, though. They have the choir ready and waiting." She carried the tray back inside.

All was silent for a moment, a silence in which the awkwardness of the situation seemed to thicken the air. Then, with a dim smile, Jaydon said, "Fucking hell."

"Dude, really . . . d'you want to go to Doodletown or something?" Despite Tyler's relief, his heart was pounding in his throat. If Sue had discovered the GoPro under the menu they would have been in deep shit. The REC light was on and the sports cam was aimed at Deep Hollow Road to the south, where at that very moment two men were placing a red-and-white barrier across the road near St. Mary's Church. The same thing was happening to the north, past the place where Old Miners Road, coming in from The Point, opened out onto the main thoroughfare. The GoPro couldn't see it, but Tyler, Justin, and Lawrence could. And there was something else: Out of the Roseburgh Nursing Home next to Sue's came eight or nine warmly wrapped elderly women, fiercely scanning the road. They talked among themselves and then, with their arms linked, strolled past the patio and out toward the intersection.

"Showtime," Justin remarked. "The crowds are going wild."

"What time is it?" Tyler asked.

Lawrence peeked at his iPhone. "Nine-thirteen. One more minute. Turn your cam, dude."

With great care, Tyler slid the GoPro, covered by the menu, to the other side of the small table and aimed the lens at Old Miners Road, which ran up the hill in a sharp S curve past the closed Popolopen Visitor Center. A couple of the old ladies sat down on the bench near the fountain and the bronze washerwoman. Others had ambled into the cemetery—to check out the accommodations, Tyler guessed.

"Omigod," Justin said softly, and nodded. "There she is."

"Right on time," Tyler reported, too excited to be cool, calm, and collected. He licked his lips and pushed Lawrence's iPhone under the menu and held it in front of the lens. "Wednesday morning, nine-fourteen a.m. As usual, at exactly the right spot."

From behind Old Miners Road a woman came walking out of the woods.

Why she follows **EXACTLY** the same pattern at the square and past the graveyard **EVERY** Wednesday morning is beyond me, but the Black Rock Witch is like Ms. Autism, unchallenged titleholder for three hundred fifty years running. Which is not, like, at all what witches are famous for. Makes you wonder if she ever gets dehydrated. Well, no. She's like a Microsoft operating system: designed to sow death and destruction, and every time showing the same error message.

So this behavioral pattern is mega interesting, of course, because: what's she doing there, and why is she coming back every week? Behold! I have two theories:

The first theory is that she's stuck in some kind of time warp and keeps repeating her past to the point of obsessive-compulsive neurosis (a.k.a. the Windows XP theory). Grim says that, long ago, they had this open market on the square in front of the church (I asked if it was right in front of the cemetery and he said they're not sure there even was a cemetery back then) and that she may have gone there to get bread and fish (which, like, totally makes no sense, because if the town had cast her off they wouldn't have been thrilled to let her shop there. Conclusion: Grim is cool, but he's just guessing). Anyway, it's not like she was going to church or anything, because heretics don't go to church (except the kind where they dance around the cross naked and smear themselves with the blood of Christ and chant psalms and stuff), otherwise we wouldn't be stuck with her now, right?

And then there's this: if you're dead (or should have been), what's the point of walking the same circuit week in and week out? Didn't they teach, like, variety in witch school? Makes as little sense as that old-fashioned, lights-on, lights-off poltergeist cliché (I mean, just speak up if you wanna say something, and don't do it in fucking Latin).

The second and more likely theory is **THAT SHE GOT THIS WAY BECAUSE HER EYES ARE SEWN SHUT**. What if we have a witch in Black Spring who **JUST COMPLETELY FROZE UP** (a.k.a. the Windows Vista theory)?

(Source: Open Your Eyes *website, September 2012)*

They watched as the woman with the sewn-shut eyes crossed Old Miners Road, passed behind the bus shelter, and came closer and closer. Her bare feet made circles in the puddles forming in the gutter. Perhaps it was instinct that propelled her, or perhaps something older and more primitive than instinct, but in any case Tyler knew it was *deliberate,* something that had no need of her blind eyes. He heard the dull clank of the chains that bound her arms and dress to her body. They made her look like one of these supermarket enchiladas rolled up in cellophane you'd rather not eat, wrapped and helpless. Tyler always found her less spooky when she walked, because then you didn't have to wonder what she was plotting behind those stitched-up eyes of hers. She was just like a rare insect, the kind you could study, but that wouldn't sting.

But when she stopped . . . she got a little freaky.

"You know what's funny about her?" Justin mused. "For a fairy-tale character she's, like, chronically ugly."

"She isn't a friggin' fairy-tale character," Burak said. "She's a supernatural phenomenon."

"Hell yeah she is. Witches only appear in fairy tales. So she's a fairy-tale character."

"Dafuq? What stone did your mother get knocked up under? That still doesn't make her a fairy-tale character. They're not real, anyway."

"So what if Little Red Riding Hood appeared in front of you?" Justin said with a gravity that couldn't be denied, let alone ridiculed. "Would she suddenly be a supernatural phenomenon? Or a fairy-tale character?"

"No, just a chick with a sick Kotex fetish," Jaydon said.

Burak snorted his cappuccino all over his shirt and Lawrence almost laughed himself into a coma. *A tad too much credit,* Tyler thought. "Aw, fuck!" Burak dabbed the stain with a stack of napkins. "Dude, you're sick."

"By the way," Lawrence said after he got himself back under control, "the Blair Witch wasn't a fairy-tale character, either."

That was an argument Justin couldn't refute, and it more or less ended the debate.

A car approached St. Mary's Church. The elderly volunteers at the fountain stuck their necks out and looked at it, but the car stopped at the roadblock and turned left. The ladies relaxed. Probably someone from town. If any Outsiders had been spotted, the old ladies would already have gathered around Gramma to walk with her, busily chattering among themselves. And if she stopped, Tyler knew (and this, more than anything else, was what truly made him ashamed of being a Black Spring boy), they'd huddle around her and start practicing church hymns like a kind of *Glee* for the near dead. The deeper meaning behind this was beyond him, but it was a brilliant example of reverse psychology: No one would ever notice the gaunt women with the chains standing in their midst if they didn't know she was there already. And no one could stomach an old folks' choir long enough to find out.

The woman with the sewn-shut eyes went past the patio right in front of them and advanced to the square, watched closely by the ladies at the fountain. Tyler turned the GoPro. It was essential for the success of their experiment that no Outsiders be there. Just as he was about to bask in the luck of their good fortune, Sue came out and stood in the doorway as if suddenly struck by this public-spirited and hitherto unseen sense of responsibility for her underage guests.

"Got any pesticide?" Jaydon asked.

Sue laughed and said, "If that worked, we would have tried it long ago, Jaydon," not realizing that it was her they needed it for, not the other witch. But Burak got the hint; he walked up to her with some lame excuse about planning his work schedule, and they both went inside together.

Justin grinned. "That woman would let you screw her even sideways, Jaydon."

"Fuck off."

"Guys, shut up," Tyler said. "It's gonna happen." He took the GoPro out from under the menu and shielded it with his body from the security cam that was mounted on The Point to Point Inn's façade across the intersection. To their hilarity, the camera was still hanging at a low, crooked angle, just as Jaydon had left it last night after hitting it with a long stick. Jaydon was like a living ordnance map when it came to the square and its surroundings, since he and his mom lived behind the butcher shop on the other side. He had said there were two other cameras that had a view of the lamppost on the eastern side of the cemetery. One was located in the bushes at the highest corner of Temple Hill, which they had neutralized by hanging a pine branch in front of it. The second camera was inaccessible. It was hidden in a window casing of Crystal Meth Church, but they had decided there were too many trees in front of it to cause real problems at night.

It was 2:57 a.m. when they hung Burak's long black cloth like a curtain from the branches of the oak tree that forked over the cemetery hedge. It was 3:36 when they wrung out the soaked curtain and rolled it up. And in all that time only one car had come down Deep Hollow Road, and it had passed without slowing down.

The only visible evidence of their operation was that the streetlight behind the curtain had gone out at 3:17, just when Jaydon cut through the exposed electrical cable that ran to the underground power box. Fortunately, the lamppost itself was not too tall, and its classical-looking fitting was aluminum, not cast iron. Easy-peasy. By the time they had cleaned everything up and had raised their toast to science, the lamppost was no longer standing against the cemetery hedge, but was neatly planted in the middle of the sidewalk, a foot and a half to the left.

Ground Zero.

So. As you can see in the clips below, she comes straight out of the woods and walks west down Deep Hollow Road. She arrives at the square, walks along the creek, up over the sidewalk, turns a kind of three-quarter pirouette at the cemetery hedge as if she's the Ballet Princess or something, and stands facing the street, as if someone had pulled her plug. I mean, we're talking serious runtime error here. A wisp of smoke rising from her hair would add to the dramatic effect. Exactly eight minutes and thirty-six seconds later, it's as if someone had pushed Ctrl+Alt+Del, because she starts walking again and disappears behind the houses on Hilltop Drive. And she does this every week, in exactly the same way (except the stupid thing is that no one knows exactly where and how she disappears—ideas, guys?).

It all happened in a flash.

When the woman with the sewn-shut eyes walked up along the creek and passed the SLOW—CHILDREN sign, the boys on the patio forgot their boredom and became so excited that they left their seats and rocked from one leg to another. They couldn't help it. It felt as if they were witnessing one of those rare significant moments in human history that would outlive even Wikipedia, like the invention of penicillin or the first explosion of the silicone breast implant. Tyler forgot his fear of Doodletown and no longer bothered to keep his GoPro out of sight of the surveillance cam. This *had* to be captured.

"O-M-F-G," Justin said, without taking a breath.

"She's gonna see it . . . she's gonna see it . . . *she's gonna see it . . .*"

She didn't see it. With an audible thud, the Black Rock Witch walked straight into the lamppost and fell backward on her butt.

The ladies at the fountain jumped up, all shrieks and hands covering mouths. Tyler and his friends looked at one another in silent, speechless amazement, their jaws down on the sidewalk. Burak had appeared in the restaurant doorway. It was as if the impact had sucked all the oxygen out of the air. It exceeded their wildest dreams. They had just floored a three-hundred-year-old supernatural phenomenon, and they had it on fucking video.

Gramma was squirming on the drying sidewalk at the foot of the lamppost, as you might imagine an enchilada squirming in cellophane. All the creepiness her mutilated face and reputation had bestowed on her had been knocked for a loop. Now she just looked helpless, like a baby bird fallen from its nest. There was no way she'd be able to stand up on her own. One of the elderly women approached her, hand on cheek, and for a moment Tyler was afraid the woman had made the suicidal decision to help her up when something totally freaky happened. In a flash, the witch was back on her feet. The elderly woman recoiled with a scream. One moment Gramma had been lying there, helpless and twitching on the sidewalk; the next moment, like in a stop-motion video, she was up and chafing against the lamppost with her chains, as if she were trying to walk straight through it.

"Jesus fuck . . ." was all Jaydon could manage.

"Did you get that?" Lawrence asked. Tyler looked down and discovered that he had just made the most dire mistake of his budding career as a reporter: In his consternation, he had let his camera dangle and shoot some super-interesting footage of the sidewalk, and had missed the witch's stop-motion trick. He felt his cheeks turn purple and cursed himself, but the others were much too engrossed in what *she* was doing to pay any attention to him.

"What's going on?" Sue asked as she struggled to see something from the doorway behind Burak. No one took the trouble to inform her.

"Look at that," Justin said. "She's trying to push right through it."

It was true. For three hundred years the witch had been passing through that very spot, and today was no exception, lamppost or no lamppost.

"She's, like, preprogrammed," Lawrence said.

"She's, like, fucking the lamppost," Jaydon said.

After half a minute of metal grating against metal, she suddenly slipped past it, did her three-quarter pirouette, and disconnected.

Justin was the first to laugh.

Burak was the second.

Then they all laughed, wild, uncontrollable laughter, and they slapped each other on the shoulders and punched each other on the arms. The humorless crones at the fountain turned around and fixed their eyes on the group of boys. They saw the GoPro and one of them shouted, "Hey, what have you got there? What are you doing with that camera, young man?"

"Busted!" Jaydon roared. "Which one of you pushed her over?"

This caused general confusion among the women, as if they were seriously considering the possibility that one of them had pushed her (that, or people over seventy lost all their talent for clever comebacks), and that made the boys laugh even harder. They were still laughing when they slid past the roadblock a minute later and ran down Deep Hollow Road, and they were laughing even harder when, two hundred yards farther on, they could no longer suppress their curiosity and stopped on the shoulder to watch the footage on the GoPro's LCD screen.

-+-|-|-|-|-

THE IMAGES SHOULD hold no surprises; you know what's there. These are the first pictures in journalistic history to feature a supernatural phenomenon going for a nosedive. They're so unique that they go viral on YouTube in a matter of minutes and are celebrated and debunked on hundreds of blogs, not to mention being endlessly repeated on Jimmy Fallon. But of course that doesn't happen; of course the images are kept secret. Still, that same evening they do achieve a certain cult status.

The boys weren't born yesterday and they know they're in for it. They figure there's only one way to escape Doodletown: to step forward on their own and play the holy innocent.

"We were just fooling around," Tyler says when they show Robert Grim a director's cut of the clip. In this version, you only see the witch walk up along the creek, bump into the lamppost, and topple over. Grim plays the images directly from the memory card. They're the only recordings from that morning still in the camera—Tyler fixed it that way. The rest is safely tucked away on his MacBook, password protected. Tyler tries to add a contrite quality to his voice by imagining a halo hanging over his head, but at a certain point he can't hold back his laughter.

Robert Grim is laughing, too. In fact, tears stream down his cheeks when he sees what a trick the kids have pulled. He laughs for the same reason the boys laugh, and for the same reason the regulars at the Quiet Man Tavern laugh when they crowd around Grim's laptop that night. None of them realizes that this is more than a bit of amusement over the witch's vaudevillian pratfall: It's a triumph, small and inconsequential though it may seem, over the very thing that has cast a shadow over their lives for as long as they can remember. Within the laughter lies a collective relief so deep-seated that it becomes a little uncanny. And later on, when Tyler realizes why, it scares him to the marrow.

"Officially, I can't approve of this, of course," Robert Grim says, after pulling himself together and wiping the tears from his eyes. But then he just starts roaring again. Without a murmur the boys agree to his proposal: In order to steer clear of the Council, they must put everything back as it had been, pay for the severed cable out of their own pockets, and spend the rest of the week picking up trash in Ladycliff Park.

While he's in bed that night, Tyler gets a PM from Jaydon:

@QT Man. Falling #ag mks evrybdy crack up.
FCKD UP!

At that point, Tyler is still dazed by the success of the lamppost test (although he gets seriously stymied while writing his report for *OYE* when Lawrence asks him, "Okay, but what does this all *prove?*"), so he doesn't yet understand what Jaydon means.

But the next day, as he's doing his cleanup work in the park and sees the faces of the people in the rain, it begins to dawn on him. Everybody seems to know what he has done, and from one day to the next he has become a cult hero. No one says a thing, but they all smile at him and silently express their support. It's those smiling faces that get to him. They should seem pleasant, but they're not. They're perverse, like they always have been. Because when these faces smile, he no longer recognizes them. They're faces that have forgotten how to smile. They're faces with too much skin on them, too many wrinkles for their years. They're faces that are leading lives of their own, and every day they sag a little further. They're flattened faces, grim faces, faces under insurmountable stress. They're the faces of Black Spring. And when they try to smile, it looks like they're screaming.

That evening Tyler lies in bed with a terrible premonition of darkness and horror, and there are two images that keep him awake until the crack of dawn: screaming faces in the rain and the falling witch. Then they fade to black.

FIVE

THE FORMER POPOLOPEN Visitor Center at the bottom of Old
Miners Road had been the property of the United States Military
Academy at West Point since 1802. Still on display in the frieze on
the outer wall was the tiled tableau with the school's motto in large,
old-fashioned letters: DUTY—HONOR—COUNTRY. Now the outpost
was abandoned and the officers at The Point went out of their way to
avoid it, but the flag with the eagle emblem still hung in the humble
museum at the visitor center, where you could find nostalgic sepia
prints of army officers dressed in tails and women wearing fur collars.
The visitor center was now closed, too. But if you happened to peer
inside, you might be able to make out a grubby black-and-white photo
hanging inconspicuously in a corner, a picture of St. Mary's Church
Square. In it, three women dressed in rags and with their eyes painted
shut were leaning forward and shaking their fists at a small group of
children in knee pants and heavy overcoats. In their clawlike hands
they held broomsticks, the kind chimney sweeps used at the beginning
of the previous century. The photo's caption read: ALL HALLOW'S EVE
CELEBRATION, 1932.

But even if the photo witches had been captured jamming their
broomsticks up the children's little behinds and spinning them around
until they burst into flames, it wouldn't have spoiled one itsy bit of
Robert Grim's excellent mood. Just after midnight on the night of the
lamppost incident, he left the Quiet Man and walked downhill, a
broad grin on his face and his laptop under his arm.

It was rare for Grim to be in such high spirits, and given the fact that he had been officially admonished by Colton Mathers earlier that day, it was all the more astonishing. The councilman's poor conservative ego had felt locked out of that lamppost business. To call Robert Grim progressive was like calling Auschwitz a Boy Scout camp, but Colton Mathers's conservatism had fallen to an altogether different, amphibian low, as if it had been scorned by evolution itself after crawling out of the primordial swamp and, out of pure misery, had turned around and crept right back in. Mathers's excuse was God; but then the Crusades were God's work, too, Grim reasoned.

And so were blue laws.

And jihad.

He walked toward Old Miners Road. The next day it would rain, a dull, persistent rain that would continue through the whole first week of October, but now it was dry and the clouds drifted through the air in dark wisps. Grim fished the keys to the former visitor center out of his pocket and went inside. He didn't have night duty, but he felt too elated to sleep. He locked the door behind him, walked behind the counter in the dusty darkness, and went down the three flights of stairs at the end of the hallway to the secret that lay sunken in the hillside.

It was no accident that the former military outpost had been built against the steep crest of the hill, since of course its main purpose had not been to house the Popolopen Visitor Center. The income that had accrued from renting the building to the private owners of the Black Rock Forest Reserve until they moved north to Cornwall in 1989 had covered most of the expenses The Point incurred for running its own covert operation: the supervision of the residents of Black Spring. For Robert Grim, the goal was subtly different: saving their damn skins.

The interior of the HEX control center looked like a cross between NASA Mission Control in Houston and a dilapidated neighborhood clubhouse. Next to the coordination room with its big screen and horseshoe-shaped computer desk there were well-maintained video and microfilm archives; the town's network provider room; a small library of the occult; a storeroom for smoke screens, which resembled theater props more than anything else (the large artifacts, such as the construction hut for when she appeared on public roads, were kept in a shed on Deep Hollow Road); a lounging area with old, stained sofas; and a small kitchen without a dishwasher. The control center had been renovated many times over the years, and modernized with both an eye toward technical progress and upstate, penny-pinching provinciality. As the HEX security chief, Robert Grim had always had the feeling that he was playing a part in a James Bond movie directed by the mentally deprived. The most painful example of this was the cardboard box donated weekly by Colton Mathers that contained instant ramen noodles and Lipton tea in fourteen different flavors.

The electric kettle had been out of service for months.

But tonight, even the thought of Mathers's petty face failed to shake Grim's upbeat mood. He entered the coordination room and bid the night shift, Warren Castillo and Claire Hammer, an almost musical good evening.

"You get laid or something?" Warren asked.

"Better," Grim said. "I've had a gala premiere." With a grin, he put the laptop on the desk.

"No!"

"Yes."

"Hero!"

Warren laughed out loud, but Claire snapped like a mousetrap. "Robert, what the hell are you thinking?" she asked. "You've already rubbed Colton the wrong way once today, and you don't want to do that again."

"What's he gonna do, bawl me out again?"

"According to protocol . . ."

"Fuck protocol. The whole town is behind me. They loved it. Absolutely loved it. They need this, Claire. Let them blow off some steam once in a while. We have enough to put up with here. And Colton's sorry ass appreciates a practical joke every now and then."

Warren raised his eyebrows. "Colton Mathers appreciating practical jokes is as unlikely as a Disney movie where everybody dies in the end of internal hemorrhaging."

"I'm just saying, be careful, Robert," Claire said. "This is going to come back and hit you hard."

"Karma's a bitch. Enough about this. Where's our lovely lady tonight?"

Warren dragged the digital map to the main screen, which marked her most recent appearances with tiny lights. One of them, somewhere in lower Black Spring near Route 293, was blinking red. "She's been on Weyant Road, in Mrs. Clemens's basement, since half past five. It's supposed to be packed with furniture. Mrs. Clemens didn't see her until she went down to get a can of corn. She's jammed between a massage chair and an ironing board."

"Doesn't take much to make her happy," Grim said.

"Mrs. Clemens was pretty shocked. At her age, she's not really big on unexpected visits anymore, she said." Warren snorted. "She called, would you believe it? I didn't say anything, but last year she requested an iPhone so she could use the damn app. I think she only uses it to Skype with that daughter of hers in Australia."

"As long as she doesn't do her Skyping from her massage chair tonight." Grim looked at the screen. "And Katherine? Is she rattled, after what happened this morning?"

"Not that we've noticed," Claire said. "It doesn't seem to have had any effect on her. Maybe she got a bump on her forehead, but you know how changes disappear when she moves from place to place. Though I'll be curious to see if there are any alterations in her pattern next week."

"Old habits die hard," Warren said. He yawned and turned to Grim. "Listen, why don't you call it a night, workaholic? We'll handle this on our own."

Grim said he'd follow Warren's advice as soon as he checked his e-mail. Claire turned her attention back to Internet traffic, and Warren continued with his game of solitaire. There wasn't anything in the mail or on *Yahoo! News,* and ten minutes later Grim noticed he, too, was yawning. He was getting ready to go home when Warren jumped up from his desk with a triumphant yell and shouted, "Home encounter! I *knew* it!"

Grim and Claire turned and looked up. Claire's mouth fell open. "No way. The Delarosas?"

Warren bopped back and forth in front of the desk, striking a balance between the moonwalk and Gangnam style. Grim couldn't decide whether he was a very good dancer or a total jerk.

Claire couldn't believe it. "And they've only been there a week! How is it possible?"

On the big screen, in greenish night vision, were live images from camera D19-063, which took in the former Barphwell plot, now owned by the Delarosas. In the middle of the street was Bammy Delarosa with a white sheet wrapped around her torso like an ancient Greek. Although the surveillance cams in Black Spring had no mics, it was obvious she was screaming. Her husband—Burt, his name was; Burt Delarosa—was in his underpants and was hopping around her in a panicky, helpless sort of way. To Robert Grim, they looked like a satyr and a maenad getting ready to make an offering to Dionysus.

Grim's experience at sizing up situations provided him with immediate reassurance. The Delarosas had run outside as fast as their legs could carry them, forgetting their cell phones in their haste. This gave Grim and his team a bit more time before it occurred to the Delarosas to call 911. In any case, the Delarosas didn't look as if they'd had the kind of experience that warranted calling the law. An exorcist, perhaps— if such a thing lay within their frame of reference.

On the right side of the screen, a square of light appeared in the darkness of the house next door and soon Mrs. Soderson came outside. More worried neighbors arrived from across the street and tried to calm the newbies down.

"Yup, a home encounter," Grim said. "Congratulations, Warren. You can split the kitty."

"Now the phone rings," Claire said. Sure enough, one second later, it did. Claire answered and began talking to one of the Delarosas' neighbors.

Warren stood next to Grim, staring pensively at the screen. "Now they're going to find out that they're stuck with us for the rest of their lives."

"Such a tragedy. Couldn't happen to nicer people."

"Who's going to do it?"

"I will," said Grim without a second thought. Although he knew that blew his chance of getting any sleep tonight, he accepted it without complaint. Having to inform newbies was no easy task and charity wasn't exactly his forte, but Grim felt sympathy for the Delarosas. They would have to revise their perception of the spiritual and the supernatural in ways that were subtle, but drastic nonetheless. Grim, born and bred in Black Spring, had never had that experience, but he had witnessed it often enough from the sidelines to know its traumatizing effects. He was a lapsed Methodist, and outside his job he would have nothing whatsoever to do with the paranormal. Yet somewhere in his indeterminate notions of the whole *spiritus mundi* he simply accepted the fact that inexplicable things happened, bewildering things, even in a world that regarded itself as fully enlightened. Still, that wasn't what was most painful: For many newcomers in Black Spring, the irreversibility of their fate, its *finality,* was their first uncanny confrontation with their own mortality. People desperately resisted the idea of their own death by looking away for as long as they could and avoiding the subject. But in Black Spring, they lived with death. They took her into their homes and hid her from the outside world . . . and sometimes they put a lamppost in her path.

The Delarosas, however . . . irreversibility and death didn't fit in with their cosmopolitan life of cool sophistication and postmenopausal career switches. Black Spring was the arsenic pill they had accidentally discovered under their tongues and had bitten into before they knew it. If Robert Grim hadn't just lost his bet, he might have felt sorry for them.

They watched on the big screen as the Delarosas were taken by their neighbors to Mrs. Soderson's house. Claire hung up and said, "They're in good hands. I promised to have a team ready in ten minutes. Who's going?"

"Me," Grim said. "Are they religious?"

"No. If I remember correctly, he was a Methodist as a boy, but he's not practicing."

"Then let's leave the church out of it."

"'Thy rod and thy staff they comfort them,'" Warren recited solemnly.

"Should you really be going, Robert? After our last run-in with them, you're probably the last person to ease their minds."

We're not going to ease their minds, Grim thought. *We're going to shake up their world even more.* "They're in too much shock to realize that. I'll take Pete VanderMeer and Steve Grant. They're on call this month. A sociologist and a doctor, and cool enough to know how to thread that needle. Oh, and one of their wives, for Bammy. That ought to do it." He threw on his coat and added, "You'll be getting them out of bed when you call, angel."

He left Warren and Claire behind in the control center and prepared for a long night.

SIX

"**HER NAME IS** Katherine van Wyler, but most of us call her the Black Rock Witch," Pete VanderMeer said. He took a long drag on his cigarette and fell thoughtfully silent.

They were in the lounge of The Point to Point Inn, sitting in vintage leather armchairs that smelled of age. The coffee table in between them was littered with half-full glasses, bottles, and thermoses. After the innkeeper prepared a room for the Delarosas, she had withdrawn to bed, leaving the dimly lit hotel bar to her guests. Pete VanderMeer and Grim were having beer; Steve drank coffee. Jocelyn was sipping from a steaming mug of chamomile tea, as was Bammy Delarosa—but not until after Grim made her down a shot of vodka. Her husband needed no such encouragement: he was already on his third shot. He wasn't altogether drunk yet, but was well on his way. *Probably a good thing,* Steve thought.

Burt and Bammy Delarosa were far from the arrogant snobs Grim had made them out to be. Steve found that he rather liked them, insofar as this was a good time to judge. Now that the initial shock had passed, they were able to take the situation a bit more lightheartedly. That wasn't to say that they had come to grips with it. They were numbed, with the same numbness that undertakers so cleverly exploit when practical matters have to be discussed with the bereaved. Tomorrow, or during the weekend at the latest, reality would hit hard, and when it did they'd be better off knowing what they were up against. In any case, now they had the chance of making the discovery within the safe confines of the hotel. There was nothing in the world that could have persuaded the Delarosas to go back to their dark, abandoned house . . . where *she* was.

Grim had gone to pick up Pete, Jocelyn, and Steve in his Dodge Ram, and the new folks had greeted them, politely but with trembling hands, in the lobby. Steve felt racked and dazed; he and Jocelyn had been asleep for almost two hours when the phone rang. But now that the coffee had settled in his stomach, his mind was finally starting to clear.

"Katherine van Wyler," Burt Delarosa said unsteadily.

"Yes," Pete said. "She lived in Philosopher's Deep, in the woods behind where Steve and Jocelyn and my wife and I now live. It was in Black Spring that she was sentenced to death for witchcraft in 1664—although they didn't call it Black Spring back then; it was a Dutch trappers' colony known as New Beeck—and it's here in Black Spring that she's remained ever since."

Behind them a block of wood crackled in the fireplace, and Bammy shot up like a jack-in-the-box. The poor woman was as nervous as a deer, Steve noticed, and there were deep furrows of tension around her mouth.

"In Highland Falls, Fort Montgomery, and of course The Point they all know that the hills and woods around here are haunted. They don't even need to know the details. You can feel it because it's in the air, like the smell of ozone after a lightning storm. But the witch is a Black Spring problem, and unfortunately we can't do anything but try to keep it that way."

He sipped his beer. The Delarosas looked forlornly at their own drinks and couldn't bring themselves to pick up their glasses.

"Little to nothing is known about her life, which only adds to the mystery. She must have come here on one of the Dutch West India Company's ships in about 1647. New Amsterdam was a bustling port city at the time. The outposts up along the Hudson, where they traded with the Indians, were very primitive, and stories went around by word of mouth. Many of them were lost over time. Katherine may have been a shepherd, or maybe she was a midwife. The role of women in the New World was to build up the community."

"By bearing children," Jocelyn explained.

"Right. They were sowing the seeds of a new civilization, you see. The settlements that the Dutch founded were mainly along the secure riverbanks. But the woods out west were full of game, and the Munsee did their trapping in what's now known as Black Rock Forest, so that's where the Dutch established New Beeck. They got along with the Indians all right. Traded with 'em. It was the English that gave 'em the jitters. New England was breathing down their neck and eager to add New Netherland to their territory. Well, that's exactly what happened the next year: The English annexed the Dutch settlements without spilling a single drop of blood. They were the ones who finally drove the Munsee away . . . but many argue that the Munsee left the area of their own free will and went north. Because by then, Black Spring had already been cursed."

"Excuse me, but what exactly does that mean?" Burt Delarosa asked.

"Bewitched," Robert Grim said, with his customary lack of subtlety. "Gone sour. Doomed."

"At least, that's what they believed back then," Bammy presumed.

"Yeah, that's one way of putting it," Grim sneered, but he slumped back in his chair at Pete VanderMeer's venomous stare. The Delarosas looked at each other and frowned. Under different circumstances, it might have been almost comical to see how perfectly synchronously they acted.

"Now, you have to understand that superstition was embedded deep in the human psyche," Pete continued. "We're talking about folks who had to manage in a completely strange world, at a time when there was absolutely no security. In Europe, they had had their share of plague epidemics, failed harvests, famine, and outlaws, and the New World was full of unknown wild beasts, savages, and demons. No one knew what kind of supernatural forces haunted the wilderness to the west of the settlements. A pretty unpleasant situation. Without science, people had to rely on old wives' tales and omens. They feared Almighty God and were scared to death of the Devil. This left an unmistakable mark on the surrounding forests—just think about the name of the hill behind our house."

"Mount Misery?" Burt asked. "We went for a hike up there just this week. Beautiful place. We could see the Hudson from the top."

"It's a nice walk. Completely harmless these days, as long as you stay on the trail. But those omens . . . You have to see them as a primitive form of meteorology, except it's not the weather they're predicting; it's impending disaster. You know the Salem witch trials, of course, which happened some twenty or thirty years later in the Massachusetts Bay Colony. They were preceded by a failed harvest, a smallpox epidemic, and the constant threat of attack by native tribes. The connection wasn't made until afterward, but that doesn't matter. From then on, fear played an enormous role in the flow of rumors that preceded tragedies. People saw the signs everywhere. Stillbirths, strange natural phenomena, rapid putrefaction of the flesh, big birds . . ." Pete grinned. "The Dutch were somewhat more down-to-earth than the Puritans, but in 1653 there was this large bird that landed on the steeple cross of the harbor church in New Amsterdam every day at sunset for three weeks, causing a huge uproar. They said it was bigger than a goose and gray in color, and it preyed on dead bodies. Today, of course, you'd figure it was a vulture—they used to appear as vagrants in these parts every now and again. But how could the colonists know? So, soon enough, this mob gathers and makes all kinds of predictions based on the bird's appearance. The city council has the poor thing shot, but it was too late: The next year, the population was devastated by smallpox. So they blamed it on the bird."

Jocelyn remembered something. "Steve, tell them the story about that doctor and the children. I don't know if Pete's familiar with it?"

"No, I'm not."

"A colleague of mine at New York Med once told me this," Steve said. "Prior to the same epidemic of 1654, a New Amsterdam doctor named Frederick Verhulst studied the behavior of children who were playing 'funeral.' The children dug holes outside the walls of the settlement and carried fruit crates out to put in their graves, walking in procession. Their parents thought they were possessed, and the game was seen as a bad omen."

"Thank God we have Wii now," Pete said. They all laughed, except for Bammy Delarosa, who could only manage a faint smile.

"There are many stories like this," Steve said. "Some pretty gruesome. Bodies have been found from that period with bricks shoved between their jaws. During the Boston Yellow Fever Epidemic of 1693, mass graves were often reopened to bury the new dead, and sometimes the gravediggers came across swollen corpses that had blood running out of their mouths, with the shrouds eaten away from around the faces. It was as if the dead person had gnawed his way out of his shroud and had come back to life in order to drink blood. Today we know that decomposing bodies swell up because of gases. Rotting organs force fluids out of the mouth and the shroud is eaten away by the bacteria they contain. But back then it was presented as scientific fact that the 'shroud eaters' were the undead who fed on the living and spread curses along with the fever, so that more dead would come to life. Church ministers would shove bricks into their mouths so they would starve."

A profound silence fell, broken only by the crackling of the fire. Then Burt said, "You know, in some towns they actually big-up the place. Tell the new residents how nice the area is—good places to eat, stuff like that . . ."

Grim snorted and choked on his beer. This time everyone laughed, even Bammy. Jocelyn pounded Grim on the back until he got hold of himself. Steve thought it was a good sign that Burt was able to make jokes. It meant he wasn't so rattled that everything he was hearing tonight was going in one ear and out the other—as long as he didn't knock back that whole bottle of Stoli.

"All well and good," said Pete when he was laughed out. "The doomsayers contributed to the insecurity and fear that grips people when strange calamity strikes. Children born blind, weird animal tracks in the mud, lights in the night sky . . . when people start believing in omens, there's a general breakdown in the way they think and live. What terrible thing awaits us? That's the breeding ground where the fear of Katherine van Wyler took root."

"So they thought she was a witch," Burt said.

"That's right." Pete's cigarette had burned down in the ashtray and he started rolling a new one. "It was the usual witch-hunt story, but it differed in a couple of respects. Not as far as the cause is concerned: She was a single woman living alone in the woods, so everyone looked down on her. By 1664, she must have been a good thirty years old, because she was the mother of two small children, a son and a daughter. Who the father was and why he wasn't there, we don't know. Word went around that she had mated with Indians. Add to this the fact that she had left the church, and it wasn't long before fingers started pointing in her direction. They said she engaged in heathen practices. Exactly what these practices entailed became the grist for one hell of a rumor mill."

"Devil worship?" Burt asked.

"Sodomy. Bestiality. Cannibalism. And, indeed, all of it the work of the Devil."

"Jesus."

"That part comes next. So it's October 1664 when Katherine's nine-year-old son dies of smallpox. Witnesses testify that they've seen her, dressed in full mourning, burying his body up in the woods. But a few days later, the townsfolk see the boy walking around the streets of New Beeck as if Katherine had raised him from the dead, like Jesus did with Lazarus. They shat bricks, I tell you. If raising the dead isn't the ultimate proof that you're messing with stuff you shouldn't be messing with, I don't know what is, so Katherine van Wyler was sentenced to death for witchcraft. After being tortured, she confessed, but they all did. God, after the wheel and the dunking stool, you'd damn well confess that you had flown from roof to roof on a broomstick. The things they did to her were horrible. Anyway, she was forced to kill the godless thing that was her resurrected son, and to do it with her own hands. If she didn't obey, the judges would kill not only the boy, but her daughter, too."

"That's terrible!" Bammy cried. "So she had to choose between her children?"

Pete shrugged. "They weren't exactly sweethearts back then. It was a cold wind that blew over from the Old World. Accusations and convictions of witchcraft were the order of the day. Katherine had no choice, so she killed her son to save her daughter, after which she was sentenced to the noose as an act of mercy. They didn't hang her themselves, though: She was forced to jump of her own accord, to symbolize atonement and self-chastisement. When she was dead, her body was thrown into one of the witch's pools in the woods for the wild animals. That's the way it usually happened. Either that, or they would be burned at the stake. Innocent, of course."

"How awful," Bammy muttered.

"Except, in this case, she wasn't all that innocent," Grim said. The Delarosas looked at him.

"Yeah, well, we don't know that," Pete said hastily. "We don't know if she was guilty of the crimes she was convicted of. Even in Black Spring, it is a little far out to make those assumptions. This much we do know: The settlers *believed* she had raised her son from the dead, and that was enough for them. Looking back, it's possible, even probable, that during her lifetime she possessed certain powers, but there's no indication that she performed miracles or used her gift to harm anyone. What's more likely is that her violent death, preceded by horrible torture and being forced to kill her own child, made her what she is now. But that's all guesswork. In the world of the occult, we don't really have a lot of reference material, you know."

"Good," Burt Delarosa said. He tossed back his Stoli. "So you guys have your own village ghost." He produced a high-pitched laugh, as if he were surprised to hear himself say those words, and he lifted his empty glass to Grim. "That's terrific. So you were telling the truth when you called me, you son of a bitch. I thought you were pulling my leg. Well . . . of course I thought you were pulling my leg."

"What are you talking about?" Bammy asked, looking bewildered.

"The day he and that woman tried to bribe us. That night he called me on my cell phone and tried it again, with some cock-and-bull story about the Wicked Witch of the West. I didn't tell you because I was shocked by how far they were willing to go with their badgering, and I didn't want to upset you. And . . . well, you know what we thought about them, honey."

"Sorry," Grim admitted, without any noticeable irony.

"You called her a village ghost," Pete said, "which is not entirely correct, but it's close. You don't seem to be having much trouble accepting the reality of something very peculiar hanging out in your bedroom. Why didn't you guys call the police when you saw her? That's the first thing most people do when they encounter an intruder. Or maybe an ambulance, given the state she's in?"

The Delarosas exchanged awkward glances and didn't know what to say. A sudden feeling of déjà vu crept over Steve, as it so often did when they were giving new folks the lowdown. It only happened a couple of times a year, if they were lucky, and usually at a more civilized hour. But the hour had nothing to do with what he was recalling. It had been eighteen years ago, with the same Pete VanderMeer, quite a bit younger then and working in the Department of Sociology at New York University; maybe less proficient in his storytelling, but with the same thoughtful calmness in his voice. What Steve mainly recollected was their fear and their uncertainty. *We were listening to a story about omens and witches, yet at no time did we fail to believe him. Not . . . after what we had seen.*

Finally, it was Bammy who spoke. "You just *felt* that she . . . well, that she was no intruder. One look at her and there was no denying it.

She felt like something *bad*." She turned to her husband. "May I tell them how it happened?"

Burt seemed to want to say something, but he waved his hand. "Whatever."

"We hadn't fallen asleep yet. We were . . . engaged with each other." Elegant blushes appeared on her cheeks and both Steve and Grim bit their tongues. In all his years as a doctor, Steve didn't think he had ever heard a more prudish description of the act, or one more aptly suited to the person uttering it. "I turned onto my back and suddenly there she was, at the foot of the bed. I saw her behind Burt. And that was the creepy thing about it. First she hadn't been there at all, and then she was, and she was looking at me. Except she didn't have eyes, only black, frayed threads, and she looked at me with them. I wish she hadn't done that."

"My wife screamed," Burt said, his voice flat and toneless, "and she squirmed out from under me as if she'd been electrocuted. Then I saw her, too. And *I* screamed. I don't think I've screamed since I had to jump into a hole in the ice during frat hazing at Jamaica Bay, but I screamed now. It's like Bammy says: There was absolutely no doubt in my mind that she was some sort of apparition, or a nightmare— except this was a nightmare that was real, and we were both sharing it. Bammy pulled the sheet up around her and ran out of the room. I followed her, but when I got to the doorway I turned around, because I wanted to see if she disappeared when you blinked your eyes, as night-mares do. But she was still there. And . . . I went back."

"But why?" Bammy asked, shocked.

He shrugged. "You know. There was a maimed woman in our bed-room. All chained up. I wanted to see if I could do something for her, I guess."

"Did anything happen?" Grim wanted to know.

At first Burt said nothing, and Steve saw Bammy's hand stiffen around his. "No," he finally said. "She just stood there. I was afraid, and I went out after my wife."

Grim and Steve exchanged glances. Pete saw the lie, too, but decided it wasn't relevant, at least not now. "Fine. So you both had the feeling that she isn't human."

"How come this isn't more widely known?" Burt asked. "I mean, if there really is a ghost haunting your town—and that's not something I'm ready to accept until I've studied it carefully—but, say it's true, it would turn science on its head. Have you ever captured her on video?"

"We have more than forty thousand hours of footage in our digital archive," Grim said. "We have cameras hanging all over town. Didn't you notice? We save the material for ten years, but then we throw it away. It gets pretty boring after a while."

Again the Delarosas stared at him. "I don't think I follow," Burt said slowly.

"What he's trying to say," Pete said, "is that we're doing everything we can to make sure it *isn't* widely known. In fact, our lives depend on it." He looked each of them straight in the eye, first Burt, then Bammy. Steve had deep respect for the fact that he didn't turn away as he was uttering these words. "Katherine's story doesn't end with her death, you see. One winter morning in 1665, four months after she was hanged, a party led by former Director-General Peter Stuyvesant himself went into the hills to see what the trappers had been up to, and they found New Beeck completely deserted. Icicles were hanging from the roofs and everything was covered in a thick blanket of snow. The odd thing, though, was that the snow wasn't fresh. There should have been tracks all over the place, but there weren't. It was as if the townsfolk had gone up in smoke in the course of one fateful night. They were never seen again. The Dutch suspected a curse, and they avoided the ghost town and the hills around it, where they felt the 'evil eye' was upon them. In June of that year, Stuyvesant returned to the Netherlands. Most of the original settlers left, and the events sank into oblivion. The only official historical documentation on the disappearance didn't turn up until more than forty years later, in 1708, in the annals of the Dutch

Republic, which include a brief account of the legend. We have that document in our archive. It attributes the exodus from New Beeck to the economic difficulties caused by the Second Anglo-Dutch War and the annexation of New York, and assumes that the settlers had been killed in a battle between Indian tribes."

"So it was local folklore," Burt muttered.

"Except," Jocelyn said, "there are those who say that the Indians had already abandoned the area the previous fall, right in the middle of hunting season. Legend has it that they were afraid, saying that the woods they once claimed had been 'contaminated.' Whatever it was, why would the Indians just walk away from lucrative trade with the settlers, and why did it happen right after the trappers had left Katherine's body in the woods?"

"Exactly," Pete said. "And there's more. Because what happened in 1713 *is* documented. In April of that year, the English settlers moved into town, renaming it Black Spring. After a week, three people committed suicide. Bethia Kelly, a midwife, killed eight children before they put her away."

"You're making that up."

"I wish I were. When they came to arrest her, she declared that this woman coming from out of the woods had whispered to her to make a choice between the children. She said she couldn't choose, so she killed them all. In the archive, there's a brief mention of local folklore having to do with the evil eye and strange phenomena that took place on Mount Misery, supposedly in connection with a witch. A month later, a party of church elders went into the woods. When they came back, they claimed to have expelled a possessed woman by sewing her eyes and mouth shut and chaining up her body. That same year all of them died, although the circumstances are unknown. But at least they were partly successful. They closed her evil eye."

"But she never went away," Bammy said with an expression of deep horror on her face.

"No, that's sort of the problem," Pete agreed. "She never went away.

Until this day, Katherine van Wyler walks the streets of Black Spring day and night . . . and appears in our houses."

No one spoke, so Grim took up the task. "We're not talking about the outdated kind of ghost who's only seen by some irritating, autistic, and neglected kid who no one believes but always ends up being right in the end. The Black Rock Witch is always here. And she's no benign sort of specter or an echo from the past like in those drippy adolescent horror-porn flicks. She confronts us with her presence like a fenced-in pit bull. Muzzled, never moving an inch. But if you stick your finger through the bars, she doesn't just feel it to see if it's fat enough. She rips it off."

Burt rose. He was about to grab the bottle of Stoli, but changed his mind. Suddenly he seemed completely sober, despite the considerable amount of alcohol running through his veins. "Assuming all this is true . . . what does she *want*? What does the damn witch want from you, for crying out loud?"

"We're assuming she wants revenge," Pete said grimly. "Whatever it is that's driving her, her death released a power that seeks revenge against the people who made her commit those terrible acts. And even though three hundred fifty years have passed, those people are us, the people of Black Spring."

"But, I mean, how do you *know*? Has anyone ever tried to communicate with her? Or, I dunno, exorcise her?"

"Yes," Bammy said, backing him up. "Maybe she's just wants to be heard. . . ."

"Been there, done that," Grim said. "Ouija boards are out of the question—don't mess with those fuckers, they'll kill you. Airy-fairy pagan shit simply doesn't work on her. Tried it all before. We've had exorcists from the Vatican who concluded she was godless, so they couldn't help us. Of course, the truth was that those pansies were scared shitless by what they found here. Priests, shamans, white witches, commandos, the army . . . it all leads to very nasty situations. In the past, they tried to behead her and set her on fire, but she just vanishes as soon as the smoke rises from under her skirt, so to speak. Now we have an Emergency Decree that strictly prohibits those kinds of stunts, because they always end in death. Innocent people of Black Spring suddenly keel over the minute someone else tries to hurt her. Stitching her up has made her mostly harmless—God only knows how they managed *that*—but if what's happening here leaks out, people will inevitably want to open her eyes and mouth. Humanity has proven time and time again that it has a tendency to cross boundaries it shouldn't. And we have every reason to believe that if her eyes open and she starts uttering her spells, we will all die. That's why we keep her out of sight. She doesn't want to be understood—she *must* not be understood. Katherine is a paranormal time bomb."

"I'm sorry, but I don't believe that," Burt said.

Pete took a sip of beer and put his glass on the table. "Mr. Delarosa, when your wife ran outside and you walked back into your bedroom, did you hear her whispering?"

His voice faltered. "I . . . I did hear something, I guess. The corner of her mouth moved. Barely visible. I wanted to hear if she was saying something."

"And what did you hear?"

"She whispered."

"And, please excuse me, but was there a moment that you considered suicide?"

Bammy shrieked, a stifled scream, and knocked over her empty teacup, which was resting on the arm of her leather chair. It hit the floor and broke into three pieces. Jocelyn rushed forward to pick up the bits. Bammy tried to open her mouth to say something, but then she saw her husband's face, and her lower lip began to tremble.

"You did, right?" Pete said. "You heard her whispering, and you played with the idea of harming yourself. That's how she gets at you. She has people kill themselves, just as she herself was forced to do."

"Burt?" Bammy asked, voice quivering. "What do they mean, Burt?"

Burt tried to speak but wasn't able, and he cleared his throat. All the color had drained from his face. "I was alone with her for only a few seconds. I didn't say anything. I was afraid that if I made any noise she would look up. I didn't want her to look up, you know what I mean? Even if she's blind, I didn't want her to see me. And I heard her whispering. Then I went out to the hallway and I wanted to slam my skull against the doorpost." Bammy flinched as if someone had struck her, and she clapped her hands to her mouth. "I swear to God, in my mind's eye I was grabbing the doorpost and smashing my forehead against it three times till it was crushed. And then . . . then you screamed, honey. That woke me up, and I ran after you. I didn't do it, because you screamed."

"Stop it!" Bammy wailed, grabbing her husband. "That isn't true, is it? I don't want to listen to this anymore, Burt. Please."

"Calm down," Jocelyn shushed. "You're safe. It didn't go on long enough to have any lasting effect."

Burt put his arm around his weeping wife and turned to Pete. For the first time Steve saw how sick and overwrought he looked . . . and that he *believed* it. "Who knows about this?" he asked, with difficulty.

"The people at The Point, right down the road," Grim said. "But just a small, highly classified division all the way at the top. I'm talking the kind of small that's not under the supervision of any commissions, to avoid the risk of leaks."

"Get out of here."

"I suspect even the president doesn't know. They used to—oh yeah. All the way back, from George Washington to Abraham Lincoln, they must have known about what was going on here, because we know from the archive that they visited Black Spring. In 1802, the U.S. Military Academy was established at West Point to help us cover it up. Don't hold me to it, but it must have been toward the end of the Civil War that The Point was deemed trustworthy enough to be given exclusive authority over Black Spring. Probably on the orders of good old Abe himself. The matter is just too delicate. Later on, when the region got developed and the risk of leaks became higher, we got organized. We went pro. And so, HEX was born."

"What's HEX?"

"That's us. We're the ghostbusters. We hide the witch in plain sight."

Burt looked at Grim with visible difficulty. "What does the name stand for?"

"Oh, it's just some old acronym that stuck. No one really knows. It's what we do that matters. Over there at The Point they let us take care of our own business, but we write up reports to keep them happy, so we have something to fall back on in case we have to close off roads or if we need a favor at the state reserve. How else do you think we could have succeeded in keeping it quiet? You can set up smoke screens all you want, but that takes money—and complete secrecy. The Point is set up to preserve the status quo because they're totally clueless as to what to do with this mess, apart from keeping it secret from the general public and from foreign intelligence services. There's no control—that's a bald-faced lie. In fact, they're shitting their pants. If they could, they'd put a big fence around us and turn the area into an uninhabited reservation, but then the blood of three thousand people would be on their hands, as many as died on 9/11. So they decided on a containment policy. Until a solution is found—whatever the hell that means—life here goes on as usual and we get subsidized for keeping our mouths shut, by way of an almost untraceable cache in the state treasury."

"It's a matter of image," Pete said. "If you have a wart on your neck, you wear high collars."

"Jesus," Burt Delarosa muttered. "Has anyone ever tried to open her eyes?"

"Once," Pete said after a long silence. "Although they never even got that far. This took place in 1967, at the initiative of the Military Intelligence unit at The Point. Nothing had happened for so long that people began to doubt if she really posed such a danger. Even in town there was talk that people just wanted to understand her and, you know, *give* her something. It was like Bammy said: Maybe she just wanted to be heard. The experiment was recorded on film. Robert, maybe you can show it to them?"

Grim took his MacBook out of his briefcase and opened it. "We use this fragment to give new folks an idea of how serious the situation is. Perception, image-forming, all that. But, let me warn you: It was some piss-poor judgment on everybody's part. The images are pretty wild. The kind of wild that they usually censor on the six o'clock news, if you know what I'm saying."

"I don't know if I want to see this," Bammy said, wiping away her tears.

"It's okay, honey," Burt said. "You don't have to watch if you don't want to." He wiggled nervously and looked over at Pete for confirmation. Pete nodded. Grim put his MacBook on his lap and clicked PLAY.

╶╂╴╂╴╂╴╂╴

THE IMAGES *ARE* shocking, no doubt about it. They're authentic, digitized Super 8 images from the sixties, and, unlike Tyler's GoPro, invoke that nostalgic film feeling that even Instagram photos can only approximate. Steve catches himself having an instinctive preference for the style, even though the colors are washed-out and his oldest son would have called him hopelessly outdated. Not that Steve is looking at the footage now; he's sitting on the other side of the lounge with his arms around Jocelyn, staring at Burt and Bammy Delarosa's faces. But he knows what the images show. Everyone in Black Spring knows. They've all been indoctrinated with them, most of them from early childhood. Steve is fiercely opposed to showing the fragment to fifth-grade children at Black Rock Elementary, so when it was Tyler's turn, and then Matt's, he tried to call them in sick. But the fines were simply too high. In Black Spring, you have to abide by the Emergency Decree.

He still remembers the showings as if they were yesterday: All the parents were there, and it was horrible. For many children, watching the images marks the point at which they become adults, and it happens much too early.

The setting is a square-shaped general practitioner's office, with Katherine van Wyler in a chair in the middle. They've managed to force her to sit down by using a wire-looped grasper, an instrument normally used to restrain mad dogs. An officer from The Point in a tweed jacket is standing at a distance, the loop of his grasper still around her neck. Two others are behind her with their poles at the ready.

But she doesn't look as if she's planning on going anywhere.

The Black Rock Witch is not moving.

There are three other men in the room: two doctors from Black Spring and the cameraman, who is providing running commentary in a deep Walter Cronkite kind of voice. The doctors don't say a word. You don't have to look closely to see the sweat on their foreheads. They're as nervous as they can be. They're kneeling in front of the witch, shifting their weight from one foot to the other to find comfortable positions while trying not to touch her. One of them has a pair of tweezers and a stitch cutter. "Doctor McGee is now going to remove the first thread from her mouth," the newsreel voice says, and you can hear his fear and uncertainty.

Grim, Burt, and Bammy—who doesn't want to watch, but watches anyway—see Doctor McGee warily push aside the quivering, dried flesh in the left corner of the witch's mouth with his tweezers and tighten the farthest stitch. He draws the knife blade along the stitch and it snaps like a rubber band. The doctor recoils and changes position. He wipes the sweat from his brow. Katherine hasn't moved. The curved black thread is sticking out of the corner of her mouth, just as it is today. We can see the corner of her mouth unmistakably trembling. Doctor McGee bends over again and a surprised expression appears on his face. The other doctor also moves in closer. The officers from The Point can't hear her whisper; they don't realize that from that moment on they are in *her* domain. "That was the first stitch," says the voice that is not Walter Cronkite's, and McGee blinks. He wipes his brow again and raises his tweezers, but his hand drops halfway there. He bends over again. "Is everything all right . . . Doctor McGee?" asks the newsreel voice, and Doctor McGee answers by suddenly raising the stitch cutter and, with the speed of a Singer sewing machine needle, plunging it into his own face again and again.

In the next few seconds, everything happens at once. The chaos is complete. A howling can be heard that chills you to the bone. The camera is knocked over, forcing the tripod against the wall, so we suddenly see the room from a nauseating perspective. The witch is no longer in her chair but is now standing in a corner of the office and we only see her lower body; the rest is cut off by the camera angle. The grasper has crashed to the floor. Doctor McGee is lying sprawled in a large pool of blood, his body in convulsions. We also see the legs of the second doctor lying nearby—at least, we assume they're the legs of the second doctor. The officers are screaming and running from the scene. Bammy Delarosa looks as if she'd like to do the same; she's holding her hands in front of her face and hyperventilating. Her husband seems too deep in shock to realize he's watching actual events.

"That," Robert Grim says, "was the last time the intelligence services got their fingers burned on the witch."

He clicks COMMAND-Q and the screen goes black.

-+-|-|-|-

"FIVE PEOPLE DIED," Pete resumed. "The two doctors committed suicide right then and there, but elsewhere in Black Spring three elderly people dropped dead in the street, all at the same time. Autopsies revealed that they had all been struck by acute cerebral hemorrhages. It's assumed that their time of death exactly coincided with the cutting of the first stitch."

Silence fell in the hotel bar. Steve glanced at his phone and noticed that the time was now a quarter past three. Bammy was in Burt's arms, shaking and crying, and the others looked uneasily at their feet.

"I don't want to go back to that house, Burt!" Bammy cried. "I don't ever want to go back."

"There, there," Burt said huskily. "You won't have to." He turned to Grim. "Tell you what, we're both pretty upset. I really appreciate your having booked this hotel room for us, but I don't think my wife and I want to stay in Black Spring one minute longer. We're full of questions, but they can wait. If my wife is in any condition to drive, we'll go stay with friends in Manhattan tonight. If not, we'll take a taxi and grab a motel in Newburgh."

"I don't think—" Pete tried to interrupt, but Burt didn't let him get a word in.

"Tomorrow I'll call a real estate agent. I'm . . . sorry you have to live with this, but . . . it's not for us. We're moving out."

"I'm afraid that's not going to happen," Pete said softly. Now, Steve realized, even Pete didn't have the nerve to keep his eyes on them.

At last Burt said, "What do you mean?"

"You said 'your' village ghost and 'your' witch earlier. I'm sorry to have to tell you this, but I'm afraid that starting tonight, it's your problem, too. She's not going to let you go. You live in Black Spring now. That means the curse is on you as well."

The silence that followed could only be broken by Robert Grim: "Welcome home." His face assumed a morbid grin. "We have all sorts of great town fairs."

SEVEN

TYLER CAME HOME from community service the following afternoon drenched with rain, his face tense. Steve was at the dining room table reading an article in the *New Yorker*, but he had had to start over again twice because his mind kept wandering. They hadn't gotten home that morning until a quarter to six, leaving him and Jocelyn feeling dull and exhausted. They had dozed off and snapped awake over a cup of tea in the kitchen until, much to his frustration, Steve could begin to make out the contours of the woods behind the house when the first sign of dawn touched the sky in the east. He had decided to skip going to bed with Jocelyn and switch to coffee—he had to get up for work at seven.

That afternoon after classes, he retreated to his office at the research center to look over a pile of Ph.D. test results but caught himself staring at the streaks of rain running down the window. His thoughts drifted to the conversation with the Delarosas.

"I don't know what's on your mind," his graduate assistant Laura Frazier said when she popped into his office to file a stack of forms, "but take my advice: Go home and get some sleep. You look like you need it."

Steve gave her a dazed smile. "Short night. My wife is sick." He was shocked by how naturally the lie passed over his lips. Christ, what a prolific liar he had become after eighteen years. *Part of the Black Spring identity,* Pete VanderMeer would have said.

"You'll get sick yourself if you don't watch out. I'm not kidding."

"I look like shit, don't I?" he said, and suddenly Burt Delarosa's cry of despair ran through his head: *Why didn't you try harder to keep us away from here, you sons of bitches?*

Now Jocelyn was in bed upstairs and Matt was doing his homework. Tyler muttered a stiff "hi" to his dad and went upstairs to hang up his wet clothes. Steve could see there was something eating at him. He knew they'd have to talk, but there was more to it than that. You didn't ask Tyler right out; you waited until he came around. That boyish vulnerability was one of the traits Steve admired in him.

And sure enough, there he is, he said to himself when Tyler came down fifteen minutes later. But he didn't look up from his article; he didn't want to give him the impression that he had been waiting for this moment to arrive.

"Mom told me it got pretty late with the new people," Tyler said with forced lightheartedness. He sat down on the dining room table.

"Don't get me started," Steve said. "We ended up pulling an all-nighter."

"How'd it go?"

"Lousy, as usual. But they'll get through it somehow. How's community service?"

Tyler turned red and grinned guiltily. "So you know."

"The whole town knows," he said, but he gave him a wink and punched him confidently in the side. Tyler was visibly relieved. "You're quite a bunch. Robert Grim showed me the images last night. It's your most sensational report so far, I must say."

"No kidding. We were shocked. And honestly, I felt kind of embarrassed for doing that to her. I mean, we expected something, but not this—not that she'd go flat on her ass. . . ."

Steve grinned but continued, more seriously. "I hope you understand that you've all been incredibly lucky. Just one mistake and you wouldn't be picking up papers in the park right now; you'd be out on that island."

"Robert is on our side, you know."

"Robert, maybe, but the Council isn't. You said yourself that you didn't know what to expect. She could have walked around the lamp-post; instead she bumped into it and fell over. God knows what else could have happened. If it were up to the Council, you'd all be in Doodletown right now."

Tyler shrugged, a gesture that left Steve a little nonplussed. "Do you have any idea what you're messing with?" he said. "Your good intentions don't make you invulnerable, you know. And I'm not even talking about *her*. The Council doesn't think highly of characters like Jaydon Holst. Was this his idea?"

"No, it was all of us," Tyler said, with eyes that didn't waver. That was something else Steve admired in him: Tyler never let others take the rap for his own behavior.

The problem wasn't so much that they had played a prank and recorded it on video: those were boyish tricks. When it came to rais-ing children, Steve and Jocelyn had always had progressive ideas, despite the restrictions of the Emergency Decree. The only thing that made the situation in Black Spring manageable—survivable, as some claimed—was that Black Spring was an indoctrinated commune. The townsfolk lived according to strict rules because they believed in those rules and accepted them without question. Children took in the commandments of the Emergency Decree with their mothers' milk: Thou shalt not associate with the witch. Thou shalt not say a word about her to people on the outside. Thou shalt comply with the visitor regulation. And the mortal sin: Thou shalt never, under any circum-stances, open the witch's eyes. These were rules prompted by fear, and Steve knew that fear invariably led to violence. He'd seen plenty of blank, pale little faces with black-and-blue patches and swollen lips on the playground of Black Rock Elementary in earlier years, faces of children who had spilled the beans with friends or cousins from out of town and had been beaten until they were fully reprogrammed accord-ing to their parents' example.

Steve and Jocelyn disapproved of these methods. They had chosen to raise their sons in well-grounded harmony and symbiosis, with plenty of room for independent thought but without losing sight of the reality of their fate. As a result, both of them had grown into kind-hearted, sensible kids, kids who inspired trust that they'd never get mixed up in any funny business.

But that confidence is an illusion, Steve thought. *For years you think you've got everything under control, and then somebody mentions the word "Doodletown" and you see how carelessly Tyler shrugs his shoulders.*

"When was the last time you visited the bunker?" Steve asked.

"Sixth grade, I think. Ms. Richardson took us out there."

"Maybe it's about time we went back there to take another look, then. Do you remember what it looks like on the inside?"

Tyler's shoulders drooped. The Doodletown Detention Center was a privately owned bunker on gloomy Iona Island in the Hudson, a little over five miles out of town and in the shadow of Bear Mountain Bridge. Part of the specially adapted curriculum at Black Rock Elementary was that all pupils be given a tour to raise awareness. "The walls and floors are padded," Tyler said.

"Exactly, and for good reason. Three weeks of solitary confinement in one of the cells out there will drive you nuts. You'd feel so miserable that you'd beg them on your knees to let you go back to Black Spring. And at that point you're still wondering what the padded walls are for. Until halfway through the third week, when you start going haywire and getting suicidal. You're under supervision to keep you from actu-ally *doing* it, but you have to *experience* it. You see what I'm saying?"

"Dad, I know what it's like," Tyler sighed.

"No, you don't," Steve said, and a cold hand closed around his en-trails as the memory flashed before him from so long ago in Thailand, when he found himself with the sheet in his hands, staring at his own dangling feet . . . how close had the intention come to reality? "That's it: you don't, and that's exactly the problem."

Doodletown was based on the idea that if the condemned had ex-perienced the witch's influence firsthand, he would be aware of the danger he posed to himself and his fellow townsfolk. And although

Steve was fiercely opposed to this form of sanction in principle, it proved extremely effective: The rate of recidivism was almost nil.

"Do you know how many basic human rights they violate with Doodletown?" Tyler remarked.

"That may well be, but you're not dealing with a dictator here. Katherine is a supernatural evil. That renders all norms invalid and makes safety our first, second, *and* third concern."

"You sound like you support it."

"Of course I don't. But did you ever notice what a puritanical bunch of bastards most of the people here in Black Spring are? It doesn't matter whether I support it or not; *they* support it. And I'd like to see you try to refute their arguments. What else can we do?"

"Come out of the closet," Tyler said, dead serious.

Steve raised his eyebrows. "And how exactly would you go about doing that? A pride parade down Deep Hollow Road?"

"Ha-ha. Seriously, in *True Blood* the vampires came out of the closet. If you go mainstream and you have scientific proof, then nobody can get around it, witch or not. It's the only thing that *hasn't* been tried."

"Tyler . . . *True Blood* is a TV series!"

"So what? The media inspire reality. Take the Arab Spring. It all started when *one* person had a dream and put it out on Facebook. Two months later, all of Tahrir Square was packed. It was social media that got all those people up off their asses. Even if you live in Iran, freedom is just a couple of mouse clicks away. Why not in Black Spring?"

"Tyler . . ." Steve stammered, but the boy was on a roll and there was no stopping him.

"I'm not the only one who's like this. All the kids feel the same way. I'm just the only one brave enough to open his mouth. We're sick of living in the Dark Ages. We want free Internet and we want our privacy. Our Facebook and WhatsApp messages are all censored by HEX like this is fucking Moscow, and sometimes they don't even get through. You can't even access Twitter here. Do you have any idea how incredibly backward we are? Your generation may be indoctrinated, but *we* want change."

Steve looked at his son with helpless admiration. "Most of the people in town don't give a damn about your Internet. They see it as one hell of a leak in their maze. Don't let anybody hear about this idea of yours or they'll cut you off even more."

"Let 'em try," Tyler sneered.

"And how did you plan on doing this? Send an e-mail to the *New York Times* with your little clip of her walking into the lamppost?"

Tyler let out an infinitely contemptuous groan. "We'd have National Geographic or Discovery Channel make a documentary, in deepest secrecy and well prepped. It'd be a media sensation, of course. The town will be swamped with journalists and scientists from all over the world. It all comes down to good preparation. If we're clear from the get-go about how serious it is and how important it is to keep her eyes and mouth shut, nothing could go wrong."

"Tyler . . . the army would have to step in! We'd be so overrun by the press and by the morbidly curious that they'd have to put the town under quarantine. Maybe they'd say they were doing it for our own safety; but no, they'd be doing it to prevent a popular uprising. A dictator you can predict, but not a witch. You'd leave them no other option than to shut us off from the rest of the world. And you think you don't have any freedom now?"

Tyler wavered only slightly. "Maybe in the beginning. But think about it. With all those cameras at the borders, we'd have the perfect platform for telling our story! The sympathy would be overwhelming. And maybe we'd even find a solution to the whole problem! Let the world figure it out. I mean, it's not like we're the first fucking town in history with a curse on our head."

Steve was perplexed. This wasn't just a passing thought. Tyler seemed absolutely convinced. But it was impossible. He remembered one of the many questions Burt Delarosa had fired off the night before in his emotional tirade: *How's it possible that something as big as this has been kept a secret for so long?* That was always what puzzled new-comers the most. Steve's reply had been a perfect summary of the impossibility of Tyler's ideals: *It all boils down to our will to survive. If this gets out, it will almost certainly result in our death. Every single time Outsiders have come here, and whether it was officials from the military or scientists of the occult, their fear and disbelief went hand in hand with their curiosity to open her eyes. It's like this desire that takes hold of them. If it didn't result in a disaster like in '67, it took a whole damn lot of bribery to get them to leave. That's why we do everything we can to cover her up. We build tiled walls around her or put a folding screen in front of her if she appears in restaurants or in the supermarket. Just last year around Easter she appeared in one of the aisles of the Market & Deli, and she decided to stay for three days. We had to put a man-sized, hollow Easter bunny over her like a big tea cozy. The Point called Grim on the carpet for that one, but they don't understand how practical you've got to be. We block the streets where she walks, we plant shrubs around her if she's standing near one of the trails in the woods . . . anything that works. And here's the biggest trick: We brag about her. Just like they do in Roswell with their UFOs. Didn't you see the brightly colored figure of a crooked old witch with a broomstick in front of Sue's Highland Diner? It looks more like the Wicked Witch of the West from* The Wizard of Oz *than Katherine, but still. Next to it is a wooden welcome sign that says:* BLACK SPRING, HOME OF THE BLACK ROCK WITCH. *Sue's Highland Diner organizes a special witch tour through the woods. Every now and then groups sign up for it, mainly pensioners or kids on local school trips, and they can pose for a photo with the witch: an actress from town. I know, sounds kinda corny and provincial. But it's the perfect cover. Because we cannot guarantee that she'll never be seen. This is a pretty touristy area, with plenty of hikers and sightseers around. Whenever somebody from the outside does happen to see her—which is rare, thanks to the good work of Robert Grim—we throw in a makeshift tour from Sue's where both the participants and the witch are actors from Black Spring, to explain what they thought they'd seen. Case closed.*

Tyler's idea of coming out of the closet was antithetical to the town's puritanical soul. It was an idealistic, rebellious idea, and in a community like Black Spring, which was governed by fear, rebellion was a dangerous thing. Every last grain of idealism would be sacrificed on the altar of safety. And Steve would do anything to keep Tyler from ending up on that altar.

"Listen," he said. "I'm very proud of you. You're standing up for your ideals. But nine out of ten people in Black Spring want to keep things just the way they are, because they fear the consequences. A proposal like that wouldn't stand a chance in the Council. Why in the world would you want to try and fight a lost battle?"

Tyler twisted uncomfortably. "I dunno. On principle. I want a life. I don't want to spend the rest of my days out here in the boondocks. Do you?" He seemed to be plucking up his courage, then added in one breath: "And I want to be honest with Laurie."

Aha, so there's the rub, Steve thought. It was all about love. He felt a pang of remorse: Tyler did indeed deserve better than Black Spring. It suddenly struck him that when his son put on his worried gaze, he bore a shocking resemblance to his mother.

"Dad, if I want to tell Laurie, will you back me up?"

"You know that's impossible."

"I know, but I'm sick and tired of lying to her. You think she never asks why she's almost never allowed to sleep over? She thinks you guys are TV evangelists."

Steve suppressed his urge to laugh—this matter was far too serious for that. Laurie was a good match for Tyler, bright and outspoken—the kind of girl who wore almost no makeup, but was naturally attractive. Tyler had brought her home for the first time seven or eight months ago. "How serious are you two, anyway?"

"I love her."

Steve sighed. "I warned you about this when you started dating. Laurie is more than welcome here. You can spend all your visiting hours on her, for all I care. But we can't let her visits overrun the curfew.

If they found out, they'd slap us with such a fine we'd have to sell the horses. You should be glad that Matt gives you his hours every now and then."

"I know that, but that's why I thought, if she just knew . . ."

"You know that's never going to happen. This isn't like telling your girlfriend you're a vegetarian or bisexual or anything. You're dealing with the whole town."

"I wouldn't be the first one, you know," Tyler said in a huff. He jumped up from the table. "Do you really think there's nobody who hasn't told their best friend from fucking Outtatown?"

"Of course there are. But those are the same people who'd yell the loudest if they found out their neighbors were doing the same. They'd go: '*I* can judge whether my friends can be trusted, but my neighbors can't.' "

"Do you know how hypocritical that sounds!"

"Welcome to planet Earth. You—"

"*Welcome to Black Spring!*" Tyler screamed suddenly—really screamed—and Steve stepped back in alarm. He realized how sensitive an issue this must be for his son. He had to tread carefully in explaining to Tyler what, in his anger, he was missing—something so obvious it was the elephant in the room.

"You cannot tell Laurie, Tyler. And believe me: *You don't want to do that to her.* The risk is just too great. You don't know how she'll react or who she'll tell in turn. You cannot burden her with this."

"But then you're saying that I can never be honest with her. After finals next year she wants to go to Europe for six months and she asked if I'd like to go with her. What am I supposed to say? 'I'd rather stay home with my inbred Addams Family'?"

"Tyler, I'm sorry, but that's what's going to happen if you go out with girls from outside. Laurie wants to go to college; she wants to travel—who can blame her? I know it's unfair, but you cannot leave this place. You can study in the city if you want to spend four hours on a train every day, but how long do you think you'd be able to keep that up? Or her?"

Tyler's lips trembled in despair. "So what are you trying to say? That I'd better break up with her?"

"Absolutely not. But you're so young. You shouldn't tie yourself down. . . ."

"I love her, and I'm not going to let this fucking town come between us!"

"So what's the alternative?" Steve asked. He tried to put his hand on Tyler's arm, but the boy jerked away. "You know the only way you could tell her would be if she were to move to Black Spring—or, let me rephrase that, *after* she moved to Black Spring. Again: Do you want to do that to her? You'd be the one deciding how the rest of her life would turn out. Would she ever be able to forgive you?"

"You decided it for me and Matt!" Tyler hissed, screwing up his eyes.

He regretted his words immediately, of course, now that it was too late. But Steve felt a shadow darken his face. It was like rubbing salt in his deepest wound: the fact that because of his unfortunate decision to come to Black Spring he had doomed the lives of his sons, doomed them from the crib. Steve looked at Tyler, turned away, and sat down.

"That's not fair," he said softly. The agitation in his voice was supplanted by pain. "What were we supposed to do? Abort you?"

"I'm sorry," Tyler muttered uneasily, but in his mind Steve heard Burt Delarosa's lamentation once again: *Why didn't you try harder to keep us away from here, you sons of bitches?* He had actually cried, his face wet with tears, and they wouldn't be his last tears, either, Steve knew. They were the same tears that he himself had cried eighteen years before. *I'm really sorry,* he had said. *The right thing to do would be to seal Black Spring off hermetically and to let the curse die with the last of us. Sure, our retail vacancy is higher than anywhere on the Hudson, and there are houses where the lights go on and off by time switches to make them look inhabited. Robert Grim works hard with the real estate agent to keep people away. But the Council, led by good ol' Colton Mathers, is hell-bent on keeping the town healthy and resisting the unavoidable problems of aging. Allowing an influx of new people is the lesser of two evils, they say. It's a sacrifice, but life here in the boondocks really isn't that bad. Okay, there are some small inconveniences, such as not being able to take long vacations, or having to register visiting hours (to avoid a Code Red, you see); and a few online restrictions, too; and, oh yes, you'd better settle down because you won't be leaving here again . . . but life's pretty good, if you stick to the rules. And let's face it, we can't organize all our politics and community affairs around a supernatural phenomenon, right? In the end, there's always hope. Hope that somehow, one way or another, the situation will . . . resolve itself.*

"Listen," Steve said, unutterably tired. "I had to spend a whole hour tying myself up in knots last night, trying to explain to those new folks why in God's name we didn't stop them from buying that house. The town policy makes me cringe, and Robert Grim as well. It's *bad* policy. If you really love Laurie, don't do it to her. There *is* no alternative."

"There is if we come out of the closet." Tyler pouted stubbornly.

"Next year you'll hit legal age. Then you can submit proposals to the Council until you're blue in the face, for all I care, and recruit as many people as you can find. If you come up with one good plan, I'm prepared to vote in favor. But until that time you will not do anything illegal, and you definitely will not do anything stupid without consulting the Council. No more bullshit with the witch, no YouTube clips, no crazy ideas. Is that clear?"

Tyler muttered something.

"You haven't got something else up your sleeve, I hope?"

"No," Tyler said impassively, after a brief hesitation.

Steve gave Tyler a quick, searching look. "Are you absolutely sure?"

"I said no, didn't I?" He jumped up irritably—they were both tired and irritated. "Jeez, Dad, what are you so afraid of?"

Steve sighed. "The last time anybody wanted to go public with this thing was in 1932 during the Great Depression. Some workers lost their jobs after the old tree farm closed. They threatened to start shooting their mouths off unless they were rehired, since of course there were no opportunities to try and find employment elsewhere. The town took a vote to set an example for other blackmailers. They were publicly flogged and killed by firing squad in the town square."

"Dad . . . it's 2012."

"Yes, and they won't do the firing squad anymore. But corporal punishments are still written into the Emergency Decree, and you'd be a fool to underestimate what they're capable of if they feel they've been driven into a corner."

Tyler was quiet for a long time. Finally, he slowly shook his head. "I can't believe this. We may be fucked up here, but that's a whole nother level of fucked-upness."

"Quote: 'Welcome to Black Spring,'" Steve said.

EIGHT

GRISELDA HOLST, OWNER of Griselda's Butchery & Delicacies, hurried through the rainy streets of Upper Mineral Valley, the upscale part of town. She was stooped over and clutching a small white bag to her chest, and the poncho she was wearing had a plastic hood from which her prematurely gray hair stuck out in dripping tufts. If the hood had been red, she might have been mistaken for the little girl from that other fairy tale . . . the one with the wolf, not the witch.

There was blood on her lip, but she didn't notice it. If the townsfolk had seen her scuttling along like that, they hardly would have recognized her, for Griselda's regulars knew her to be a strong woman—moody perhaps, marked by life, but widely respected. For many, Griselda's Butchery & Delicacies served as the local hangout, even more than the Quiet Man on the other corner of the square. At the Quiet Man, they got drunk and forgot. At Griselda's, they were sober, with memories written in furrows all over their faces. Maybe it was because Griselda had a face just like theirs that they always found their way to her to rehash the latest town gossip over a plate of something meaty. The people knew her past. They never mentioned it, as if the telling blows and makeup she used to cover her bruises had all been gestures of love. They never mentioned her husband, the real butcher Jim Holst, who couldn't cope with Black Spring and had vanished without a trace seven years before—except perhaps for an anonymous report in a newspaper found in a Boston gutter: *Unknown man throws self in front of train.* They all knew, but none broke their conspiracy of silence.

For Griselda's part, she knew that most of her loyal customers secretly missed Jim despite her suffering, although they wouldn't even admit it in front of an inquisition. Jim's Butchery & Delicacies had been famous for its goose breast pâté, a delicacy that Jim himself had concocted and made fresh every day. Compared with that refined charcuterie, Griselda's vinegary Holst pâté was more like pulverized head cheese. Yet people had been buying it for a good seven years now, and Griselda kept making it for them. Behold a typical Black Spring ritual of tacit sympathy: The squeeze of the hand, the touch of the cheek, and at night Griselda's Holst pâté would lie unopened in the garbage can and they'd all think: *Would she be crying? Or is she really as strong as she lets on?*

But as Griselda walked up the hill past the luxury farms in Upper Mineral Valley, stocky and skittish, she didn't look like a strong woman at all. She looked like an exile. She was taunted and she was cursed; she was spat on and she was abused.

Hey, you filthy whore. How 'bout spreadin' y'r legs again?

This from Arthur Roth, who didn't know her name—not anymore, at least—as she stepped away from the cell beneath Crystal Methodist Church.

Fuck off, you sick bitch!

And this from her very own son, Jaydon, half an hour earlier.

And after every cruel word she told herself that they no longer reminded her of Jim's callused hands tugging hard on her purple nipples, that his fists no longer caused her any pain, that she could no longer smell his breath, foul with the smell of vodka and goose breast pâté.

Don't you like this, Griselda? Isn't this why you married me?

Griselda stopped at an orchard on the side of the road and scanned the hillside. There was nobody out there to see her. Everyone was indoors watching the local news or *Law & Order,* with the heat turned on for the first time that fall. She quickly hoisted her bulky frame over the fence and climbed past the orchard and along the side of the steeply sloping field until she came to the edge of the woods. The ground was soggy and she slipped twice, scraping her hands. When she reached the other side, breathless, she scrambled up the tree-covered moraine and finally relaxed a bit. There were no paths or cameras here, all the way up to Ackerman's Corner.

In the woods the air was heavy with the smell of dampness and leaf mold caused by the rainwater leaking down through the thick foliage. Someone else might have found it peculiar that no birds or crickets could be heard and that there were no insects, but not Griselda—not in Black Spring. She stumbled on a bit, panting, with aches flaring up below her rib cage. Finally, she reached a dry streambed, carved into the black bedrock in earlier eons by meltwater. The streambed was spanned by a fallen tree over where it turned sharply to the left, and there she came to a halt.

Standing under the fallen tree trunk was Katherine.

She was shrouded in shadows, and her rain-drenched, formless dress stuck to her emaciated body, making her seem even more small and frail than she was. Griselda wasn't a tall woman, but she was still at least a head taller than the witch, who was unusually delicate, almost like a child. People didn't get much bigger back then, Griselda supposed. The witch was not moving. The rainwater that leaked through her saturated headscarf gathered between the threads in her shriveled eyelids and dripped down her cheeks from the torn bits of flesh. It looked like she was crying.

"Hi, Katherine," Griselda said shyly. She cast her eyes to the ground. "I wanted to bring an umbrella for you, but the rain ain't bothering you, now, is it?"

The woman with the sewn-up eyes didn't stir.

Griselda dropped to the ground at Katherine's feet and sat at an angle with her back to her, groaning from the pain in her joints. She didn't mind getting wet and dirty; she just had to pause a minute to catch her breath. She knew better than to look at the witch when she spoke to her, just as you wouldn't look at a wild animal when you entered its territory. The witch towered over Griselda like an idol. The whispering from the corner of her mouth was little more than a sigh. And although Griselda was so close to the witch that the heavy, ancient smell overwhelmed her, the rain and the woods drowned out her whispers and there was nothing on earth that could make her move closer yet . . . or touch her.

Griselda removed a paper sack from her bag, and from this she took out a paper plate with a slice of Holst pâté on it. This she placed on the ground beside her, in front of Katherine's bony, dirt-smeared feet. Rainwater dripped from the hem of her dress and onto the pâté, so Griselda pulled the plate forward a bit. There was still the occasional drop from the trees overhead, but at least that wasn't polluted by the dress.

Griselda looked around. They were alone.

"I brought you an extra-thick slice," she began. "Because I want to apologize for what Jaydon did, Katherine. With those *friends* he got. You know what I mean. They shamed you."

The woman with the sewn-up eyes didn't stir.

Suddenly Griselda began pouring her heart out. "It's terrible what they done to you. What a mean trick! Did you get hurt, dear? I gave him a piece of my mind; you can take my word for that. And he won't get out of this one easy. I'll make him pay for his sins, you hear me? I'm just so scared, so awful scared! He was laying low for a little while—my boy Jaydon, I mean—but that's all changed now. I just can't get through to him anymore. He won't talk to me, not even about his fastballs or the girls he's taking out or all the things he likes. I feel so powerless! I can deal with anger; do it all the time. I've had my share of anger, as you know. But not that indifference of his. Sometimes I wonder if I'm doing it all wrong, but I don't know if I should get tougher or ease up on him. You know what we've been through. It hasn't been easy for him. And then something like this happens. . . ."

A pool of rainwater slowly began to form around the pâté on the plate at the witch's feet. Griselda didn't see it. She continued: "Oh, dear, don't get me wrong; they were disrespectful to you. But it wasn't his idea, he says. Jaydon is so easily influenced by his friends. It was probably that Muslim boy he hangs out with, that Buran. I bet it was him—it's just the kind of thing his kind would do, right? And Jaydon? Oh, Jaydon can be a handful, but he never means no harm. If you could just see how he helps around the shop . . . deep inside, he's really just a fragile child."

But then she heard his voice come roaring through her mind, so loud and sudden that it startled her and made her look around: *Fuck off, you sick bitch!*

While everybody in Black Spring seemed to know what had happened, Griselda hadn't heard about it until that morning, when the first loose-lipped customers came into the butcher shop. It seemed like half the town came out to catch a glimpse of the dumbfounded expression on the butcher's wife's face, and as word spread that she hadn't known, even more showed up to see for themselves. That Schaeffer woman, who married that rich surgeon for you-know-what, even came back twice, with the excuse that she had forgotten to pick up a slice of Holst pâté. Mrs. Schaeffer had never bought any Holst pâté.

Some showed signs of indignation, but most appeared to find it all rather amusing. Griselda was shocked. She had just made up her mind to contact Colton Mathers, Head of the Council—on which she, as a leading and upright citizen, also held a seat—when Mathers himself called her on the phone, right in the middle of the noon rush. Griselda slipped into the back, leaving her customers in the lunchroom and at the counter wild with curiosity.

The old councilman was livid. He repudiated Grim for coming to a compromise with the boys and sidelining the Council. To avoid a general revolt, their only option had been to give the boys an official warning, although the good man stressed in no uncertain terms that taking a more heavy-handed approach in the name of parental authority would serve Jaydon well. Griselda twitched when Colton Mathers said, "Believe it or not, the town actually seems to *approve* of these scamps and their little trick."

After that, she got frightened. The fear tightened itself around her stomach over the course of the afternoon, as if a great, inevitable calamity were approaching like an express train. She wasn't afraid of what was in store for Jaydon, nor did she fear for the image of the shop. Like all the townsfolk, Griselda lived in constant fear of Katherine van Wyler's evil eye and the day it would turn upon her. But while everyone knew that the curse had been fatal to Griselda's ill-tempered husband, no one knew that since the day she got free of him, Griselda had in fact been *grateful* to Katherine, and that her fear had been converted into a bitter determination to free herself of the witch's evil as well. And so it was that for seven long years, in all secrecy and under penalty of something far worse than Doodletown, Griselda had been offering Katherine gifts and trifles and sweeping the sidewalk where Katherine would be walking the very next day. She'd entrusted her with all the secrets and stories she had picked up from town, the juiciest bits of gossip she happened to overhear in the butcher shop, and pointed the finger at the guilty in the hope of getting into Katherine's good graces so that she and Jaydon would be spared should the worst ever happen. She straightened Katherine's headscarf if the wind blew it askew (with a long stick, of course) and rearranged her iron chains if they seemed to cause her discomfort. She reshaped the witch into a goddess she worshipped, believing less and less in the old legends that clung to her and more and more in the witch herself. Griselda would do anything for her, anything except the one thing she could not do . . . anything but open her eyes.

"But," she once told the witch confidentially, "I know that one day someone will come along who *will* perform that service, Ms. van Wyler,"—that was before they were on a first-name basis—"and I hope on that day you'll remember that I've always been good to you."

Except now all that she had so painstakingly built up over seven years may have been undone by Jaydon with a single stroke.

That's why she had to clearly show whose side she was on. She had waited for Jaydon in the kitchen, and even before he had fully entered, she had slapped him in the face with the back of her hand. Jaydon screamed and recoiled against the counter. The slap reverberated like a gunshot and filled the kitchen with an explosive tension. Never had she struck her own flesh and blood before; Jim's fists had done that enough for the both of them. But now she had no choice: There was no going back.

"What were you thinking?" she said in a voice cold with rage. "What the *hell* were you thinking? What have you got, shit for brains?"

"What the fuck, Mom!"

Griselda's hand shot up once more and this time her palm struck Jaydon's face. He flailed his arms and tried to back away, but again he bumped up against the counter. Griselda felt heat rising in her face, the same heat she had felt when Jim came at her with that glazed look in his eyes and his fists raised. But as soon as she saw this strapping young man flinch, she knew she had him exactly where she wanted him: ambushed.

"How can you endanger us like that? Did you think I wouldn't find out? The whole town knows. How can you be so stupid?"

"What is this?"

"Shut your big mouth, you!"

Jaydon was genuinely taken aback. "Jesus, relax, everything's been taken care of. Grim has us picking up trash in the park, which is seriously moronic because they pay the park attendants to do it all over again. But okay, whatever."

"I don't care what Grim is making you do. You're dealing with me now."

"Like you matter." Jaydon had wavered, but he was pulling himself together, and his face assumed the defiant expression she hated so much. "The Council said . . ."

"This isn't about the Council!" she spat out. "This is about you and me, don't you get it?" She glanced around nervously and lowered her voice. "What if someday her eyes open; have you ever thought about that? Do you think she'll spare you if you mock her? Do you have any idea what you're getting us into?''

To her great dismay, Jaydon began to laugh, not from pleasure but from a condescending kind of pity. "Seriously, Mom. You got issues.''

He was about to stalk off, but Griselda grabbed him by the neck of his T-shirt—she had to reach up to do it—and threw him back against the counter. "You're not going anywhere, mister.''

"Don't you touch me,'' Jaydon snapped, tearing free from her grip by throwing up his arms.

"You know what happened to your father! Do you want to end up like that?'' That hit home; Griselda saw his face freeze. Despite the fact that the man had repeatedly beaten his son black and blue, Jaydon would have gone to hell and back for him—damned if Griselda knew where the man had earned that respect. Even though Jaydon was now nineteen and his father had been dead seven years, the feeling hadn't diminished. "That's what I mean," she said. "I'm trying so hard for both of us. You think you're helping by making a fool of her?''

Jaydon's eyes radiated disgust, contempt, and hatred. She tried not to register the hatred, but it was there, like oil in a puddle of still water. "If she opens her eyes,'' he said, "we're all gonna die.''

He turned around and Griselda clutched at him, begging now: "That doesn't have to happen, don't you see? I'll make sure we don't die; not you and me, Jaydon. Listen . . .''

He turned on his heel. "Fuck off, you sick bitch!''

SMACK!

Before she knew it, her hand had struck out again, harder than ever this time. A second later, white pain exploded in her head and she was knocked backward onto the kitchen linoleum. Her lower lip was throbbing and she could taste the metallic tang of blood. It took a while before she realized what had happened.

Jaydon was towering over her in the doorway and looking down, his fist in his left hand and his mouth half open. "I told you not to touch me," he said softly. He pushed the palm of his hand against his jaw and put pressure on it. "You're no fucking better than him."

Then he left, and what had hurt the most were not his words, not his fist, but the look she had seen in his eyes. Through her pain she saw a playground swing: the swing that in another life, in another place, she might have pushed him on. They would have laughed, the two of them.

Still, somehow she had pulled herself together, as she had done her whole life, and now she was here, in the woods. She felt queasy, weak. Reflected in the rainwater that was gathering in the streambed she saw a face she didn't recognize: slack cheeks of waxen skin, bags under her eyes, swollen, chapped lips.

The woman with the sewn-up eyes didn't move.

The offering sat at her feet, untouched.

"Tell me what to do, Katherine. Tell me; give me a sign so I can make amends. I ask so little of you, and you know I've always been good to you. So spare us, please, when your day comes. Let us be healthy. Let us be free of sickness, free of sin, free from your eye. It can't be as evil as they're all saying, right?"

Absentmindedly, she tilted the paper plate and let the rainwater run off. Then she stuck her finger into the pâté, took a big curl, and thoughtlessly put it in her mouth.

"Haven't I been punished enough? Just look at my face. I look ten years older than I am. I'm not saying it's your fault, but it's the situation that gets to you. My arthritis is getting worse, not to mention the scars on my body."

Her goddess towered over her, motionless. Griselda took another fingerful of pâté and slowly licked it off.

"You took my husband, and good riddance. You know I'm grateful that you took him from me, even though it hurt. It's not the fact that he's gone that's painful, but the memory of when he was still there. But life goes on, as you well know. You get back up on your feet. There are times when it's tolerable, but it never really goes away. It's a mark I carry with me. I carry it for you, just like the burden they put upon you. I know how you feel, Katherine. I know what it's like. And that's why I'm asking you this one thing: Don't take my boy, and don't take me. Please don't ask that of me."

And as Griselda continued to offer up her supplication, she ate the entire rain-drenched slice of pâté. It wasn't the taste of the meat that she liked so much as the structure of the liver, which stuck to the words on the roof of her mouth and weighed them down so they could tumble from her lips.

She was so lost in her prayer that she didn't notice the witch turning her head toward her.

"I should go now," Griselda said. "It'll be dark soon. Not that I wouldn't like to stay with you a little longer, but people will notice if I walk down the streets after dark." In fact, being alone with the witch after nightfall was the last thing Griselda wanted, and night fell quickly in the woods. "Arthur Roth in Crystal Meth is still the same. I stopped by to see him just before I got here. Colton Mathers wants me to put him on half rations, so now I only bring him food every other day. His bones are starting to show. I think they want to get rid of him, but it seems so inhumane to do it this way. That's not how civilized people behave, is it? I'm sure he's on the agenda for the next Council meeting, but I'd be surprised if they make any real decision this time."

Arthur Roth had been a thorn in the side of the Black Spring Council for years: a former hardware store owner and a depressed alcoholic who had lost his house in September 2007 and his mind two months later. Since then, he had threatened to blow the town's cover by talking openly about what was going on in Black Spring. The four times they'd sentenced him to Doodletown had only made his insanity more persistent. Nevertheless, the Council hadn't dared to have him committed to an asylum outside of Black Spring for fear of the suspicion he might arouse before he'd killed himself. As for pulling the thorn out themselves . . . no one had ever actually uttered the words. After all, they were civilized people, here in Black Spring.

Griselda pressed her index finger into the last bits of pâté and licked it off. "Couldn't you maybe pay him a visit sometime?" she asked. "I'm sorry to bother you with this, and I know you don't like church and all, but maybe you could make this one exception? He's down below, in the cell block. Really, it would make it so much easier . . ." She turned her head shyly, and gave the witch a quick glance for the first time that night. "Maybe you could whisper something in his ear."

In a flash, Katherine was bending over her. Griselda's body jolted from the sudden chill and she fell over backward with a scream, landing in the muddy streambed in almost exactly the same way she had smacked down onto the kitchen linoleum earlier in the day. Fear washed over her in gray waves and mixed with the rain as she was forced to look into that mutilated face, the stitches set into the dead skin like a black zipper over blind eyes, and she scrambled backward, clawing the mud with her hands in the face of her own death . . .

And lay still.

The woman with the sewn-up eyes hadn't moved at all.

Griselda raised herself on her elbows and listened to her heart pounding erratically in her temples. She began to feel woozy, as if she were floating. Katherine van Wyler was still standing farther up in the streambed, a dark, dripping idol padlocked in chains in the last gloomy light of day. For a moment, Griselda feared she was going to faint, but the thought of waking up in the dark, in the domain of her goddess, gave her enough strength to turn over, scramble to her feet, and take to her heels, without so much as a word of good-bye.

The offering, in the form of a cleanly licked and rain-soaked paper plate, was left lying in the streambed. Much later that evening, when the Black Rock Witch moved, she accidentally stepped on it.

NINE

IN THE THREE weeks following the lamppost test, the boys from *Open Your Eyes: Preachings from the Witch's Nest* made solid progress in their mission to gather so much scientific evidence that they could make Black Spring go not only mainstream but immediately viral as well. During those three weeks, the wedge between Tyler Grant and Jaydon Holst also became painfully evident. It had always been there, of course—Jaydon had been unpredictable since childhood, and dangerous—but it had lain dormant, like an underground fossil now finally exposed by the inevitable quirks of fate.

What started it was the October 15 message on the *OYE* website:

Next step: the #double-dare whisper test
Posted 01:29 P.M. by Tyler Grant

The whisper test wasn't the first experiment after the collision Tyler had had with his dad over Laurie. That had been their fiercest quarrel in ages—in fact, he couldn't remember them ever having had a more violent clash. Tyler and Steve hardly ever got into fights, just as Matt and Jocelyn rarely did. It had rattled them both so deeply that it had affected the other family members as well. The next afternoon, Tyler had come to help his dad and Matt in the stable, and as he passed Steve a bale of hay they exchanged a glance that signaled the end of the rift between them. This particular hatchet had been buried, but the pressure in Tyler's chest had remained. He hadn't been able to tell his dad all his plans, of course, but it stung him that Steve hadn't approved of the things he *had* told him.

In the days that followed, he had mostly avoided his parents. Once his community service work was finished, he stayed away from home longer after school, eating at Laurie's or with friends in Newburgh. He spent his afternoons roaming aimlessly through the city or logging onto the free Wi-Fi at Starbucks to work on *OYE*. Until now, he had always done this from the comfort of his bedroom with the Wi-Fi disconnected while his parents slept, then put it online away from the watchful eye of HEX at school the next day, but now he felt he needed to be even more careful. Maybe he was being paranoid, but it was out of his control. Laurie had asked what was going on and Tyler had inadvertently pushed her away, creating tension between them. He found he didn't feel much enthusiasm for getting it on with her, either, something they usually did well and at length. It didn't feel right; the lie rose like a wall between them.

And at the end of the day, racing back home up the road that wound between the large homes of Cornwall on his Diamondback Joker, Tyler thought about what awaited him at the end of the tunnel of trees. He was becoming increasingly aware that he'd be going down this road in the dark for the rest of his life. Maybe the people behind those windows were watching him go by and seeing a healthy American boy on his way home after a long day. A boy in a free country, almost done with school, who would spread his wings and chase his dreams. And no one, no one knew what was going on just a few miles down the road. No one knew that this boy would remain in the dark forever.

More than anything, it proved that something had to change. Tyler didn't want to be that boy.

The results of the Ray-Ban experiment raised new questions, as all scientific problems do. Tyler had uploaded the raw footage onto the *OYE* website in order to avoid future accusations of a hoax, but as an introduction he also edited a short video in the style of TylerFlow95. Here we go:

-l-l-l-l-

WE SEE A group of boys surrounding the Black Rock Witch at a safe distance in the alley behind the Market & Deli. Tyler has put "Brooklyn's Finest" by Jay-Z and Notorious B.I.G. under the video and overlaid the images with a black-and-white grunge layer, so the whole thing looks more like a hip-hop video clip. Using one of Grim's grabber sticks from community service, they push Burak's Ray-Bans underneath the witch's headscarf. The glasses balance on the bridge of her nose, slightly askew, but one more push, and for the first time in three hundred fifty years Katherine van Wyler is wearing a trendy, expensive accessory to go with her iron chains. "Who's my bitch now?" Burak raps, and the boys break and pop as Jay-Z and B.I.G. assure us: "Take that witcha, hit ya, back split ya . . ."

Of course, there's a lot of the usual jokes, but let's jump to the shot in which Katherine is moving farther back into the alley behind the supermarket and the boys are hurrying after her. Once they turn the corner, the witch is gone, but then the boys find what they're really after: Burak's Ray-Bans. Or what's left of them. Amazed, excited shouts as the camera jerks and zooms in on the asphalt and Tyler says, "Careful, don't touch them. . . ."

The Ray-Bans appear to have melted away—there's no other way of describing it. One of the lenses is cracked; the other is wavy like softened plastic after it's been heated. The glass is held in place by burned, bubbly, molten plastic, one arm of the frames jutting out of the remains like an antenna. You can still see the Ray-Ban logo. And there's something else: a black, crusty, layered substance that is clearly gooed *onto* the frames and is not part of the actual construction. It has the texture of insulation material bulging from a crack in a plastered wall. "Jesus, what is that?" someone asks. "God, it stinks!" another shouts. We see Tyler putting his hand into a freezer bag and picking up the glasses. "They're still hot . . ." he says breathlessly. The glasses stick to the asphalt and make a popping noise as they tear free. Then

Tyler holds the evidence up to the camera and declares, "This is a historic moment."

The next shot is a cabinet in a chemistry classroom: *James I. O'Neill High School, Highland Falls,* reads the subtitle. Lawrence VanderMeer and Tyler, the cameraman, are hanging on the lab assistant's every word. He's a dapper, gray-haired guy with tobacco-stained fingers, and he's examining the remains of the Ray-Bans under his microscope. "So you really don't know?" Tyler repeats, excited because that's exactly what he had hoped for, but still visibly disappointed, as if he had actually . . . well, expected *something.* The lab assistant turns off the light and says briskly, "Be damned if I know what it is. It's too badly burned to identify. Given the smell there's probably some sulfur in it, but the structure seems more organic. But, guys . . . what on earth did you *do* to those glasses? To get glass to melt you need a temperature of fourteen hundred degrees. But the plastic arm is still intact, you see? And that's impossible. Because if the glasses had cooled off that quickly, the second lens would have cracked as well."

OMG, 1400 degrees! Is it possible that the Black Rock Witch uses so much energy to manifest that she reaches temperatures that high? Is this some unknown, supernatural phenomenon? And what about that burned-on goop? Sulfur, but with an organic structure, says Mr. Mason at O'Neill High. Of course, we couldn't tell him our theory, but—drumroll, please—could we have found the first tangible evidence of the existence of **ECTOPLASM**???

For the uneducated among us: "Ectoplasm" is a term coined by French physiologist Charles Richet for a substance that can be exteriorized or projected by a medium or by spiritual energy (says Wikipedia). We've all seen photos of tripping mediums barfing up this gross cloud of mashed potatoes. Usually the mediums were fakes and it *was* mashed potatoes, which is exactly why the existence of ectoplasm has not been recognized by science. But even so, ectoplasm has been connected with ghosts ever since, like, the first ghost was seen. Even today, when that chick with the milkshake in her throat shows up in *The Grudge,* she appears as this puffy cloud in the upper corner of the bedroom. And in *The Blair Witch Project,* there's this "blue jelly" stuff all over the illiterate hippie's backpack the night before the witch gets him.

I mean, we don't want to jump to conclusions, but holy shit, this is exciting! This requires a thorough scientific investigation. We at *OYE* will carefully store the evidence in our archives for National Geographic to pick up. NG: you can get it for free from Tyler's house, in exchange for a new pair of sunglasses (Ray-Ban, says Burak, preferably the type rb8029K Aviator Ultra, the limited edition).

-+-|-|-|-

AGAINST ALL EXPECTATIONS, they almost screwed up the whisper test. That was because the opportunity arose more or less accidentally, before they were able to weigh the options and discuss them at length. Looking back, Tyler decided that even if they had been given enough time, it still would have been one hell of a big risk. But sometimes science took place in the crater of an erupting volcano and there was nothing you could do about that.

That Sunday afternoon, Tyler had decided to go for a walk with Lawrence and Fletcher in the woods behind their house. The trees cast blazing colors across the sodden paths and shone with extraordinary brightness in anticipation of the end of the month, when they would fade and drop their leaves. When the path veered sharply to the left and went up the hill to the outlook point, the boys instinctively followed Philosopher's Creek, which was out of reach of the hidden cams that projected the entire Mount Misery trail system onto HEX's monitors.

Lawrence and Tyler were strolling along, casually discussing the practical details of the whisper test, when Fletcher suddenly strained against his leash and began to growl, ears cocked.

Tyler wrapped the leash twice around his wrist and braced himself.

In the distance, they heard excited voices and something stirred in the foliage. Suddenly Fletcher began barking wildly. Tyler and Lawrence exchanged startled glances and hurried after Fletcher to the place where there was a split in the soggy streambed, with the creek branching off and the surrounding slopes growing narrower. Burak, Jaydon, and Justin were on the left bank with the Black Rock Witch in their midst. They were poking her body with long branches. When they heard the dog, Burak and Justin looked over their shoulders and raised their hands, grinning broadly.

"Jesus," Tyler muttered. "Easy, Fletcher. Down!" He tugged on the leash and pushed it into Lawrence's hand. "Hold on to him and don't come any closer, or he'll freak."

Lawrence nodded and Tyler ran to the others. "What the hell are you doing? Cut it out!"

"Well, if it isn't our fearless leader," Justin laughed. "We're doing scientific research. We're proving she's made of solid matter."

"And she is. Look," Jaydon said, and with unnecessary roughness he jabbed the witch in the shoulder with the tip of his stick. Katherine tottered and turned her head slowly to where she had been stung, but she didn't move from her spot.

Tyler was disgusted. They were mocking the witch. Sure, *he* may have been the one to come up with the idea for the lamppost test, but that was just a prank gone wrong. Mocking the witch was a no-go; you didn't need an Emergency Decree to figure that out. What Jaydon was doing shocked Tyler. Jaydon had embarked on a slippery slope that would take him irrevocably to the abyss.

"Cut it out," Tyler said again, and he pushed Jaydon's arm hard, more confidently than he felt.

Jaydon's glance froze and grew dark. He lowered the stick and turned around, two years older and a head taller than Tyler, and spoiling for a confrontation. Tyler felt his heart pounding in his throat, but he didn't back away. "Dude, you're sick, baiting her like that. I don't want you fucking around with our research. You'll blow our cover."

"That dog of yours; he's the one who's gonna blow your cover," Jaydon said. Tyler saw something in his eyes he didn't like at all, something that frightened him, something that had been smoldering within Jaydon since the day his father had left to meet his ill-fated death. Behind them, Fletcher started barking again and Lawrence was on his knees, trying to keep him calm.

"We agreed we'd only do experiments together, and only in ways that help our research. The Council meeting is next week, and you'll fuck up our chances for free Internet and privacy if they see you messing around like this." Tyler licked his lips nervously, then decided to take it one step further. "Get your act together, or you're out of *OYE*."

"And who made you boss all of a sudden?" Jaydon said, moving in closer.

"Um . . . we did?" Lawrence intervened, and Tyler closed his eyes in prayerful thanks.

"It's *his* website," Justin said with a silly grin.

"Yeah, and his plan," Burak said.

Jaydon stared at him coldly and Tyler was catapulted back to the past. They were ten and twelve years old and both in elementary school, Tyler in fifth grade and Jaydon in sixth because he had been held-back that summer. It was less than a year after Jaydon's father had left without a trace, but back then Tyler Grant was too young to make the obvious connection. All he knew was that you didn't turn your back on Jaydon if you knew what was good for you because he was the kind of jerk who wasn't stingy about passing along the punches he had received at home.

One day while they were playing soccer during recess, Katherine appeared amid the children on the field behind the school. Some of the kids were frightened, but Miss Ashton told them to move their game a little to the left and keep on playing. "Remember: We run to our teacher or parents as soon as we see her, and then we go on with whatever we were doing as if nothing happened," she said. Andy Pynchot, a cocky little boy one year Tyler's senior, suggested using her as a goal post and was rewarded with a firm slap on the back of the head. When Miss Ashton finally clapped her hands and the children ran inside, much relieved, the ball had rolled outside the lines not far from the witch. Tyler and Jaydon were the closest and Tyler was about to go get it, but Jaydon had looked at him with the same cold eyes as he did now, seven years later, and little Tyler became frightened—not of the witch, but of Jaydon. Later, when he was able to see the bigger picture, he imagined that wild animals must feel the same kind of uncontrollable fear when they first inhaled the smoky air of a forest fire. Then Jaydon did something appalling: He ran up to the ball, bent backward, and kicked it at the witch, hitting her like a sledgehammer. Katherine doubled over and the leather exploded with a loud bang as the witch disappeared.

All those images shot through Tyler's mind in the few seconds that he and Jaydon stood face-to-face in the woods. Seven years was a long time, and since then they had hung out together off and on. But the foul taste the incident had left in his mouth had never gone away, and Tyler had never forgotten that cold look in Jaydon's eyes. If a boy of twelve had been able to kick a soccer ball at the witch with so much pent-up rage, what would the same boy be capable of at nineteen?

Finally, Jaydon lowered his shoulders and grinned. "Don't cry, faggot."

Tyler relaxed a little, but remained on guard. "Listen, this is not about who's boss. I just don't want to fuck this up. We're not taking any chances. We may be free soon, so just keep it together, okay?"

"No prob. Best friends forevah."

Tyler rolled his eyes. "Do they know she's here yet?"

"Nope," Justin said. "App says she's somewhere in Lower South, and there's no new alert since then. We just bumped into her here."

"We were just screwing around, that's all," Burak said.

Tyler walked back to Lawrence and gave Burak a frigid look as he passed. Burak caught his gaze, didn't understand it, and probably felt hurt. But Tyler couldn't make it any clearer: Sure, Jaydon and Justin would stoop this low, but he hadn't expected it of Burak. He turned aside and said, "So can somebody please send an app? We're not that far off the trail, and there are fucking hikers around."

"Sure," Jaydon said, and pulled out his iPhone, maybe to show that he truly meant well. Tyler was bending over to calm Fletcher down when Jaydon let out a surprised cry. Tyler's head jerked up. The witch had taken a vigorous step forward and had almost bumped into Jaydon, who had been busy with his text message. Startled, he took a few steps back. The witch stood there motionless, the black stitches sealing her eyes and mouth standing out like hastily made scratches against her pale face.

Jaydon forgot the phone in his hand and all of them fell silent. Fletcher stopped barking and switched to a low, bestial growl. Maybe there was danger lurking within Jaydon, but Katherine possessed a much older, primordial power, and with that one step she had reminded them who was at the top of the food chain. *Something's gonna happen here, dude,* Tyler thought. *Something pretty creepy, I think.*

"Hey," Jaydon said shyly.

The witch stood facing him, motionless.

"Sorry? What was that? What did you say, Katherine?"

He tilted his head, listening.

Tyler's pounding heart suddenly overwhelmed everything around him.

"What do you want me to do?" Jaydon asked. "Really, Katherine? You want me to touch your boobies?"

Justin and Burak doubled over and shrieked with laughter. Tyler and Lawrence didn't laugh, but they did exchange glances, and Tyler thought, *Please stop it; you're way out of line. Don't mock the witch.* Keeping a safe distance, Jaydon cautiously reached his hands forward and pretended he was fondling Katherine's breasts as he bumped and ground his hips obscenely.

"You haven't got the guts," Burak said, egging him on.

"Oh no? I'd fuck her, all right," Jaydon said. Suddenly he bent over toward the witch and bellowed into her face, "*You filthy whore! You'd like that, wouldn't you! Dirty cunt! That's how you did it back in your day, huh?*"

Fletcher started howling and sprang forward so suddenly that Lawrence almost fell over. Tyler grabbed the dog by his collar to help control him and yelled, "Jaydon, knock it off!"

Jaydon turned to the others with a foolish grin. "Twenty bucks," he said. "Twenty bucks for the one who takes a picture of her tit. Naked, I mean. I want to see what a seventeenth-century tit looks like."

"Get the fuck out of here," Tyler said. "That is so wrong."

"Oh, come on," Jaydon laughed. "I'm sure she wouldn't mind, would you, Katherine? You don't mind, do you?" He scurried around behind her and continued with a high little voice: "No, Tyler, I don't mind at all! In fact I'm getting a little wet just talking about it! You want to come and see for yourself, Tyler? You want to feel how wet my panties are?"

More laughter. Katherine van Wyler endured the humiliation silently, seemingly unaware. Maybe there was no awareness behind those closed eyes, Tyler thought—no human awareness, at any rate. But you couldn't be sure. Maybe Katherine was waiting for her moment, as she had been waiting for centuries in this dormant state. The very idea made Tyler's insides churn.

Jaydon had gone back to the HEXApp on his iPhone when Lawrence suddenly said, "Wait. We can record her."

They looked at each other. It took three seconds for Tyler to consider the possibility: The dense silence of the woods and the fact that they were out of camera range created an opportunity that wouldn't come again anytime soon. The excitement ignited a blazing flash in him, and he said, "Oh, fuck. Okay, but make it quick."

They used Fletcher's leash. Tyler let him loose and Lawrence led the dog farther downstream, holding him firmly by the collar. Jaydon handed over his iPhone and, without stopping to think about it, Tyler wrapped the leash around the phone several times and tied it off. Then they knotted it at the far end of the long stick that Jaydon had used to poke the witch.

In the distance they heard the cackling laughter of children. The boys looked around, startled. The sound was coming from the south but carried in a strange way beneath the leaf canopy. Probably hikers. They listened for a while but heard nothing more.

"Come on, quick," Burak said, and he took the stick from Tyler. "You got this?"

Tyler took the GoPro out of his pocket and began shooting. "Okay, Sunday, October 21. This is the whisper test. Wait . . ." He took a few steps back. "All right. Go."

Jaydon turned on the voice recorder on his iPhone and whispered, "Okay, everybody quiet . . ." Burak raised the stick in the air like a fishing pole and the iPhone swung forward on Fletcher's leash. Moving cautiously, he held it in front of the Black Rock Witch's face. Tyler saw that Burak's hands were trembling and that he was having a hard time keeping the phone still. Then he shifted the fishing pole to the left so the phone smacked into Katherine's cheek with a fleshy thud, right in front of the corner of her mouth with the severed stitch.

For a full minute, no one made a sound. When Burak finally reeled in the fishing pole and Jaydon plucked his iPhone from the air, they all cheered and clapped their hands for another successfully completed stage in their experiment. Yet Tyler was only lukewarm in his enthusiasm; while the others shared their excitement, he had turned off the GoPro. He walked over to Jaydon and they all bowed over his phone with appropriate respect. On the display, the voice recorder asked if he wanted to PLAY the file or make a NEW SAMPLE.

"This is Katherine's dead-whisper," Jaydon said, as he gave the phone a portentous shake. His thumb hovered over the touch screen, as if to demonstrate that he had the guts to play the sound file. "This may well be the most dangerous recording in the world. You could kill somebody with this."

"Yeah, so who's sacrificing himself?" Justin asked. The others laughed, but not convincingly. No one was willing to volunteer for this one.

"Not yet," Tyler said. "First we find somebody from outside. Then we'll listen, in a secure environment. Jaydon, can you send it to me by Bluetooth? That's a signal they can't pick up."

"Sure," Jaydon said, and he sent the sound file. Tyler accepted it on his own phone.

"You gonna put it online?" Burak asked.

"Of course not. This shit is fatal. You don't fuck with it. Delete the file as soon as it's finished sending, okay? I don't want any accidents to happen."

He glanced sharply at Jaydon and Jaydon grinned back. Then their phones indicated that the file had been transferred. Jaydon tapped his thumb on his screen a few times and said, "Okay, it's gone."

Jaydon's face brightened and he slipped his phone into his pocket. Tyler imagined himself reaching his hand into that face and feeling nothing but darkness.

-+-|-|-|-

A FEW DAYS later, a new clip is launched on *OYE*. We see the camera zooming in on Tyler's iPhone, making its way through a noisy school auditorium until it stops on a cheerful, strapping seventeen-year-old in a baseball cap and headphones. "Hey, what's up, dude?" he asks, and Tyler says, "Hey, Mike, wanna do me a favor?" Mike smiles at the camera and says, "Sure, we'll pretend you didn't just ask me to listen to your little music clip and that I hadn't already agreed to say, 'Hey, what's up, dude?'" His friends crack up and Tyler says, "Cool. Let's do it one more time."

"Hey, what's up, dude?" Mike says, and Tyler says, "Hey, Mike, wanna do me a favor?" Mike grins. "Sure. Is this spontaneous or what?" "Yeah, it really is," Tyler says. "Hey, Mike, what's up, dude?" "Hey, Tyler, can I do you a favor?"

Everybody is in stitches again, but let's skip to the next shot, where

Mike has taken off his headphones and exchanged them for two ear-buds attached to Tyler's iPhone. "Mike here, from Highland Falls," Tyler points out, "is now going to listen to the sound file. You ready for it, Mike?" Mike gives him a thumbs-up and Tyler clicks PLAY.

At first, nothing happens. Then Mike winces and pushes the plugs deeper into his ears, as if he has to strain to hear what's being said. Tyler looks on, mesmerized. "What is this, anyway?" Mike asks, but Tyler gestures for him to be quiet and keep on listening.

"So what did you hear?" he asks when the file has played completely and Mike has taken out the earbuds.

"Just some whispers," Mike says. He looks a little flustered.

"But what did they say?" Tyler presses.

"How should I know? It wasn't English. It wasn't any language I knew. Just jabbering. What is this, one of those messages you play backward and when it enters into your subconscious it actually says, *'DIE, MOTHERFUCKER, WORSHIP THE DEVIL, MOTHER-FUCKER!'*" He bellows out these last words, to his friends' hysterical laughter. Tyler says, "Yeah, something like that. But . . . what did you *feel?*" Mike's expression changes to one of contempt, and he says, "What did I feel? Man, what have you been sniffing?"

Tyler turns the camera on himself and says, "Theory confirmed. Subject unharmed—mission accomplished."

TEN

AUTUMN HAD BEEN mild, but two days before Halloween it suddenly got cold. The old-fashioned mercury thermometer outside the Quiet Man indicated a mere forty degrees, the kind of biting fall chill that hits unexpectedly after a relatively long transitional period of milder temperatures and sinks right into your bones. On October 31 the sky over Black Spring was steely gray and pregnant with rain, which blew around in the upper atmosphere but never really fell.

Early that morning, at the closed-off intersection of Deep Hollow Road and Lower Reservoir Road, along the lower corner of Temple Hill Cemetery, the Wicker Woman was set up: a gigantic reed dummy that would be set afire that night during the festival. People had to climb tall ladders to festoon the dummy with blackened iron chains, which were fished out of the smoldering ashes with pokers every year to be reused the next. Liza Belt's sewing studio donated a tailor-made scarf to tie around the dummy's head, and bunches of straw were stuck into its eyes and mouth. The ritual was older than the residents of Black Spring themselves and due to its heathen character, it was challenged year after year by Colton Mathers and the parish councils of both the Little Methodist Church and St. Mary's Church. And each year the All Hallows Committee triumphed by arguing that they couldn't break with tradition, as burning the Wicker Woman was the highlight of the annual Celebration of the Witch: Black Spring's cover for Katherine in plain sight of the Outsiders who'd flock to the town from all over the county.

The argument was bogus, of course. The truth was much more primitive: The ritual itself was woven into the community's soul, and no one wanted to do away with it. Whether Christian, Jew, Muslim, or atheist, all the people of Black Spring were equally eager to lawfully circumvent the ban on meddling with Katherine van Wyler at least once a year. That morning, townspeople brought in gifts from every corner of town, each one bigger than the next, and silently shoved them into the opening under the giant Wicker Woman's skirt. Many would touch the dummy nervously as they did so, falling to their knees for a moment or making a sign to ward off the evil eye. Some brought food: Children tossed candy and apples between the woven reeds, parents brought plates of their favorite dishes or baked pies, and there were those who hung strings of garlic from the iron chains. Others brought objects: candles, homemade wickerwork, guest towels, soap, curling tongs, an old Bernette sewing machine, everything that could be sacrificed to Katherine to ensure another year free from doom. There were also gifts of more dubious quality: John Blanchard, the sheep farmer from Ackerman's Corner, showed up with a dead lamb; a young mother from town insisted on burning a plastic bag full of her newborn baby's dirty diapers; and Griselda Holst donated a calf's head, a delicacy especially ordered from the slaughterhouse for the occasion. These artifacts would be provisionally concealed by gifts of a more mundane nature before the first Outsiders arrived.

Steve and Jocelyn Grant were too practical to engage in that sort of idolatry. They had let Matt and Tyler dutifully add a drawing or a carrot to the stake every year when they were younger and watched from the crowd as the Wicker Woman went up in flames. Now the boys were too old to work up any enthusiasm, so the ritual had been shelved along with so many other childhood customs. Steve had always felt a bit uneasy about the symbolism of the burning witch. And even worse, the smoke clung to your clothes for days. He attended the Wicker Burning only for the same reason that he had always been fascinated by the early January Christmas tree bonfires of his youth: because every man gets hypnotized by big fires, and a column of heat in your face was a welcome finish to a bleak fall night.

But that part was yet to come. Black Spring had a lot more in store than just the offering ritual that day.

The kitchen of Griselda's Butchery & Delicacies was a hive of activity that morning. Griselda had hired six extra people to get her traditional goodies delivered to the food stand on the town square on time: potato salad, tapas, roasted meat on the spit, special green witch's stew (pea soup with meatballs) served from a real copper kettle, and, of course, large plates of Griselda's own sour Holst pâté. Griselda wasn't the least bit interested in making money from the event, but any local entrepreneur would have been crazy not to profit from the two-thousand-plus outside visitors that the festival attracted.

After all, she said to herself, it was all in honor of Katherine.

At around three o'clock in the afternoon, when it really started getting crowded, the main streets of Black Spring were closed off and the stands with candy and geegaws formed a horseshoe around Crystal Meth Church and the cemetery. Orange and black ribbons hung from the trees, and carved jack-o'-lanterns were planted on stakes below. The square was full of people dressed as the Black Rock Witch: some with pointy hats and waving broomsticks, others with the more traditional sewn-up eyes. Children got their faces painted and had a ball on the bouncy castle in front of Sue's Highland Diner. Shrieking with delight, they took swings at the papier-mâché witch piñatas that were hanging from the trees and ended up buried in candy, or had themselves weighed on the special witch scales set up on the church square. If a child weighed no more than two ducks—which happened every now and then—he or she would be declared a witch and chased around by a group of pitchfork-brandishing actors from Black Spring dressed in seventeenth-century rags.

Robert Grim found this popular amusement rather corny. A few years ago, by way of experiment, he had submitted a proposal to reintroduce medieval torture games like goose pulling and cat burning (because everybody knew that charred cat cinders were lucky), but it was rejected due to legislation against animal abuse and crude morals. The committee was not amused.

For Grim, October 31 was traditionally the most hectic and exasperating day of the year. Trying to supervise the arrival of so many Outsiders required a good dose of empathy and patience, traits that Robert Grim possessed in scant quantities. In Grim's humble opinion, the people of the Hudson Valley were ill-bred, loud, beer-swilling wife beaters and, worst of all, they lacked the common sense to take full advantage of their geographic location. To the east they had the Hudson to collectively drown themselves in, and to the south they had Bear Mountain State Park, where they could mate unashamedly with beavers and white-tailed deer and effectively implement their own extinction. But so far no one had seized these golden opportunities. For these and other reasons, after doing the obligatory round of inspections with the officials from The Point, Robert Grim spent the rest of the day at his post in the control center, which in turn meant a day of suffering for his colleagues.

The witch—the real one—had decided to stand in the disabled parking space behind Town Hall at a little after eleven-thirty, and there she stayed. The parking space was less than three hundred yards from the center of all the activities as the crow flies, but it was a perfectly workable location. Grim had had the approach to Deep Hollow Road fenced off. Behind Town Hall he had created a fake building site, guarded on all sides by a battery of well-instructed workmen. Katherine herself was enclosed in a toolshed. In the unlikely event that she should join the festivities that day, there were six possible scenarios at hand. The last time something like that had happened was in 2003, before they had acquired the barrel organ. The wench had spent the entire celebration standing imperiously on the town square in front of Sue's. After a heated debate, they had decided to set up a Black Spring billboard behind her and hang a banner that read: GET YOUR PICTURE TAKEN WITH THE *REAL* WITCH! After they pinned a button on her that said: WELCOME TO BLACK SPRING, no one believed she was real. All the children wanted to have their pictures taken with the funny lady. It turned out to be a relatively safe and especially lucrative business: All the parents gladly paid five bucks to get a shot.

A number of babies had cried pitifully, but that's what babies are for.

Today, however, the festival was smooth sailing. The inspectors from The Point had left, Grim thought of reinforced concrete, and the people partied, the people partied.

At four-fifteen Tyler Grant and his friends sat in the shelter of the hedge near the fountain and the bronze washerwoman statue. They ate cotton candy and stared with unspoken envy at the passing stream of Outsiders. Jaydon was helping out at his mom's food stand that day, but he was on his break and had joined them for a minute.

Lawrence held up five matches. Each drew one and they all revealed them at the same time. Burak had the one with the burned end. It took a few seconds for the truth to sink in: He had been chosen for the whisper test. He cursed. "Right. Let the Turk do the dirty work."

The others laughed, but their hearts weren't in it. The laughter sounded nervous to Tyler—affected, filled with relief that they hadn't been chosen for the test. A chilly gust of wind stirred the leaves at his feet and the leaden sky seemed like a dome descending over Black Spring. Tyler shivered and pulled his head down into his collar. *All this is going to change real soon now,* he thought.

And it would, but not the way Tyler expected.

At a little before five, as Katherine van Wyler was continuously whispering corrupted words in ancient languages inside the toolshed behind Town Hall, and Fletcher moved restlessly in his sleep two miles away in his kennel, Griselda Holst stealthily withdrew from the festivities. She hurried across the cemetery to the back of Crystal Meth Church. No one noticed when she opened the heavy wooden door to the chancel with a skeleton key, slipped inside, and shut out the din of the celebrations. Hands on the cold walls, Griselda went down the spiral staircase, descending deeper and deeper into the foul smell of old stone, moldering wood, seeping water, and human disease. An unpleasant chill crept from the walls into Griselda's joints: In the vaults beneath the church it was always winter, and always night.

Arthur Roth was slumped against the bars of his cell, and Griselda knew in an instant that he was dead. He was naked, and in the light of the bulbs on the wall, his skin had taken on the purple, pallid color of dead fish, stretched taut across his emaciated rib cage. Roth lay in his own excrement, one hand limply cuffed to the bars, the veins on his arm like exposed power cables.

Griselda's heart was racing, but even so, she was strangely relieved. Now that her ordeal was finally over, she wouldn't have to go down that ghastly stairway anymore to feed him or hose him off or listen to his insane cackling echoing from the vaulted ceiling, as if the space beneath the church were teeming with lost souls. Griselda felt no shame, only the slow, endless drizzle that always saturated her mind. She hadn't starved him; she had only followed Mathers's orders. She had done her duty to serve Katherine.

She took a broom from the utility room and stuck the handle through the bars, poking Roth's body. He remained limp. Griselda looked around, seized by a sudden panic. She froze, realizing she was alone in the dark below the church with the dead body of Arthur Roth—his *presumably* dead body. Common sense told her she ought to make sure, but doubt made her thoughts run wild, turned reason into foolishness and logic into a dream. It was the same irrational doubt she had felt years ago, in the silent echoes after Jim had beaten her up or forced himself on her. She groped for the key ring, and that simple act helped her to get a grip on herself.

Griselda opened the cell and warily knelt beside the cold, starved body, pressing her scarf to her mouth against the stench. It was not anxiety she felt when she realized the man was still breathing, but a vulnerable kind of wonder. *He's still alive,* she thought. And when Arthur

Roth opened his eyes and his hand snapped around her wrist like a trap, she didn't even have time to scream.

Oh, there was screaming, all right: children being chased by witches and carny folk, teenagers being thrown from the bucking rodeo bronco, the elderly competing at horseshoes, and all their shrill screams rose high above the streets of Black Spring, where the low-hanging mist distorted it into dissonant whispers. "You filthy slut," whispered Arthur Roth, hypothermic and starving, but far from dead. "I'm going to screw you," he whispered, and he clasped Griselda to him with his legs and pinched her breast hard with his free hand. Aboveground, people danced to the old folk tunes played by the fiddlers' quartet—Griselda could hear the muted sounds make their way through the air vent as she faintly, distantly calculated her chances, no matter how slight. She found herself outside time, and his eager hand, tearing at her blouse, could hurt her no more; Jim's hands could hurt her no more; he was dead and she smelled cotton candy and popcorn, roasted poultry, and sausages in oil.

And at ten past five, as Steve Grant and his youngest son, Matt, ambled among the throngs of people at the fair and ate freshly baked churros from grease-stained paper bags; and as Griselda Holst grabbed the broomstick in a supreme effort and brought it down again and again on Arthur Roth's bleeding head in the vault beneath Crystal Meth Church, screaming the name of her husband with every blow, an unusually large owl descended on the church's spire. It was a magnificent bird, and from its great height it spied on the crowds with superhuman concentration, as if it were observing rats in a trap. Not many people saw the bird in the gathering dusk, but those who did would later claim to have heard the sound of mighty wings as it flew away, and they identified the owl on the Cross of God as an omen of impending disaster.

ELEVEN

MATT ASTOUNDED STEVE by leaving an offering after all; when they crossed the intersection, he walked up to the Wicker Woman, took a pennant out of his coat, and put it on the pyre with all the other gifts. Though not condemning Matt's action, Steve was shocked. If Matt had tossed a couple of churros under her skirt, it would have been an impulsive adolescent prank, but he had brought the pennant from home.

"What did you do that for?" he asked when Matt came back.

"No reason," Matt said matter-of-factly. "Just wanted to give Gramma something."

"But why one of your pennants? You won it in a contest; it's a keepsake for later on."

Matt shrugged. "This is the one from preliminaries, when I had just come back from that injury, remember? Nuala wasn't broken in yet and I came in fourteenth. Then it was summer vacation, and after that I went to junior high, and things got a lot better." He hesitated, then added, "Besides, if you sacrifice something that isn't important to you, what's the point?"

Steve looked at him in amazement. He wondered what had driven Matt to this sudden, foolish expression of superstition. Apparently the pennant symbolized the low Matt had hit a year and a half ago; by burning it he would gain closure and ward off similar bad luck for the future. Steve got the idea, and strictly speaking, he shouldn't have been surprised that such superstition had cropped up in his own family, considering where they lived. He had just never noticed it before.

"*Is* there a point?" he finally asked, raising an eyebrow.

But Matt surprised him again by saying, "Does it matter?"

No, thought Steve. *Not as long as it means something to you. People find hope, comfort, or confidence in making the sign of the cross or not walking under a ladder, just as you find hope and confidence in offering a pennant to the witch. Magic exists in the minds of those who believe in it, not in its actual influence on reality. Even my thirteen-year-old son, who has to accept the fact that reality in Black Spring bends just a little differently than it does anywhere else, seems to understand that. Who can claim to know his own children?*

The Wicker Burning started at six. The surrounding stands had been cleared and taken down by order of the fire department, and The Point to Point Inn had collapsed its canopy. People crowded into the streets in endless rows behind the fence, which had been placed in a wide circle around the Wicker Woman. The audience spread out at least fifty yards in all directions to witness the spectacle. Steve and Matt had found a pretty good spot on Deep Hollow Road. Jocelyn texted that she was standing farther back. She had gone to the market with Mary VanderMeer, but Steve couldn't find them in the crowd. He had no idea where Tyler was.

The crowd observed a moment of silence and prayer. Then the executioner stepped forward with a leather hood over his head, holding a burning torch aloft. He roared gravely—*Ten points for character development,* Steve thought—and set fire to the gasoline-soaked mound of offerings at the foot of the Wicker Woman. The flames licked at the reeds for a few seconds but soon blazed upward, and a sigh of awe ran through the crowd. Simultaneously, the fiddlers struck up a rousing melody, and within the fences a group of folk dancers twirled around the burning witch like druids.

For eight minutes she burned, and, at their peak, the flames rose higher than the rooftops of the surrounding houses, reaching up like grasping fingers. Then the Woman tilted backward, her face to the sky as if in one last godless incantation, and collapsed. Sparks swirled in the cold October evening. When the fire department finally directed the crowds to move back in order to let the pile of blackened ash smolder, their clothes already stank of smoke.

The PA system switched on and Steve recognized the voice of Lucy Everett, one of the regular collaborators at HEX and chairman of the All Hallows Committee: "Ladies and gentlemen, boys and girls, with this fantastic spectacle our wonderful celebration has come to an end! To make the cleanup easier, the bars and restaurants around the square will now close. You can go back to the parking lot on Route 293 by following the fire department's instructions. Your buses will be waiting for you there. Have a super duper Halloween and a safe trip home, and we'll see you next year!"

Steve hid his smile while the crowds of Outsiders slowly began to disperse for a night of trick-or-treating and Halloween parties in Highland Falls, Highland Mills, and Fort Montgomery. It was an ingenious diversion, but he detected the implicit order between the lines. The pretext of the fire department closing the town's bars and restaurants at 6:30 on the most lucrative day of the year . . . you may as well say: *Get in your bus and get the fuck out or we'll set our wild dogs on you*. But because Lucy managed to act like an overly enthusiastic employee of the local community center, no one doubted her integrity, and the crowds filed out neatly as they were told. Steve knew that coordinating the send-off was a detailed process meticulously organized by HEX. The surveillance cams ran overtime; nothing could be left to chance. The market closed, downtown died out. At about eight o'clock, the last bone-chilled teens making out in the woods would be chased away, and by nine Black Spring would be back in the hands of Black Spring.

And there was no trick-or-treating here.

On their way home, Steve and Matt bumped into Jocelyn and Pete and Mary VanderMeer. At the house they found Tyler, Lawrence, and Burak, and that's where Steve first heard the rumor that something serious had happened. Tyler read out a PM from Jaydon Holst: "Arthur Roth dead as a dodo. OMG all that blood, fucking sick!" The journalist in Tyler absorbed this information and went on a roll. "That means he saw it, right? He hasn't replied since, but maybe HEX is intercepting his messages. . . ." Steve and Pete exchanged glances, but refrained from theorizing for the time being. They kept an eye on the HEXApp for updates, and Steve went out to walk Fletcher.

At nine-twenty, HEX gave the green light and they all bundled into two cars for the traditional closing of the Halloween festivities: the public Council meeting at Town Hall. Only Matt stayed home, despite his fierce protests; the meeting was closed to anyone under sixteen.

In the slow procession of seven or eight hundred townspeople making its way through the ID checks, rumors ran rampant. Steve greeted a few friends, shook their hands, and shrugged when they asked him questions. He was surprised to spot Burt and Bammy Delarosa, hidden away in long, dark-gray coats, their arms wrapped around each other.

"How's it going?" he asked.

"We're hanging in there," Burt said. "We just came from the celebration. Quite memorable, I must say. So we figured we might as well take in the entire Black Spring experience."

Steve smiled and leaned in. "Keep your eyes open," he said with a muffled voice. It was the most sincere advice he could think of. "It may be pretty intense tonight, but don't get too involved. They know you're newbies. You've got a lot against you right from the start."

Steve, Jocelyn, and Tyler found seats in the sixth row from the stage, to the left of the center aisle. Pete and Mary sat down beside them, the Delarosas one row back and a little to the left. Steve noticed that the sign advertising local businesses, which was usually right behind the podium, had been replaced by a placard that read: LET US TRUST IN GOD AND EACH OTHER. Struck by unbridled cynicism, he was suddenly reminded of the run-in he had had with Tyler. *Come out of the closet?* he thought. *Maybe if Easter and Halloween come to fall on the same day and Colton Mathers breaks into a lively round of "Walpurgis Night."*

A little before ten, the subdued buzzing died down and the mayor took the floor. He invited the members of the Council to take their places at the panel table—only six of them, as Griselda Holst was absent due to illness. Steve tried to catch Pete's eye, but his neighbor was looking with derision at the stage, where the mayor was helping Colton Mathers to his place behind the podium, and where Robert Grim had also found a seat. Pete had once confided in Steve, the two of them sitting on the sociologist's back porch, that in his humble opinion the administrative order of Black Spring was the greatest pantomime since the tribunal of Pontius Pilate that had convicted Jesus Christ.

"Good," the mayor said. "I would like to turn the proceedings over to Mr. Mathers, who will open the meeting with the traditional passage from Psalm 91."

It was so quiet in the auditorium you could hear a pin drop. The old councilman, patriarch of the community, began to speak in a solemn monotone. The man exuded a strange sort of magnetism; even Steve was aware of it. It was as if he were sucking all the available air out of the hall. Mathers was old, but not in a fragile way. He was massive, like a cathedral. " 'He that dwelleth in the secret place of the most High,' " he intoned, " 'shall abide under the shadow of the Almighty. Surely He shall deliver thee from the snare of the fowler, and from the noisome pestilence. Thou shalt not be afraid for the terror by night; nor for the pestilence that walketh in darkness; nor for the destruction that wasteth at noonday. A thousand shall fall at thy side, and ten thousand at thy right hand; but it shall not come nigh thee. Only with thine eyes shalt thou behold and see the reward of the wicked.' Ladies and gentlemen, it is my duty to inform you that Arthur Roth, detained beneath Little Methodist Church for repeatedly violating the Black Spring Emergency Decree, passed away earlier today of cardiac arrest. God rest his soul."

There was a moment of charged silence, then a frenzied cheer rose up from the crowd. People began to applaud. Others looked around with contorted, uncertain faces. "He's finally dead, the swine!" someone yelled, and this was met with laughter.

Pete bent over to Steve and whispered, "He's lying through his teeth."

"Right," the mayor said. "Let this be the first item on the agenda. Since the case of Mr. Roth is a town matter and we've always treated it as such, I feel it would be good to continue to regard it as a town matter. As far as we know, Arthur Roth has no family or relatives, neither inside nor outside our community. Because of his unrelenting threats to pervert the day-to-day running of things here in Black Spring, we were forced to pass a ruling—democratically, of course—to sequester him from society. Unfortunately, his presumed brain fever was never cured. The question now is what to do with his body."

"Burn the motherfucker!" someone yelled.

"Yeah, offer him up to the Wicker Woman!"

New laughter erupted.

"Well, we can't just go out and burn somebody, can we?" the mayor said, punctuating his words with the kind of pompous laugh reserved for government officials after telling a not-quite-successful joke that's doomed to die a painful death. Yet the people in the audience didn't care. In the glow of the lights hanging from the roof beams, they looked feverish and forbidding, like obsessed townsfolk from times past. Steve saw Robert Grim looking at the audience with deep revulsion and was suddenly filled with a similar horror.

Gripped by an impulse, Steve stood up and said, "Was he seen by a doctor?"

The murmuring stopped and the mayor looked at him quizzically, clearly thrown off-balance. Steve felt the gaze of hundreds of townspeople focus on him and he cleared his throat. "I mean, I was just wondering whether his death has been officially recorded on a death certificate."

"Oh, he's dead, all right, I guarantee it," said the mayor.

That's not the same thing, Steve thought. "I understand that, but only a doctor can determine the cause of death with any certainty. I've heard from someone directly involved that the way he died was rather bloody." A disconcerted sigh rose from the audience, which gave Steve the self-confidence to continue. "As a doctor, I don't see how that would be consistent with cardiac arrest. The person directly involved is Jaydon Holst, son of Council member Griselda Holst, who was given the task of taking care of Roth. And who now, on the day of his death, appears to be sick. Given the fact that this is a town matter, I'm sure you won't mind telling us exactly what happened?"

A buzzing of approval. Tyler gazed up at his dad with something close to idolization, which did not leave Steve unmoved. Meanwhile, up on the stage, the mayor was looking to Colton Mathers for help.

Mathers chose his words carefully: "Mrs. Holst did indeed find him dead in his cell. She is extremely upset, which is why she is not with us tonight, and I don't think anyone can fault her for that. Mr. Roth had undressed himself and had inflicted serious injuries upon himself in several places, but I will not elaborate on the details. Mrs. Holst panicked and first called her son, then me. When I arrived, I determined that a combination of blood loss and hypothermia had led to cardiac arrest, which resulted in death."

A pretty fucking obvious example of quackery, Steve thought. He, too, had put all the pieces together, and had come up with a similar scenario, except his differed from Mathers's account on one significant point: If Griselda Holst had just found Roth dead, it wouldn't have made sense for her to call her son first. Griselda was a strong woman, toughened by her sad history of domestic violence, and it was hard for Steve to imagine her panicking. If she had been thinking rationally, she would have called Mathers and never involved her son. But that's exactly what she *did* do, and so she *had* panicked. Something else must have happened down there.

And besides, if hypothermia had played a role, under what conditions were you keeping him prisoner beneath the house of God?

Steve's hands went moist and clammy and he noticed the sour taste of doubt in his mouth. He was still on his feet when the truth suddenly got through to him. The vast majority of townsfolk looking up at him from their seats were living under constant pressure and in unbridled fear of what was out there on the streets. *How far will they go?* Steve thought. *What might they be capable of if the pressure builds too much?* Maybe the rumors were true and they *had* starved Roth to death. Maybe things had gotten nasty in some other way today, even before such a stage had been reached. Did it matter? It was still a Black Spring affair, and the consequences were the same.

No, a headstrong and idealistic part of him insisted. *We still have human dignity. That stays intact, even if everything around us falls apart.*

"I just think he deserves a proper autopsy like anybody else. That's all," Steve said, and he sat down. Jocelyn grabbed his hand and squeezed it gently.

"Duly noted," the mayor said. "The problem is that we cannot declare Arthur Roth legally dead because he no longer legally exists. It would only raise a host of questions. The Council has passed a resolution—six yeas and one nay—to bury him anonymously and dishonorably, without a tombstone and outside the cemetery grounds." An outburst of exultant cheering. "However, as behooves a democratic community, I would like to put this to the vote by means of—"

"Doctor Grant is right!" Pete VanderMeer shouted suddenly, rising from his seat. The mayor frowned, but despite the power of his office, he was not able to muster the authority to quell the interruption. "Are you really asking us, in the name of democracy, to vote to whisk away a dead body so we can all wash our hands in innocence? That's not democracy, that's a popular tribunal."

"What difference does it make?" a surly-looking man on the other side of the aisle said. "We need to get rid of him one way or another. And he doesn't deserve any better."

"But it's a farce!" Pete said. "Come on, people, we're not barbarians, are we? If we go down that road, we're one step away from a lynch mob."

"So what do you want to do with him?" the man on the other side of the aisle yelled contemptuously. "Hand him over to the authorities?"

"No," Pete said. "But at least have a doctor draw up an official death certificate. He is a human being, for God's sake."

A loud bang thundered through Town Hall. Everyone winced and jerked their heads forward. Colton Mathers had pounded on the podium with an old-fashioned wooden gavel, and fire was blazing from his eyes. "In . . . this . . . house . . . no one will take the name of the Lord in vain," Mathers spoke with all the authority the mayor lacked. "The Emergency Decree says: What comes from Black Spring stays in Black Spring."

"That's not what the Emergency Decree says—it's what Katherine says," Pete mumbled as he sat down, but no one heard him except Steve and perhaps his wife, Mary.

"But let us demonstrate that our decision-making process is indeed democratic and that everyone here is heard by putting these two gentlemen's motion to the vote."

Steve cursed silently. Mathers knew puritanical stubbornness would prevail over common sense, and he'd even managed to give the matter a righteous twist. Pete knew it, too, and kept quiet. Suddenly a grotesque image arose in Steve's mind: Colton Mathers and Griselda Holst wrapping Arthur Roth's corpse in a duct-tape-sealed Hefty bag and dragging him up Mount Misery on a homemade bier of broomsticks, to take him to his anonymous and dishonorable final resting place.

The old councilman showed no emotion at all when he gave the floor back to the mayor: "Well, the question is, are we going to give Arthur Roth official recognition by having a doctor draw up a death certificate? All those in favor, raise your right hand."

Admittedly, some hands went up, but Steve didn't need to turn to see that they were few—marginal, even. Of all the Council members, only Grim had irritably raised his hand.

"Looks like an open-and-shut case to me, so the motion is rejected. If no one has any objections"—the mayor quickly glanced around the hall as a formality—"I would now like to bring the Council's motion to a vote: The Council moves to give Arthur Roth a dishonorable burial, without a tombstone and outside the cemetery. All those in favor, raise your right hand."

With a loud rustling of clothes and cracking of elbow joints, the hands went into the air. A few necks turned triumphantly to the group clustering in row six, who remained seated with their arms crossed. Steve didn't return their glances, but he looked over his shoulder and his eyes met those of Burt and Bammy Delarosa, who looked absolutely bewildered.

"The motion is passed," Colton Mathers said, bringing the gavel down with a loud bang.

-+-|-|-|-

"IT'S A GOOD thing you never started a practice in town," Jocelyn said, "or you would have lost half your patients tonight." They were lying together in bed and listening to the wind, rapid and fierce. Temperatures had dropped below freezing.

"They're a bunch of medieval religious fanatics," Steve said. "They don't need a GP. They need a barber-surgeon."

"It's the religious fanatics we've got to live with, Steve."

He rolled over toward her, yawning, and said, "Most of 'em could use a little bloodletting. I happily volunteer."

Jocelyn began to giggle uncontrollably and kissed him. "You did make someone proud tonight," she said, after pulling away. Steve raised his eyebrows and she continued: "Tyler. I saw how he looked at you. He really admired the way you stood up for your ideals, Doctor. I think you both needed that, after the fuss about Laurie."

I hope so, Steve thought. *Maybe it'll clear the air for a while, but it won't wipe away his worries. He's just come face-to-face with the fact that the situation is never going to change. The puppet show he witnessed tonight only confirms it. And it's at odds with everything he believes in.*

They made love and fell asleep in each other's arms. Steve dreamt that Katherine van Wyler appeared in their bedroom, a dark monolith amid the shadows, except her eyes were open and gleaming with demonic life. As soon as he was awake enough to realize what he had seen, he shot bolt upright and kicked off the blankets. Jocelyn was fast asleep on her side of the bed. Steve felt that his eyes were bulging and his upper body was covered in cold sweat.

Of course Katherine wasn't there, but he got out of bed and walked to the landing even so. Katherine had appeared in their bedroom twice during their marriage to Black Spring. The first time, before Matt was born, she had been standing in the bay window at night, as if she were looking outside. Steve and Jocelyn had stayed in bed, paralyzed, observing her as you might observe deadly animals from a wildlife observation hut. The second time had been a few years ago, when she'd stood at their bedside for three days and three nights. Jocelyn had insisted they sleep on the couch.

Steve checked out the entire house, including the downstairs and the garage. He turned all the lights on—if he were to bump into her in the dark, he knew he would scream. He checked all the doors. That was pointless, but it still made him feel more comfortable. The house was quiet, deserted. Only Fletcher was there, looking up at him curiously from his basket and whining softly.

Christ, go back to bed, he said to himself. He shivered from the cold, spooked by his own delusions.

Nevertheless, he had to stifle a cry when the wind blew a branch against the bay window, and without thinking twice he dove into bed. Steve bit his lip at his own stupidity and soon fell asleep.

TWELVE

TYLER CAME DOWNSTAIRS at a quarter past eight the next morning. The other family members were already at the breakfast table, Matt with bags under his eyes and an open history book at his elbow, Jocelyn still in her bathrobe. The smell of fresh buns from the oven usually made his mouth water, but today it left him cold. He pulled up a chair without saying a word and began chewing apathetically on a cracker.

"Wow, someone had a good night's sleep," Matt commented.

"Cut it, douche bag," Tyler snapped back.

Jocelyn put her knife down on her plate and said, "Hey, come on, guys. . . ."

"All I asked was how he slept," Matt protested. "Don't be so touchy, dude. Jeez . . ."

"One big happy family," Steve said. "Hurry up, guys, or you'll miss your bus."

"It's Staff Development Day," Tyler said. "Forgot to mention it."

"For real?" Matt cried out. "How did *you* get so lucky?"

"It's for high school, not junior high." The lie was out before he knew it. Until that moment he hadn't realized that he was planning on playing hooky. It troubled him, being able to lie so easily to his dad, especially since he didn't feel even slightly guilty about it. Of course you didn't let your parents in on everything, but something essential had changed in their relationship since he disavowed his father's one important question: *You haven't got something else up your sleeve,*

I hope? With that, he had set out on a course that he could no longer easily depart from.

"Good. Then you can take the dog out," Steve said.

Tyler shrugged and pulled another cracker from the box. Matt hugged Jocelyn and Steve good-bye and left for the bus stop. When the back door slammed, Jocelyn grumbled, but she didn't chase after him. Instead, she poured herself another cup of coffee. Everything was fine: same shit, different day. Suddenly Tyler felt the need to throw up. He put his cracker down. Sweat burst from his pores and his stomach went into a spasm.

You haven't got something else up your sleeve, I hope?

Nothing was fine. Yesterday's events were pressing down on his guts like a rock. When the meeting began and Jaydon still hadn't checked in or shown up, Tyler was initially furious. They needed him to raise their complaint about privacy and Internet policies, since he was the only one in the group who was of age. Tyler understood that the situation was different now that someone had died, but at least Jaydon could have responded to their zillions of apps so the others could have come up with a plan B.

Tyler had always felt that everything he was doing for *Open Your Eyes* was based on common sense. But was there any common sense in the desperate, shattered feeling that had come over him after the grim opening of the Council meeting and the vote on Arthur Roth? In no time, his morale had hit rock-bottom. Did he really believe that the same people who had screamed, *Burn the motherfucker!* and *Offer him up to the Wicker Woman!* would be willing to pass a positive judgment on something as stupid as their right to Twitter and Facebook? It was ludicrous. For the first time, Tyler realized that bigger forces were at play here.

Thou shalt not be afraid for the terror by night; nor for the pestilence that walketh in darkness.

But he *was* afraid. And every time he wondered whether trying to change those forces was a good idea, he thought of Jaydon in the woods jabbing the witch with his stick, and the thought that had occurred to Tyler at that very moment, suddenly, out of nowhere: *Something's gonna happen here, dude. Something pretty creepy, I think.*

No more bullshit with the witch, no YouTube clips, no crazy ideas.

They won't do the firing squad anymore. But corporal punishments are still written into the Emergency Decree.

We may be fucked up here, but that's a whole nother level of fucked-upness.

Welcome to Black Spring.

"You okay?" Steve asked with a frown. "You look feverish, maybe a bit under the weather."

Tyler blinked. "I'm fine," he said, and struggled to put a smile on his face. "Not really awake yet, I guess."

He left the table, ran the last few steps to the bathroom, and hung over the toilet, but nothing came up. Tyler splashed water on his face and looked at himself in the mirror with bloodshot eyes. *Let it go,* he thought. *Let them all go to hell. It's none of your business.*

But it was. And if he didn't open his mouth, who would?

Back in his room, he turned on the radio and cranked the volume up to full blast when he recognized a Train song. The stirring melody raised his spirits a little. He apped Lawrence to ask if he was on the bus, and Lawrence apped back that his dad had been easy on him after last night's meeting and had called him in sick, so they met at nine-thirty at the boulders in front of their houses. Fletcher jumped up on Lawrence, wagging his tail and leaving muddy marks all over his jacket.

"Hey, calm down, boy!" he said. He patted the dog's head and Fletcher barked. Tyler suggested they go into the woods, but Lawrence said, "Haven't you heard? The witch is at Burak's house."

"Burak's?"

"Yeah, that's what the HEXApp said this morning. I haven't heard from Burak, but usually his parents let him off after the Council meetings."

They decided to walk in that direction. The Şayer family lived in Lower South near Popolopen Lake, in a house on Morris Avenue. Burak's parents were Turkish and were among the tiny group of practicing Muslims in Black Spring. Tyler had always been puzzled about how that influenced their attitude toward the witch, but Burak usually just shrugged if anyone asked him about it. As far as Tyler knew, Burak himself didn't go to the mosque in Newburgh, but that didn't keep Jaydon from taking him down a peg or two with jokes of a highly politically incorrect nature.

They had just reached the town square, where the festival cleanup activities were in full swing. One of the town workers was spraying the big black stain of ash at the intersection with a high-pressure hose when Tyler got a message from Burak:

Jaydon here, trippin. Pls come asap!

They ran the last half mile to Burak's house with Fletcher in the lead, and Tyler felt sick, on the brink of losing control.

"Dude's gonna go too far one of these days," Lawrence panted.

Yeah, and leave him to it. It's none of your business, Tyler thought again. But that wasn't true, and if things got out of hand, he was partly responsible.

The Şayers' car was gone, which meant Burak's parents weren't home. They crossed the lawn and went around to the backyard, using Fletcher's leash to tie the dog to one of the poplars. Evidently Fletcher hadn't yet noticed that the witch was nearby because he began to sniff the hedge energetically. Tyler tried the back door. It was open.

"Hello?" he called. Lawrence followed him through the kitchen when the bead curtain leading to the living room clattered open. It was Burak. His eyes looked wild, bordering on panic.

"Tyler, you have to . . ."

But then Lawrence saw it, and his voice sounded like a sob. "Oh, Jesus fuck . . ."

It was a surrealistic nightmare. The living room behind Burak shimmered in the semidarkness because the drapes were closed and heavy with a spicy odor, the way you might imagine the mist in *The Arabian Nights* to smell. Tyler saw immediately where it was coming from: Long incense sticks were burning on the coffee table and mantelpiece. And next to them was Katherine. Usually there were no overt religious symbols in the Şayer household, but now countless amulets dangled around the witch like blue peacock eyes, tied to lengths of string tacked to the ceiling. In an eerie repetition of last week's episode in the woods, Jaydon was standing in front of Katherine with a stick in his hands, only now there was an X-Acto knife duct-taped to the tip. He had used it to cut away the rags of her dress, which hung down like a drawbridge to expose Katherine van Wyler's dangling, pale purple right tit.

A flash of bright white light as Jaydon took a picture with his iPhone. The flash revealed it all, more than Tyler ever wanted to see, burning onto his retina the horrifying image of Katherine's black nipple on the soft, dead vaulting of her breast. It wasn't sexy, as some strange, exotic breasts could be. It was repulsive, obscene. And there was more: Jaydon hadn't cut carefully. There were scratches in her bare flesh. A drop of dark blood was slowly leaking from one of them.

That one drop of blood, that black nipple in Jaydon's camera flash, those blue teardrop eyes on strings were what Tyler would never forget.

"Lawrence . . . Tyler," Jaydon said with raised eyebrows. "I hope you haven't come to spoil my party, or you can both get the hell out of here."

"What the fuck are you doing?" Tyler stammered. He was nailed to the ground. Oh, Jesus. Just now, when he needed to keep his head straight, it was all slipping away. This was way too much for him. This was unreal.

"What the fuck were you thinking, showing my PM to that fucking ol' man of yours, who had to share it with the whole fucking town?"

Jaydon practically shouted those last words, and spit was shining on his lips. The stick with the X-Acto knife shook in his hands.

"You should have stayed in touch!" Lawrence yelled. "We were calling and texting you all night! Where the hell were you?"

"Maybe I had more important shit on my mind than your fucking tests. Mathers gave it to me today with both barrels and then some! And all because that faggot there couldn't keep his mouth shut."

"Dude, I just want you outta here, now . . ." Burak said, sounding desperate. "If my parents find out what you did in our house, they'll kill me."

"You're sick," Tyler said softly, his glance still locked on the witch's hideous black nipple. "You're playing with everybody's lives. If the Council ever found out about this, you'd get a lot worse than Doodletown." He dug around in the pocket of his jacket and took out the GoPro, but as soon as Jaydon saw the camera he lunged at Tyler with his knife stick. Tyler screamed and shrank back, bumping into Lawrence.

"Oh no you don't," Jaydon said, and the look in his eyes made Tyler put the GoPro back in his pocket. Jaydon had lost it. Completely. "The only one who's filming or taking pictures today is me. The best fucking pictures in human history. The bare tit of a ghost." He roared with laughter. "I'll send them to Justin and I'll send them to Burak, because this is probably the first tit Mohammed here has ever seen and I know that he'll want to go back to his room and jack off to it later on. But if anybody opens their mouth about this, I'll tell them all about the website and your tests. I'll drag you all down with me."

"Get that fucking knife out of my face!" Tyler said sharply.

"Whatever you say, dude," Jaydon said, and in one fluent move he turned around and brutally jabbed the X-Acto stick at Katherine. The blade was only an inch long, but it disappeared completely into her drooping tit. The witch's body jolted backward and shuddered as if it had received an electrical shock. Her scrawny hands clenched convulsively. When Jaydon withdrew the knife, it released a gush of blood that spattered all over the carpet.

"Fuck!"

"Now look what you've done!" Burak shrieked, pointing at the carpet. "My dad's gonna kill me!"

Lawrence turned away and stumbled backward, tears on his cheeks. The witch was hanging forward in her chains, exposing her breast even more. The wound had split her nipple and blood was forming in dark spots on her dress. *Go on, disappear,* Tyler thought. *Get lost before it gets any worse. . . .*

He tried to control his voice, but it shook nonetheless. "Dude, this is sick—this is abuse. You can't do that to her."

"Who cares? She's a fucking ghost! If she pops up somewhere else later she'll be as good as new."

"But you can't humiliate her like that, she'll . . ."

"That bitch murdered my dad!" Jaydon roared, fiercely brandishing his spear. Tyler recoiled once again. "That bitch raped my mom! Don't tell me what to do, because she's got it coming!"

"Jesus," Tyler said, raising both palms in the air. "Listen, I don't know what happened yesterday, but let's talk about it. There isn't anything we can't solve together, right guys?"

He turned to Burak and Lawrence for help. Burak understood what he was trying to do. "Yeah, he's right. Just calm down."

"Don't try to fucking calm me down. We've been making nice to her long enough. Plan's changed. We're not going public anymore."

"What do you mean?" Tyler asked, but he knew very well what Jaydon meant. Something in Jaydon had snapped, something that had started a long time ago and had come to a climax yesterday. And at the root of it all was the witch. Jaydon didn't want to keep plugging the holes, didn't want to foster understanding anymore. If they were to go mainstream and the authorities moved in, it would no longer be possible for him to . . . Oh, Jesus. To take revenge. What the hell happened down there under the church? What's come over him? And why is the goddamn witch still here?

"I mean that *OYE* doesn't exist anymore," Jaydon said, eyes narrowing. "I'm in charge from now on. We're doing things my way. And I meant what I said. If anyone here blabs I'll show them all the videos, all the reports, all the messages. You're all going to Doodletown. Don't forget my mom's on the disciplinary board, and believe me, they owe her big-time. She'll make sure they believe my side, not yours."

He hurled the stick with the X-Acto knife into a corner with a crash, tore himself away from the others, and charged through the kitchen and out of the house. The rest were left in the sickly incense clouds, shaken, as if they'd just been hit by a hurricane. No one said a thing. After a few moments, Tyler turned to the witch, trembling.

"How's she doing?" Burak asked gloomily.

"I don't know, man." She still hadn't moved. She just stood there, bending over as far as the chains would allow, her bleeding breast dripping onto the carpet. One of the blue amulets now dangled against her headscarf. Katherine curled her fingers in . . . pain? Despair? They were trembling, in any case. To what extent was she aware of the humiliation? Tyler honestly didn't know. The witch's humanity was a mystery that no one had unraveled yet, just like her decision to appear and disappear at will. That's what made her so freaky.

"Katherine?" Lawrence asked. He approached her cautiously with quivering lips. "Katherine, I'm so sorry. This should never have happened. It was Jaydon; he did it. *We* never wanted to . . ."

"Dude . . ." Tyler put his hand on his arm.

Lawrence shrugged and wiped his tears away. "I don't know what to do."

"What's with all the amulets, anyway?" Tyler asked Burak.

"They're the *nazar boncuğu*—they protect you from the evil eye. When my mother came downstairs this morning and *she* was here, she hung this freak show all around her, and now they've gone to the mosque to pray for her to leave. Fuck, I probably ought to be pray-ing for her to leave myself, because if they come home and she's still here, and they see her like this . . ."

"Have you got an old sheet or something? Just tell your mom and dad you couldn't stand how she stares at you so you covered her with a sheet."

"She's blind."

"You know what I mean. They'll never check underneath. But we've got to get that blood out of the carpet. Maybe we can . . . do you have a broom? Maybe we can push her upright, carefully. To make her stop leaking."

"Fuck, I'm not gonna touch her."

"And what about the website?" Lawrence said. "Jaydon has seri-ously flipped. He sounded like he meant it."

"We'll go on without him," Tyler said fiercely.

"I dunno . . ." Burak said.

"What? Are you just going to let him threaten you?"

Burak shook his head with doubt. "Yesterday I was chosen to do the whisper test, and today she suddenly appears in my house. That's gotta mean something, right?"

"It doesn't mean jack shit," Tyler said, but he sympathized with Burak's anxiety. "Listen, you don't have to do the test if you don't want to. I'll do it. In a controlled environment, with you guys around. Noth-ing can go wrong. It's not like you'll kill yourself straight off. You have to measure it out properly. There are lots of people who've heard her whisper and they're still around to tell the tale."

"I don't know, Tyler," Burak said again. "I don't think it was a coin-cidence. I think she's trying to tell us to stop. Your experiments, going public. She's doesn't want us to do it. I'm sorry, man."

"But . . ."

But before Tyler could figure out what to say—he was truly at a loss—it all toppled over the edge into the abyss. The bead curtain was shoved aside and Jaydon came in, his fingers clenched around Fletcher's collar. Jaydon had taken off, spotted the dog in the backyard, and changed his mind. Maybe he wanted to get even with Tyler; maybe he just saw an opportunity with the witch close at hand. Whatever his motives, he'd come up with the fatal idea to sic Fletcher on her. Tyler didn't know whether the dog normally detected her by her scent alone or by something more primitive, but the incense must have diverted him. Now that he'd caught sight of her, his growling swelled to a savage howling that filled the Şayers' small living room, and he pawed the air like a pit bull.

"Jaydon, don't!" Tyler screamed. He tried to jump in between Fletcher and the witch, but Jaydon provoked the border collie by yanking on his collar, and Fletcher was deaf to his master. His lips were drawn back from his teeth. He barked ferociously, mad with rage, and then Jaydon let go.

Fletcher slid across the floor. For a moment Tyler thought he had him, his fingers grasping his fur. But then the dog reached the carpet and his legs gained traction. With a terrific guttural snarl—louder than barking, wilder than growling—he threw himself at the witch. His powerful jaws closed around her right arm. The witch's body, dangling forward to the left, now jerked to the right, and for a moment Fletcher hung by her chained arm, shaking his head furiously, tearing skin and tendons. One second later, with a howling shriek, the dog flew across the room and slammed against the wall.

In that moment of absolute shock and bewilderment Tyler felt a hypersensitive jolt to his nerves from an electrical charge that seemed to come from *outside* his body. Every hair stood on end. Adrenaline flooded his veins. His terror seemed to actually sharpen his awareness to an extreme, and even before he turned around he knew that the witch had gone up in smoke . . . and that he'd been so close that it must have been *her* that he'd felt, the moment she disappeared.

The blue amulets swayed like mad pendulums.

Wailing, Tyler dropped down beside Fletcher. The dog lay on his side, whining and breathing too fast, groggily raking his foreleg across his snout, as if he had accidentally stuck it in a wasp nest. Tyler carefully took his head in his arms and stroked him. Fletcher licked his hands, and Tyler, who would normally have pushed him off, let him.

Jaydon hesitated in the doorway. "Is he . . . ?"

"*Fuck off!*" Tyler roared, lunging at him. Jaydon jumped and twisted his mouth until there was nothing left of his lips but white skin and wrinkles. He stood there irresolutely for a few seconds, then took to his heels.

-+-|-|-|-+-

LAWRENCE STAYED WITH Burak to help him clean up. When Tyler left the house, the early November cold hit him harder than before. It sank into his bones and blended with the inner chill that clung to him after witnessing Jaydon's cruelty. He let Fletcher drink from the stream that ran past the town square. The dog lapped greedily, plunging his muzzle into the water and drinking in thirsty gulps. By then Tyler was sick with worry. There were no visible injuries, no scorch marks or cuts on Fletcher's tongue or the roof of his mouth, but the dog was visibly shaken. He padded nervously behind Tyler, head low to the ground, tail between his legs. Every bird that took flight made him look around with wide, staring eyes, and when a car came around the corner, he jumped into a hedge, whining. Tyler's hushing didn't seem to help.

Back home, he took Fletcher upstairs and put him in the tub, where he gave him a lengthy soaping with dog shampoo and rinsed him off with warm water. Fletcher, who hated water with a passion and usually retaliated by soaking both bathroom and master, submitted to the treatment quietly. Tyler was relieved that Steve and Jocelyn had gone to work, sparing him the need to explain. He had no idea what he would have said.

There was only brief contact, he told himself. *Naturally, he's upset, but maybe it's not that bad. There's no need to expect the worst.*

But when Fletcher crept into his basket and Tyler offered him his favorite biscuit from the tin in the kitchen cabinet, the dog just sniffed it and looked up at Tyler with big, sad eyes.

All afternoon Tyler felt rattled, as if he were constantly on the brink of a migraine attack that never came. He checked the HEXApp almost compulsively. At two o'clock it reported that Katherine was standing in the shop window of Clough's Used Books, but there were no details. Apparently all traces of the incident had been erased . . . on her, at any rate. Because at about four, just before his parents came home and when over at O'Neill, his Spanish class had probably just ended, Fletcher started shaking all over.

"What's the matter, boy?" Tyler whispered, his nose buried in the dog's fur, sniffing the smell that had become so familiar to him over the years. "It's all over. Take it easy now."

But Fletcher whined softly and Tyler felt the lump in his stomach swell as if a storm was in the air, a storm that couldn't be averted.

Fletcher didn't eat that night, instead lying silently in Jocelyn's Limbo. Jocelyn and Matt watched *American Idol,* Steve was engrossed in a magazine, and Tyler aimlessly surfed on his laptop. Fletcher didn't sleep. He sniffed every now and then and stared bleakly into the distance. When the TV produced a loud noise, he began to growl softly.

"What is it with that dog?" Jocelyn asked. "He's wound up like a spring. It's getting on my nerves."

"Oh gosh, don't tell me Gramma's back," Matt joked. Tyler was afraid to look up from his laptop.

That night he lay wide awake, staring up at the ceiling. He couldn't shake the images of that killer look in Jaydon's eyes; the exposed, torn nipple; Fletcher catapulting through the room. It was the first time he had seen the witch stand up for herself and not just passively occupy space in a corner. And how bad was the situation now? What would be the consequence of the events *he* was partly responsible for?

There are forces at work here beyond your control.

That's a whole nother level of fucked-upness.

It took a long time before he fell asleep, totally exhausted. And when he finally did, he dreamt of owls, big owls with silky wings and golden eyes that hunted in the night.

-+-|-|-|-

THE NEXT MORNING, Friday, Fletcher came into the kitchen whining and wagging his tail. Tyler gaped at him as if he couldn't believe what he was seeing. Jocelyn had the day off, so he had thought she might be able to keep an eye on him. But when Fletcher actually took a few nibbles of his food, Tyler allowed himself a glimmer of hope . . . a hope that maybe things weren't so bad after all.

At two o'clock that afternoon Jocelyn went out for groceries. She had been about to lock the dog up in his kennel, she later related—when all of them, in a state of growing despair, were trying to reconstruct the day's events, while Tyler kept his mouth shut, numbed. But Fletcher did something he had never done before: He growled at Jocelyn. So she scolded him, and finally he let himself be taken to his kennel, head hanging guiltily between his front legs. Then Jocelyn went to town and thought no more about the dog, at least not until Tyler came home from school at four-thirty and noticed that the door to Fletcher's run was ajar and the kennel was empty.

Even though it was getting dark, Steve and Tyler went out to the woods behind their house armed with flashlights and Matt biked through the neighborhood and along Deep Hollow Road, whistling and calling.

"Fletcher may have a mind of his own, but he never goes far, and he knows the woods like his own backyard," Steve said confidently. "If he's there, we'll find him."

"And what if we don't?" Tyler asked. The gathering darkness hid the fear that showed on his pale face and trembling lips, and the new, overpowering sense of guilt that gripped his heart. Steve didn't answer, because it simply didn't seem like a realistic option. Of course they'd find Fletcher. But they didn't, and that's when Steve, too, began to worry. Later that evening they searched again, assisted by Pete Vander-Meer, but in the dark it was a wasted effort.

At half past nine, as Jocelyn whimpered yet again that she could have *sworn* she had shot the bolt and was pondering the dreadful possibility that Fletcher had ended up under a car, and when Tyler's condition mounted to what could best be described as early hysteria, HEX sent out a text alert for people to be on the lookout for a black-and-white border collie, owned by the Grant family of 188 Deep Hollow Road. Fletcher was officially declared missing.

THIRTEEN

THAT NIGHT FLETCHER didn't come home, even though they left the back door ajar and stayed up until four in the morning. At first light Pete and Mary VanderMeer came to the back door. Mary had made muffins—a kind gesture, although the children were still asleep and only Steve had an appetite. Jocelyn, still in her bathrobe, asked if they'd like a cup of coffee, but she was unable to pour without spilling. After becoming fully awake, she began weeping quietly and couldn't seem to stop.

"Don't worry, Jocelyn," Mary said, standing up to get a towel from the kitchen. "We'll find him. I'm sure he'll be wagging his tail when he walks in the door as if nothing happened. You know how dogs are. They always find their way home."

"But Fletcher never runs away!" Jocelyn cried.

Once is enough, Steve thought, but he said nothing. He had accepted the reality that Fletcher was more likely dead than lost. *It's cats that always come home. Cats are drifters, gangsters. If a dog runs away from home, it turns into one of those dramatic episodes that almost never has a happy ending. The faithful old pooch who wouldn't hurt a fly but chases a rabbit into the woods and ends up in a trap and dies. The beloved hound who never runs off but climbs out of his basket one day and gets run over on a busy road. It's gruesome, the way a dog meets his fate. It almost seems predestined.*

At ten past eight, Robert Grim came to the door. He looked remarkably alert for such an early hour. "We've studied the images from the camera on Deep Hollow Road, from the minute Jocelyn left for groceries until your son got home from school. We're sure your dog didn't escape from the street side, because we would have seen it. The cameras behind your property haven't registered anything, either. But they're focused on the trail, not your backyard."

"But that means he's almost sure to be in the woods, right?" Jocelyn asked hopefully.

"That would be my guess," Grim said. "But here's something reassuring: I've driven Route 293 twice, from the golf course all the way to the south side of Popolopen Lake, and there was nothing on the shoulder. The app's full of sympathy from people who are keeping an eye out, and if he's in town, we'll see it on camera. That dog is sure to be back soon."

That's not what you think, Steve said to himself.

He took Pete and Grim out to the backyard. "Here, take a look at this." He pulled out the bolt from Fletcher's kennel and stuck his fingers through the wire mesh. "Jocelyn says she's sure she shot the bolt. I believe her. You don't put your dog in his kennel without bolting it; that just doesn't make any sense. And look at this." He pushed the gate against the lock and let go. It bounced back and stayed ajar. He did it again, and again the gate sprang open. "You *have* to slide the bolt shut, otherwise it just won't close."

Pete looked at it and nodded. "So you think the kennel was opened from the outside."

"Absolutely."

"But by whom?"

Grim jerked his thumb over his shoulder. "You didn't make a lot of friends in town at the Council meeting Wednesday night. Don't get me wrong: your idealism was moving; your performance . . . a bit reckless."

"You don't think—" Steve began, but he cut his sentence short. A gust of wind blew past the eaves and he shivered for no good reason.

"I don't know," Grim said. "Say somebody wanted to take revenge and came up with a plan to poison your dog. They must have come and left through the woods rather than taking the trails, or the security cams would have caught them."

"That seems unlikely," Pete said.

"Yeah, but not impossible," Steve muttered. "Do you really think they'd pull it off?"

"Coming up with a scheme like that? Definitely," Grim said without a trace of doubt. "But the strategy is too complex. If you want to waste a dog, you slip into the yard and feed the mutt a bowl of poisoned Purina. Making off with a live dog would draw too much attention. Especially here."

Why don't you say what you're afraid of? Steve thought. *What we're all afraid of, but nobody dares to say out loud: that no matter how insane it sounds,* she *had something to do with it. It doesn't fit the pattern, but you're thinking it anyway, or you wouldn't be here. We're talking about a dog, for Christ's sake.*

Steve realized that Grim must have read his mind, because the security chief pulled his head down into the fur-edged hood of his coat. He said nothing for a moment, then seemed to reach a decision. "Maybe we ought to go for a little walk in the woods. It's still early and there aren't any hikers out yet. If he's fallen into one of the mineral ditches or gotten himself stuck in the barbed wire, he may very well be alive."

"Good," Pete said, as if he had been waiting for a command like this one. "I'll go put on my boots. The trails are bound to be soggy."

-+-|-|-|-

THEY CLIMBED AT a brisk pace along Philosopher's Creek, which left the nature reserve from the side of their property before dipping under Deep Hollow Road, where it fed into the sewer. As the streambed began to narrow they took the trail to the left and up the hill. They decided to start on the ridge and comb out from there to the south and west: the part of Mount Misery that belonged to Black Spring. Without having to mention it, they all knew, with a certainty that was both instinctive and unconscious, that Fletcher still had to be in Black Spring.

The trail was indeed soggy, and Steve, who was already sorry he was wearing sneakers, soon felt his socks become drenched. When he had gone inside to put them on the kids were up. Tyler was pale and withdrawn and said nothing. Jocelyn and Matt had their preliminaries that afternoon, but Jocelyn said she'd call them off if they hadn't had any news yet. She wanted to be there in case Fletcher came home.

They reached the two leveled rocky outcrops that formed the top of the mountain. Passing the highest one on the left, they climbed the stony hewn path to the southern vantage point. When they got there, Pete threw back his head and stretched his back.

"You okay?" Steve asked.

"Yeah, just catching my breath." He sat down on a rock and lit a cigarette.

There was history on the hilltop. For the Munsee, who had built their settlements on the lower slopes, it had been a holy site where they buried their dead. In the seventeenth century, Dutch trappers had built a lookout post on the main summit, but all traces of it were gone. From here, the terrain took a steep dip into the valley, where the tongue of the continental glacier had reached during the Ice Age, and where the Hudson had carved its path at a later time. Steve stared at the cultivated land, the river, the fields, and the buildings of Fort Montgomery and Highland Falls, the Bear Mountain Bridge, and, in the distance, Peekskill. The vast grayness and silence had something medieval about it, something malignant. It gave off an unmistakable charge that seemed to come from all sides but was concentrated behind the ridge to the south, where Black Spring was. It reeked of a past of cruelty and human disease, a past ruled by fear. Here terrified settlers had engaged in heinous atrocities; here they had hanged witches. Having fled to the New World, but with the scars of the Old World still etched in their skin, they had burned casks of pitch and herbs in the streets to drive away the tainted pestilential air while carrying their dead in sinister processions to be burned on pyres, all the while spreading the disease by excising their infected buboes. And here their descendants were driven one by one into the Hudson on a winter morning, never to be found.

In that context, and with that charge in the air, anything was possible. Someone might have taken Fletcher away and poisoned him or bashed his brains in with a rock. *Does it make any difference,* Steve thought, *that three hundred fifty years have passed and we now have what we like to call civilization?*

"Come on, buddy," Grim said, placing a sympathetic hand on his shoulder. "We won't find your dog this way."

Steve nodded and turned aside. He felt tears stinging his eyes, and for the first time he realized how deeply Fletcher's disappearance was affecting him. There was still the possibility that they would find him alive and well, although Steve had little faith in it. But damn it, he loved that dog.

They descended into the shelter of the woods. A bit lower down, where the terrain leveled off, Pete came to a halt. On the trail in front of him was a circle of ivory-greenish toadstools, so perfectly round it seemed unnatural.

"A fairy ring," said Pete. "My mother used to say that if you counted more than thirteen toadstools in a ring it meant that witches had danced there, and you had to walk past with your eyes closed to ward off doom. Later I stopped believing in witches, so I did it as a balancing exercise."

He winked, but almost imperceptibly. Steve squatted down and stuck out his hand, but Pete stopped him. "Watch out—they're poisonous. They're death caps."

Steve pulled his hand back and muttered, "It seems so . . . *intentional.*"

"Oh yes, that's why they call 'em fairy rings. Fungi grow like weeds, and rings like this can pop up overnight. It used to scare the crap out of people, but in fact it's a perfectly natural process. The fungus grows underground in all directions, and when the nutrients are exhausted the fruits grow upward. Nature is a mystery, but like so many mysteries, there's almost always a logical explanation."

Steve was slightly amused to see that all three of them were reluctant to be the first to go past the ring. Finally, Robert Grim took the initiative, followed by Pete. Neither of them shut his eyes. Steve wondered if they might have done so if they had been alone.

On impulse, and embarrassed by that stupid fit of superstition that had briefly undermined his determination, Steve kicked one of the death caps and broke the ring. The others hadn't seen him do it, and he hurried to catch up with them.

They didn't stay on the trail, but scoured the area across the wooded bedrock outcrops and unnamed streams. The slopes were covered with densely packed ferns and empty acorn caps, pried open by some animal. Every now and then they whistled or called, but after a while they stopped. If Fletcher was nearby, he wouldn't be able to miss their noisy rummaging through the undergrowth.

It was Steve who suddenly broached the subject. "When was the last time she caused trouble on her own?" he asked, trying to make his voice sound neutral. "Apart from '67, I mean."

"That we're sure of?" Pete asked. "Wow, that's going way, way back. Good heavens, I doubt anyone who was there to see it is still alive. In '32, when that nasty business happened with those workers they executed from the old tree farm, none of us had even been born yet. But Katherine didn't have anything to do with that. People have always stirred up trouble, and that's something that'll never change—it comes in waves. Of course, there's the story of the six Point officers who came back from Berlin in '45 and were said to have been found hanged from a tree near the witch's pool, right here in these woods, but that's a tall tale. Old William Rothfuss, who's senile and waiting to die in Roseburgh, used to claim that the official story—that they died at the front—was a cover-up, and that he was one of the men who had taken them down. But he'd only tell you that after a few shots of bourbon at the Quiet Man, and the story that the witch's pool is still there is total bull. I can show you the place where it used to be, where they dumped her body, but the whole area was reforested when the logging industry hit the Black Rock Forest in the nineteenth century. The pool is long gone."

"Never believe an alcoholic," Grim said, "except if he's paying."

"Of course, the number of suicides is unusually high in these parts. Always has been. That's mostly due to social isolation, depression, and ongoing pressure. You know, like in Japan, where people work so hard that at some point something just snaps inside them. This is the same thing. I think the fact that Katherine follows her same old pattern every day is the only reason the situation here is livable. It's been so long since things got out of hand. Back in '67, I had just turned twenty, and you, Robert . . . when were you born?"

"August 17, 1955, the night Hurricane Diane hit the Hudson Valley and flooded it," said Grim. "They say the river puked me out."

"I wouldn't be surprised, you old shipwreck. But see, even you were just a kid. She's so damn stable, Steve—that's been our salvation. The ones who sewed her eyes shut, God knows how, did us a huge favor."

Pete stood still for a moment with his hands on his hips and looked around. The vegetation had become denser; trees were blocking out the daylight, and scrambling over the stumps and moldering trunks was tiring.

Grim took over and said, "The last time she really departed from her pattern—or so we suspect—was in 1887, when Eliza Hoffman disappeared into the woods. No one knew what had led her to do it, but the public outrage that followed made The Point decide to establish HEX."

"What happened, exactly?" Steve asked, familiar only with the gist of the story.

"Eliza Hoffman was the daughter of a prominent New York family that had only recently moved to Black Spring," Pete said. "I heard this story from my gramps, who heard it from his father before him. He was the owner of one of the old bleacheries that had prospered in Black Spring back in the eighteenth and nineteenth centuries thanks to the clean spring water coming down from the hills. But by 1887, bleaching had become a dying trade: after they passed strict environmental laws and dry cleaners and Laundromats started to pop up in the cities, it pretty much forced the traditional bleacheries out of the region. Business wasn't exactly booming for old VanderMeer, is all I'm saying. Anyway, one day the Hoffmans lost sight of their little girl while they were out in the woods. She was never seen again. Poor kid wasn't even eight years old. They called in searchers with tracker dogs and they dredged Popolopen Lake, but no luck."

"So they put it down to kidnapping," Steve assumed.

"That's right. But the people in Black Spring knew better. For three days, the water in Philosopher's Creek turned a deep blood red and countless dead ermines floated to the surface, after collectively drowning themselves for no apparent reason. The water was undrinkable for days. My gramps had to shut down the bleachery for a week, which didn't do the business any good. But the weird thing was that the blood didn't come from the ermines, because they had all drowned. My gramps said that it seemed as if the earth itself was bleeding."

Steve wasn't sure whether he believed that. Not for the first time, he noticed that even if accepting *one* supernatural reality came relatively easy, it didn't mean that a second one would follow . . . because he simply lacked the willingness to believe. "It doesn't sound like Katherine," he finally said.

"That's the odd thing about it. No one knew why it had happened. Or where the little kid was."

"But . . . ermines?"

"We still have some of them in formaldehyde," Robert Grim said. "They saved a few when they burned the carcasses. You can come and look at them sometime if you like, although they're nothing special. Just old, dead animal."

"And nothing like it ever happened again?"

"Nope," Pete said. "And it would have been swept under the carpet if it weren't for the facts that Hoffman had previously been a prominent judge in New York and that the case had stirred quite a bit of interest. An article appeared in the *New York Times* with the suggestive title 'Is Mount Misery Haunted?' As far as I know, that's the only time any of the major media reported on what's going on here. They even tried to link the case to, and I quote, 'the folklore concerning the disappearances in Black Rock Forest of 1713 and 1665, which were said to have something to do with a witch.' When The Point got wind of that, they decided to act."

"And so HEX was born," Steve said.

"Exactly. And that was pretty easy by that time, since Black Spring had been self-governing since 1871. Before that it was part of the municipality of Highland Mills, and the town council met in Black Spring. It was a tough one for the mayor, having that double agenda. Every week councilmen would arrive from Highland Mills, Central Valley, and Harriman, unaware of the situation. But Katherine doesn't adapt to administrative shuffling. The curse is only on us. The Point granted autonomy to Black Spring and founded HEX under terms of confidentiality, to enable us to fend for ourselves. They supervise the ins and outs and channel money to us, but otherwise they don't want to get their fingers burned. And who can blame them? They're scared shitless."

Steve waded through a pile of fallen leaves. "That word will get out?"

"That something like this is even possible, and that they can't send in the army to deal with it."

"Oh, Jesus," Pete said. He had come to such a sudden stop that Steven almost bumped into him.

There was a bit more light here. To the right of the game trail they had been following, three slender, dead trees broke through the thinning November canopy. They may have been silver birches, but the trunks were so old and weathered that it was difficult to tell. They swayed in the wind, groaning gently, their bare branches as jagged as black, crystallized lightning against the steel gray sky. Pete looked up, and now Steve saw what he was looking at: Hanging at least fifty feet up, almost at the top, was Fletcher.

The border collie hung with his head and forelegs caught in a forked branch, the fur on his upper body bunched up because of his hanging weight. He was in no way mutilated, not even visibly disfigured, and the fact that he was unblemished imparted a sinister quality to the cadaver, as if it might open its eyes at any moment and start barking. But you didn't have to get up close and make a diagnosis to know that would never happen. Fletcher's eyes were half open and glassy, and his tongue drooped out of his mouth, pale and desiccated. Despite the late season, the ants had found him first.

"Is that Fletcher?" Grim asked, although he already knew the answer.

"Yeah, that's him all right," Steve sighed. How was he supposed to tell them about this at home? Fletcher was part of the family. They had all been crazy about the damn dog—not just Jocelyn and himself, but the boys, too. It all seemed so pointless. Pete patted him on the back, a simple gesture that, at such a moment of emotional dismay, was as moving to Steve as it was encouraging.

"This isn't the work of some animal torturer," Grim said. "No man would climb up so high in a tree and risk his own life to hang a dog."

No one said a word. They were only about five minutes from the trails, yet an imposing silence seemed to have descended on the forest.

"Is there the slightest possibility that your dog could have climbed up there himself and slipped?"

Steve grimaced. "No way. Dogs aren't climbers. And just look . . . look at the tree. There's something very wrong here. You see it, too, don't you?"

It was true, and they all knew it. Something was terribly wrong with what they were seeing, something about the atmosphere of this place. It was *dead*—that's what was wrong. As a doctor, he knew he should be approaching this in a scientific way, but he felt incapable. The sudden presence of the three skeleton trees in the middle of the windswept wilderness did not seem accidental, nor did the way they were grouped together, or the fact that Fletcher had chosen this particular place to die. There were small mountain ashes growing around, but they did nothing to dispel the sense of hidden darkness encompassing the dead trees, as if something from last night was still clinging to them. Even the air here was still, cold, and unchanging. All at once, Steve was certain that Fletcher had met a *bad* end, that there had been nothing good or peaceful about his death.

Maybe it would have been different if we had walked past that fairy ring with our eyes closed, he thought. *Maybe Fletcher wouldn't have died.*

It was a stupid thought, it was bullshit, it was the kind of superstitious madness that he didn't want to submit to . . . but it was also true.

Later I stopped believing in witches, so I did it as a balancing exercise.

"I don't like this at all, Robert," Pete said.

"Call me crazy," Grim said, "but doesn't it sorta look like the dog jumped down from the top of the tree by his own doing? That he somehow managed to hoist himself all the way up . . . and then hanged himself?"

A coldness descended on Steve, a chill of such elementary intensity that it pressed down on his chest and made it hard to breathe. In his mind's eye, he suddenly saw Fletcher with big, frightened eyes, clambering up the withered tree trunk, lured by a crooked, whispering female form. In a druidic symmetry, dangling from the two other dead trees by lengths of Manila rope were the bodies of both of his sons, Matt and Tyler. Their eyes were open and stared at him accusatorily with cloudy, ivory-colored corneas that made him think of the toadstools in the fairy ring, the ring he'd broken. . . .

With a jerk he turned away, his hands on his knees. He squeezed his eyes closed until he felt dizzy. When he opened them again he saw spots, but at least they obliterated the grotesque image from his mind.

"You okay?" Pete asked. Grim was already on the phone. Steve didn't like the expression on his face. There wasn't a trace of his usual lively cynicism.

"To be honest, not really," he said. "I want to get the fuck out of here."

"Let's go back down," Pete said. "Rey Darrel's Rush Painting has a ladder that must be tall enough to get him down. That poor critter deserves a decent burial."

-+-+-+-+-

BY THE TIME Steve came out of the woods for the second time, now with Fletcher's lifeless body wrapped up in a blanket (he didn't have the heart to put him in a garbage bag), his head had cleared and he could consider the situation more soberly. The charged atmosphere, the strange agelessness he had felt up there, now seemed like something from a dream. Instead, a much more worldly thought occurred to him: that there were moments that stuck with you your whole life, and they almost always had to do with life and death. This was such a moment: Steve stumbling through the gate of the backyard, the bundle in his arms, aching and sore from the deadweight, the other three members of his family coming out to meet him in tears. It was a moment that would have a deep impact on all of them for the rest of their lives, and it was never to be forgotten. Indeed, it was to be cherished . . . for the confrontation it presented meant acceptance, and that was a first step toward the day when the pain would stop and warm memories would begin.

They held a makeshift funeral near the flower bed where honeysuckle grew in the summer, behind the horse pen where their property bordered on Philosopher's Deep. Fletcher had always liked it there, Jocelyn said. The vet had dropped by earlier in the day. Grim had wanted to have an autopsy performed, but Steve had appealed to him to leave the dog with the family. Grim had given in. According to the vet it was an open-and-shut case, and the worn patches on his coat told the story: Fletcher's hanging weight had closed off his windpipe and the dog had choked to death. Nothing more to make of it. But Jocelyn told Steve afterward that when she led the man to the kitchen to wash his hands, she saw him make the sign of the horns . . . the gesture to ward off the evil eye.

Finally, the moment came when the family was alone, and they used that time to mourn. They lowered Fletcher, wrapped in his blanket, into the newly dug hole and folded the blanket over him. They reminisced. Matt and Jocelyn cried and held each other. Tyler stood beside them, his face shocked and preoccupied, and he didn't say much. He kept looking around, as if to reassure himself that he was still there. Steve was worried about him. Tyler's way of dealing with setbacks was to withdraw into himself, but he usually also showed a certain down-to-earthness that was not at all in evidence now.

They threw flowers into the grave, then damp earth. Steve was reminded of something he had said to the Delarosas about children playing funeral prior to the smallpox epidemic of 1654: *The children dug holes outside the walls of the settlement and carried fruit crates out to put in their graves, walking in procession. Their parents thought they were possessed, and the game was seen as a bad omen.*

He dismissed the thought. Jocelyn took the boys inside and Steve walked to the stable to get the shovel. Paladin and Nuala snorted restlessly when he came in—quietly and consolingly in a strangely nostalgic way, as horses do. He hugged them and went back out to fill in the grave.

-+-|-|-|-

IT'S A LITTLE after four when Robert Grim returns, bearing bad news like the prophet of doom from an ancient Greek tragedy. Except this bad news comes in the form of a video fragment. "The only fragment we've been able to find from all the Mount Misery security cams," Grim says, "but it tells it all. I thought you guys ought to see it."

They gather around the coffee table with the MacBook in front of them and Grim clicks PLAY. First it's hard to make out what we're seeing; we seem to be looking at a hazy photo negative. Then Steve realizes that these are infrared images. There's moisture on the lens, which blurs the image somewhat, yet in the dark anthracite tints he can still distinguish trees, and something that's clearly a trail. At the bottom of the image are the numbers: 2012/11/02, 8:57 p.m. *Yesterday,* Steve says to himself.

What the footage shows next is so frightening that his whole body turns ice cold. Everyone is startled, but Tyler most of all: He recoils, biting the palm of his hand, and tears fill his eyes. Two figures appear, pale white and luminous in night vision: the witch, striding like a phantom at a masked ball, with Fletcher at her side. The dog sniffs here and there, even wagging his tail a little. Steve realizes why this seemingly innocent image is so appalling: None of them has ever seen Katherine acting *determined* before. Until this image, showing the two walking together into the night, side by side, to meet Fletcher's death.

"This is extremely alarming, you understand," Grim says. "I've consulted with the Council and we're trying to keep this under wraps to avoid public unrest, but we're baffled. This is something completely new. Did anything happen to Fletcher that could have provoked this? If so, I need to know, guys."

Jocelyn and Steve slowly shake their heads. "He's usually scared stiff of her," Jocelyn says, deeply shocked. "Look at how he just walks along with her. . . ."

"It's all *your* fault!" Matt suddenly explodes. "You didn't give her anything!" As Steve looks at him in bewilderment, he adds, "At the Wicker Burning! You didn't want to offer anything to her, and now she's taken Fletcher!"

"That's completely unrelated," Steve says. "How can you even think something like that?"

"What do *you* know?" Matt is crying, and he pulls himself away from his mother. Steve sees Grim's distressed expression and he thinks, *This is only the beginning. We'll be hearing a lot more of this crap reasoning in the days to come. The impulse to point the finger, to assign a scapegoat. If this gets out, we're in deep shit. You know that, don't you?*

"Tyler? Did anything happen with Fletcher that you know of?"

Tyler shakes his head rapidly, lips trembling.

"You didn't run across *her* while you were taking him out?"

"No."

Steve gives him a probing look and says, "If anything bad happened, please tell us, okay? This is about our safety."

"He's right," Grim chimes in. "Don't worry. If you guys have been messing around like you did with that video you made, I won't tell the Council. Of course you never wanted this to happen. I just have to know about it. Something very serious is going on, do you understand that?"

There are tears in Tyler's eyes and his lips are trembling even more, and maybe, just maybe, they've pushed him so far that he's going to say something—but then there's a loud crash, and it will be a very long time before anyone thinks back to this moment again, the moment *before* the moment that would cause all the others to be forgotten. Steve has just enough time to turn his head toward where the noise came from—the sound of heavy wood violently slamming into the ground—and he sees, through the French dining room doors, through the window to the backyard, something that his brain cannot fully comprehend. He sees a horse stampeding toward him. He sees straining muscles. He sees foam on black flanks, he sees rolling eyes, he sees flailing hooves. Like exploding crystal, the window is pulverized, and through the curtain of glass shards Paladin comes leaping into the dining room. The horse skids across the dining room table, which crashes to the floor as its legs give way. Paladin's legs also collapse and the horse rolls over on his flank, mad with fear. His hooves trample splinters from the interior French doors.

The Grant family and Robert Grim dive for cover as if bombs are falling. No one screams; the violence with which the bolting horse has appeared seems to have sucked all the oxygen from the room. Then the animal rears up, graceful, surreal, decapitating the dining room lamp, and Jocelyn and Matt dart forward in a spontaneous effort to rein the stallion in. But Paladin isn't the only one who has broken out of the stables; at that very moment, and in a blind panic, Nuala gallops through the backyard gate, around the house, and heads in a westerly direction down Deep Hollow Road. It's sheer luck that there isn't any traffic—lucky for the traffic and lucky for Nuala. Several surveillance cameras record her movements: first the one near the parking lot at the trailhead where Philosopher's Creek ends, then the one on the corner of Patton Street. Inside the house, Jocelyn and Matt are finally able to calm down the confused stallion. The animal snorts and knocks over chairs, but Jocelyn's stern voice is getting through. Steve helps Robert Grim to his feet, and he is convinced that if his heart were to go any faster, his rib cage would burst apart.

All around them, people come out of their houses. The VanderMeers—Pete, Mary, and Lawrence—hurry over, and so do the Wilsons across the street, and many others. The HEX cams show how they're drawn to the Grant home like a magnet, then to the area behind it. In the control center, Warren Castillo and Claire Hammer look at the screen with open mouths. They watch as Steve, Tyler, and Grim emerge, too, to see what it was that spooked the horses so badly. Claire quickly switches over to a new camera and feels herself becoming sick.

The image shows a small group crowded together on the sandy bed of Philosopher's Creek.

Swirling in the dark oozing water are unmistakable trails of blood.

FOURTEEN

THAT SUNDAY THE silver bell over the door of Griselda's Butchery & Delicacies didn't stop ringing. Usually Griselda was closed on Sundays, but today she got it in her mind to do her community duty and open the lunchroom for the anxious townsfolk who had attended church services in droves and now needed to talk about what was going on.

It was a sunny autumn day, refreshingly cold and with a pale but intense light that was reflected in the puddles along the streets. Yet a gloominess had fallen over Black Spring that could be read in people's faces. They shied away from the hills that morning, haunted by the polluted smell of the woods and streams that hung so heavily in the air. To Griselda they looked like people on the run: making their way to Crystal Meth or St. Mary's, drawn by the sound of the carillon and compelled by the need to share their fear and faith with one another. Rules strictly prohibited both the Reverend and the Father from preaching about Katherine—there might be Outsiders in attendance— but they got around the rules by encouraging their parishioners not to give in to the "terror by night" and to "put their trust in the Lord God." At least that's what Mrs. Talbot, one of Griselda's early customers, said, because Griselda and God weren't really on the same wavelength and she had spent the entire morning in the kitchen making preparations for a busy lunchtime. According to Mrs. Talbot, someone in the church choir had risen up from the pew when Reverend Newman was pronouncing the benediction and shouted, "This is hogwash! Why don't you talk about what's really goin' on and what we oughta do about it?"

The voice had broken off and dissolved into a sob, and the people had exchanged anxious glances and kept their thoughts to themselves.

But at Griselda's, they were eager to speak their minds. The bloody creek and the death of the dog were the talk of the day, but even in that intense climate the townsfolk didn't forget what the poor butcher's wife had had to put up with recently, and they all came over to buy her meat. They bought it and they ate it. It was as if they were saying: *Give us your meat, Griselda, and let us eat; give us your meat and we will share your burden. . . .*

"Who the hell could have rattled Katherine so much?" Mrs. Strauss asked out loud while munching on her warm mutton sandwich.

Some of the guests muttered distractedly and whispered names. Old Mr. Pierson's frail but firm hand grabbed Griselda as she passed by. "It's that damn Internet," he said, his masticating jaws pulverizing the meatball on his fork. "I always told you: nothing good will come of it. What are we going to do when it's not a dog but one of us, next time?"

A number of old folks nodded in agreement, but there was sneering laughter as well. Griselda handed the old man a napkin (after unconsciously dabbing at the sweat on her forehead), as there was thick gravy dripping down his chin.

The Schaeffer woman, wife of the surgeon, was already waiting at the counter. "Oh, sweetheart," she said, "you have so much to put up with. Such a brave soul. Gimme a slice of that Holst pâté, and make it a nice thick one today." Usually Griselda loathed Mrs. Schaeffer, but she noticed that the woman was clutching her little bag with white knuckles and that her fingers were trembling as she handed over the money. The poor creature was scared to death.

Give us your meat, Griselda, and let us eat; give us your meat and we'll all get through this together, . . .

Griselda was also out of sorts, and all those folks in her lunchroom just made her more jittery. It had only been four days since that Arthur Roth mess and she hadn't yet recovered from the shock. And now there was this new rumpus.

They held a crisis meeting of the Council. The last time she had seen Colton Mathers, he had taken her in hand and whispered gently but urgently, "Calm down, Griselda. You've done well. It was a natural death. No one ever has to know." This time they were on the bank of Philosopher's Creek, the entire Council along with a number of the HEX staff looking silently at the stream, afraid to get even one step closer to the cursed water. Blood welled up from the bottom of the creek in several places and swirled around lazily like trails of red ink. There was too little to saturate the water, but rusty deposits were already forming on the banks. The phenomenon, unnatural and blasphemous, possessed a dark magnetism, and the sight of it made Griselda shiver.

What had happened that had caused Katherine to express her dissatisfaction so strongly? Like many of the townsfolk, Griselda was obsessed with the idea that she herself was at the root of it. The difference was that, in Griselda's case, it had to be true. Last night she lay awake, tossing and turning. The sheet had irritatingly crept up between her buttocks and she was surrounded by the penetrating smell of her own sweat. More and more she had convinced herself that she was failing somehow, that Katherine was personally singling her out and might appear in her bedroom at any moment with open, milky eyes, silently pointing her finger at her. . . .

Even now, while she cleaned the coffee machine in broad daylight, the thought made her feel queasy.

There was a disturbance in the street and the whispering in the lunchroom died down. Griselda peeked outside. In front of the cemetery, a small group of people were swarming around sheep farmer John Blanchard, who was making wide gestures with one hand and holding one of those small, flat computer thingies with the other—a tablet, they called it. Griselda slapped her dishtowel over her shoulder and stood in the doorway. The little bell jingled over her head.

Believe it or not, the sheep farmer was actually preaching. "Damnation! Damnation! Didn't I warn you all when lights appeared in the night sky earlier this month, and isn't it true that the witch has now killed the doctor's dog? I told you, but you wouldn't listen. Isn't it true that owls have been flying during the day, that she made the earth bleed, and that the doctor's horses have run wild?"

"Yeah," one of his listeners chimed in. "Isn't this all the fault of that Dr. Grant with that blarney he talks?"

"No," said John Blanchard, "for the wrath is not his alone to bear. My sheep have been restless since the birth of the Two-Headed Lamb. They refuse to eat. Didn't the Lord say to Jeremiah that the people would be punished because their ancestors had forsaken Him? And didn't He say that the punishment would have four faces: the plague, the sword, famine, and, uh . . . eh . . ." The sheep farmer touched the screen of his tablet. When it didn't respond, he tapped it several more times irritably. "Exile!"

Liza Belt, the tailor, came over to Griselda and said, "If they've gone and published the Old Testament as an e-book, too, I will personally eat my mother's big family Bible. Good grief, is that John Blanchard?"

"Yes," Griselda said, "and he has followers."

Blanchard's voice was vigorous and resonant, and the fact that he was preaching doom with the local, trusted Highland accent made it more uncanny than corny. "Confess your sins and glorify Him—that's the only way to ward off the Evil Eye, good people. Adulterers, reveal yourselves! Homosexuals, reveal yourselves! Pedophiles, foreigners, brother-killers, reveal yourselves and confess thy sins! Let us sing together . . ." He tapped the screen a few more times and lost his temper. "Does anybody know how this cocksuckin' thing works?"

"You have to get a real one, not some garbage from Best Buy," somebody from the crowd said.

"No, this came with a subscription to *Autoweek*," Blanchard said absently. "There, I got it." He turned the screen toward his followers. It showed a karaoke hymn on YouTube, and shrill organ music emerged from the little speaker. But because he was outside and far away from a Wi-Fi spot there was a delay between the image and the sound, so that the words kept flashing up too late, and the people who were singing along—and there were certainly quite a few—couldn't keep up with the melody.

If your Lord should heareth this, Griselda thought, *He'd wish he had never started in on His Creation.*

Not much later, Blanchard and his congregation were chased away by members of the HEX staff. Things remained restless all afternoon, and at five-thirty, when the last of the townsfolk had finally left and Griselda Holst had flipped the sign on the front door to CLOSED, she felt both drained and relieved.

+-|-|-|-

THAT EVENING, IN the comforting twilight of her little home at the back of the butcher shop, Griselda did something she hadn't done in twenty years: she medicated herself with drink. Not beer; Jim had always drunk beer, and Griselda thought it stank of barley and sweat and Jim's grasping hands. Griselda drank wine. And good wine, too. She had bought the bottle the year before at Market & Deli to save for guests, but no guests ever came, and now she remembered that she had hidden it under the meat cooler so Jaydon wouldn't polish it off. Griselda despised alcohol in principle, but if ever there was a good time to violate her regime, it was tonight. Because just before dinner, as she was stirring a big panful of hash, the thought occurred to her so naturally that it must have been there all afternoon, slumbering: *When are you going to butcher something for her . . . when are you going to bring her your blood offering?*

There was a certain logical balance to the idea that was impossible to deny. Griselda had given the witch pâté. She had given her a dead calf's head. The witch had taken a live dog. So apparently it hadn't been enough: Katherine wanted a live offering.

Another person probably would have wriggled out of their duty by

counting Arthur Roth as an offering, but, in an odd way, Griselda was
too pragmatic for that. Here, too, there was an undeniable balance:
Griselda had begged the witch to visit Roth and finish him off; and
though she'd wound up doing it by herself, wasn't there a certain poetic
justice in the fact that she'd done it with a broomstick? But it was no
offering; Griselda understood that. She had acted solely on her own
behalf. With every blow to that miserable, mutilated head, she had
further freed herself from Jim and gotten even with her past. The intense aching of the muscles in her arms, which prevented her from
raising them above shoulder level even today, was a liberation.

Griselda sat in her chair at the window and poured the wine into a
tumbler. The bitter taste made her wince, but after a while it settled in
her throat and didn't seem so bad. She was a robust woman, but she
was not accustomed to alcohol, and halfway through the second glass
she began to feel woozy and her thoughts started to run free.

Jim used to slaughter cattle, mainly for small farmers from the
Highlands who would bring him a calf and a couple of lambs each year.
In the back of his workshop he had an old shackle-and-hoist sling, a
manual grinder for making lamb sausage with hog casings, a cold
chamber for aging, a smoking cabinet, and a curing bath for ham.
After his death, Griselda had sold all of it—she ordered everything
from the wholesaler's these days. The workshop still smelled a lot like
blood, but that was the smell of metal and spilled oil from Jaydon's
bike. The Holst butcher shop was no longer a high-quality establish-
ment, but at least she had been able to keep the business running.

And although Griselda didn't have her husband's expertise in
slaughtering, she knew how it was done.

*What are you getting yourself into, Griselda? You really want to sac-
rifice a cow to her? You know how much damn legislation there used to be
from when Jim was always whining about it. First of all, you can't trans-
port cattle yourself. An inspector has to come to check everything before
you can even sharpen your knife. Then a tester comes. You think they're*

going to check the box for "sacrifice" on their stupid forms? If you do this illegally, you could lose your license, and if Katherine isn't satisfied, you'll lose a whole lot more. . . .

But did any of this really matter, or was she listening to the voice of cowardice? The same voice had told her not to leave Jim, and look how that had turned out. Besides, she wouldn't do it in the workshop anyway.

It would have to happen somewhere up in the woods.

Systematically, she began running through all the possibilities. She knew a couple of local farmers who might sell her a calf under the table, and some of them still did their own slaughtering, but Griselda regarded them as her competitors. She didn't want to go down that road. Then she remembered all the hoo-ha on TV last week about the Muslims in the city and their ritual slaughtering business. They had just had their Ramadan, or whatever you called those weird things they do where they slit the throats of goats and let the blood spray all over their mosque. Surely those people could slip her a goat, Griselda thought scornfully. But she'd rather give her own blood than meddle with *them*, and that was over a week ago, anyway. They were probably all out of goats.

You're forgetting the most important thing. What do you think people will say when they see you walking through town with a goat on a rope? "There's that Wacky Griselda. What's she up to now?" There's no denying that you've always taken advantage of their pity, but if they suspect that you're getting mixed up with the witch, they'll make you their scapegoat.

Thanks for nothing, she thought, filled with contempt. *I'd be doing them a favor!*

And what about all those damn cameras?

Griselda stood up and grabbed the back of her chair. The living room was spinning around her in a wide, nauseating motion. She stumbled to the kitchen and hung her head over the sink, breaking out in a sweat.

She had to abandon the idea. It was crazy, and far too dangerous.

There was a knock at the back door.

For a moment she froze at the counter, unable to think, overcome by a single thought that filled her mind with acidic terror: It was Katherine. Someone had opened her eyes, and she'd come to demand her sacrifice. Her eyelids would be frayed from the severed threads, and she would seize Griselda with her dead gaze, whispering because she had failed in her duty. . . .

She turned off the tap and staggered to the back door. With waxen fingers she pushed aside the old-fashioned lace curtain and peered out. In the dim light of the outside lamp she saw not Katherine but Jaydon, waiting impatiently with his hands in his pockets. Griselda tried to laugh, unlocked the door with trembling hands, and opened it.

"Sorry, I didn't have my key," Jaydon mumbled.

"You look terrible! What happened?" Griselda stared at Jaydon's face, hidden in the shadows. His right eye was swollen and had turned an ugly purple.

"Got into a fight," he said.

"Got into a fight? With who?"

"I don't want to talk about it."

It was as if time had come full circle. Jaydon's black eye. Arthur Roth. The violent collision Griselda had had with her son here in this kitchen. Jim's fists beating the nine-year-old boy black and blue. Jaydon had seen and experienced more than enough domestic violence; one look at his black eye and Griselda felt a rancid belch rising that filled her nose with the sour smell of alcohol.

"Honey, they beat you up, let me see . . ."

Jaydon waved her off before she could touch him. "Mom, it was my own fault, okay?" His voice broke. "I said something stupid."

"But that doesn't give them any right to lace into you like that, does it?"

Jaydon muttered something, flung the big blue Market & Deli shopping bag containing his gym clothes into a corner, and ran upstairs, where he slammed the door behind him. Griselda watched him leave, dismayed, and stood indecisively in the kitchen. After a few minutes, she threw the rest of her wine down the sink and poured herself a glass of milk. Halfway through the second glass she realized what kind of impression Jaydon had made on her: the impression that he was scared to death.

She stared at the Market & Deli shopping bag, and suddenly she knew what she had to do.

-+-|-|-|-

FORTY MINUTES LATER, hidden away in her raincoat and with the shopping bag stuffed under her arm, she crossed the lawn and headed for the driveway. A strong wind had blown up in the course of the evening. She drove with enthusiasm—to put it mildly—swinging way out at the first bend and jumping the curb at the next as she made her way to Deep Hollow Road. By the time Griselda's taillights flashed an hour and a half later as she turned her old Dodge back into her driveway, there was little left of her erratic driving style. Somewhere during that ride in the dark, Griselda had completely sobered up.

Clutching the shopping bag to her bosom, she went to the workshop. When she came out another half hour later—it was close to one o'clock by then—the shopping bag was sewn shut with needle and thread, except for the far side, where a thick bunch of peacock feathers protruded. These she stuffed under her coat.

Griselda would bring Katherine the most prestigious offering that lay in her power to procure . . . and that could stay hidden in a Market & Deli shopping bag.

Confidently, she had driven down Popolopen Drive to the petting zoo near the Presbyterian church in Monroe. It was a modest little park with some goats, some ducks, and a peacock. She parked the Dodge in a dark spot between two streetlights and crossed the street. Then she peered through the chain-link fence. No peacock in sight. A car approached and Griselda jumped behind a tree. Frantically, she wondered what to do next. She couldn't just show up with a stupid duck in her arms. Twenty minutes passed—she was losing precious time. Then she remembered what she had read back home when she had Googled "how to catch a peacock": that peacocks often slept in trees.

She looked up and saw tail feathers hanging from the shadow of the big oak near the pond.

Idiot! she said to herself. *If you're such a hero, don't just stand there dawdling!*

And so she glanced around to make sure she wasn't being observed, threw the shopping bag over the fence, and hoisted herself up. Griselda, who had her stature and overtaxed arms working against her, but the power of the simpleminded to her advantage, somehow succeeded and landed in the bird droppings with a thud. She scrambled up on her weak, trembling legs, brushed off her scratched hands, and got to work.

First, she knocked the peacock out of the tree with a large rock.

The bird ran off amid piercing shrieks. Griselda pressed herself against the tree trunk with her heart in her mouth, convinced that half of the town of Monroe was now wide awake. The racket the bird made was excruciating, not to mention highly unbecoming for such a prestigious robe of blue feathers. Griselda hoped Katherine wouldn't find it irritating.

Ten minutes later, she stole out of the shadows, the blanket from the shopping bag spread out and ready. The bird stood in front of the mesh wire eyeing her suspiciously. When Griselda got closer, it hurried away, dragging its tail feathers behind it like the train of a gown. Griselda chased the peacock into a corner of the zoo. If anyone happened to come along now, she'd be screwed: There was no way she could pass herself off as the owner, and if she were to be taken to the police, she'd have to explain the meaning of all this. But Griselda had such blind faith in Katherine that she didn't even look around. She tossed the blanket over the bird and threw her full weight on top of it.

Back in Black Spring, she hurried past the enclosure of the trailhead behind the former Hopewell residence, at the foot of Bog Meadow Hill.

She shivered at the prospect of having to enter the woods, where pitch-darkness reigned and where she would be alone with the wind and with *her*. But Griselda forced herself not to think about it and continued on her way. The peacock in the shopping bag was silent. Griselda was afraid she might have broken its wing in the assault; it had made a noise as if she had stepped on a box of eggs. The bird had moaned balefully, but halfway through the journey back home, it fell asleep. Every now and then Griselda assured herself that it was still alive by sticking her hand inside the bag to feel the movement of its delicate little body.

Making her way through the ink black night was madness, but finally she found Katherine just where the HEXApp said she'd be: in the woods behind the fields of Ackerman's Corner. By studying the map, she had had a vague idea of which trails Katherine would be standing near, but Griselda didn't want to risk taking the trails because they would be under extra surveillance now, even at night. So she worked her way through underbrush, so dense that she had to turn back in places. The offering in her arms grew heavier with every step. The smell of mud and mold and forest decay was almost unbearable. Griselda's plump body screamed with pain, and she panted with exhaustion. She was almost about to give up when Katherine suddenly appeared right in front of her, barely detectable in the opaque darkness.

Griselda's blood froze.

"You startled me, Katherine," she said, her mouth dry. "It's me, Griselda." The sound of her own voice in the darkness made her hair stand on end, and it cost tremendous force of will not to give in to the primitive urge to turn tail and run. The witch stood there, a motionless black silhouette, everything around her suffused with death.

Griselda glanced around. She was in the middle of a group of tall, old pine trees. She kept telling herself that the bewitching of the creeks wasn't any more ominous here than it was anywhere else, that she only had to walk down the hill to be back in familiar town environs, away from the heathen, malevolent power that seemed to linger here.

Katherine had come to this spot, driven by ancient instinct. The witch would be good to her, if Griselda was good to the witch.

She dropped to her knees, her left kneecap sinking into something slimy. She jumped back as if she had been electrified. Warily, she groped along the dark forest floor until she felt something moist, lukewarm, and elastic. It wasn't long before Griselda's butcher hands recognized what it was: a pig's heart. Suddenly she was angry, even insulted, which calmed her fear. Someone else had been here before her. That dirty coward! Whoever it was must have been trying to get on Katherine's good side. Carelessly, she tossed the filthy thing into the bushes and wiped her hands on her pants.

Now that the altar was free, she knelt before her goddess.

"Oh, look at you. I'm so sorry, Katherine. I may not be as good a speaker as Colton or John Blanchard or any of the others, but my heart is in the right place, just keep that in mind. I failed with my sacrifices, and I want to thank you on my bare knees for pointing that out to me. I should have known better. Please accept my peace offering; it's the most beautiful one I could think of." With timid pride she added, "It's a peacock."

Katherine stood motionless in the dark. Griselda rose and took the roll of hemp rope from her coat pocket. The peacock moved around nervously in its shopping bag and began to coo softly.

"I don't want to ask too much of you, but do you think you might make everything the way it was before? The creek, I mean, and all that . . . I know you didn't mean any harm, but you gave the townsfolk the heebie-jeebies—and me too, to be honest. I've brought you a live sacrifice, just like you wanted. I know you got no use for a nasty organ like that. Whoever brought that filthy thing here, anyway? If I find out, I'll show her, the bitch, don't you worry about that!"

Griselda started in on her task. She had left her butcher knives at home, because the last pieces of the puzzle had suddenly fallen into place on the way back from the petting zoo. What if Katherine wasn't entirely pleased with a pool of warm blood on her bare feet? Then her offering might be entirely misinterpreted. It would have to happen in a clean and dignified way, and it didn't take long for Griselda to figure out how.

She gnawed off two yards of rope and tied one end around both handles of the shopping bag. Then she took a pair of wax earplugs out of her pocket—she used to put them in every night because of Jim's snoring, and she still did it out of habit—when she realized something that made her stop dead in her tracks.

The witch wasn't whispering.

Only now did Griselda realize how utterly silent it was in the woods.

She listened carefully, turned her ear to Katherine, and counted to sixty. Silence.

Deeply moved, and overwhelmed by something that, in all simplicity, may have been closer to friendship than Griselda had ever known in her life, she kissed her own bare hands and reverently blew the kiss toward the witch. "Thank you, dear," she said with a quavering voice. "Thank you for welcoming me."

No longer afraid, and now ready to come closer, Griselda threaded the hemp through one of the links of the iron chains around Katherine's body, taking great care not to touch her, despite everything. She knotted the remaining end to a long, thick branch. Standing behind the witch, she wrapped the rope around the branch until it was tight; then she lifted it up like a fishing pole, causing the shopping bag to rise from the ground. As soon as it was hanging from the witch's body, the peacock began erupting with its icy shrieks. Griselda's eyes opened wide, bulging in the darkness. Up here in the woods, the bird's screeching didn't sound out of place at all, but terrible and melancholy, like the call of a dead man. Griselda moaned, but kept on going. With all her strength, she raised the shopping bag as high as it would go, then began to walk the tightened rope around Katherine, unwinding it from the branch as she went, until the rope was tightly wrapped around her, and Griselda knotted the far end to the handles of the shopping bag.

With great relief she paused to catch her breath. Too bad it was so dark; she would have liked to see the result of her hard work. But there was no doubt in her mind that Katherine would be satisfied. When it came time for her to disappear later tonight, the peacock in the shopping bag would burn and rise like a phoenix.

Once more, Griselda came closer.

This time, to rearrange its feathers.

FIFTEEN

JUST BEFORE SEVEN-THIRTY on Monday morning, Marty Keller called to tell him he'd better come up right away, and even before Robert Grim cut off the conversation, his thoughts wandered off to dwell on a tempting fantasy in which he bit off Colton Mathers's scrotum, spat it out, and beat his convulsing testicles to a pulp with a croquet mallet on his mother's old butcher block. It's wasn't a very soothing thought, but it gave him a joyless satisfaction nonetheless.

After the call, Grim and Warren Castillo slipped on their rain capes and hurried up the hill along Old Miners Road. It was a murky morning and the wind was rising. There wasn't a soul to be seen out on the street. Those who didn't have to go to work that morning bolted their doors and shut their curtains against the storm. Those who did called in sick in large numbers, reported Lucy Everett—the telephone lines were so red-hot she had only been able to monitor them via random checks. Grim knew that the real storm people feared wasn't raging outside, but within. He had felt the anxiety of the townsfolk, and it was finally getting to him as well.

Katherine, what are you up to, girl? Who got a rise out of you?

Warren, almost ten years younger than Grim, had trouble keeping up with him as they trod along the wet roadside. "How bad is this going to be, you think?" he asked, panting.

"Nothing we can't deal with," Grim said, but his voice sounded strangely hollow. After the crazy incident with Grant's horses on Saturday afternoon, Grim had thought he had the situation more or less under control. It had almost given him a heart attack when it happened, of course, but the animal hadn't been up to any mischief and was soon calmed down. It had bolted in a blind panic, broken out, was probably frightened by its own reflection, and had jumped right through it. Grim had had the Grants' horses moved to Saul Humfries's pasture on the other side of town . . . because the source of their supernatural terror was right behind their stable, where Philosopher's Creek ran along Steve Grant's property.

When Grim had seen what was going on at the creek, he had understood that the situation was not under control at all. In fact, the situation had never been so royally fucked up.

Mathers had said he wanted to keep it under wraps, and Grim had almost exploded.

"Listen," he said, "I got animals running wild, I got a dog who committed suicide, and Mount Misery is excreting its own goddamn placenta. You go ahead and scatter bread crumbs in the enchanted forest; I'm reporting this to The Point."

"You'll do no such thing, Robert," the old councilman said with the kind of dogged passion only seen in very small children and dangerous religious fanatics. But Grim also heard doubt in his voice, and a deep bedrock of weary old age.

"We have no choice. Katherine never bothers with house pets. For the first time in a hundred and twenty years she's changed her pattern, and no one knows why or where this is going to lead."

"Exactly. And that's why we have to find out what happened before we make any brash decisions. This is a town matter. Black Spring has always taken care of itself, and we will take care of ourselves now."

"But we *don't* know—that's just it!" Grim cried in dismay. "This is a unique and entirely precarious situation. The people are scared shitless. And who can blame them? We've got to put the authorities on standby in case the whole thing escalates."

"Mr. Mathers is right, Robert," said Adrian Chass, one of the other Council members. "What can they do for us over at West Point, besides watching from behind their bulletproof windows as things here spiral out of control?''

Griselda Holst nodded passionately and said, "Trust in the Lord."

"This is a fucking fiasco." Grim shook his head. "Sorry, I can't go along with this. I have an obligation."

Mathers's bony fingers slipped around Grim's wrist like a poisonous snake. "The decision of the Council is binding, Robert. If you refuse to comply, I will discharge you from your position."

Grim cursed Colton Mathers and the midwife who had delivered him. Not that he himself had such a high opinion of the folks at The Point: He had dutifully filed his reports year after year, but usually he regarded them as nothing more than a bureaucratic pain in the ass whose friendship had to be maintained in order to keep the money flowing. But now things were different. Grim wanted to send them a sample of the creek water and have it lab-analyzed ASAP. He wanted them . . . well, he wanted them to *know*. Maybe it would only add to the *appearance* of safety, but it felt like the right thing to do. That damn creek water had given Grim a serious case of the howling fantods, and every bit of reason that he could cling to was welcome indeed.

But Mathers was afraid, and fear overruled clearheaded reason. It made the councilman unpredictable, drove him into a corner. And like Steve Grant, Grim understood the potentially dangerous consequences: the primitive human urge to channel fear, transform it into rage . . . and find a scapegoat. It was a devotion bordering on fanaticism, and it was happening all over town. Who had mocked the witch? What had changed to make her want to punish us? Everyone looked close to home for some unusual recent event and made the obvious connection. The Wicker Burning. The coming of the Outsiders during the festival. The woman next door, who had painted her garden fence that ugly terra-cotta. Dr. Grant—because after all, it had been *his* dog.

Colton Mathers blamed the blood that had clung to the hands of the butcher's wife since last Wednesday at a little after five. Grim could only guess at what had happened, but whatever it was, it wasn't exactly kosher. The Holst woman had been found in deep shock at Roth's side—and now, Katherine's rumblings. For Mathers, it was a no-brainer.

It's too much of a motherfucking honor for you, you orc, Grim thought, *to have your private hotline with God* and *influence on the witch as well.*

In any case, Mathers had had Roth buried out in the woods, his corpse wrapped in a Hefty bag and sealed with duct tape, and the death was never reported to The Point. Now it was a matter of waiting for lightning to strike. Colton Mathers wanted to keep the intelligence services outside their door. The Council voted—five for, two against—and Grim had his back against the wall.

Since the blood first showed on Saturday, the seven-member HEX staff had been on high alert getting the situation under control. There were reports of the same phenomenon occurring in the Spy Rock Valley Creek, which emptied out more to the west, at the site of the historic waterwheel across from Town Hall. When the sun rose on Sunday morning, it provided a forlorn sight: For the first time since its restoration in 1984, the waterwheel wasn't turning. Fences were erected to block the entrance to the trails in the reserve, there and on Mount Misery. The creeks continued to bleed. Not enough to saturate the water, and they probably could have told hikers that there was rust in the springs, but Grim didn't want to take any chances. No one knew if the pollution was harmful, or how the situation would develop. It scared the shit out of the animals, and Grim readily trusted their instincts.

To make matters worse, Sunday was a gorgeous day, so a good many hikers had to be sent elsewhere. Grim had posted an army of volunteers in State Trooper uniforms at every barrier, who had told the hikers that the Military Academy was conducting a large-scale drill involving gunfire. And there *was* gunfire: it came from the HEX sound-effects library.

For the first twenty-four hours, he had three people following Katherine like a shadow. Initially she had appeared in a broom closet on Sutherland Drive (the discovery was purely accidental, after the house dachshund had started throwing itself against the closet door in a furious rage). Then she had ambled back and forth a bit on the steep, enclosed fields of Ackerman's Corner, and on Sunday night, she had stayed out in the woods. It was her old random pattern, nothing to indicate a behavioral change. The weather had turned frigid and her escorts were getting bored to extinction, so Grim had sent them home.

That, as it turned out, had been his biggest mistake since running out of espresso on Sunday and switching to Red Bull. Robert Grim felt as if he was having a caffeine convulsion and was just about to snap an artery.

He called Marty, who steered Grim and Warren through the rainy woods. The kid came running up to them in great agitation, with drenched sneakers and a face that had last night written all over it. "Just a little farther up," he panted. "Robert, this is fucked up. . . ."

Christ on a bike, Grim thought when he saw it. His jaw nearly dropped with a crash to the sodden forest ground.

The witch was standing among the ferns, dripping wet, her small form saturated and dark with rainwater. In a fraction of a second, she managed to evoke the illusion of standing at a poultry market with a peacock under her arm. *Am I really seeing this?* Grim thought incredulously—but then he noticed that someone had tied a blue, sewn-up shopping bag around her waist, from which an enormous fan of peacock feathers proudly protruded. Countless green and blue peacock eyes with dark pupils looked out at the three of them, as if Katherine herself had opened her eyes and was staring them down.

The thought hit Grim like a slap in the face. If Grim had seen the witch amid the *nazar boncuğu*—the blue, tear-shaped amulets warding off the evil eye—in the Şayer living room a few days ago, he would have been immediately struck by their eerie resemblance to what he was seeing now. But he hadn't, and Robert Grim had never in his life had such a strong premonition of intensifying power . . . *bad* power.

"The bird is still alive," Marty said.

"You gotta be kidding me," Warren said.

"For real. I just heard him chirkling. Or curkling. Or whatever it is that a peacock does."

"Give me a break," curkled Grim.

"And that's not all," Marty said. "There was an organ lying in the bushes—I think it's an animal heart, but I'm no anatomist. Then we have that twig doll over there"—he pointed to a sort of braided cross of willow branches dangling from a branch not far away—"which is, like, totally ripped off from *The Blair Witch Project*. I don't get it, because in the film it was this evil thing from the witch herself, and why would anyone want to give her something like that? And, um, discount coupons from the supermarket."

Grim and Warren stared at him.

"There's something written on the back. The rain has made it run, but I think it's Bible verses."

The peacock in the shopping bag let out a piteous cry.

"Motherfuckers!" Grim hissed. "Mary, call Claire. Have her send out an alert that the situation is under control, and that contact with the witch is still prohibited. Mention the Emergency Decree and what people can expect if they ignore it. Tell Claire to search all the relevant security images. I want to find the assholes who did this and hang their scalps on the wall."

He took his box cutter out of the pocket of his coat and stepped forward.

"What are you doing?" Warren asked.

"Cutting it off, of course! These jokers have no idea what they're letting themselves in for. She's already getting wound up, and if people start tying junk to her, God knows what she'll do next. What if somebody drops dead of a stroke, like those old folks did in '67? What the hell were they thinking?"

"Just be careful, okay?"

Grim noticed that the witch's dead, sunken lips, where murky drops of rainwater had gathered, were moving slightly, causing the wet stitches in the left corner of her mouth to tighten. He concentrated on the voice of Marty Keller, who now had Claire on the line, and on the sound of the rain in the woods. The witch was whispering, but Grim didn't listen, violently forcing Katrina & the Waves in his head to keep him from focusing on her words.

He cleared his throat and stepped forward. The peacock in the blue shopping bag rustled softly. A shudder passed through its plumage. Katherine's hands hung limply at her sides. Grim reached out with the box cutter . . .

. . . and the witch grabbed hold of the peacock feathers.

Grim jumped back, tottered, and was caught by Warren Castillo. He let out a stifled cry. It had been one compelling movement, deliberately made, as the poor bird's tail feathers stuck out just within reach of a swift twist of the wrist, and now her scrawny, cadaverous fingers closed around them like a wolf trap. As the three of them watched, the bird's life ebbed away. The brilliant green and blue flowed out of the peacock eyes and faded to a mournful gray. The thin feathers around them curled inward, crumbled into powder, and dissolved in the wind.

The bird didn't rise like a phoenix, it roasted like a chicken. Thin wisps of smoke rose from the shopping bag and gave off an appallingly vile smell—not of burning but of *charring,* like a dried piece of charcoal breaking up in your throat and filling your windpipe with hot ash. Grim imagined that opening an old tomb in Pompeii would smell like that.

"I'll . . . I'll call you right back," Marty stammered, and he cut Claire off. "Jesus, did you see that? I mean, did you *see* that?"

No one bothered to answer. Katherine stood facing them, motionless. Something in the way she held the undoubtedly dead bird gave them the impression that she was mocking them, as if with that one simple act she was reminding them who was boss here in Black Spring. Grim tried to appeal to reason, but he felt the world tilting crazily, straightening itself out, and skidding to the other side. He was in the grips of a strangling panic, and for the first time in his life, he wished with all his heart that he had never been born in Black Spring and that Katherine was someone else's curse.

-+-|-|-|-

KATHERINE HELD ON to her peacock.

Instead of disappearing and popping up somewhere else, as she usually did every seven hours or so, her pattern changed. From that moment on, she began wandering through town, the shopping bag tied around her waist and the bunch of dead peacock feathers in her hand.

"I think she's happy with her offering," Warren Castillo concluded at a certain point, but no one knew if that was true or not.

By Monday evening, while all of America's networks were covering the run-up to the next day's presidential elections, Philosopher's Creek had turned a murky red, as if a great white shark were swimming somewhere in the waters and had bitten a couple of hikers in half.

Katherine had made her way to Town Hall, with her peacock in tow.

SIXTEEN

AT THE LOW point of his stupor after Fletcher's death—at half past one on Monday night—Tyler lay in bed, naked but for his underpants, his body covered with goose bumps and his nipples dark, hard nodules. The normally gentle but well-formed lines of his ribs and muscles looked sunken and pale in the glow of his MacBook screen saver. He stared at the ceiling and listened to the ticking of the heating pipes, counting off the passing of seconds. The window guys wouldn't be coming to repair the back window until tomorrow, so the house was drafty and the radiators had been working overtime for the last few days.

Tyler was beyond exhausted, but sleep eluded him. He changed positions, shivered restlessly, and pulled the blankets up to his waist. He had no idea how he'd gotten through the past forty-eight hours with so little sleep, but one way or another, he had managed it. It made him despondent, overwrought, frustrated. He didn't want another night like that.

Just before midnight, Laurie had texted:

> Tyler, how RU? Miss you, let me hear from you, OK?
> Love, Laurie

Tyler had clicked the message away and turned off his phone. He didn't feel capable of answering her. It was as if Laurie were in another dimension, where the images that kept flashing through his mind in a sickening repetition—Katherine's nipple, Fletcher, the horses—didn't exist. He had surfed to a webcam site in search of easier consolation, but nothing could excite him much in this condition.

Finally, he had worked up something in his blog's content manager, but of course he didn't put it online:

Total wash-up. Think I'm brain-dead. Can't think clearly. Brain feels slammed, as if Paladin trashed my head instead of the living room. Wish I had some weed or something. Gotta keep cool or I'll explode. Got a bottle of tequila from downstairs and threw a party in my room—a one-man fiesta à la TylerFlow95, you bitches. Think I'm gonna puke. If I don't puke, I'll never drink another drop of alcohol.

No idea what the next step's supposed to be. How things turned out. Hubris, Icarus, all that crap? Yeah, it's my fault. *OYE* was my project. Proper preps, check. Articulating vision, check. Tolerance, check, anticipating, check. But there's no tolerance for Jaydon's madness, no anticipating. How he stuck that knife in her tit. FUCKED UP. I don't want to think about it, but I can't get it out of my mind. How he sliced her nipple like a piece of rotten fruit, or a piñata. Why did I ever let Norman Bates join?

He's DANGEROUS. Big fucking period. Stay out of his way. Don't let yourself be tempted the way you did yesterday. Real manly man, standing up for your rights. He didn't even give a fuck. As if he understood why he deserved a punch in the mouth. Freaky, no? You saw how he was looking at you. As if he had it coming and he knew it, like after-school detention.

Went to the creek today. Dad says we can't go anywhere near there because we don't know if it's dangerous or not—look at what happened to the horses. But horses sense things differently, and I don't think it has the same effect on us. Personally, I think it is dangerous, but in a whole nother way. It fucks with your brain. Those trails of blood in the water. Like party streamers. Hypnotizing you.

Anyway, shot some doc but don't feel like editing. Why should I? *OYE* is dead and buried. A grave in the backyard, just like Fletcher.

Oh, Fletcher. Dad, I'm sorry. Mom, I'm sorry. Matt, I'm sorry. Without me Fletcher would still be alive. Dad knows I know more. I can tell by the way he looks at me. He asked me once, but I didn't say anything. Is he waiting for me to confess it on my own? But I can't, wouldn't know how. And what Katherine did was just a reaction—Fletcher struck first. Can we blame Katherine for wanting to get back at us? We killed her children, we hanged her, we sewed her fucking eyes shut. Who wouldn't be pissed? And jeez, why am I saying "we"? Paranoia. Maybe I'm losing it. Things are falling apart. Reality check: HER EYES MUST NEVER BE OPENED. After 300 years of bottled-up powers she'll explode like a supernova.

I'm shitting my pants. Never been so scared in my whole life. Why did I call our project *Open Your Eyes*? It's weird how things make so much sense at first and seem so fucked up later on.

It was always meant as a call to Black Spring. Why does it sound like a call to the witch now?

A floorboard creaked on the landing.

Tyler listened, paralyzed like a salamander on a rock, feeling himself run hot and cold at the same time. The sound moved, followed by an unmistakable groaning of the stairway joints—the gently placed footsteps of someone who didn't want to make any noise. Tyler recognized Matt, as you come to do with the sounds of the people you live with. He wondered what Matt was doing downstairs; there was a bathroom up here on the second floor, too. Maybe to get something to eat. Tyler suddenly felt hungry himself; he hadn't been able to swallow a thing all day. Maybe a bite of something would get rid of the heartburn he'd gotten from the tequila . . . if he could manage to keep it down.

He listened for a little while. Silence. Tyler pressed his palms against his eyes until he saw stars blossom, but suddenly he sat bolt upright and opened his eyes wide. There were rapid footsteps on the stairs. Thumping, a quiet bump, a muffled curse: Matt had stumbled. Hurried steps on the way to their parents' bedroom. Tyler stared into the darkness and listened to the agitated, sleepy voices. He couldn't make out what they were saying.

The food's gone, he thought stupidly. *The witch has eaten it all. Tomorrow they'll take Matt and you to the woods and leave you there for the wild animals.*

When he heard Fletcher's name he threw off the blanket and sneaked down the hall on bare feet. Light was pouring from his parents' bedroom, and Matt glanced over his shoulder at Tyler.

"Go to sleep, it's one-thirty . . ." he heard Jocelyn moan from under her pillow. Steve growled something and Matt bounced nervously from one leg to the other.

"What's going on?" Tyler whispered.

Matt turned to his big brother. "I dreamt I heard Fletcher scratching at the back door. As if we had accidentally locked him out in the cold, you know? And then I went to look, and it wasn't until I got downstairs that I remembered he was dead. Except he was still scratching at the back door. I saw his shadow in the light of the outside lamp."

Tyler sighed. He saw the circles under Matt's eyes. In his oversized T-shirt, he looked like the little kid who was still hidden inside him, who had every right to show up now and then at age thirteen—when he was having a nightmare, for instance. "Dude, you're dreaming," he said. "Go to bed, bro."

"But the outside lamp *went on,* Tyler, and that means—"

Then they heard it: a muted barking in the distance that seemed to be coming from the woods behind the house. For a second Tyler thought he was only hearing it in his head, a phantom sound emerging from the depths of his exhausted mind like some sort of psychological reaction to what had happened over the last few days. Because yes, it had *sounded* like Fletcher, no denying that. But then he heard the barking again, clearer and closer this time, as if the dog making the noise were standing near the horse pen in the backyard, and now there was no doubt in his mind: that was Fletcher barking.

It was almost comical the way they all snapped into action: Tyler

stormed down the stairs, closely followed by Matt, then Steve and
Jocelyn, who stumbled out of bed. Downstairs, Tyler stepped through
the rectangle of icy moonlight falling through the back door and onto
the tiles. He saw that the outdoor lamp was off. The lamp had a time
and motion sensor, and if anything had moved earlier, it was gone now.
It was unusually dark downstairs because the chipboard covering the
window in the dining room was blocking any incoming light. They
hadn't yet bought a new dining room table, and the empty, boarded-up
darkness seemed gloomy, like an old boiler room in a factory.

Tyler unbolted the back door and turned the key. The cold outside
air chilled his naked skin when he opened the door. Matt wriggled past
him and stared outside.

"Boys, you'll catch your death," Jocelyn said, but Matt raised an
index finger and said, "Shhh!"

He cocked his head and listened.

Silence.

Then the barking came again, flatter and yet more *present* without
walls to dampen the sound. It came from the left, somewhere in the
massive blackness that was Mount Misery. Tyler's breath caught in his
throat and Matt turned around with a wild look in his eyes. "That's
Fletcher!"

"Don't be ridiculous, Matt," Steve said matter-of-factly. He joined
his sons in the doorway. The barking had moved, this time to the right.
It didn't sound happy, the way Fletcher had always barked when he
was running after branches. Nor did it sound angry . . . "hunted" was
the right word, and somehow sad. Still, that sound . . . Could you recognize a dog from his bark, the way you could distinguish people's
voices—and in the dark, if you were all worked up and scared? Because
of course it couldn't be Fletcher. They had buried the dog on Saturday
afternoon, and now he was at the far end of the backyard, wrapped up
in a woolen blanket, in a shallow pit behind the horse pen. The earth
was damp and the blanket would have started to grow moldy by now;

his gums may have already decomposed, and the white spots on his fur would no longer be white.

The barking in the distance reached a high, ghostly yowl, and Tyler felt chilled to the bone.

"Just listen—it *is* Fletcher . . ." Matt whispered, losing control of himself.

"Fletcher is *dead,* Matt," Tyler said. "And, anyway, he sounded really different. Did you ever hear Fletcher howl like that before?"

"No, but he's never been dead before, either."

There was no arguing with a fool's logic, and it made the corners of Tyler's mouth taste like scrap iron. Matt leaned outside and began to call the name of the dead dog, nervously trying to keep his voice down. It would have been impossible for Tyler to explain why this filled him with such horror, yet it did, and he had to turn away, shuddering. Even Steve seemed to sense it, because he grabbed Matt around the waist and pulled him inside.

"Knock it off!" he hissed. "What the hell would the neighbors think if they heard you? There's a dog on the loose out there, but it's not Fletcher. Fletcher is dead."

"And what if it's *her*?" Matt protested. "If she can cast a spell on the creek, she can . . . I dunno. *She's* the one who killed him!"

Steve was unnerved. Jocelyn wrapped her arms around her body—she was only wearing a nightgown—and said, "I don't think it sounded like Fletcher, to be honest . . ."

"Stay inside," Steve said, slipping into a pair of rubber clogs that had been lying under the radiator, next to Fletcher's basket. The basket was still there because nobody'd had the heart to store it in the shed. A human fragment of grief, but now it seemed more sinister, as if they had been unconsciously waiting for reasons that they themselves didn't quite understand . . . and may not have had any control over.

Steve went outside and Tyler slipped out after him. Jocelyn called to him, but Tyler pulled the door shut and ran after his dad. The damp cold hit him like a sledgehammer. It was less than forty degrees out and the patio tiles he was walking on barefoot were covered with wet leaves, which sent the cold up through his ankles and spread it to every inch of his body. Tyler began shivering uncontrollably. He clutched at his waist, trying to rub himself warm. It didn't help. Steve turned toward the noise and was about to say something, but changed his mind. Tyler thought he saw a glimpse of relief in his dad's eyes.

The barking had stopped. There was just the rustling of the wind and the babbling of the creek, out there in the dark . . . the creek, where the blood would no longer be red, but black. It was a full moon and their breath blew around in luminous white plumes.

Then the barking started up again, deeper in the woods this time, and Tyler suddenly knew with irrational certainty that it *was* Fletcher. It was impossible and it was true. On a cold fairy-tale night like this, such things could easily be true.

"I understand why Matt thought it was Fletcher," Steve said suddenly, his voice strangely flat. "It *does* sound like him. But all medium-sized dogs sound the same. There are dozens of dogs in town, and it could be any one of them."

In the dark, Tyler couldn't tell whether his dad's casual attitude was sincere or not, or whether he was just trying to convince himself.

It became quiet again.

They listened for a few minutes, but there was no more barking. Steve turned around and seemed to be making a decision. "If that dog's walking around loose, we'll have to catch it before more bad things happen," he said. "I'll send a text to Robert Grim. You coming back in with me?"

Tyler thought of the howling they had heard earlier. He leaned his head back and looked at the cold stars, clearing the haunting thoughts that fluttered through his mind. Then he scoured the backyard, distinguishing the shapes of the horse pen; the mound that was Fletcher's grave; the stable, now empty and dark. Something was moving there. On the edge of the roof crouched a snow-white cat: lean, on the hunt.

Steve touched his arm and said, "Come on, you're freezing."

When Tyler looked again, the cat had disappeared.

"What is it?" Steve asked.

"I thought I saw a white cat. On the roof of the stable."

"It must have been the moonlight."

Tyler paused for a moment, then turned around.

The pebbles on the path glistened in the light of the full moon as if they were showing them the way home.

-+-+-+-+-

NO DOGS WERE reported missing in town and no one else had heard the barking. When Tyler got home from school, Steve told him the creek had stopped bleeding that morning, and that by midday the water was as crystal clear as it always had been. HEX dutifully combed the woods, but was unable to discover anything unusual. They were frankly optimistic. The escaped dog must have come from Mountainville or Central Valley on the other side of the reserve, Steve guessed, and was undoubtedly back with its master. After the window people left, he and Jocelyn went to the Warehouse Furniture Showroom in Newburgh and picked out a new dining room table. While waiting for the delivery, they brought the old pine table down from the attic. The strong "fresh start" vibes of it all made Tyler feel iffy. By now the people in town would be relieved that everything was back to the way it used to be, which was good enough for them.

Tyler was not relieved. He was more ill at ease than ever, and an ever-increasing sense of desperation was hanging over him. Everything around him felt wrong, disrupted.

It had taken him a long time to fall asleep that night. He had sat in his bedroom window, blankets over his shoulders, the pale moonlight reflecting in his eyes, and had heard the voice of his younger brother: *No, but he's never been dead before, either.* These words came back to him at school during geography when he got a PM from Lawrence:

Did you hear that dog last night?? didnt know if i should tell
you this but i shat my pants, thought it was Fletcher!

"Tyler, is there something you need to tell me?" Steve asked suddenly as Tyler was getting ready to go upstairs that evening. It was just after eleven and the networks had called Ohio for Obama, earning him another four years in office.

"No. Why?" He gave his father an open, honest look, but inside he cursed himself. Was it so obvious?

"I don't know. You've been so quiet lately."

He shrugged. "A lot's been goin' on, huh?"

"I suppose so." Steve looked at him, searching for what was going on behind his eyes. Tyler practically felt like a billboard. "You going to be okay?"

"Sure."

Steve smiled and said, "Well, whenever you're ready, give me a holler." Tyler managed to produce something like a smile and ran up the stairs. At that moment he hated his dad for seeing through him so easily; it was a fiery, hostile stab, the strength of which surprised him and even hurt a little. It forced him to acknowledge that things changed, and not all for the good. Seldom for the good, when he got right down to it.

When the clock in the downstairs hall chimed one, he jumped into his jeans, put on two sweaters, and loaded up his stuff in his Adidas sports bag: Maglite, GoPro, iPhone, and the half-full, folded-up bag of dog kibble he had brought upstairs from the pantry earlier in the evening. Something else they hadn't thrown away yet, even though Fletcher would never be there to eat it. He listened for a minute on the landing, then decided he couldn't risk taking the creaking stairs. When he'd assured himself that everyone was asleep, he opened his bedroom window as quietly as he could, put his hands on the sill, and lowered himself down the unstable trellis until his sneakers found the mortared upper edge of the kitchen window more to the left. Cautiously he pushed the window ajar. The hinges and the casement stay gave out earsplitting squeaks and Tyler thought his whole plan was fucked. His parents would be wide awake. They'd find him hanging from the ivy trellis and send him straight back to bed.

But they didn't, so Tyler jumped down, sank to his knees, and rolled over the ground.

He stole noiselessly into the VanderMeers' backyard and called Lawrence on his phone. It took ten minutes before a sleepy head finally appeared at the window; Tyler had been calling without letup and had ended up maliciously pelting his window with pebbles. "Sorry, I fell asleep," Lawrence hissed. After another five minutes he finally climbed out and dropped from the sun porch roof to the patio.

"I told you to set your alarm, didn't I?"

"I slept right through it." He stuck his hands in his pockets and rubbed them against his thighs to warm them up. "Jesus, it's cold. So what's up?"

"We're going into the woods."

Lawrence hesitated, as if reconsidering his earlier promise, as if Tyler's idea had lost all its logic and sense now that it had been exposed to the starlight glittering among the turbulent clouds. "I don't know, man. I haven't heard shit tonight."

"I want to be sure."

Neither of them spoke as they took the Highland Trail on the other side of the creek, which ran steeply up the side of the ridge. Every now and then they saw the glowing LEDs from the security cams in the trees high above them, but the app said the witch was in town, not up here in the woods. Tyler was all too happy to risk being seen by HEX because the trail eased his mind a little, just as lighthouse beacons must have eased the minds of the old seamen on stormy nights long ago. The darkness was monumental. Every sound—a snapping twig, the rustling of the wind, the nervous call of a night bird—was magnified to spectacular proportions, as if the night itself were acting as a natural amplifier and the woods teeming with secret life. Here, at age seventeen, he was still the child he thought he had left behind long ago, and he understood the vulnerability of who they were and what they were doing—two children, alone and wandering through a vast, dark forest.

After a while he took a handful of dog kibble from his bag and began to scatter it bit by bit across the trail.

"Fuck, man." Lawrence watched him uncomfortably. "That looks way too much like the beginning of a fairy tale to me. One of the bad ones, where you get eaten by the big bad wolf in the end."

Tyler flashed a smile. "I think you're mixing them up." They talked like little boys around a campfire: muffled, hushed. Tyler dropped a piece of kibble and began to whistle softly.

"You really think that helps?" Lawrence asked. Tyler shrugged, and after a while Lawrence joined in. In unison, their whistling sounded like high-pitched, shrill bird calls, as frail and glassy as a dead symphony. It made the hair on the back of Tyler's neck stand on end. They both stopped at the same time and stood shoulder to shoulder. The ellipse cast by the Maglite jumped from tree trunk to tree trunk.

"I really feel like a moron, you know that?" Lawrence said, laughing foolishly. "That wasn't Fletcher last night. I said it sounded like him, but Fletcher's dead. We saw how Jaydon sicced him on the witch, right? So she got back at him. What the fuck are we doing here, Tyler?"

"Do you think Jaydon is afraid?" Tyler asked. "That she'll get to him, too, I mean?"

"No, I don't think so. At first he was—that's why he didn't hit back when you punched him in the face. But I don't think she's after him. Fletcher bit her with his bare teeth. Jaydon's knife was on a stick. They never touched skin to skin."

"I think he's much more dangerous if he knows that," Tyler said.

"Why?"

Tyler shrugged. It was a gut feeling; a premonition, if you will—he couldn't explain why he knew it was true. The look in Jaydon's eyes before he so violently drove the X-Acto knife into Katherine's nipple kept coming back to him, and Tyler had come to the conclusion that this went far beyond reckless bravado, juvenile delinquency, or even lunacy.

This was a whole nother level of fucked-upness.

They had walked for about fifteen minutes when Tyler came to a halt. They'd gone up quite a steep incline, and somewhere on the left there were large rocky outcrops that formed the top of the hill, behind which lay Aleck Meadow Reservoir and Lookout Point. The shaft of light from the Maglite shone brightly over the impenetrable jumble of tree trunks and fallen branches on the hillside, but it didn't reach farther than about ten yards and revealed nothing. He turned around and directed the Maglite down the path they'd come up over, where the scattered trail of dog kibble disappeared in a grisly tunnel of trees. Tyler was just calming himself with the thought that, as in every fairy tale, you only had to follow the trail and retrace your steps along the path to get home when something moved down there in the darkness.

Tyler abruptly stopped moving the dull circle of yellow light and listened to the sound. For a second he didn't even know if he could still hear it. Then: crunching undergrowth, rustling leaves, the stealthy movement of an animal of some kind. Lawrence cocked his head, his mouth pursed and tense.

Tyler's right hand reached reflexively into his sports bag and took out the GoPro. He turned it on and pressed REC. In the dark, the LCD screen lit up like a solid, green-and-black stain.

Once again they heard the sound, lower down on the trail. It came closer. Tyler felt his blood shoot up to his head. The palms of his hands got clammy and the Maglite almost slipped out of his fingers; his mouth, however, had gone completely dry.

"Fletcher?" he whispered.

"Oh, Jesus, shut up," Lawrence moaned.

"You hear it, don't you?"

"That's not Fletcher down there, it's a deer or a fox or a fucking raccoon; it could be anything. I want to get the hell out of here."

The sound shifted to the right of the trail, seemed to distance itself on the slope but came back again. It was a *fast* sound, hurried, and Tyler knew it was no deer or raccoon; what was moving out there was driven by a hunting instinct and was making its way through the crackling undergrowth on rapid paws. The night seemed to be breathing, swelling, and waiting to burst. Tyler's legs began to feel like rubber. Pattering there in front of them in the dark was unmistakably a dog.

"Oh, Jesus, it *is* him," Lawrence said with a husky voice. "Fletcher!"

Driven by an uncontrollable impulse, Tyler sprang forward to leave the trail and go into the woods, but Lawrence grabbed him by his sleeve and pulled him back. "Oh no, you don't! You stay right here!"

"Fletcher!" Tyler hissed again, and he whistled quietly. Lawrence joined him. For a moment Tyler imagined he could hear panting . . . and then he was convinced that he hadn't imagined it, that it was really there. Again it moved. There was no doubt that Fletcher was within earshot—if it *was* Fletcher, of course, but why act as if it wasn't? He couldn't be more than fifty feet uphill, although sound carried in strange ways at night. But why didn't he come? Tyler imagined Fletcher out there, sniffing in the dark, blind and deaf, his tongue lolling in his mouth, and unable to find his way home . . .

Thou shalt not be afraid for the terror by night; nor for the pestilence that walketh in darkness.

It was Colton Mathers's voice and it was in his head, but it didn't give him any measure of reassurance because it was immediately followed by another voice, popping up out of nowhere, as if Katherine herself were whispering in his head: *Nibble, nibble like a mouse, tomorrow everyone will die.*

Suddenly Tyler had a brain wave, as cold as a handful of black ice. The Maglite began to shake uncontrollably and he grabbed hold of Lawrence. "They say Katherine raised her son from the dead, right? Isn't that why they hanged her? Do you believe that? Do you believe she can raise the dead?"

"Fuck off." It sounded like a sob.

"What if she . . ."

"I don't know. But I don't think it's Fletcher out there, man. If it *is* Fletcher, why doesn't he come?"

"Fletcher!"

"Stop it!"

The air filled with a wild flapping, and in a flash a snow-white owl flew through the ray of the Maglite. The boys screamed and jumped into each other's arms. The bird shrieked, and with powerful wing-beats disappeared in the direction of the dilapidated wooden cabin on Lookout Point, where they'd spent many a summer night as children and where you could have the best picnics in the world, but which would surely be made of cake if you let this owl guide you, with ginger-bread roof tiles and white sugar window frames. And all at once Tyler knew for certain that he didn't want to see what was slinking around them in the dark, even if it really was Fletcher, because if Fletcher was dead, then this was a horror that would instantly strip you of your sanity.

The next thing he knew they were running, and Tyler heard it coming after them, reducing the distance between them with laugh-able ease. The Maglite cleaved the path in front of them in a freak light show. Sometimes Lawrence was up front and sometimes Tyler, and they would scream at each other, "Not so fast, wait for me!" but neither of them slowed down. At some point Tyler thought he heard the jin-gling of metal, and it made him think of the buckle of Fletcher's collar.

Of course the trail of kibble ended not much farther down the hill. You know how it goes with such trails that are meant to lead little boys out of the woods. Yet, oddly enough, that soothed Tyler's panic, and deep in his heart he felt a strong sense of belonging because he knew exactly where they were: out in the middle of nowhere being chased by a nightmare straight out of a fairy tale, and at the end of the trail was Black Spring. At the end of the trail was always Black Spring, the end-of-the-line from the cold outside world, where no one knew their names or their way of life.

After that his memory began to fade; his consciousness must have shut down in an instinctive attempt at self-preservation. Apparently they had reached the end of the trail, because the first thing he became aware of was stubbing his toe against something and flying headfirst into Philosopher's Creek. Ice-cold water swirled past his face, stiffened his cheeks, and soaked into his clothes right down to his naked skin. His mouth opened wide to let out a scream and was filled with liquid sand. That brought him back to reality, and half a beat later Tyler was up on his knees, gagging and slapping the water out of his face. Later he would realize that he had been tottering on the edge of madness at that point; the idea that he had ingested water and sediment from *that* creek was more than any sane person could bear. He clearly heard a click in his head, like the opening of enormous iron floodgates . . . and then Lawrence dragged him up and Tyler splashed onto the bank.

They stumbled over the enclosure, staggered down the path to the backyard, and dropped onto the lawn in front of the horses' stable, utterly exhausted.

And because it was the only conceivable reaction to madness, they burst out laughing.

"This is the part where we're supposed to find a whole potful of gems and gold, and everybody lives happily ever after," Tyler said, which made them laugh even harder.

"Here's your cam," Lawrence said when he was all laughed out. He handed the GoPro to Tyler; it must have fallen out of his hand when he tripped and ended up in the creek, but the waterproof casing had saved it. The Maglite, sadly, had drowned.

Tyler scrambled to his feet, his clothes heavy and cold and dripping with creek water, his wet hair sticking to his forehead in strands. His teeth started chattering and there was nothing he could do to stop them. "What the f-f-fuck was that?" he stammered inarticulately.

Lawrence shook his head. "I didn't see anything."

They gazed at each other and uttered a hollow laugh, but quickly stopped. Indecisive and shivering uncontrollably all over, Tyler just stood there on the lawn. To his amazement, he saw that the red light on the GoPro was still on. The tough little sucker had filmed the entire thing.

Astonished, he turned it off.

-+-|-|-|-+-

TYLER CAN'T BRING himself to look at the footage until two days later.

He inserts the GoPro memory card into his MacBook and stares at the screen with glassy, dazed eyes. Things have changed: His muddy clothes, reeking of creek water, now smell of laundry detergent and are nicely folded in his closet. Katherine has changed, too. She hasn't been doing her disappearing trick for a few days now because she's apparently walking around with a large shopping bag containing a dead peacock (this has not quite escaped Tyler's attention, despite the state he's in) and appears to be rather attached to it. At the moment she's a little farther up in the woods behind his house, but Tyler hasn't gone to take a peek. He's had enough of the witch, enough of shooting doc. Besides, the woods are still closed off to hikers; there are fences everywhere and there are volunteers from HEX dressed as State Reserve park rangers at the trailhead.

The clip lasts twelve minutes and forty-four seconds, and because of its sheer size, Tyler puts the file on his external hard drive.

Then he looks at the images and sees something terrifying.

He hits PAUSE and stares at it, lost in thought.

Suddenly there's frantic pounding on the back door downstairs. Slowly, as if coming out of a trance, he looks up. He remembers that he's home alone. In a reflex that comes from being a video blogger he snatches the memory card from the USB drive, sticks it in the GoPro, and puts the cam in his pocket. He rushes down the stairs, to what will be the last and most shocking report from his career as a journalist.

It's Lawrence who's pounding on the door. As soon as Tyler opens it, Lawrence drags him out by the arm. "Come with me, *now*," he says. "We've got to stop them."

"What . . ." Tyler begins, then thinks, *Jaydon*. He doesn't know how he knows, but he knows. They run to the backyard gate and down the path to the creek, and it's like a video being played backward: They're right where Tyler fell into the creek a few nights before. It takes three seconds to take stock of the situation and to grasp how serious it is, how completely and indisputably fucked up it is. Instinctively, he takes the GoPro out of his pocket and starts shooting.

The images are shaky, but images don't lie. A hundred yards to the left near Deep Hollow Road are the fences, abandoned by the volunteers. The camera sweeps to the other side and we see who the volunteers are: Jaydon, Justin, and Burak, in heavy boots and State Reserve uniforms. *Those sons of bitches have offered their services and Grim has fallen for it,* Tyler thinks. Staggering in their midst is Katherine, unnaturally bent as if her spinal column had been broken, and they're driving her forward the way you drive cattle, using broomsticks with the heads torn off. Judging from how the witch is moving, she's in a panic. Her sewn-up mouth is a crooked grimace of horror and she's desperately clutching the charred peacock feathers that are sticking out of her—*This is unreal,* Tyler thinks—Market & Deli shopping bag. She keeps trying to turn away and walk off, but they roughly push her back. Jaydon beats her with his broomstick and her body doubles over, forcing her to walk the other way. Why she's so attached to that stupid peacock is a mystery to Tyler, but she is; desperately, she puts up with the abuse rather than vanish and have to leave her shopping bag behind.

Then the images blur; we see pink spots from Tyler's fingers since he's holding the GoPro out of sight, we hear running footsteps, we see the jolting forest floor. We also see splintered fragments of a security cam that's been knocked out of a tree: no room for subtlety this time.

"Oh Jesus stop!" Tyler shouts in one breath. "Leave her alone!"

"Mind your own fucking business. Stay and watch or get the fuck out of here."

"Don't make it any worse than it is. You can still stop this thing!"

"She killed your dog. You should be grateful. Everybody just stands by and watches, but at least we're doing something. Walk, whore!" A new blow and the witch sways on her feet, trying to keep her balance.

Stumbling. Khaki fatigues, suddenly very close. Sky spinning. Sewn-shut eyes and rapid, desperate steps in jangling chains. Hands grasping shoulders. A broom handle sweeping through the air like a whip; Jaydon means serious business. Tyler shrinks back and we see grass, we see the streambed, we see desperate faces overhead. Again Lawrence and Tyler jump forward and there's fighting, there's cursing. Then Lawrence is struck by a sickening blow from a stick and he hits his forehead against one of the boulders in the creek. Panting, Tyler turns him over and we see a deep cut in pale skin and dark hair smeared with blood.

"Lawrence, you all right?"

"No. Stop them."

Burak looks down at them, hesitating, stick in his hand. "Bastard!" Tyler roars as he helps Lawrence up, and Burak runs back to the others.

Just when Tyler sees what they're up to, the images reveal it as well, and we hear the smothered cry from Tyler's throat, more animal than human. They've driven the witch to the lower reaches of the creek. Farther on we see the hole of the tank that once collected the creek water from the culvert running under Deep Hollow Road but is no longer in use. The hole is a little less than a square yard, and the metal plate that normally covers it, overrun with mold, is now lying on the nearby bank.

For the last time Tyler sprints up to them, screaming for them not to do it, to stop while they still can, but it's too late. The wildly shaking images show Jaydon giving the witch a vicious push with his stick and her falling helplessly into the tank. It's not deep; she knocks her head against the concrete edge and her attackers roar, her attackers gather rocks, her attackers stone the witch. Tyler sees it all; he sees how two sharp rocks hit her face at the same time and split it open, he sees how her headscarf is torn off and he sees blood and he sees more rocks. He vomits on the ground as Katherine finally gives in. The smell of burning shopping-bag plastic rises as she disappears. And still rocks are bouncing and tumbling, now against the concrete sides of the empty tank.

"He's got a fucking camera!" someone bellows. A new rock whizzes in Tyler's direction and he ducks just in time to avoid it. In a flash we see Jaydon's face coming toward us, a mask of pure psychopathic rage, the kind of face that screams at you to run if you want to live and tell the tale, and that's just what Tyler and Lawrence do. Their salvation is that they're so close to home; if this drama had taken place farther into the woods, they easily would have been caught. But here there are more cameras, here there are people who might be home, and the chase is called off. Yet Tyler, unaware of this, slams the back door so hard behind him that the pane rattles in its frame, and he turns both latches before he and Lawrence fall to their knees on the kitchen floor and burst into tears.

But now they're not crying like the little boys they still were until two nights ago; this is the crying of boys who have just become adults because of events that are too big for them to bear on their own. And while they're crying, the image goes black.

SEVENTEEN

LATER THE SAME afternoon Steve suggested they go get the horses and settle them back in their own stable, but Jocelyn's face clouded over at the idea.

"I don't know, Steve. I don't have a good feeling about it, so close to the creek and the woods and all. . . . How can we know if it's safe?" She looked outdoors through the new window. The air in the dining room was still heavy with the smell of fresh paint from the retouched window frame, but the fragrance of Jocelyn's vegetarian quiche in the oven was slowly taking over.

Steve shrugged. "*We* stayed here, didn't we? Nothing happened to us."

"Yes, but it's different with people," Matt said, as simple as that. He laid down his pen on top of his homework. "I don't want Nuala to end up hanging from a tree, too, Dad."

"The creek's been back to normal for two days now," Steve said. "And there's no indication that things are any different than they were before, or that the horses are in any kind of danger."

"Unless a certain person forgets to shut the stable door," Matt remarked. He seemed shocked by his own comment, but it was too late: Jocelyn's expression changed into a mask of offended distress.

Steve was taken aback. "What kind of goddamn presumptuousness is that!" he exclaimed.

"Well, it's true, isn't it? Gramma can't use her hands, and Fletcher didn't unbolt his kennel by himself, you know!"

"We don't know how Fletcher got out. But if your mom says she bolted the kennel, you have no right to doubt her. I want you to apologize."

"I'm not going to apologize for something that—"

"Apologize!"

Matt slammed his book on the floor and jumped up from the table. "I'm sorry, all right? Sorry you guys can't take it if somebody speaks the truth for once!"

"Matt!"

But he had already run upstairs and slammed his bedroom door. Steve was aghast. He looked at Jocelyn in the pale four o'clock light, but she lowered her eyes. "Well done," she sighed.

"You should have said something yourself, then," Steve snapped, nastier than he had intended. He understood that Matt's irrational outburst was just his way of dealing with his grief, but it made Steve angry nonetheless. He didn't know how to deal with Matt's mood swings, especially when he got downright mean. Jocelyn was better at it. One of the things that had always held their marriage together in the Black Spring whirlwind was the natural division of roles they had settled into within the family, from which they rarely deviated. It created context and order in an environment where turmoil was all too common. And when it came to matters of the heart, reason was a virtue. One of the aspects of that role division was that Jocelyn took care of Matt while Steve was responsible for Tyler. It wasn't entirely black-and-white, of course, but that's what both of them—all four of them—knew to be true.

"I don't mean just Matt," Jocelyn said. "It's affecting both of them. Tyler hasn't come out of his room for days. This is going to leave scars, Steve." She gestured angrily at the waning daylight. "There's something out there that killed our dog, and there's nothing we can do about it."

"To be honest, Matt's reaction seems like a perfectly natural expression of grief to me. Crude and unreasonable, but normal. His grief is seeking an outlet, and he's not fighting it. He wants to blame people. He'll come back and apologize, I'm sure."

"That's not the point. You're trivializing the situation. Fletcher gets buried. Fine. We buy a new table, we get everything nicely painted, we make like none of it ever happened. But it did, and you see the traces right there in front of you."

She pointed at the dark tiles that had the dents of Paladin's hooves hammered into them. Steve stared at her and sighed calmly in an effort to salvage the situation. "What surprises *me* is that Matt got so worked up about the fact that we didn't offer anything up at the festival. Remember how he went on about it on Saturday? We didn't offer anything, so it's our fault that Fletcher is dead. I hoped we had given Tyler and Matt a bit more reason than that. He almost sounded like the people from town."

"What do you expect?" Jocelyn exclaimed. "What the hell does he know? Maybe that *did* cause it, maybe it *is* our fault. Are you trying to say that isn't a natural reaction?"

"Jocelyn," he said, "you're talking nonsense."

"Not at all. I'm not saying that's how it happened; I'm just saying that we don't know how Fletcher ended up in that tree. And we'll never know. *That's* why Matt is scared, Steve. And Tyler . . . have you even sat down and talked to Tyler in the past few days? Aren't you worried about how he's *distancing* himself from everything?"

"I did ask him about it."

"That's not the same as talking."

"Sweetheart, he prefers to solve his problems himself, now. That, too, is perfectly normal for his age."

"Nothing's normal here. This town is bewitched, Steve. And it's not just Katherine. It's everything, it's the sounds we hear at night and it's that creek behind our house that was full of blood for three days— *blood,* do you realize that? And it's the people. Do you really believe this won't have a lasting influence on the children? Or on us?"

He looked at her, nonplussed. "Jocelyn, I'm not pretending it never happened. I'm just trying to preserve the peace. That's the only reasonable way to deal with this. Just like we've always done."

She was standing directly across from him now, and she was hopping mad. "But everything's changed now, don't you get that? We've lived here in relative peace for eighteen years and we could stand it because we weren't in any immediate danger. But now Fletcher's dead, so don't you say we're not in danger, Steve! Don't you dare say that!"

"It seems like everything's back to normal, and—"

"Nothing's back to normal, and I don't want you to pretend it is! It's your fault that we . . ."

She didn't finish her sentence, but she didn't have to. *So there we have it,* he thought. The sly dig, the final argument to chasten Steve when all others had failed, because no matter how much time had passed, this was still what could strike him at the core. He knew what Jocelyn had wanted to say: *It's your fault that we live here, so* you *do something about it.* Steve felt shaken, as if he had bumped into an invisible pane of glass. Was this still the issue? How was it possible to live together in perfect harmony for years and years, only for something like this to come barreling out of the blue and put them in a zone of full-fledged alienation? Boulders or no boulders, it was for Steve's career that they had moved to Black Spring, while Jocelyn had given up her own. The old wound had lain buried for more than fifteen years— *In a hole in the backyard, just like Fletcher,* he thought absentmindedly. But sometimes what lay buried came back . . . because buried wasn't always *buried.*

She read the indignation in his face and touched his arm, but he pulled away and grabbed her wrist. "Just remember," he said, "that *I* was the one who argued against having a second baby. If you aren't pleased with the way they've grown up, think about the fact that you could have avoided half of it."

Of course that wasn't fair; of course he shouldn't have said it. Jocelyn's lips quivered, then she tore away from him and went to the kitchen without saying a word. Steve was left behind in the dining room, which felt more abandoned than ever.

Christ, how could I have thought that everything was all right? he said to himself. *Katherine, what on earth have you done to our family?*

From the kitchen came a stifled cry, then the rattling of the baking sheet in the oven. Soon the smell of burned pastry filled the room. Steve closed his eyes as Jocelyn noisily shook the failed quiche into the trash can and let the pie plate clatter into the sink. Her face stained with tears, she pushed by him and went upstairs. Steve entered the kitchen and looked into the trash can. There was little left of the edges, but the center of the quiche still looked pretty good. He slid it cautiously onto a plate, cut the burned pieces away, covered it with aluminum foil, and left it on the counter. Then he went outside. He caught himself about to take Fletcher's leash from the hook out of habit, then remembered he had stored it in the shed along with his basket yesterday.

He walked briskly, hands in his pockets, straight into a howling wind that numbed his cheekbones. He crossed the golf course and continued a few miles past the tall fence enclosing West Point, away from Black Spring. Fuck, maybe Jocelyn was right—maybe he had been too quick to shrug it all off. He sincerely tried to recall what had gotten into them two nights before when they thought they'd heard Fletcher barking—even if only for a minute or two. Bullshit, of course; he refused to believe it. It seemed far away now, blurry, like the chill that had overtaken him in the woods when he found Fletcher dead, or when he'd damaged the fairy ring. These were irrational moments that weren't at all like him. It felt foolish, embarrassing. *Buried is buried,* he thought. *And that's the end of it.*

But maybe it wasn't foolish for the rest of the family. And despite the fact that it hurt Steve more than he was willing to admit, didn't that make him responsible?

Later I stopped believing in witches, so I did it as a balancing exercise.

Steve decided to talk to Tyler as soon as the opportunity arose.

-+-|-|-|-

THE LOW-PRESSURE SYSTEM in the house lasted all evening long, but at least Jocelyn and Matt ate some of the quiche. Tyler didn't even come downstairs; he muttered something about having to study for an exam and wanting to be left alone. That night Jocelyn and Steve each lay facing the wall on their own side of the big bed, unspoken words trembling in the empty space between them. He lay awake for a long time but finally fell asleep from exhaustion.

The next morning at breakfast Jocelyn said, "Maybe I will bring the horses back after we're finished riding this afternoon. I think you're right. It probably won't hurt them."

Steve nodded and felt something relax inside. "You want me to come along with the trailer?"

She shook her head. "Matt and I can manage."

Nothing else was articulated, but at least it was a start, and he didn't want to force anything. Times of tension between them never lasted long, but this had been different, more delicate, and it required careful treatment. He thought about it during the day at the university, and as he was raking the leaves in the backyard that afternoon he came to the conclusion that they weren't so bad off after all. Jocelyn and Matt were hooking up the trailer to the car in the driveway. Steve inhaled the cold autumn air deep into his lungs—it was one of those November days that held the first subtle traces of winter—and comforted himself with the thought that there must be people in town who had done much worse than they had.

He was still working in the backyard when Jocelyn came outside in her riding gear and screamed, "Steve!" She sounded anxious. "Steve, right away!"

He dropped the rake into the pile of leaves and ran to the kitchen door. "Something's wrong with Tyler," she said. "He's not responding . . . I can't get through to him."

She took him to the living room. Tyler was sitting on the couch in the twilight with his legs drawn up close to his body. It took Steve less than three seconds to come to a diagnosis: The boy seemed about to drop into a psychotic episode, or was already having one. The toes of his bare feet were curled up and cramped, his hair was tousled, his knuckles were white. He was staring into the far distance with big, unseeing eyes. Steve recognized that expression from psychiatric patients who were willfully struggling to disengage themselves from reality. It was the expression of someone moving from the light into the darkness, and Steve suppressed a sudden burst of staggering fear.

He lowered himself to his knees in front of Tyler and put his hands on his shoulders. "Hey, Tyler, look at me . . ." He shook him gently to awaken him from his stupor. Tyler yielded to his movements immediately, which alarmed Steve even more. He had expected his body to be as constricted as his fingers and toes. Resistance would have been a sign of consciousness. But Tyler's body was behaving like a doll filled with straw. Steve put his hand on the back of his neck and squeezed his vertebrae tightly with his thumb and forefinger.

"What's wrong with him?" Jocelyn asked, aghast. She knelt beside him as well. Matt had popped up in the open French doors and was peering at them in terror.

"Shock," Steve said. "Get me some water, Jocelyn."

Jocelyn did as he asked and Steve sat down on the couch next to his son. He took him in his arms and rocked him gently back and forth. Tyler's body felt cold and clammy. "Hey, son, it's going to be all right; everything's going to be all right," he murmured, and he kept on repeating the words like a mantra. But inside he cursed himself: He had known that it *wasn't* all right from the moment Robert Grim had questioned Tyler, right before the horses had gone crazy. He had seen it in his eyes. Why hadn't he tried harder to fish it out of him? *Idiot.* "What are you doing, son? Scaring the daylights out of us." He held his son even tighter. "I'm here with you, Tyler. No matter what happens, I'm always with you. It's going to be all right."

Finally, his attempts bore fruit and Tyler began shuddering in his arms. The blind, boneless expression on his face began to thaw. His lips quivered and released a soft, stifled moan. His eyes opened wider and became moist. His hands moved upward, trembling, and fell help-lessly back down.

Jocelyn came back with a glass of water and a towel and put them on a stool in front of them. Steve hardly noticed, because at that very moment Tyler looked up at him with such a fragile expression of mis-ery and despair that Steve's heart abruptly filled with almost drunken love and a sickening feeling of regret.

"Listen, Jocelyn. Why don't you go riding with Matt?"

"But I can't leave him like this. . . . Is he going to be all right?"

"He'll be fine. I think the two of us need a little time together, here."

He gave her a meaningful look and Jocelyn understood. "Come on, Matt, let's go," she said, directing him out of the living room. She closed the French doors behind them, smothering Matt's fierce pro-tests. Then they left through the kitchen door and everything got quiet.

Okay, kiddo, here we are, Steve thought. It was a peculiar moment, and it felt as if a balance had been struck. Here they were, finally alone: he and his eldest, he and his boy. As if both of them had been waiting for this for a long time—not only since that strange night a few days back, when Tyler had followed him outside on bare feet, and not even since that fight about Laurie early in October, but longer, much longer. Steve had brought his son back from a faraway place in the darkness, and he knew that what was waiting to be dragged out into daylight would not be good, yet the feeling that prevailed right now was that of deep, overwhelming love.

He made Tyler drink. The boy spilled some of the water on his gray sweatpants, wiped it off, and wept silently for a long time. Steve held him close until he eventually calmed down. Then he had him drink some more and said cautiously, "It's pretty bad, huh?"

Tyler nodded with pale, wet cheeks. It took at least a couple of min-utes before he was finally able to speak. When he was ready, three weak, imploring words dropped from his lips: "Help me, Dad."

And Steve swore that he would do everything he could to help him, literally everything.

-+-|-|-|-

AN HOUR LATER, just before Jocelyn and Matt were due to come home with the horses and plenty of questions, Steve and Tyler took the Toyota and drove out of town on Route 293, then took 9W through Black Rock Forest. As soon as they crossed the pass and descended into the valley, a feeling came over Steve that they were in forbidden territory, and he had to suppress the urge to keep looking in his rear-view mirror to see if they were being followed. Ridiculous, but it was there nonetheless, and he wasn't able to shake it.

They didn't say a word during the entire ride.

They drove along the Hudson and into Newburgh, parked near the Washington's Headquarters historic site, and found a bar in the center of town with few people and lots of dark corners. Steve ordered two root beers and asked for the Wi-Fi code. It took him twenty minutes to read through a selection of the reports on Tyler's website and to watch his videos, with increasing dismay—and, he had to admit, silent admiration. None of them were as shocking as the images he had seen at home—thank God those weren't online—but each and every one contained spectacular and highly incriminating material, to say the least. Then he made Tyler erase it all and leave no trace. The boy gratefully set to work.

Watching his son and drinking his root beer, Steve came back to himself with a shock. *Don't you see what a dangerous game you're playing? You're destroying evidence. More importantly, you're renouncing the morality that you and Jocelyn have always placed such a high value on. I hope you're fully aware that you're offering Tyler an escape from a sordid game that he was a major player in.*

But hadn't Tyler been punished enough already, being forced to witness the atrocity committed by his so-called friends? He had had to come face-to-face with the consequences of his stupidity. Tyler had gone through hell and back in the past twenty-four hours. A fit like that didn't come out of nowhere. He hadn't even been able to summon the courage to check the HEXApp for Katherine's whereabouts, afraid that Armageddon might have hit the town. When Steve had assured him that nothing unusual had been reported, and that the witch had resumed her normal pattern after the stoning, the relief in Tyler's eyes had been overwhelming.

"I'll have to report this. You understand that, don't you?" Steve finally said, breaking a long, painful silence after Tyler had told him his story.

Tyler nodded slowly, afraid.

"This has gone from bad to worse. People are going to get killed if your friends continue down this path. I can't bear that responsibility."

Tyler said he understood.

"This isn't your fault, okay? That Jaydon has totally lost it—he needs help. Someone's got to put an end to this." As he said this, he realized that he had been speaking mostly to himself, trying to justify the plan that was slowly dawning on him. He shook his head with doubtful certainty. "No. Not your fault."

"I just don't get it," Tyler said. "I mean, Burak's part in this. Jaydon's nuts and Justin's just a jerk, but Burak . . . he used to be cool."

"Well, he finally snapped," Steve said, more forcefully than he intended. "You know that's what Black Spring does to some people."

But that didn't seem to sink in with Tyler. He finally looked up at his dad. "I'm scared for what's gonna happen to him."

The truth was that Steve was terrified of what lay in store for all of these boys. Something had to happen, that much was obvious. They had broken all the laws of the Emergency Decree; they had caused Fletcher's death and had jeopardized the lives of everyone in Black Spring. Maybe Doodletown really was the kind of shock therapy they needed to make them see what the hell they had been doing . . . although in his heart of hearts, Steve feared Doodletown wouldn't be the end of it. Tyler's part alone was enough to put him in Doodletown. If the images of the stoning were not handled with the utmost care, it might well lead to a popular insurrection.

A chill suddenly gripped him. *Those fucking idiots don't deserve any better than to take full blame for their imbecility. What Tyler did, he did out of idealism. Should he be punished for that?* Steve's mouth went dry when he found himself remembering his own suicidal thoughts in the Thai beach bungalow so long ago, during Jocelyn's first pregnancy. That's what Doodletown must be like. And then he remembered Tyler's infinitely fragile, begging eyes: *Help me, Dad.*

Steve had made his decision. And now, while his son was destroying the result of months of effort, and Steve couldn't help but feel that they were blowing a unique opportunity to actually make progress— that in fact they were driving Black Spring back into the seventeenth century—a persistent doubt kept gnawing at him, a doubt about whether he was doing the right thing.

"Okay, done," Tyler said.

"Is it completely gone?"

"Yeah."

"Everything?" Steve was looking for more confirmation.

"Yeah. All content has been deleted and I've cancelled the URL."

"And it can never be retrieved?"

"Not exactly. The address will be in quarantine for thirty days. In case I wanted to restore it, or whatever. But the domain registration is anonymous, so no one can see my details. Unless they call in the law." Tyler hesitated. "You don't think they're going to go that far, right?"

Don't be so sure, Steve thought. *What if they get West Point involved?* But even then, chances were slim that Tyler would be picked up, he figured. If Jaydon was arrested, he'd rat on him, that much was certain. Maybe the other two would corroborate Jaydon's story, although they were more likely to keep their mouths shut about the part they played in Tyler's project, afraid of further consequences if they were found out. So it would all boil down to a single accusation by a deranged perpetrator who had been driven into a corner, and even in Black Spring they knew that desperate needs led to desperate deeds.

You've set off on a road full of pitfalls, Steve, with no way of knowing what the consequences might be. Maybe this kind of intervention isn't going to help Tyler at all—did that ever occur to you?

Oh, fuck off. No way am I going to send my son to Doodletown. Over my dead body.

"So can they uncover the history in any other way?" he asked. "I don't know, automatic backups or something?"

"Only through Mike."

"Who's Mike?"

"Classmate. From Highland Falls. He builds websites and has his own server. He let me put my site on his server for a crate of beer."

"So you let somebody from outside . . ."

Tyler shrugged. "What the hell does he care? He thinks it's some kind of private collection of all my YouTube vlogs. Which it was in the beginning, because that's how I got started, just to bore Mike and keep him from poking around in my shit."

Steve closed his eyes and took a deep breath. When he opened them again, he saw that Tyler had picked up his phone and was tapping the screen with his thumbs. "What are you doing?"

"I'm texting him. I know the guy. For another crate of beer, he'll get rid of all the backups today."

Next, Steve made Tyler erase his browser history on both his laptop and his iPhone, as well as his chat conversations and the entire folder of video clips and Word docs that had anything to do with his project. The GoPro memory card was last. Only the video of the stoning was left on his desktop.

Steve rubbed his cheeks, making a chafing sound, and suddenly got worried. "Do the other guys still have material on their computers or phones?"

Tyler shook his head. "The agreement was that we would only log in outside of town. I think everybody did it at school or in the library.

We think the iPhones HEX distributed last year are bugged with key-loggers, so we decided to ban their use for the project."

Steve looked at him, all at sea, and Tyler produced a faint smile. "A keylogger is like an app that allows you to see what's happening on a computer or phone from a distance. It passes on all the keystrokes so you can see exactly what websites someone is visiting. Way handy if you want to find out if somebody's cheating on you."

"Right. So you're sure there's nothing else? They're going to search everything; I want you to be well aware of that."

"Jaydon took a picture of . . ." He made a curvy gesture and looked away with embarrassment. "You know, what I told you about. You have to tell them that, Dad. They should take his phone away immediately if they're going to arrest him. But that's it, as far as I know."

Let's just hope you're right. "Anything else?"

Tyler thought for a minute and shook his head. "Oh, wait!" He turned red and began searching his phone. Steve half watched what he was doing and noted that, curiously enough, he was paging through his sound files. He clicked on one.

"Do I want to know what this is?" Steve asked.

Tyler shook his head and looked at the file with regret and disgust. Then, with two taps of his thumb, it was gone.

Steve settled the tab and soon they were walking along the Hudson, heads pulled into their collars and hands in their pockets. They saun-tered all the way past the yacht basin to the enormous pillar that was part of the Hamilton Fish Bridge. They paused below the bridge and stared at its reflection, a glistening orange in the black water. The northeast wind tugged at their hair and their clothes as if it were trying to drive them back to Black Spring. But the river flowed farther, away from the darkness that surrounded them. Past the city it emptied into the New York Bight, and beyond that into the Atlantic Ocean where, much farther east, the new light would always break sooner than up in the hills where they belonged.

"Tomorrow, you're going to talk to Lawrence," Steve said. This was the last piece of the puzzle, and if that fell into place they had at least a chance. "You trust Lawrence, right? You're going to tell him what we did and that no matter what happens, he has to keep his mouth shut and stick with our story. Make it clear to him that this is the only way he can get out of this unharmed. If Jaydon blabs, they'll question you both. Is Lawrence up to it, you think?"

Tyler shrugged.

"And you. Are you up to it?"

He nodded slowly. He looked like a convict on death row being asked if he could handle his last walk to the scaffold. Steve put his arm around him and felt a shock run through Tyler's body.

"No one will have to know," he said. "Only you and me."

The boy stared with dark-rimmed eyes at a gravel barge that was making its way steadily down the river with a soft rumble of the engine. Steve understood that not only was Tyler afraid, but he was also plagued by guilt. The boy had character. Steve knew few people with as strong a sense of justice as Tyler. He well remembered how proudly Tyler had looked at him when he stood up for his ideals at the All Hallows Council meeting. And suddenly he realized that he might easily be burdening his son with something he'd never be able to come to terms with.

He's gonna have to, Steve thought. *There's no alternative. Maybe it'll haunt him for a while, but it will pass, like all things pass in the end.*

The surge caused by the barge had reached the pillar and sloshed against the boulders with white-crested waves. Steve was suddenly angry at himself for having such misgivings. He'd protected Tyler out of love. Parents loved their children and protected them at any cost. Hadn't Tyler himself asked him the question not long ago for his blog: Who would Steve save, his own child or a village in Sudan?

Of course you saved your own child. That's what love was.

"Okay," Tyler said eventually. He shivered, and Steve pulled him close and rubbed him to warm him up.

"Good. Be strong, son, and everything will be all right. You didn't deserve this."

"Are you going to tell Mom?"

"No." The thought hadn't even occurred to Steve until that moment, but it felt like the right thing to do. "This is just between you and me."

Tyler nodded. "Okay." He was silent for a few seconds, then he quietly added, "Thanks, Dad."

They stood there and watched the cold, dark water flow past them. It was a moment with his oldest son that Steve would never forget. Suddenly he wished with all his heart that they could step onto a barge together, leave Black Spring behind, and just follow the current, past the New York harbors and into the new dawn. That's where things would assume their true form. In a flash of déjà vu, he heard Matt's sarcastic laugh: *Yes, Dad. Who would you save, Tyler or me?* Steve had given the obvious answer that evening, and Tyler had faultlessly sensed that he was being politically correct. The truth was that it made you feel uncomfortable if you really preferred one of your children over the other. Steve had treated enough parents at New York Med to know that it was a perfectly natural thing, but when you were forced to look into that mirror yourself, it became downright embarrassing.

Tonight, though, at the end of the pier and with his arm around his oldest son, he wasn't ashamed to admit it, because it was the truth. Despite the fact that Steve loved Matt and Jocelyn with all his heart and would probably go out of his mind if anything should happen to either one of them, Tyler would always be number one.

-+-|-|-|-+-

YET AS HE lay in bed that night, the doubt was still there . . . like a pilot flame in his head that refused to go out completely.

Jocelyn had apologized for her outburst and Steve had apologized for his ugly remark. They had all been under enormous pressure. The unexpressed accusation remained buried, but for the sake of a reconciliation, it would have to do. As they lay together in the dark, Steve calmly told her what had happened with Tyler—at least, the version of the story he would also tell HEX. He had never been good at lying to his wife and had never had any reason for it, but now the stream of half-truths came out of his mouth with astonishing ease, and he was slightly distressed to discover that he wasn't even ashamed of himself. Jocelyn was shocked, and praised him for the fact that he had managed to wheedle all that out of Tyler. She apologized once again for accusing him of handling the situation badly, but Steve pressed his forefinger against her lips and kissed her. *Not bad for a dress rehearsal,* he thought, *but any more sorries from her and I'll go nuts.* They made love, and the love was by all means sincere: At least on that front he'd be able to look at himself in the mirror.

He lay awake for a long time and listened to the soft hiss of the flame in his head. *God, I hope I did the right thing. I truly believe my heart is in the right place.* But love was a mysterious, deceptive force, and one of the few areas in which Steve didn't trust his powers of judgment the full hundred percent.

EIGHTEEN

THE CREEK STOPPED bleeding, but the town was haunted.

There were hubbubs and riots—small rebellions that Robert Grim had the security guards forcefully nip in the bud. All week long there were extra church services. The ancient call for an exorcism arose, and people lit candles on the gravestones at Temple Hill Cemetery for the repose of the dead. In the meantime, the IT specialists at HEX were working overtime to keep up with the flood of e-mails, chats, and apps about omens and the end-times. Thank God it was still only within the confines of the town, but you never knew what these idiots would get into their heads. "You see, the Mayans were right!" supermarket clerk Eve Modjeski e-mailed to her friend Betty Chu at the nursing home. Eve Modjeski was a featherbrained fool with rather nice tits but too much forehead, for whose creation Grim would gladly have parted with a rib—although after the Mayan remark he might be inclined to yank it right back and replace it in his own body, with or without Eve attached.

For the first time since time immemorial all seven of the HEX staff were working twenty-four/seven to keep the public unrest under control and to try to pinpoint the cause of Katherine's agitation. The frantic phone calls alone were proving to be a full-time job.

"The prophet of doom called again," Warren Castillo said when Grim came back from creek-water inspection on Tuesday afternoon.

"John Blanchard? That's the seventh time in two days."

"I know. I told him I was going to hang up, but then the wacko said he wanted his lamb back. I asked him what lamb, and he said the two-headed lamb."

Grim pulled a sour face. "That ugly fucker we put in the archive?"

"He said he wanted to eat the fetus to cleanse him of his sins. He said God had given it to him and that it was his duty to do penance. I said that if his stomach was up to a hefty dose of formaldehyde he could come and get it. He thought I was serious and wanted to make an appointment."

"Ugh. Primates don't come any lower than that."

Despite the clearly visible tightened measures implemented by the HEX staff and the sympathy of many of the townsfolk who offered themselves as volunteers, there were also critical voices, not the least of which was Colton Mathers's. "You were appointed to prevent such disturbances, but from all appearances it looks like you've seriously shirked your responsibility," the councilman raged over the phone. "I want you to make sure we get some peace and quiet around here, and that the ones responsible do not escape punishment." Grim, who was summoning up a mental image of Mathers's pancreas and adorning it with a large tumor, assured him that they would do everything in their power *without* the help of The Point, and he hung up before Mathers had a chance to respond.

The criticism didn't only come from above: That same evening the windows of the former Popolopen Visitor Center were smashed with bricks. The perpetrators—some drunk and dissatisfied construction workers—were caught in the act and spent the night in the vaults beneath Crystal Meth Church.

By then, Marty Keller had discovered who had pulled the joke with the peacock: fellow Council member and butcher's wife Griselda Holst, of all people.

"Her?" Grim exclaimed in shock. "You can't be serious."

"I am," Marty said. He showed Grim what he'd been able to recon-struct from the security cam images. Holst had left the butcher shop the previous Sunday evening at 10:58 p.m. with, sure enough, the big blue shopping bag clutched under her arm. The cameras along Old Miners Road showed her old Dodge leaving town in the direction of Highland Mills. At 12:23 she had returned, parked in her driveway, and sneaked into her house. Sticking out of her shopping bag was a profuse bunch of peacock feathers. It was so blatantly obvious that it made Grim furious: as if the old cow was poking fun at the system. Not much later, the images showed Griselda Holst walking into the woods.

"Grow a fucking brain cell!" Grim shouted with a voice that stuck in his throat.

Marty shrugged. "She probably thought Katherine would disappear before dawn and that the bird would get toasted before anybody found out."

Warren grinned. "But instead she shows her gratitude to the Holst woman and parades around with it all week long. What a scream!"

"But why? Why a peacock?"

Claire had brought in a Harvard University Press reference work from their library of the occult, and she paraphrased as follows: "For the Persians, the peacock was a symbol of immortality because they believed peacock meat was impervious to decomposition. Which is not true; it's supposed to be very dry and hardly edible. Let's see . . . in the Middle Ages the peacock was a bad omen because its cries were thought to evoke rain—well, they were right about that—and according to Paracelsus, a German astrologist and occultist, the cry of a peacock at unusual times foretold the death of someone from the family to whom the bird belonged. Oh, yes, finding peacock feathers brings luck, but keeping them in the house is very unlucky. Is any of this helpful?"

Grim sniffed. "The butcher woman doesn't really strike me as the type who gives a fuck about the symbolic value of her offering."

"Yeah, right," Warren said, chuckling. "She's too stupid to find her own ass. Have you ever tasted that pâté of hers? Tastes like she extracted the fat directly from her paunch with a liposuction needle and injected it into the terrine."

"Warren, you swine!" Claire said. "A little respect, please. She's had a tragic life, with that husband of hers."

"That may be true," Grim said, "but that doesn't give her the right to pull a stunt like that."

But that was only the beginning. Marty and Warren dove into the video archive, and by Wednesday evening they had uncovered Griselda Holst's peculiar habit of calling on the witch beyond the eye of the cameras. The pattern was always the same. Every Thursday, rain or shine, when Katherine was up in the woods, Griselda would sneak out behind a couple of parked cars or along a hedge and disappear into the bushes, clutching a white plastic bag. About an hour later she would return—bag gone. Grim was baffled. How could they have missed this? And what on earth was the woman *doing* when she was with Katherine?

The next morning they wired Marty with a mic and sent him over to Griselda's Butchery & Delicacies, while Grim, Warren, Claire, and the others intently watched the live images from the butcher shop's surveillance cam on the big screen.

"What'll it be?" came the brash voice of Griselda through the speakers.

"A pound of peacock pâté, please," Marty said. Warren burst out laughing and Grim gestured for him to keep quiet.

Griselda, instantly tense, hesitated. "Holst pâté, you mean?"

"No, peacock pâté," Marty said, straight-faced.

"I . . . don't carry that."

"How about peacock pie, then?"

"I don't sell any peacock meat."

"Aw, bummer," Marty said. "No peacock filet, either?" On-screen, it was easy to see that Griselda didn't know how to handle the situation. "I thought I might give it a try, since Katherine is such a big fan."

Griselda relaxed a little and smiled. "Ain't that right," she said. Wasn't that just a hint of pride in her voice? "She must be. Why else would she hang on to it so long?"

"Yeah, no matter what they say, the person who gave her that peacock really knows how to avert a crisis. That's why we wanted a peacock, too." Griselda blushed and Marty made eager use of the opportunity. "You know, my partner and I always organize these Katherine theme nights where we act out whatever the witch is doing. Over the weekend we tied Gaudi, our Chihuahua, to the branch of a tree. We laughed so hard we thought we'd piss our pants! Wait, wanna see a selfie?"

Griselda's smile disappeared instantly and her embarrassment evaporated. Beneath it was a layer of petrified rage. "You dirty little whippersnapper!" she roared. "Mocking my Katherine! Get the hell out of here, you!" She yanked an enormous salami off the shelf and stormed around the counter, right up to the awestruck Marty, who just about flew out the door, its little bell jingling maniacally. "You deserve Doodletown, mister man!" Griselda shrieked after him. "Be careful, or I'm gonna report you to the Council! You're Grim's whiz kid, aren't you? I'll find out what your name is!"

She marched back inside with all the grace of a Ukrainian warship and slammed the door behind her. Back in the control center Warren howled like a wolf and roared, "Give that woman an Oscar!"

Grim still couldn't connect Griselda's activities with the death of the dog or the bleeding of the creek, but meddling with the witch was strictly forbidden because the risks were simply impossible to foresee. Grim had no choice but to inform Colton Mathers. The councilman met with him in his country house, which was enclosed by a rusty old fence on the top of the Hill of Pines as if it were the Frankenstein mansion itself. With an increasingly deeper frown, the old relic listened to the facts, and finally he amazed Grim by saying, "Let it go, Robert. Mrs. Holst is an upright woman and she's been under intense strain lately. Besides, we have to wait and see what the consequences of her actions are. Maybe it won't be all that bad."

Grim couldn't believe his ears. "But she—"

"I'm glad you brought this up," Mathers continued as if Grim were nothing but smoke, "and we certainly have to keep our eye on Mrs. Holst, but for now my advice is: Let sleeping dogs lie."

Robert Grim, who had wanted to scream in his face that the sleeping dogs had been awake for ages, that in fact they were stalking the town streets with foaming mouths and menacing teeth, turned homeward empty-handed and thought, *He's covering up for her because of the Roth business. How long is he going to keep up this dirty game?*

The answer came right away: *Until you grow some balls and stand up to him.*

But Grim was attached to his job and he kept his mouth shut. And that evening, after the storm had subsided and the witch had finally given up her weird predilection for the dead peacock, he thought maybe it was better this way. Against protocol, even hypocritical, but so be it. Everything seemed to be back to normal. No one wanted to talk about what had dominated every conversation up until then; people wanted to forget their anxiety and erase all memory of it. And so did Robert Grim. He began to believe that a small miracle had occurred: Black Spring had gotten through Katherine's miseries relatively unscathed.

That was his frame of mind until early Saturday evening, when bad news came knocking at the door.

-+-|-|-|-

PETRIFIED AND NUMB, the members of the HEX staff who were present at the time—Claire, Warren, and Grim—listened to Steve Grant and Pete VanderMeer tell their story. It was mainly Steve who did the talking. This was where they were at: Jaydon Holst—son of the intrepid butcher's wife, for God's sake—had systematically terrorized the witch and stabbed her with a box cutter, then sicced the Grants' dog on her. As revenge for Fletcher's death, Jaydon, Justin Walker, and Burak Şayer had reported to HEX as volunteers to gain free access to Katherine, and Grim had fallen for it. The shocking, horrible results of that blunder were revealed in the footage that Grant's son had shot.

After the clip finished playing no one said anything for a long time. The cramped lounge area in the control center seemed too small, as if all the air had been sucked out of it and they were slowly being asphyxiated. Grim felt his heart make a number of unexpected, prancing leaps before resuming its normal rhythm.

The stoning. Oh, sweet Jesus, those few frames where you could see them hurling rocks in her face.

Suddenly a thought as vivid as a heap of burning phosphorus struck him. *They could easily have snapped the stitches on her eyes.*

Claire's mouth fell open and she was the first to speak. "When was this? Thursday afternoon, you said?"

Steve nodded. "It must have been before four, because that's when Matt and I came home."

Her eyes grew bigger and bigger, and Grim didn't like the expression in them at all. "Can you be more precise?"

Steve turned to the MacBook, tapped the video file with two fingers, and opened the properties menu. "Look, there it is. Content created: Thursday, November 8, 2012, 3:37 p.m."

"Oh my God." Claire slapped her hands over her mouth. "That's when that old lady died."

Grim didn't know what she was talking about. "Who?"

"Rita Marmell. She was a patient at Roseburgh. She had a stroke Thursday afternoon while she was playing cards. Her doctor said it was completely unexpected because she was in relatively good health, but these things happen at her age, so I didn't think anything of it. It said on the death certificate that she was declared dead at a quarter to four, after CPR failed."

Pete VanderMeer and Steve exchanged shocked glances. "Isn't that exactly what she did back in '67?" Pete said. "When those doctors were trying to cut her mouth open. Three elderly people in town dropped dead of strokes."

Warren understood what he was getting at. "Years go by and she's just standing there, like a chained hibernating bear. But get too close and . . ." He clapped his hands and everyone jumped at the hollow sound.

Like a chained hibernating bear, Grim thought with a sudden shiver. *Waiting for . . . what?*

"Apparently she sends out this freak energy when she's under great physical or emotional stress," Warren said. "And it makes the weakest among us just . . . snap."

"If that's true, then these kids killed that woman," Grim said, his voice flat. Under the harsh, unforgiving striplights, the group looked pale and gutted, but at the same time restrained. What if this were to leak out in town, God forbid? *If you want to know what restraint looks like, take a good look around you,* he thought, *because this is the last you're going to see of it for a long time.*

"Good." Grim took off his glasses and began polishing the lenses. "We've got to bring those jerks in as quietly as possible. If this leaks out before they're safely locked up, all hell will break loose."

"And you think that won't happen if people find out afterward?" Pete remarked.

"It probably will, but at least these boys won't get lynched."

"I hope not."

Grim stared at him. "You don't really think . . ."

"What do you think the Council will decide if word gets out that the boys are responsible not only for last week's panic and the death of Steve's dog, but also for the death of an elderly woman? Master Mathers will insist that it's one of his town matters and he'll get everybody to vote on it under the guise of democracy. But if this isn't handled with delicacy there'll be total anarchy. Haven't you noticed how frightened people are out there? They'll be capable of just about anything when they find out who caused it."

Warren brightened up. "And that's why we're going to be one step ahead of them. We'll pick 'em up quietly and try them under the laws of the Emergency Decree."

"Right, and what does that say about willfully causing a 'serious threat to the municipal public order,' which I'm pretty damn sure covers stoning as well?"

"Come on, Pete, that's just a stupid old law from the eighteenth century," Grim snapped.

"The Emergency Decree *is* the law here. Don't be so sure about that."

"Listen, this is bullshit. We still live in America, for fuck's sake. I don't know how long it's been since any incident occurred that fell under that particular law, so the statutes have never been adapted to contemporary criminal legislation. We'll figure it out in the Council."

But the others avoided each other's glances and looked at the floor with visible discomfort. Warren was the only one who dared to open his mouth. "People have been sent to Doodletown for far less serious offenses."

"Guys, come on!" Grim shouted with disbelief. He felt cornered, and that fed his anger. "You don't really believe that, do you? I don't want to jump the gun on the sentence, because that's up to the entire Council, but don't worry, we'll come up with something trendy. I'm sorry, but I can't keep this quiet. What they did is criminal, make no mistake. Who knows what those fuckers will cook up the next time? Maybe burn her, because that's what we do to witches, after all. Do you want to wait for that to happen? If things had turned out just a little bit differently we'd all be dead by now."

"I'm well aware of that," Pete said softly.

Then Steve spoke up. "Tyler and Lawrence are terrified of these guys, especially Jaydon. Also of what's going to happen after they're released."

"Let's cross that bridge when we come to it," Grim said. "I'm assuming they won't be seeing the light of day for a while."

"Say, you have the authority to call in The Point if you think it's a good idea, right?" Pete asked, suddenly hopeful. "Now would be a good time. If Mathers wants to keep it internal, like the Roth case, the town will be under even greater strain. Releasing some of the pressure might not be a bad idea, with a little outside supervision."

Grim laughed bitterly. "Listen, my friend, if that was at all possible I'd be on the phone with them right now. The Council has forbidden me from alerting them about what happened last week."

"*What?*"

"Because of Roth. If I don't obey the order I'll lose my job."

That was true, but this new development was shocking enough to justify acting on his own initiative. Robert Grim couldn't exactly nail down why, but VanderMeer's words had upset him in some indefinable way. People were slowly losing their minds, and if this persisted, nothing would ever be as it had been before. He knew it would probably be wisest to neutralize the situation and stay one step ahead of Mathers, but Mathers wouldn't stand for it. Grim guessed that the councilman wouldn't go so far as to fire him—after all, who could replace him?—but he couldn't exactly be sure. Colton Mathers was a life-form who had a lot in common with a marshy swamp: immune from evolution and sucking up every little mishap in its stinking depths, where it would never be forgotten.

"I don't think you should go that far," Steve said suddenly. Pete was surprised, but Steve shrugged. "I know there's no way to justify this, but if you go to The Point, the Council will be on your ass. I think you'd be better off keeping everyone calm and trying to get the Council to use their heads."

"Exactly," said Grim, who swept his doubts aside, and in so doing made a terrible miscalculation. "I'll inform the Council tonight and we'll get that scum off the street. It'll be all right. We may be Black Spring, but we're not animals."

NINETEEN

GRISELDA HOLST CAME to the conclusion that her sacrifice had been a supreme achievement. For the first time since the birth of her son she felt something that was both spine-chilling and blissful: unsurpassed happiness, the way other people were made happy by a sultry summer breeze or the smell of lilac bushes growing against the wall of a garden house. Tragically, Griselda's happiness only lasted for four days, until it was permanently cut short on Saturday evening with the arrest of her son.

At first she had felt offended—put on the spot, even. She had prepared such a lovely offering, but Katherine, instead of disappearing, had refused to vanish, so the sacrifice was never completed. Not only that, but now there was a fairly good chance that Griselda would be unmasked. After closing the shop on Monday, she had had the urge to go and ask what the deal here was, but she didn't dare, fully aware she ought to be careful. The next day, however, when it began to look as if she might have gotten away with it, she began to see things differently. Katherine had held on to the peacock because she wanted to show everyone how grateful she was to her friend, Griselda! And, lo and behold, the creek stopped bleeding. It began to dawn on Griselda that what she had done was nothing short of an act of heroism. Silently, she took intense pleasure in her achievement and engaged in frivolous fantasies. If only the people knew, they'd carry her through the streets on their shoulders. There'd be a great party with dancing and singing, and everyone would want to eat her pâté. Still, Griselda didn't long for recognition or fame. All she wanted was the good favor of her beloved Katherine.

Saturday came and she stood behind the shop counter in a particularly good mood. As the specialty of the day, she had made her "lukewarm meatballs à la gravy." People poured into the shop, as if they all secretly knew that she was their savior. Even Mrs. Schaeffer greeted her wholeheartedly and bought a two-pound rump steak like it was nothing.

That evening, Griselda lay in bed watching *Saturday Night Live* with a tray full of liverwurst and a sense of satisfaction when she heard a loud banging on the door downstairs. She was surprised; no one ever came to visit her, and Jaydon had shut himself up in his room after dinner.

"Jaydon, the door!" she screamed. Nothing, only the thumping from his stereo in the attic. *"Jaydon!"*

Resentfully, she slid into her slippers and went out to the hallway in her pajamas. She was about to go upstairs and give Jaydon a piece of her mind—how often had she told him that his affairs with his friends were *his* business, not hers? But there was more pounding, even louder this time, and she lumbered back down the stairs, grumbling all the while. As she turned on the light in the shop the doorbell began ringing nonstop. "Yeah, yeah, yeah, I'm coming," she snarled, shuffling around the counter. "I'm not sixteen anymore, you know!"

Behind the braided window curtain were three hefty figures. There—Jaydon's friends, just as she'd expected. She unlocked the door and was about to greet the visitors with a harsh *Couldn't you guys have called him on his goddamned phone?* but the words died on her lips. It was Rey Darrel and Joe Ramsey from Rush Painting, accompanied by Theo Stackhouse, owner of the garage on Deep Hollow Road where Jaydon had had some lousy-ass job last summer, as he had called it himself. Three big, overblown guys full of testosterone who looked as if they were about to pop. Only now did she notice Colton Mathers in their wake, two heads shorter and hidden away inside his overcoat. Rey Darrel's Chevy was idling in the distance, lights still on.

Griselda looked nervously from one face to another. "What can I do for you guys?"

"Is Jaydon home?" Darrel asked abruptly.

"What mess did he get himself into now?" She looked suspiciously over her shoulder and the men took the opportunity to squeeze right past her and enter the shop. "Hey, what do you think you're doing! Colton, what's this all about?"

The councilman looked at her with a contorted mask of anger. Suddenly Griselda was struck with fear, burning fear. "These officers of the law have come to arrest Jaydon, Griselda. You'd be well advised to let them do their work without any resistance."

"Arrest? What on earth for?"

The three men ignored her and walked around the counter to the private comfort of Griselda's home. "Hey, get back here! This is my house! Jaydon!"

Colton Mathers placed his hand on her arm and called her name, articulating each syllable, but Griselda, in the spur of the moment, turned and went after the intruders, who had shamelessly started up the stairs. They couldn't just do that, could they? With a shock, Griselda realized that indeed they *could* if the situation called for it. Black Spring's local police force consisted of nothing more than a bunch of volunteer officers supervised by the HEX staff, who were called in for internal matters. There were no clear rules for carrying out arrests and it often came down to improvisation, but who could you turn to and complain about the lack of a search warrant? The authority was standing downstairs in the shop, waiting.

Ramsey, Stackhouse, and Darrel followed the music and went straight to the attic. The first of the three slammed Jaydon's bedroom door against the wall with a house-shattering bang. Griselda was right behind them, out of breath, and saw Jaydon, who had been gaming on his laptop in bed, sit bolt upright.

"Jaydon Holst, you are under arrest for breaking just about every goddamn law in the Emergency Decree," Rey Darrel said. He almost shouted it out, and for the first time Griselda realized that the men were not only worked up about their task but were also sincerely outraged. "You have the right to remain silent, but I wouldn't count on an attorney, you stupid little fuck." With a loud crash he hurled Jaydon's desk chair to the floor.

"Are you out of your mind?" Griselda screamed. She grabbed him by the sleeve, but Darrel freed himself with a simple twist of the arm.

"What the fuck?" Jaydon stammered. He turned to Griselda for help. "Mom . . ."

"What kind of psychopath are you?" Theo Stackhouse asked, his lips white with rage. He walked up to Jaydon and grabbed him by the arm, fusing his hand to the boy's skin. "This is not what I hired you for! You fucking ate lunch at my house with my wife and kids, every single day!"

"Theo, chill out, man. What's this all about?"

"*You're* the one who should've chilled out!" he roared, and Jaydon shrank back. "Not so tough without a stone in your hand, are you?"

Jaydon raised both his palms. "Listen, that was just a joke, nothing more."

"I'll show you a joke." With one quick move he grabbed Jaydon's wrist and twisted his arm onto his back. Jaydon bent forward and screamed.

"Stop it!" Griselda screamed, but Darrel held her back with fingers that felt like steel cables. "Rey, I'm never going to sell you that ground beef you like so much unless you tell me *right now* what the hell you think you're doing!"

"Sorry, Mrs. Holst. Orders."

"Why don't you just call me Griselda, like you always do?"

But Darrel roughly pushed her aside and grabbed Jaydon's free arm. "You're coming with me," he ordered. They dragged him past Griselda and out of the room. Ramsey snatched Jaydon's laptop from the bed, pulled the charger from the wall, and tucked it under his arm.

"Wait!" Griselda shouted. Holding on to the banister for support, she heaved herself down the stairs after the group of men. She felt her heart racing like mad and she was panting like a runner, but what kept her on her feet were her son's terrified cries for help. She reached the stairs to the ground floor just in time to see Darrel jab him violently in the back, so Jaydon flew down the last few steps and fell flat on his face in the doorway to the shop. Blood spurted out of his nose. In a blind rage, Griselda threw herself on the man in front of her, Joe Ramsey, but he had grabbed the banister, and despite her impressive weight it was as if she had crashed against a wall.

"Don't hurt him, you monsters!" she wept. "Keep your dirty hands off my son!"

Lying facedown, Jaydon groped in his pant pocket for his phone, but Theo Stackhouse planted a leather boot on Jaydon's wrist and he screamed. The garage owner took the phone and stuck it into the pocket of his coat.

"Motherfuckers!" Jaydon wailed. "I have rights, too, you know!"

"Not anymore," Stackhouse said.

He gave him such a hard kick in the small of his back that Jaydon bent in half and coughed up a gob of saliva, and at that moment all Griselda could see was Jim; at that moment all Griselda could see was her late husband kicking her son, and a red haze of madness spread over her vision.

"Enough!" thundered the voice of the councilman above all the other noise. "Stand up, boy."

His face contorted with pain, Jaydon scrambled to his feet and held the doorpost for support, but he did manage to stand up without the help of the arresting team. He pressed his wounded wrist against his chest and blood dripped from his upper lip. With tear-filled eyes clouded with pathological hatred, he looked up into Colton Mathers's steel face.

"Young master Holst, I am arresting you in the name of God for the repeated and disproportionate violation of the Emergency Decree, the stoning of Katherine van Wyler, and for maliciously endangering the lives of the almost three thousand residents of Black Spring. May the Lord have mercy on your soul."

Darrel and Stackhouse grabbed Jaydon and led him past the counter. "Mom, you saw what they did to me!" he cried. "Tell everybody! She saw how you beat me up, motherfucker. You're not getting away with this!"

But Griselda could barely hear him. She could no longer think clearly. Everything had become a blur. The only thing she could hear was: *The stoning of Katherine van Wyler.* At these words, her brain had shut down with an audible click. *The stoning of Katherine van Wyler. The stoning . . .*

"Don't hurt him," she said, but the words were spoken hesitantly, almost like a question.

Oh, dear God. Did he say STONING?

"For heaven's sake, Colton, what did he do?"

As the others took Jaydon away, the councilman gave her a highly abridged version of the charges, but it was enough. Griselda's thoughts twisted and turned and plummeted in an insane free fall. "It is my duty to tell you this because you are his mother, Griselda, but I am not here in my official capacity. We have decided that it would be better if you . . ."

But Griselda wasn't listening; she had started hyperventilating, and in her thoughts she was with Katherine, not with a desire for reconciliation—oh, was reconciliation even possible after something like this?—but solely to wash her feet with her tears. She took one clumsy, off-balance step toward the hat rack.

"Griselda, what are you doing?" Colton Mathers asked quietly.

"I have to . . ." *go see her,* she had almost blurted out. "Go with him, of course."

"You're not going anywhere."

"But I . . ."

Mathers grabbed her with both hands and pushed her gently but firmly against the wall behind the counter. She felt his crooked, gouty right hand drop to her breast. She smelled his breath, a heavy, intensely penetrating, predatory smell, and her mouth closed with a wet, audible plop.

"Quiet now. I'm on your side, Griselda. You know that, don't you?"

"Yes . . ."

"Good. Trust me."

"But what—"

"No, Griselda. Trust me. Do you trust me?"

"I trust you . . ."

"I want you to repeat after me. Can you do that?"

"Yes."

"Repeat after me, Griselda. I, Griselda Holst . . ."

"I, Griselda Holst . . ."

"Resign from the Council of my own free will . . ."

She looked at him with shock. "What?"

"Resign from the Council of my own free will . . ." His hand clamped around her breast and *squeezed*, painful and cruel. "Say it, Griselda. I want to hear you say it. Resign from the Council of my own free will . . ."

She was horrified now and tried to wrest herself from his grasp, but to no avail. "But why?"

"Because I know, Griselda," the councilman said with a sincere sadness. "I know you've been going to the witch and I know you gave her the peacock. I know you visit her on a regular basis; I know it all, and I don't want to try you officially, but by God I will if you don't resign voluntarily. Repeat after me, Griselda: I hereby resign from the Council of my own free will . . ."

She blushed scarlet and looked at him with big, guilty eyes. "Colton, I . . ."

"*Repeat after me!*" the old councilman suddenly roared in an

238 «« THOMAS OLDE HEUVELT

unconcealed frenzy, and a dizzying chill jolted through Griselda's body. *"Repeat after me, Griselda! Repeat after me! I, Griselda Holst, resign from the Council of my own free will!"*

"Resign from the Council of my own free will," she moaned, cowering. Now that his mask of restraint had fallen away, Mathers's face had become a repulsive web of tendons and creases, and dangerous but absolutely not senile old age.

"And I will not do anything to impede the investigation in any way . . ."

"I will not impede the investigation . . . Ow, Colton, you're hurting me."

"Or go anywhere near the witch, not even once."

"You don't understand . . ."

"Say it!" A searing pain shot through her nipple as he squeezed even harder.

"I won't go anywhere near Katherine anymore!"

The councilman relaxed and his face became composed, as if a layer of clouds had broken open under his skin. "Very well, Griselda. May God have mercy on you, too."

He straightened his overcoat and walked out the door without saying another word. The little bell jingled gaily, as it had always done. Griselda dropped to the floor and began to cry.

-+-|-|-|-|-

JAYDON'S ARREST WAS followed by a shadowy interval in which Griselda felt an almost pathological need to make things clean, first herself and then the shop, thoroughly and repeatedly, to try to wash away the filth of her body and soul. She did it in a daze, as if she were hovering over herself, transcending her body, a floating balloon of confusing images that followed each other like fever dreams: Colton Mathers kicking Jaydon's corpse; townsfolk with blank, empty faces who knew what Griselda had done and were throwing stones at her (instead of the medals she deserved); Mathers's hands on her breast, his randy breath down her neck.

Oh, Katherine, what's happening to me? I'm going crazy.

She shuddered at the thought of the councilman's touch, which somehow had been much more horrible than Arthur Roth's. With Roth it had been sheer lust, and she could simply disassociate herself from it. When Colton Mathers squeezed her nipple she had seen on his face the sick concentration of an inquisitor, and it was as if she had been looking through a deep chasm into a distant, long-gone past.

I'm on your side, Griselda.

But Griselda had lived long enough to know that no one was on her side, not Colton Mathers, not Jaydon, and certainly not the townsfolk who ate her pâté. Only Katherine had always been on her side. But now that had changed. Every time she dozed off to sleep that night the same image appeared before her: Katherine strolling up and down Deep Hollow Road, sniffing the air like a beast of prey and searching with blind eyes for Griselda, for it had been her son who had stoned Katherine, her flesh and blood who had taken the peacock away from her. Again and again Griselda awoke with a jolt, her body cold and clammy with sweat. She spent the whole night tossing and turning, caught between two extremes: If she wanted to pay her debt to Katherine she would have to remain faithful to her, but if she wanted to keep Jaydon from harm, she would have to choose his side.

At first light on Sunday she called Town Hall, but no one answered. She tried calling Mathers, but no one picked up there, either, just as she expected. At HEX she got Robert Grim on the line, who reluctantly told her that Jaydon had been interrogated and was now in solitary confinement in Doodletown awaiting his trial, as were his friends. Grim added that Jaydon, unlike the others, was of age, and that he, Grim, wasn't obliged to pass this information on to Griselda.

"Please don't hurt him, Robert," she begged. "No matter what he did, and no matter what you think of me, don't hurt my son."

"Of course not," he said tersely. "They'll be treated like anybody else."

"When Jaydon was arrested they pushed him down the stairs and kicked him hard."

There was silence; Grim was struggling to keep his voice even. "I'm sorry about that. That shouldn't have happened."

But it *had,* and that was only the beginning. The news of the stoning spread through Black Spring like a virus, no longer whispered but trumpeted loudly in lunatic shrieks. Suddenly the carefully repressed fear had returned, and in its shadow came the panic, the rage, and the insinuations. It was as if the clock had been turned back a week. But the very fact that they had foolishly believed the danger was finally behind them made the indignation all the more distressing and the fear all the more paralyzing.

From her bedroom window, Griselda peeked out over the square and saw crowds of people gathered in front of Crystal Meth Church and the Quiet Man. Sometimes they yelled slogans to fan the flames. It wasn't long before people started banging on the windows of the lunchroom. Amid the furious screaming, Griselda tried to distinguish the voices of townsfolk who had always treated her kindly. She hid behind the curtain and desperately waited for the hysteria to blow over, but as soon as dusk set in, dark clouds of smoke could be seen rising in the west and the fire engine sirens began to wail. Someone had taken a crate of empty beer bottles, filled them with gasoline, tossed the sucker through the window of that Turkish friend of Jaydon's—that Buran—and set the house on fire. The family was away for questioning and escaped injury, but the downstairs burned out and the house was declared uninhabitable.

The Şayers were an easy scapegoat, of course. Griselda had earned more respect than them over the years, but the next day her customers abandoned her, and that afternoon two men from the Lower South came with baseball bats and smashed her glass display cases to smithereens.

As soon as she was finally able, she closed the shop and darkened the windows for her own protection. Despondently fishing splinters of glass out of the ground beef, Griselda was struck by a chilling realization that she couldn't put into words but that felt indisputable nonetheless: As each individual gave in to the collective hysteria, Black Spring was deteriorating into a state of insanity.

What remained was a horror: the soul of the town, which was irreversibly bewitched.

TWENTY

THE TRIAL WAS held on Tuesday evening in Memorial Hall, and the whole town showed up. When Steve arrived with Jocelyn and Tyler and saw the rows of people waiting at the entrance, he immediately understood that the humble building had not been made to accommodate such a large crowd and was about to burst at the seams. While about eight hundred individuals had shown up for the All Hallows gathering, now there must have been almost two thousand.

Tyler had begged to be allowed to stay home, but someone from the Council had called and told Steve that his son's presence was mandatory. Suddenly Steve's heart was pounding in his chest like a piston. He tried not to let it show, but at dinner that night he hadn't been able to swallow a thing, and Jocelyn had asked if he was coming down with something.

"Probably just nerves," he'd said—and wished he could tell her what he was nervous *about*.

Tyler had been interrogated in the Town Hall on both Sunday and Monday. Steve had put up a big stink, insisting that he be present because Tyler was underage, but in the end he had had to back down and wait in the reception room with Pete and Lawrence VanderMeer, who had an ugly stitched-up cut on his forehead. When Tyler came out, Lawrence was next. Steve asked how it went and Tyler said it wasn't so bad. Their laptops, phones, and Lawrence's iPad had been seized for inspection on Sunday morning after Jaydon had started to blab. Steve prayed that they hadn't made any mistakes, but Pete's open outrage over how Jaydon had tried to drag his friends down with him was a lucky break and would surely work in their favor. As they strolled home a little while later without Pete and Lawrence, Tyler said he had gotten the impression that Burak and Justin had kept their mouths shut. Although he wasn't all that talkative, it sounded as if Tyler had been fully cooperative and had feigned ignorance when asked about his alleged website rather than obstruct the interrogation with his silence. Steve could only hope that Lawrence would be able to do the same.

He had been moderately optimistic . . . until the phone call this afternoon from the Council, that is.

The crowd choked the corridors all the way to the back of Memorial Hall and blocked the entrances for those who were still waiting in the cloakroom. Steve, Jocelyn, and Tyler joined the people standing to the left of the rows of folding chairs, but as soon as the ubiquitous guards caught sight of them they were directed to the second row, where seats had been reserved for them next to the VanderMeers. As they made their way through the knots of townsfolk, Steve felt their eyes upon them. Each grim face was marked with fear or rage.

"What a pathetic sight, huh?" Pete said with a smile after they had taken their places.

Steve was shocked. "It's way too crowded here. If panic breaks out people will be trampled to death."

"I'm afraid they're deliberately cranking up the turmoil. Did you see that?" He pointed to the stage. Hanging behind the podium and the placard reading: LET US TRUST IN GOD AND EACH OTHER was a large flat-screen. Steve felt the blood drain from his face. The idiots were going to use the video images to cause a riot.

"They're not going to bring in those boys, I hope. If they do, they're leading them like lambs to the slaughter."

"If they do, we're in deep shit," Pete said. "If they don't, we'll still be in deep shit."

There was some commotion in the back of the hall. People were stumbling over the last rows of seats and shouting, pushed forward by the surging masses behind them. The guards raced forward to clear away a quarter of the last rows in order to create more standing room. With increasing concern, Steve noticed that the emergency exits were already blocked. Even on the balcony people were gathering in flocks.

"Let the elderly sit down, folks!" someone shouted. "Offer your seats, act like good Americans!"

When the Council entered in close formation and sat down behind the podium—six of them, Steven noted; the woman from the butcher shop was missing—the buzzing finally died down. Suddenly it was so improbably quiet that not a footstep, rustle, or cough could be heard. It was as if everyone was holding their breath in expectation of what was to come.

Colton Mathers took the floor without any opening words by the mayor. His voice was deep, commanding, and unapproachably calm. The resonance carried through the silence like waves on dark water. " 'Give me thy judgments, O God, and I shall judge thy people with righteousness, and thy poor with judgment, and shall break in pieces the oppressor.' Psalm 72. My dear fellow townspeople, we have come together this evening to pass judgment concerning an appalling crime and a blasphemous mockery that affects us all: the stoning of Katherine van Wyler this past Thursday, November 8, by the young gentlemen Jaydon Holst, Justin Walker, and Burak Şayer, concluding in the subsequent death of our most beloved Rita Marmell. God rest her soul."

Of course everyone had heard the rumors, but now that the word was out, a sigh of fury and disgust rolled through the audience, and for a moment everyone shared in the common dismay: believer and infidel, man and woman, old and young.

Adrian Chass, a Council member whose lack of good taste in clothes was exceeded only by his lack of spine, cleared his throat and began reading from a sheet of paper, with less than half of Mathers's charisma. "Ladies and gentlemen, Mrs. Marmell lost her life as the result of a fatal intracerebral hematoma of the brain at exactly the same time as the stoning, bearing indisputable similarities to the incidents of

'67, when one of the stitches in Katherine's mouth was removed." He coughed. "The implications of the irresponsible and heinous acts perpetrated by these young men are enormous and could have happened to any one of us. You probably noticed that I am speaking in terms of perpetrators, not of suspects. I am doing so on the basis of the conclusive evidence that we are now about to show you to persuade you of the barbarity of this crime."

Steve saw Robert Grim shut his eyes on stage, and his admiration for the security officer rose. Grim had been against it—against the whole damn procedure, probably.

The flat-screen suddenly showed the familiar woods behind his house and what had happened there a few days ago. Sitting beside him, Tyler dropped his chin to his chest and shuddered convulsively. Steve wished the boy could have been spared this moment, but Tyler was being forced to experience the whole thing all over again: the taunting of the witch with sticks, the fight in which Lawrence was wounded, the cries of despair, and the wet thuds of the rocks bouncing off bewitched flesh. Steve squeezed Tyler's hand, but the tears had already filled his eyes. Jocelyn, who had refused to see the images until now, clapped her hands to her mouth.

Then the screen went black, and the townsfolk lost it. The idea of the stoning was bad enough, but actually seeing it with their own eyes ignited their blind rage like burning phosphorus. Jaws dropped. Dire cries went up. People burst into tears. "Where are those murderers?" someone yelled. "Every one of us could have died!" screamed another. "We'll get them!" yet another howled. The screamer laughed, a manic, whinnying laugh, as if he didn't quite believe the seriousness of what he was saying; but then his scream resounded as one furious, vindictive shout: "Get them!" People in the back of the hall swarmed forward and fell over one another, as if all were under the illusion that the suspects themselves were being presented on stage. And had that been true, Steve didn't doubt for a minute that they would have been lynched on the spot. Chairs fell over, clothing was torn, people lay on the ground, ankles and wrists were sprained. The guards had a great deal of difficulty keeping everyone under control.

"Stay calm!" the voice of the mayor boomed through the speakers. "Please, folks, just stay calm!"

"Steve, are we safe here?" Jocelyn asked, looking at the chaos behind them with clenched fists.

"I guess so, at least for now." The uproar was too far back and too many people had stood up to keep the mob in check. The mayor continued trying to calm everyone down, but Steve saw Colton Mathers look over the crowd—*his* crowd, Steve thought—with a triumphant gleam in his eyes. Of course, the old councilman had known this was going to happen all along.

Finally things settled down and the medics were able to move a number of injured people out. Then Adrian Chass took the floor again, although his voice was drowned out by the din of the crowd. "Your outrage is understandable, folks, but please stay calm. Mr. Grim and his fellow staff members have assured us that the incident has not had any further impact on Katherine's patterns. We all know she doesn't change her behavior without reason . . ."

"What about the creek, then?" someone shouted from the middle of the hall. Many applauded him.

"We've now found an explanation for that," Chass said. "Unfortunately, the stoning is not the first crime that Mr. Holst has recently committed. There are several witnesses who testify that one week earlier he disgraced Katherine by tearing her clothing apart and exposing her breast, after which he stabbed her with a knife and sicced a dog on her. It was the Grant family dog, and, as you probably know, the direct contact caused the animal's death."

Once again there was an outburst of rage, and Steve realized that the dangerous, sultry atmosphere in Memorial Hall was beginning to look more and more like a primitive popular tribunal. Someone raised a rallying cry, and soon the masses took it over like a rioting street mob: "Bring 'em in, bring 'em in, bring 'em in!" Steve understood that they were on the edge; it wouldn't take much to make the overwrought populace snap, and for the first time he saw undisguised fear in the eyes of Pete VanderMeer.

Chass tried to make himself heard above the noise but was barely successful. "The perpetrators have been arrested and are now in custody, ladies and gentlemen. What we would now like to do . . . Ladies and gentlemen, please calm down. What we would now like to do is to take a moment to acknowledge two brave young men, Tyler Grant and Lawrence VanderMeer. As you have all observed, they did everything in their power to prevent their peers from carrying out their acts of savagery, and despite the undoubtedly enormous pressure they went to their parents with the incriminating material. We call on each and every one of you to follow their admirable example and not withhold any breaches of the public order. Tyler and Lawrence, please stand up."

Tyler flinched and looked at Steve. All Steve could do was nod and urge him to stand. *Humor them, son, just for now,* he thought. He couldn't say how intensely relieved he was. The boys' presence was purely ceremonial. Painful for them, but without consequences.

Reluctantly, Lawrence and Tyler rose to their feet and looked around, utterly miserable, while loud cheering and applause broke out all around. Tyler nodded quickly and dropped to his seat as soon as he could.

"Well done," Steve whispered, but Tyler turned his eyes away.

"All right," Colton Mathers said. "Since the question of guilt is not an issue and the perpetrators have confessed, I as prosecutor will move right on to the sentencing—"

"Let's throw stones at 'em till they're dead!" someone roared, and he was answered with shouts of approval—of course they wouldn't *really* do such a thing, because, after all, they were civilized people.

"—and as we are accustomed to doing, this case will be dealt with legally according to the laws of the Black Spring Emergency Decree as drawn up by our forefathers in 1848. Ladies and gentlemen, by committing this act, Holst, Walker, and Sayer, the very dregs of our society, knowingly jeopardized the lives of every one of us. They were born and bred in Black Spring and are fully aware of the laws *and* the dangers concerning the mocking of the witch. Investigation reveals that each of them was fully compos mentis, including Walker and Şayer, who are minors. May it be ever clear that such extraordinarily pernicious behavior will not be tolerated in our community and deserves extraordinary treatment. But, fellow townspeople, they are not the only ones who have violated the Emergency Decree in the past few weeks." Bewildered glances, tense silence. Mathers, trembling with rage, continued with his litany: "There are those among you who have begun to associate with the witch. There are those among you who have sought her out. There are those among you who have brought her blasphemous offerings, and there are those among you who have spoken to her. To all those concerned, I have but one thing to say: *You . . . are . . . endangering . . . all of us!* You are *not* to associate with the witch! We are damned! You know the Emergency Decree and you know what doom awaits us if Katherine opens her eyes! Damned, people, damned!"

Steve listened to the councilman's sermon in a state of near hypnosis and again he felt the strange magnetism that the man exuded. Mathers was like a preacher of hellfire and brimstone who called down terror from the pulpit, and it had its effect: Steve realized he was afraid, just senselessly afraid.

Mathers continued: "Those acts will be met with uncommonly harsh measures. What we need is a deterrent. Yet none of your crimes are as reprehensible as endangering the entire town, which is what these boys have done with their disgraceful treatment of the witch. According to the laws of the Emergency Decree, such behavior shall be punished with a public flogging, to be witnessed as an example by the entire community." A collective wave of dismay . . . and, oh yes, of instinctive, bestial excitement. Robert Grim stared at the councilman in disbelief. A terrible, heartrending cry rose up from Mrs. Şayer, but Mathers thundered right through it: "So this is my sentence:

Mr. Justin Walker and Mr. Burak Şayer will be brought to the town square within forty-eight hours to each publicly receive ten lashes with the cat-o'-nine-tails on their bare skin, as tradition prescribes. Mr. Jaydon Holst, because of his twofold crime and because he has reached the age of majority, will be brought to the town square within forty-eight hours to receive twenty lashes with the cat-o'-nine-tails on his bare skin, as tradition prescribes. This is to be followed by three full weeks at the Doodletown detention center for all three of them, after which the delinquents will be allowed to reenter society under close supervision and with the proper psychological guidance."

If Robert Grim had not jumped up to the podium at that moment, the chaos caused by this new, explosive mixture of powerless rage and suppressed tension would probably have reached incalculable proportions. But that's exactly what Grim did; with outstretched hands he strode across the stage. "No, no, no! This is wrong—this is not what we agreed to, Colton. What the hell are you getting us into?"

"This is our law, Grim!" The councilman held the rolled-up Emergency Decree like a rod in his hand and waved it back and forth. "Yes, it may be strange in our day and age, but what can we do? We must hold these boys up as an example."

"But not like this!" Grim shouted, and he turned to the audience. "People, we're not barbarians, are we? Use your common sense, folks. This is no Sharia. We can deal with this in a decent manner. We'll come up with an appropriate alternative, with the aid of The Point."

Scornful laughter from the crowd, which Mathers gratefully made use of. "West Point doesn't know what it's like to live with a witch's curse. West Point is powerless in the face of evil. We are living under a bell jar, and we can only fall back on the good Lord . . . and on each other." He opened his arms wide, as if he were Jesus himself. "In Black Spring we take care of our own, under the eye of the Almighty God."

"Does God want us to beat up our children?"

Mathers's Adam's apple bobbed up and down convulsively. "He that spareth his rod hateth his son!"

"This is a kangaroo court!"

"This is a town matter. And as we do in all town matters, the voice of democracy will be heard."

The Widow Talbot, from the wealthier part of town, stood up and said with perfect composure, "I tend to agree with Mr. Mathers. We can't just send them to Doodletown three times in a row and turn them into psychological wrecks, can we? That's what happened to Arthur Roth, and it destroyed his sanity. Honestly, I think that's much more inhumane than a good cracking of the whip for a mere five minutes."

Steve sat looking at the scene in disbelief, and he felt the hairs in the nape of his neck stand on end. This was turning obscene fast. If this woman, this very model of respectability and refinement, could stand up with such sangfroid and declare herself in favor of public shaming, of public torture . . . then the floodgates were open.

"Besides," Mrs. Talbot continued, raising a finger, "if people have indeed been so irresponsible as to associate with the witch, I think it's a good idea to set an example for everyone. You have my blessing."

An approving hum, but nervous nonetheless, watchful.

"And what is wrong with simple custody?" Grim insisted. "We have a cell block under the church. We can strip them psychologically and convince them of the seriousness of what they've done. We . . ."

"You've made your point, Grim," someone in the audience called out. "Why don't you just sit down?"

The voice met with general approval and Grim looked around helplessly. Steve felt an instinctive need to stand up and speak out against this charade, but Jocelyn grabbed his hand and pressed it hard against her stomach. "I don't want you to say anything, Steve. Think of Tyler and Matt."

He looked at her in amazement, but when he saw the fear in her eyes, it all became clear. The last time, with Arthur Roth, the townsfolk had forgiven him for his reckless idealism. This time would be different. The collective madness was too far gone; the meltdown was irreversible. Right now they were heroes because they had tracked down the parasites who had stoned the witch and smoked them out of their holes . . . and it might just be better to remain heroes.

"They'll take a vote," Jocelyn whispered. "Have faith in their common sense."

"I'm sorry, but I don't." He looked at Pete for support, but Pete was staring into the distance with the vacant expression of a man who has just seen his worst nightmare come true. His fingers were clenched around Mary's, and Steve saw that he had absolutely no intention of standing up.

Think about Tyler. You knew this was going to happen.

But not . . . this!

Come on, who are you kidding? Of course you knew. Keep your mouth shut or you'll pay the price.

"Dad, I want to go home," Tyler whispered anxiously.

Steve looked at his son and grabbed his hand. It could have been Tyler up there on trial. He could entertain all the fantasies he wanted about floating down the Hudson with his son, but if he didn't appreciate what was at stake now, he might well forfeit his chances. So Steve leaned back . . . and said nothing.

The rest of the trial passed by in a haze. Mr. Şayer made an emotional appeal. His house had already been destroyed; could they at least show mercy for his son? He spoke about building bridges and getting past ethnic differences. He spoke about humanity and decency. He spoke with a heavy accent and was dragged away by enraged onlookers as he wouldn't stop speaking. A fight broke out, and Mr. Walker tore himself loose from its core, threatening to go to the media if they went ahead with their punishment. But neither the menacing looks of the townsfolk nor the councilman with his Doodletown were needed to reveal the obvious: that Mr. Walker was a broken man who would resign himself to the situation. And wasn't there a hint of acceptance on his face? If it had been someone else's son, he would have voted in favor.

Griselda Holst also objected in tears. She was given the most time because the townsfolk liked her the most. Still, Steve understood it was just a formality and wouldn't make a bit of difference. The people smelled blood and were eager to vote. The butcher's wife reminded the crowd of Jaydon's tragic history of abuse by his father and the emotional damage that had caused this atrocity, and she concluded with a plea to let her Jaydon be treated rather than punished. "Please, dear friends. We know each other, right? Don't you all come to see me every week to buy your steaks? Your hamburgers? Your veal cutlets? Your chicken wings? Your pâté?"

"Get that woman out of here before she starts listing the whole fucking meat department!" some smart-ass shouted. It was a tasteless joke, but the comedian got what he wanted: Griselda was led away, weeping uncontrollably.

It was finally time to vote. The councilman asked all those in favor of the sentence to raise their right hands. Many hands went into the air, including those of three Council members. Then Mathers asked everyone who opposed the sentence to raise their right hands. Steve raised his hand high . . . and to his enormous relief he again saw many hands in the air. And now, too, there were three Council members among them—including Robert Grim, of course. Steve felt a spark of hope. The vote had been indecisive. It was impossible to tell which held the majority. That meant that a large group had had the common sense to silently turn away from this mockery, thank God.

While the written vote was being prepared, Grim took the floor once again: "Folks, don't be stupid. I know this is what the Emergency Decree says, but it's a joke. Keep this in mind: If the moment ever comes that we are freed from Katherine's curse, will you be able to look each other in the eye with this on your conscience? Will you be able to dance around the church and sing, 'Ding-dong! The witch is dead,' if there's blood on your hands? Please be sensible!"

Then began the endless, shuffling procession past the podium, where four packs of printer paper had been ripped out of their packaging, and people were given felt-tips to write down an anonymous "yea" or "nay." Because they were up front, Steve, Jocelyn, and Tyler were among the first voters. Steve dropped his makeshift ballot into the voting box—the same box that had been used only a week earlier for the presidential elections. Last week they had been voting for who would get the key to the White House for the next four years, Barack Obama or Mitt Romney. It was an absurd link with a reality that Black Spring had completely lost sight of.

It took at least an hour before everyone, including those who had trouble walking, those in wheelchairs, and those who had been waiting in the cloakroom and up on the balcony, had voted. The sorting and counting of the ballots by Council members took another twenty minutes. Steve lost sight of Jocelyn, Tyler, and the VanderMeers and had never felt so miserable and alone, despite the fact that many townspeople grabbed hold of him and wanted to know exactly how events had unfolded. At a certain point he became aware of a sudden, hyperreal image: The people around him not only resembled but actually *were* people of yore, wearing rags that stank of mud and disease. If he were to walk outside, Deep Hollow Road would be a cart track, the bell in the steeple of an ancient nearby church would be chiming, and the year would be 1664.

Steve was both relieved and dead tired when Colton Mathers finally asked for order in the hall. "Ladies and gentlemen, thank you for your attention. I shall test your patience no longer. With one thousand three hundred thirty-two votes for and six hundred seventeen against, the demanded sentence has been accepted."

A shock wave of horror shuddered through Memorial Hall as people realized how many of their neighbors and friends, in the safety of anonymity, had been seduced by sensationalism and gut feelings. There was cheering and there was anger, there were those who cried and those who screamed for a rebellion, but most were satisfied that justice had been done.

The councilman continued: "The sentence will be carried out this coming Thursday at the place of the traditional All Hallows Burning, at the intersection of Deep Hollow Road and Lower Reservoir Road.

It is the duty and responsibility of each and every one of you to witness the sentencing. I therefore suggest that we set the time at the first light of dawn, to reduce the impact on the public order and your own work schedules. Let us pray that we learn a lesson from all of this and put this mutiny behind us once and for all. Lord, our Father . . ."

Mathers led them in prayer, and most of the community joined in. These were people who had known each other all their lives, who respected each other and loved each other in their own peculiar ways, as they usually did in small upstate towns. But Steve noticed that they had all undergone a radical change. He felt it even more strongly when they slunk away a little while later, silently and with averted eyes. A resignation had fallen over the townsfolk that Steve found even more uncanny than the earlier tension.

They looked like people who knew they had done something dreadful, something irreversible . . . and something they could easily live with.

TWENTY-ONE

BLACK SPRING PREPARED for execution of the sentence as if it were a holiday. The original seventeenth-century cat-o'-nine-tails was taken out of the display case in the Town Hall's small Council Chamber. It was a fine specimen: a nicely decorated rod with nine leather cords, each one two feet long with a knot at the halfway point and little lead balls at the far end. The instrument had not been used since 1932. Colton Mathers brought it to Dinnie's Shoe Repair especially for the occasion and instructed her to impregnate the leather with oiled wax so it could stand up to vigorous lashes without snapping.

Theo Stackhouse, who had been a garage owner and car mechanic the week before, eagerly accepted the office of town executioner and was summoned to the stables of the councilman's estate on Wednesday night. He practiced first on a leather saddle, to master the art of flogging, and then on a floundering, bound calf, to prepare himself for the reflex of living flesh. That night before he went to bed he took two Advils for the intense aches in his upper arm, but despite the pain, he slept like a baby.

Griselda Holst didn't sleep at all that night. Even though her own flesh and blood was about to become the center of attention, she felt overwhelmed by a sense of submission. And she was not alone: All the people of Black Spring seemed to have succumbed to the same resignation. If he hadn't been too painfully attached to the matter, Pete VanderMeer, as a sociologist, might have drawn similarities with countries in which people willingly submit to Sharia law. It was precisely for this reason that no one would stand up in protest or notify the authorities.

Even those who had voted against the sentence thought perhaps it was all for the best. They just wanted to get it over with so they could get on with their lives.

So instead of worrying about Jaydon's fate, Griselda spent the night praying to Katherine. On her bare knees, on the little rug beside her bed, she asked for forgiveness for her apostasy. As penance, she tried to chastise herself by whipping her back with Jaydon's belt. But it all felt a bit clumsy and awkward and as soon as it really began to hurt Griselda thought, *This is not my thing,* and stopped.

If instead of going through all that hassle she had been looking out the window, she would have seen her son, Justin Walker, and Burak Şayer being silently escorted through the cemetery by nine burly men. The accused were led into Crystal Meth Church, where they went down the same circular stairway that Griselda had taken so often to keep Arthur Roth alive. In the vaults, Colton Mathers read the sentence aloud. At first the boys thought he must be joking, but soon the screaming began—first startled, then frightened, then hysterical. It was a hideous screaming, a bone-chilling expression of pure human suffering and desperation. And as soon as the door had been shut with a bang, they found themselves alone underground with the dead of the surrounding graveyard, and it seemed as if the dead were screaming with them.

The screaming woke the owls. It woke the weasels.

And somewhere in Black Spring, the witch stopped whispering . . . and listened.

The next morning, November 15, people began arriving before daybreak to assure themselves of a good spot. Just like at the Wicker Burning two weeks earlier, the intersection was blocked with crowd barriers that were placed in a circle around the wooden scaffold. The scaffold itself had been built by Clyde Willingham's construction company: a six-foot-high platform, nine feet square, with something on it that looked like an A-frame swing made of wooden trestles. The crowds gathered far out into the rainy narrow streets around the intersection. It was typical overcast New York weather and they all wore ponchos and rain hoods that glistened in the light of the streetlamps, but they were considerate enough to leave their umbrellas at home in order to keep from blocking the view. Sue's Highland Diner did a brisk business selling steaming coffee and cocoa from an outdoor stand to ease the pain of waiting. Those lucky enough to have friends living in nearby houses sat high and dry at upstairs windows. Many of the old and rich had gathered in the rooms of The Point to Point Inn, which had been made available at criminal hourly rates to compensate for the necessity of transferring Outsiders to out-of-town accommodations.

Of course Robert Grim was in charge of the practical implementation of all of this. He had hermetically sealed off the town on all sides, put up fencing, and posted voluntary patrol officers at the borders. It was tricky, but with careful planning, the roads only had to be closed off for one hour before the first flush of rose began bleeding into the east. As all retailers had been ordered by the Council to reschedule or cancel Outside services, the roadblocks went almost unnoticed, and only a few cars had to be turned away.

Robert Grim was disgusted. He was disgusted by all of it. He was disgusted by the people and their hypocritical, disguised lust for blood. He was disgusted by their opportunism and their treachery. He was disgusted by Mathers, by the executioner, by Katherine, and by the boys who had stoned her. And he was disgusted by himself, because he didn't have the guts to stand up to this disgusting circus.

At a few minutes past 6:30, the big moment finally arrived. Out of Crystal Meth Church proceeded the court, through the cordoned-off alley across Temple Hill Cemetery to the scaffold. Up front was Colton Mathers, imposing and severe, flanked by the two Council members who had voted in favor of the sentence. They were closely followed by a group of security guards led by Rey Darrel. Jaydon Holst, Justin Walker, and Burak Şayer were brutally dragged forward in iron chains, as inhumanely as they themselves had driven the witch a few days earlier. Their upper bodies were stripped bare, and panic was written all over their faces. Behind a second group of security guards the executioner rounded off the parade wearing a ceremonial hood to cover his face, although everyone knew who he was.

There was no cheering. There was no uproar. There was only an uneasy, doubtful murmur that rose from the crowd. Now that the moment they all had been waiting for had finally come, now that they were able to see with their own eyes the monsters who had stoned Katherine, they all seemed to suddenly remember that, despite the terrible charges, these were also human beings, two of them still children—human beings they had lived with and with whom they would be forced to live in the years to come. Eagerness gave way to shame, excitement to uncertainty. Only when the procession reached the crowd standing at the bronze statue of the washerwoman, someone yelled *"Murderers!"*, and a number of no-brain cretins began to throw large pinecones at the prisoners did the crowd dare to look up . . . pale, but with glistening eyes.

Now they had a show to watch and they didn't have to reflect upon themselves.

Screaming, the boys tried to dodge the pinecones, which left nasty marks on their naked skin. One of the security guards took a hit on the cheekbone. Without a moment's hesitation, he and two others threw themselves onto the agitators to douse the fire before it spread.

Farther on, at least forty yards back on the east side of the intersection, Steve, Jocelyn, Tyler, and Matt stood facing the spectacle. Not much of the disturbance reached them at that distance, but they did sense the unrest, which was rippling through the crowd like rings in water. Steve and Jocelyn had had an all-out fight. Immediately after the vote on Tuesday night, Jocelyn had taken Tyler home because the boy couldn't take it any longer. She'd blamed Steve for not taking the initiative. Moreover, she was categorically opposed to having Matt attend the flogging. She had screamed at Steve—actually *screamed*—and Steve had screamed back that *she* had forbidden *him* to step up when the moment had been right for it. Now the sentence had been passed and all parents were obliged to bring children age ten and up to witness the frightening example being set. Skipping duty was a no-go.

Steve was hurt, but he understood that Jocelyn's anger and distress had to do with the situation. As she couldn't fight that, she turned on him.

Judging by the faces in the crowd, we're probably not the only household in Black Spring where the dishes were flying through the kitchen yesterday.

And so he threw his arms around his family and pulled them close, and he prayed—not to God, but to common sense—that they would get through this one way or another.

Jaydon, Burak, and Justin were led onto the scaffold. Wild with fear, their eyes raced over the crowds for a last way out, a last hope, a last trace of humanity. The guards tossed the chains—locked to their wrists with tie wraps—over the wooden A-frame, and pulled the other ends so far down that the boys were forced to raise their arms up in the air and stand on their toes. Then they linked the chains to the railing and left the scaffold, exposing the prisoners to the crowd. Their wiry bodies were pale and blue in the cold air, their jutting rib cages wet with rain. Three all-American boys in sneakers and jeans, hanging like animal cadavers in the slaughterhouse.

The Crystal Meth carillon began to play. The people in Highland Mills and Highland Falls would have thought there was an early morning funeral going on. The carillon played, and at the crossroads Jaydon screamed, *"People, you're not going to let this happen, are you?"* He had purple hypothermic blotches on his cheeks, and saliva flew from his lips. *"What kind of fucking freaks are you? Please, do something, while you still can!"*

But the crowd was unrelentingly silent as the executioner climbed up the scaffold.

With long slow steps he circled the condemned, the rod of the cat-o'-nine-tails in his right hand and the lead-tipped leather cords in his left. The hood with its holes and his muscular build made him look like a hideous vision from a horror flick. Justin tried to scramble away from the mask like a frightened animal, but he only swung on his chains, legs kicking in a jig, and his wailing could be heard in the distant streets. Burak spat at the mask, but the executioner didn't flinch and kept on going. With a yank of both hands he snapped the leather tails tight, making a threatening whipping sound that resounded through the crowd.

And Jaydon spoke to the mask, so softly that even the people in the first row couldn't hear, only the executioner himself. He said, "Theo, please. Don't do this."

And in that one brief moment that he faced his executioner, that moment of utter darkness that would remain with him forever, he knew it wasn't Theo behind the mask, but a torturer from bygone years, Katherine's year; a torturer whose name and face he didn't know and never would, because when this was over, when the mask came off, it would be 2012 again.

The executioner walked around behind him.

The carillon played.

People licked their lips.

People shut their eyes.

People prayed.

The cat-o'-nine-tails was raised.

With brutal, terrible lashes that reverberated against the surrounding buildings, the naked backs of the three boys were flogged. The nine knotted tails sliced through their skin, and like claws the lead balls sank into their flesh. The second lash already drew blood. The boys screamed their lungs out in sounds that were unearthly and animalistic, like pigs being flayed alive with blunt knives. One by one the flogger went past them, one by one the cat-o'-nine-tails ripped them open, one by one that dreadful, excruciating pain, with no time to recover, to gasp for breath, to plead for release.

The sound of the flogging rang out over the crowd, who looked on in terror. Each of them felt the lashes as if they had landed on their own skin. They rang out through the whole region, through the valley and down the river to the south. They caused molecules in the air to whirl for miles around. Even if you had held your ear against the metal skeleton of the Bear Mountain Bridge that morning you would have sensed the tremor of the lashes, as delicate as the flapping of butterfly wings. Yet nobody did, as nobody knew what was going on in Black Spring. The people in the daily rush-hour traffic between the towns of Highland and Peekskill were listening to WJGK and WPKF. On the road, on their way, on their phones, eating commuter breakfast bagels from paper bags. America was waking up. Good morning, America.

When the executioner raised his arm for the eighth lash, a shudder of alarm suddenly ran through the crowd. People began screaming and pointing, and words were whispered from mouth to mouth: "The witch . . . Katherine . . . the witch . . . Katherine . . . the witch is here . . ." Everyone on the west side of the intersection looked up at the same time and saw Katherine van Wyler standing on the center balcony of The Point to Point Inn. Maybe it was a burst of collective delusion, or maybe it was a dark miracle, because as soon as they noticed her, every soul in the crowd saw the same nightmarish vision: The witch's evil eye was open. Like a shepherd over her flock, she looked out over the torture unfolding at the intersection . . . and *laughed*.

In a heartbeat, the vision vanished, but everyone was convinced that they had seen it. Had *lived* it. Katherine was indeed standing there, but of course her eyes and mouth were stitched-up, just as they always had been. Yet her appearance in their midst did not seem like an accident. From one moment to the next everyone knew with unshakeable certainty that the witch had set this all up, that with her degenerate whispering she had somehow brought out the very worst in all of them as part of some diabolical plan. How else could they, such righteous people, have unresistingly become entangled in such savage, depraved, and immoral practices?

This realization evoked such a primordial fear in the throng that they scattered in blind panic, stumbling about and trampling each other underfoot. It was total pandemonium. The people on the east and south sides of the intersection didn't realize what had happened, but soon the tumult spread there as well, and everyone began pushing back to get the hell away. Even Colton Mathers did nothing to stop the fleeing crowd.

Only the executioner appeared to be unaware of the sudden change in atmosphere. He had finished his work on Burak and Justin. They hung from their chains, writhing in pain, their backs a chaos of open flesh, the seats and legs of their jeans dark purple, and their heads drooping down like an imitation of the passion of Christ. With undiminished vigor, the executioner continued to flog the bloody, unconscious body of Jaydon Holst, which shook like a puppet with every lash.

When the executioner had finally counted twenty lashes, the church bells fell silent. The large number of people still present at the intersection slunk away in disgrace and shame, following the crowds who had stampeded off at the sudden appearance of the witch. Some looked up at Katherine and made a gesture to fend off her evil eye, but most just gazed in the direction they were heading: away from *there*. No one spoke. Many wept. Everyone wanted to erase the event from their memories and no one, no one, would mention it once they got home.

The security guards climbed onto the scaffold to release the mangled bodies. They were carried away on stretchers—facedown—and taken in a van to the office of Dr. Stanton, general practitioner, for proper treatment. It took a long time for the van to clear a path through the throngs of people. The scaffold was destroyed—the blood-spattered planks would meet the wood chipper that same day. Street sweepers came in to clean up the intersection. The Point to Point Inn hung a canopy over Katherine, and the roadblocks at Route 293 were taken away. By about nine o'clock, there was no sign whatsoever that earlier that morning almost three thousand people had gathered at the intersection and had unanimously been swept away in mortal fear.

A new day had dawned in Black Spring.

TWENTY-TWO

NOVEMBER PASSED LIKE an unwanted guest, overstaying its welcome. When the first day of December finally came, Tyler felt exceptionally relieved. He had wrestled with his midterms, but luckily the drop in his grades wasn't as bad as he had feared. Only Spanish was a fuck-up. During the spring semester he'd have to pull out all the stops to get a satisfactory grade on his finals.

Like everyone else in Black Spring, Tyler was trying hard, bit by bit, to resume normal life after November 15, to forget the events of that day, as well as to shake off his guilt. Eventually he succeeded, more or less. The tension between his parents had been palpable throughout the house during that period. It was probably unreasonable to blame himself for saddling his father with his secret, but he did anyway, and no amount of rational thinking could change it.

Matt had nightmares for a while, and one afternoon Jocelyn confided in Tyler that Matt had wet his bed. Tyler felt sorry for his little brother. He helped him brush Paladin and Nuala that evening, and although they didn't talk about it, they both valued the rare moment together. Not long after that, Tyler asked if he could use Matt's laptop to google some homework. When he opened Safari he saw a gay porn site in Matt's history. Tyler bit his lip, pretended he hadn't seen it, and realized he loved Matt more than he would ever say out loud.

A week after the fifteenth, Robert Grim came over to return his laptop and iPhone. He took Tyler aside and told him with a meaningful look, "No matter what you did, if you do it again, I'll see it. Is that clear?"

Tyler turned full sunset and looked at the floor in silence. Did Grim know? Of course he did. Or at least he had strong suspicions. He must have seen the quarantine for the *OYE* website URL. Why hadn't he taken action, or at least said something to Tyler? It was beyond him— until that evening, as he lay in bed and realized that if *OYE* had leaked, the conservative Council probably would have shut down the entire Internet in Black Spring in response. Grim, that badass son of a bitch, had kept his mouth shut to prevent Black Spring from turning into a second North Korea. Tyler fell asleep with a smile on his face, and the next day his conscience felt just a little lighter.

There came a day, early in December, when only after coming home from school and seeing the empty spot that had once been occupied by Fletcher's basket was Tyler reminded of the dog's death, the nightmare in the woods that had followed it, and the horrific stoning. Tyler was surprised and felt a little guilty, as if he would be held accountable for trying to leave it all behind. But time passed, and some wounds healed faster than others . . . although there would always be a faint scar to remind him.

On Jocelyn's birthday, December 4, the weather was stormy and bleak. The house, which had been so highly charged for so long, felt as warm and cozy as ever. The VanderMeers came over with a birthday cake. Laurie came, too, and was allowed to stay overnight. Tyler had put effort into making a photo collage of the family—including Fletcher—and Matt had written a hilarious poem for Jocelyn that made her laugh until she cried. After Jocelyn opened her presents, Tyler was surprised to discover two early Christmas presents for the kids, which they unwrapped in front of the fireplace. Tyler's came in a flat box. When he tore off the paper and saw it was a new MacBook, he looked at his dad with his mouth open wide. Steve nodded with a warm smile. *This one's without keyloggers,* the smile said. Tyler was deeply moved by his dad's trust, and did his best to keep from tearing up. He swore with boyish loyalty never to betray that trust, and he gave his dad a big hug.

There was a lot of hugging that night. It was as if everyone in the family felt a need to touch skin. At one point Tyler saw his parents sitting together on the couch, their hands tightly interlocked. They didn't notice him looking. For a while, Tyler had hardly dared to wonder how things would go between them from here on out, but at that moment Katherine seemed very far away.

After Jocelyn's birthday, the depressing and somber weather broke and they had a week of moderate frost. It had snowed, and during the sunny days that followed, the woods glistened crisp and clear in all their splendor. The horrific events that were bearing down not only on the Grant family but on all of Black Spring with the slow certainty of approaching asteroids would bring an end to the beautiful week, and every possible beautiful week that was to come. But that week, everything still seemed fine. Not exceptional, the way some days in every human life are exceptional, but just normal, and perhaps that's enough. TylerFlow95 made a video blog on his YouTube channel for the first time in two months. Regular viewers may have noticed that Tyler didn't laugh as much as he had before, but he did a pretty good job, and Tyler himself was proud of it. He and his girl saw a lot of each other that week, kindling renewed passions. Tyler was loyal in every way he could be, and it was exhilarating not to have to think about honesty for a while.

That Saturday Steve told him that Jaydon, Justin, and Burak were finished with their stretch at Doodletown and would be returning over the next few weeks under psychological supervision. Tyler absorbed the news mostly untouched. Until then, the only emotion he had allowed himself to feel was a vague missing of Burak, the way you missed an old friend who's grown apart over time, maybe even beyond repair . . . and Doodletown wasn't exactly the place you'd send a get-well card to. He didn't give it much thought until the following Wednesday, when he was biking through town and saw a broken figure lurching through the snow along Deep Hollow Road, hunched down in his coat, his face overshadowed by a baseball cap. At first Tyler took it for an old man oddly dressed in a young dude's clothes—until their eyes met in one frozen moment and he saw it was Jaydon. A shock jolted through Tyler's body. Jaydon was badly emaciated, his cheekbones jutting out like a skull, and he walked slowly, his body slouched over. His hands trembled as if he were suffering from Parkinson's. His eyes were dull and dead, and there wasn't even the slightest sign of recognition in them. Deeply upset, Tyler stood on his pedals and raced home.

That night, after Jocelyn had gone upstairs, he and Steve were on the couch watching TV when Tyler suddenly burst into tears. He cried long and hard and Steve calmed him, held him tight, told him everything was all right. But nothing was all right, nothing could ever be all right, because it was the last time they would hold each other, and what would they have done differently if they had known? What could have been less perfect than that intimate embrace of a father and his son? Jocelyn came hurrying down the stairs in her slippers and gazed at Steve with worried eyes, but Steve nodded to her and she left them alone. This was a moment for the two of them. For a long time they sat there, enfolded in each other's arms. Tyler didn't need to talk, and that's the way he preferred it. His dad understood. He loved his dad. His dad loved him.

Looking back, that may have been the only thing they'd be sorry for later on: that they hadn't said it out loud.

-+-|-|-|-

JUST BEFORE FOUR o'clock the next morning, the casement stay in the bedroom window, which was slightly ajar, was lifted up by a long, slender instrument. The window was carefully pulled open. Cold air rolled into the bedroom. The hinges squeaked softly, like a watchman's futile warning, but Tyler slept through it all.

Pale hands took hold of the windowsill and a shape hoisted itself laboriously into the room. It moved with much greater difficulty than Tyler had a few weeks before, after his nighttime adventure in the woods, but it succeeded nevertheless, driven by a distinct willpower.

The shape lowered itself onto the floor and stood there, unmoving. Then it crept up to the bed.

A floorboard creaked.

Tyler moved in his sleep, turning away from the noise.

The shape didn't move.

After some time, it crept closer.

Tyler was lying on his stomach, one naked arm raised above him, his left cheek flat on the mattress. He slept when the figure took something from its pant pocket, something that lit the room with a pale, artificial light. Fingers groped over the touch screen, searching for something that everyone else had overlooked.

They found it.

As the shape brought the iPhone to Tyler's ear, its hands trembled so violently that it had to grasp its wrist with the other hand to hold it still. It pressed the iPhone against Tyler's ear and pushed PLAY.

Tyler mumbled in his sleep. After a while the mumbling turned to moaning, but he didn't wake up.

When it was over, the shape played the file again.

And again.

And again.

PART 2

-|-|-•-|-+|-|-|-•-|-|-|-|-|-|-|-

2NITE? #death

TWENTY-THREE

AS IN SO many fairy tales, the cruelest part is often overlooked: It's not the depravity of the witch, but the mourning of the poor woodcutter over the loss of his children.

As a doctor, Steve Grant knew that being prepared for the death of a loved one dulled the sharpest edges of pain by helping people gradually adjust to the idea of losing someone precious, not only by allowing them to take in the mourning process in small doses, but also because the willingness to accept the worst would soften the blow. Psychological bullshit, of course, and not a luxury Steve had been permitted. The horrors had struck with such sudden and relentless force that they had blasted his brain into a place of darkness with one terrifying stroke. The man who woke up on that fateful Friday morning of the fourteenth, shaved, and went to the Newburgh Mall with Jocelyn after work was simply no longer present in the man who laid himself to rest that night on the floorboards beside Tyler's bed—not in it, because Steve couldn't bring himself to erase Tyler's imprint from the mattress.

What had completed the darkness was that last ghastly torment, that unsavory, fairy-tale cruelty: that they hadn't been able to cut his body loose . . . because *she* had been with him.

He was vaguely and somewhat disturbingly aware that they ought to be together as a family now, but in the twilight realm that Steve inhabited, such an idea had little meaning. Comfort and support were mere concepts. Steve was lost in shock, far removed from a stage of manageable grief, and was simply unable to offer or receive consolation. Besides, there was no family, as such, anymore—that unit had been destroyed. Right now, Jocelyn was sitting in a bucket chair in the coldly illuminated waiting room of St. Luke's Cornwall Hospital in Newburgh—*her* child was still alive, Steve thought spitefully—and Mary VanderMeer was seeing to her, as was her father. She would have to manage on her own for the time being.

Sometime that evening the phone had rung, and moments later Pete had come in with red-rimmed eyes. Steve couldn't say exactly when that was because his sense of time had been knocked for a loop, but the mortician from the funeral home (which had the oddly macabre name of Knocks & Cramer) had already left and he had sat at the dining room table, facing an untouched plate of Chinese takeout. It was mid-September, Tyler and Matt were sitting across from him and provoking each other with Tyler's GoPro.

"They were able to clean out most of Matt's right eye," Pete said. "They pumped his stomach, and he's out of danger. But his left eye is a different story, because the adhesive has settled in the cornea. It had hardened even before he was brought in."

"Yes," Steve said. The late summer sunshine slanted into the room. *I bet you don't want to know what I think,* Matt was saying into Tyler's lens, and Tyler said, *No, I do not, brother-who-smells-like-horse. I'd rather you took a shower.*

"Steve?"

Steve suppressed a grin, then looked up at Pete in confusion. "Yes?"

"There's a real chance of permanent injury, do you understand that? It started etching onto his cornea. He may be blind for life."

"Right, okay," he said. He had absolutely no idea what Pete was talking about. In his mind, Tyler said, *Let's bring the question closer to home. If you had to let somebody die,* o padre mio, *who would it be: your own kid or the rest of our town?*

All traces of the grin instantly disappeared from Steve's face.

"Did you hear what I just said?" Pete asked insistently.

"Yeah, right."

Pete grabbed his hand. Curious how delicate and soft his neighbor's hand felt. *Curiously unbecoming,* he thought. "Steve, you've got to go to them," Pete begged. "I'll drive you to Newburgh. They need you now. Your wife needs you. I know it's a mess, but damn it, man, you have another son and he's in the hospital fighting for his life." He raised and dropped his hands. "Goddamn it, it's not good for you to be here right now. . . ."

He started crying again, and Steve, who had been oblivious to most of what Pete had told him, slowly raised his head. His consciousness had reached a rare here-and-now moment, and he knew that he had to cling to the *here,* although he wasn't sure why. "I can't go, Pete," he said. His voice was calm and polite. "I have to stay here."

But Pete's shoulders were shaking uncontrollably. Steve put an arm around him and thought, *I'm comforting my neighbor for the death of my son.* The irony was absurd, and Steve had to bite his lip to keep from laughing out loud. Laughing would be considered inappropriate, he supposed. He felt a stab of pain and his face twitched. Oh, that's right: His lower lip was swollen, purple, torn. He had bit it to shreds before they had found him that afternoon, crouching against the banister on the landing upstairs, knees drawn up, fist jammed into his mouth, eyes bulging, throat swollen, hair standing on end. Now the blood was seeping into his mouth, and its taste of copper wire was good, pulling his dangerously drifting mind back to reality. If he were to laugh now, he'd probably start screaming soon afterward, and then he'd lose his mind.

That's politically correct, Dad, said the Tyler in his head, and that set off the time loop all over again, except now Steve tried to remember what the last words were that he had heard Tyler say that morning . . . and he couldn't.

-|-|-|-|-

WHAT HE DID remember with crystal clarity were the infinitely trivial moments before they came home. Like sheets of tracing paper, his mind tried to lay them over what had taken place at home in an effort to find reference points and similarities: *What was he doing when we left Walmart? What were we doing when he took the rope from the stable?* Nothing came of it but the hellish refrain of fragmented memories: *If only . . . If only . . . If only . . .* A torture machine that lashed into his brain and fed on his feelings of guilt.

He and Jocelyn had both finished work early and had decided to do some Christmas shopping, although they ended up mainly strolling in and out of coffeehouses and candle shops. They had already given the boys their big presents on Jocelyn's birthday after the November low, so for Christmas they had decided to keep it simple but festive. Steve wanted to pick up some special meat at the Walmart Supercenter, and Jocelyn was looking for a nice outfit to wear the day after Christmas when they were due to fly to Atlanta to visit her father for a few days. There was no indication that today wouldn't be like any other day. The air wasn't any heavier or more oppressive than usual; the people who elbowed their way through the mall were as inconsiderate as they always were. Steve and Jocelyn took a minute to watch and clap politely as a group of street dancers coalesced from the crowd and performed an impromptu routine in front of The Bon-Ton. And all the while, an unspeakable drama was unfolding at home.

Now, in the coal-chute darkness of his shock, and sitting in Tyler's bedroom where everything still breathed of Tyler, Steve wondered— his thoughts calm and composed, but treacherously irrational, had he been able to judge them with full lucidity—what they would have done if they had known. Could they have prevented anything? How tempting it was to blame Jocelyn for wanting to browse in Barnes & Noble so long, or himself for insisting on stopping at Starbucks—oh, motherfucking idiot, how could he have been so stupid? If only they had come home sooner. . . .

They had loaded their bags into the Toyota. From the parking lot, where most of the traffic turned right toward I-84 and I-87, they took a double left onto Broadway. It was only a couple of traffic lights to 9W, which would take them out of the city and switchback to the left into

Storm King State Park. From that point it was only five miles down Route 293 to Black Spring. Five miles between them and what hung irrevocably over their heads, like the crescent scimitar of the pendulum, the legendary torture machine of the Spanish Inquisition. And with every mile they covered, the glistening steel descended ruthlessly upon them, the whoosh of the razor blade coming closer and closer: first right, then left, then right, then left, a violent antique clock that heralded the end of everything they knew, everything they loved.

The ride home. Every detail sparkling like a gem in his mind. The low-hanging sun that blinded his eyes from the rearview mirror. The pale light over the Hudson. Jocelyn's suggestion that they eventually get a new dog. Every time he reexperienced it all, he wanted to scream at the phantom-Steve and phantom-Jocelyn, to make them turn around and drive away, far away, as if by doing so they could negate what had happened. But it was like watching a horror movie in which the dramatic finale had already been decided upon, and they were driving inevitably toward it.

Past the golf course, bearing off to the right up Deep Hollow Road. Crossing the creek, into the driveway. The house stood empty in the December sunshine, holding its breath. They carried the bags to the front door and Jocelyn laughed at his awkward struggle to haul all the bags and stick the key in the lock at the same time. Steve knew what was coming now. She kissed him, and the Walmart bag slipped from under his left arm and hit the ground, out of reach. Jocelyn leaned over to help him, said he was lucky it hadn't been the Christmas tree balls. Laughter broke the silence in the house—a silence they had become accustomed to since Fletcher wasn't there to jump all over them, wagging his tail and barking like the good dog he was.

The hallway; the stairs. Oh, God, the stairs.

What waited for them upstairs, now only forty seconds away.

Jocelyn went on to the dining room to open the mail, Steve to the kitchen to fill up the freezer. At that moment, a sudden draft stopped him dead in his tracks, and he looked up. Steve wasn't superstitious, but he knew that everyone was endowed with certain biorhythmic qualities that functioned like premonitions, and it was as if he could already hear the distant shrieks from the torture chamber. That draft, that gust of whirling air, was the steady swing of the pendulum, now just inches above him, and only seven hours later Steve would lie in Tyler's bedroom wrestling and writhing to free himself from the leather straps that bound him to the rack.

He closed the freezer door and picked up the bags of presents. Back to the hallway, up the stairs. Steve tried to cry out to him: *Get the fuck away from there, only twelve more seconds, twelve seconds and everything is going to come to an end, now only ten, ten seconds and the blade will have descended far enough to* . . .

But he didn't listen. He walked up the stairs . . . because he didn't know.

He had thought there would be enough time before dinner to go for a short run.

The door to the bedroom opened and Pete VanderMeer came in. He was startled when he saw Steve sitting on the floor beside Tyler's bed. What Steve didn't know was that most of the blood vessels in his eyeballs had burst, shrouding his eyes in a red film.

"No, get the hell out of here, this is bullshit," Pete said. He pulled Steve up by the arm. Steve wanted to protest, wanted to keep the air that Tyler's lungs had exhaled that same morning from entering Pete's lungs, or worse, from escaping through the door; because Tyler was *his, he* wanted to make sure that air was preserved. He wanted to keep Tyler alive.

"Now, listen to me: You're in no condition to make decisions, so you're going to do as I say. We're going to the hospital. Your wife is in bad shape. Mary is doing all she can, but you need each other, now more than ever."

He directed him out of Tyler's room, touching Tyler's door where Tyler had left his fingerprints. Steve willingly let himself be led out, mainly because Pete had to be removed before he erased all traces of Tyler's presence.

"I'll stay with you guys so Mary can come home and get some sleep. Lawrence is with Mary's parents in Poughkeepsie. She didn't want him . . ."

. . . *to be here in Black Spring,* Steve heard himself completing the sentence. A vicious jolt shot right through his heart. *Good idea. If she got Tyler, it stands to reason that Lawrence is next, right?*

Pete took him to the landing, and for the second time that day, Steve was confronted with the sight of his youngest, that delightfully happy kid who could sometimes drive him up the wall, but who was now halfway down the hallway, sitting on the floor, his head thrown back. He had sealed his own eyes with Liquid Nails construction adhesive and his mouth was twisted in a horrible, silver smile. That was because it was stuffed with death caps. Matt was drooling. Chunks of the poisonous toadstool were dribbling down his shirt. He was trapped in the middle of a fairy ring that was growing through the cracks in the floorboards, and it was as if he thought the only way to free himself was to eat them all. *But every time he picked one, a new toadstool popped up in its place and the ring closed around him once again.*

The caulking gun lay outside the ring on the floor.

Matt had witnessed something that had stripped him of his sanity in a single, dazzling stroke.

Steve turned around and, quite consciously, felt the steel of the pendulum slice his body in half. He felt himself voiding, as if his intestines had fallen out through the hole, but it wasn't anything physical that slid away from him; it was everything he had ever been up to this point. The sensation was so real that it almost made him laugh.

Tyler had hanged himself with a length of rope from the stable. He had thrown it over the crossbeam, wrapped it around his neck, and kicked the stool away. The fall had had little effect and had not broken his neck. Instead, death had come slowly and painfully, had taken him with his full consciousness intact.

Dry traces of tears ran from his glazed, swollen eyes. There was horror on his death mask, and a deep, dark sorrow.

And only now did Steve see Katherine van Wyler standing erect and gaunt behind the dangling corpse—the Black Rock Witch, who, like the Red Death, had come like a thief in the night, and now he knew, now he knew for sure: Tyler, his son, his Tyler, was dead.

As Pete VanderMeer led him across the landing seven hours later, he began to scream.

TWENTY-FOUR

NOT SENDING MATTHEW Grant straight to St. Luke's in Newburgh was the most difficult decision of his career, but Robert Grim took the responsibility and accepted the consequences. The absolute low in a nightmare of already unprecedented proportions was only reached when Jocelyn, screaming, was pulled from the stairway over and over again while Steve sat downstairs at the dining room table and stared into the void with such ghastly concentration that it seemed as if his entire brain had simply been erased.

It was Mary VanderMeer who had called Grim. He and Warren arrived at the Grant house only three minutes later, just as Walt Stanton, the GP, was pulling up—*Here again,* he thought with a shiver, as if the curse was somehow concentrated on that particular place and had now reached full power. Pete told him that he and his wife had been startled by the terrible screaming and had immediately come over to help out. Not that there was much they could do, but at least they had pulled the parents away from their dead son, and that was good.

Matt was lying on his back on the marble countertop and Mary and Jocelyn were pouring cold water from the tap over his face. When Stanton saw the remains of the toadstools in the sink he asked sharply whether Matt had ingested them. Without waiting for an answer he flipped the boy on his belly and stuck his finger down his throat to make him vomit.

In a flash, Grim saw Matt's eyes.

Oh, Jesus, those eyes.

The opaque, ivory-colored plastic layer made it seem as if his eyeballs had been punctured with needles, had drained out, and then congealed again in their sockets.

While Warren helped with Matt, Grim ran up the stairs, and that's where his emotions set out on their flight of madness. Tyler Grant, that charming, sympathetic local boy, a mere teenager, had hanged himself from the crossbeam. The reason was instantly clear: She was standing right behind the dangling body. Abruptly Grim's field of vision turned pearl gray. All sound was muted; Jocelyn's wailing faded into the distance. He bit his tongue viciously and waited for the world to swim back into focus. He forced himself to flip the switch. Grief would have to wait; right now the important thing was to secure everyone's safety.

Stanton climbed the stairs two steps at a time and slapped his hand over his mouth. "Sweet Jesus. Oh, sweet Jesus."

Tyler's bare feet hung a yard above the floorboards, toes down, Katherine's dirty, bedraggled dress behind them.

"What do you usually do in cases like this?" Grim asked.

Stanton looked at him, shocked, failing to grasp what he was saying.

"Suicide, I mean."

"Oh." Stanton shook his head vacantly, running his hand through his hair. "I'll have to report it to the district attorney. The state troopers will want to carry out an investigation, certainly after what happened to his brother."

"Right, but *she'll* have to be gone first."

Stanton looked with loathing at the perfect fairy ring of toadstools, which were growing from the cracks between the floorboards halfway across the landing. Grim hadn't even noticed them . . . and the sight so horrified him that his flesh began to creep and his legs began to stagger. He summoned all his strength to force his reason and intuition to focus on what needed to be done.

"Those are death caps," Stanton said. "Robert, I've got to get that boy to the hospital."

"Impossible. If you take him in like this they'll call in the troopers right away. If we don't report it along with Tyler's suicide, they'll suspect parental abuse and start making inquiries."

"But he's got to go to the hospital!" Stanton almost shouted. "I don't know how much he's eaten, but that fungus is deadly. And those eyes—"

"Take him to your office and do the best you can do for him."

"You know I can't do that. I've sworn an oath as a physician."

"And I've sworn an oath as the HEX chief of security. I'm taking responsibility. Do what I say: Help his little brother."

"I *can't* do anything for him at home! What if it takes three hours for her to go away? That kid is in mortal danger! These people have already lost one son, Robert."

Grim's eyes passed over the dark spot in the crotch of Tyler's jeans. In dying, the boy had released his bladder. Grim turned away. Why did it have to be so cruel, so undignified? It was beyond him. Nevertheless, he finally felt the familiar calm descend on him that he recognized from his years of dealing with fucked-up, hectic situations, which allowed him to turn off his morality with only a dim, oppressive sense of pain, like anesthesia wearing off. Stanton couldn't do that. What bothered him probably wasn't the idea of breaking his oath with the AMA—risky as that was—but the terrible truth of what had happened. Grim grabbed his shoulders. "Listen, Walt. Don't you think I wish there was another way out of this mess? But in emergency situations, the interest of the town comes before the interest of individuals, you know that. We have no choice. We can only hope that the parents don't catch on. I'll let you know as soon as we're done here. Now, hurry up and get going. I don't care how you do it, but save the boy, for God's sake."

Stanton remained where he was for two seconds, torn by doubt, but then he did something unexpected: He walked up to Tyler, reached up, and closed his eyes. It was a tender, compassionate gesture, and Grim was glad he had done it. Then he ran down the stairs and Grim called after him, "Make sure the parents don't notice!"

Stanton left with Matt, and soon Grim heard his car in the drive-way. That was one less thing to worry about. Yet the next few minutes were a succession of chaotic fragments. Jocelyn's initial hysteria had turned into confusion. She wanted to start calling people, and Grim had to tell her that the calls would have to wait. Mary sat down with her on the couch. At one point she said she had to take the chicken breasts out of the freezer for tonight, and Mary assured her that it had been taken care of. Grim grew worried. He looked to Steve for help, but Steve was still sitting at the dining room table, numb and not able to move. It was twenty minutes before Jocelyn noticed that Matt was gone, and Grim told her that Stanton had taken him to the hospital. Jocelyn began to cry and wanted to go back to Tyler. It was a fucking mess.

While the VanderMeers took care of their neighbors, Grim took Warren upstairs. They discussed their options. Katherine stood mo-tionless behind her prey, like a lioness guarding a carcass from a pack of rapacious hyenas eager to gnaw on the remains. With growing horror, Grim sensed that she wasn't going to leave. This was not uncalculated. This was an ordeal.

She wanted Tyler's parents to suffer.

Just as she had once suffered.

At least her intentions are clear now, right?

Warren shook his head. "I don't know, Robert. We've never had to move her before."

That was true. HEX was endlessly creative when it came to hiding Katherine, but protocol told them never to touch her. If they were to provoke the witch, someone else in town could die, someone with a weak heart or a thin cerebral cortex . . . someone who would sense her vibrations and simply drop down dead.

Across the landing, Katherine stood motionless.

She was whispering her depraved words.

She was challenging them.

Come and touch me, fellas. Come and touch me. Let's see who's going to die this time?

Suddenly Warren ferociously kicked the death caps, breaking the fairy ring. One of the buttons rolled right up to her corpselike feet.

It came to halt touching her gnarled, brown toenails.

"Katherine," Warren said, and he cleared his throat. "Hey, Katherine."

Grim's mouth became as dry as parchment and a choked, nerve-jangling moan escaped his lips. He wanted to pull Warren back, but he felt nailed to the floor. It was tacitly understood that they would *never* speak to the witch. The fact that Warren was doing that now was almost more ghastly than everything else.

"You got what you wanted. The boy is dead." Warren's voice sounded gurgly and trapped, as if there were a glob of petroleum jelly stuck in his throat. "Let us do our work now and get the hell out of here."

Katherine stood there motionless.

No: The fingers of her right hand twitched.

Something was going on behind those stitched-up eyes.

She was mocking them.

Warren drew a step closer. "Hey, haven't you done enough?"

"Warren, stop it," Grim whispered, revulsed and stricken with a maddening fear. There was no doubt in his mind who in Black Spring was pulling the strings, and until this threat was behind them they were entirely at her mercy. "Get the fuck over here before you end up on a rope, too."

Time dragged on. Forty-five minutes and counting. They went downstairs. Grim tried to wake Steve from his shock, to no avail. Outside, the sky was bleeding.

Warren suggested they carefully push her away with brooms. Where to? Down the stairs, if necessary; the fall would make her disappear. Just like when those assholes used sticks to drive her into the tank at Philosopher's Creek in order to pelt her with rocks. Grim saw the dark rings under Jocelyn's eyes and hesitated. Risk the life of some old bugger from town? Morality was shifting as surely as time itself.

Back upstairs. Warren with a broom, Grim with a mop. Cold drops of sweat tingled on their foreheads. With extreme caution they began poking Katherine gently with the ends of the handles. Her brittle body yielded, but she didn't budge—except she kept turning her dead, stitched-up face to wherever she felt herself being prodded.

It was as grotesque as it was loathsome, but Tyler's body was hanging in the way.

Neither of them dared to push the situation.

"I want to go to my baby!" Jocelyn's heartrending cry resounded from below. Grim and Warren exchanged startled glances, and soon Pete VanderMeer came upstairs. He was clearly overwhelmed, but he had brought an extra broom with him. Grim felt a deep appreciation for the man.

"How's it going downstairs?" he asked quietly.

"Messed up," Pete said. "How did you think it was going? But Mary's making her a nice pot of chamomile tea." He laughed briefly through his tears. It was absurd indeed: as if chamomile tea was the solution to such unutterable misery.

The three of them tried to force Katherine around Tyler's body to the right, and she finally took a staggering step to the side. Grim felt his heart pounding. Warren pushed harder . . . and in a flash the witch was *in front of* the hanging boy, right in their midst, and Grim could have sworn he heard her hissing. With a jolt the group sprang apart. Warren stumbled over his own feet and ended up on his ass in the remains of the fairy ring.

The rest unfolded with terrifying speed. *"Jocelyn!"* someone shouted from below—Mary, Grim realized—but in his shock he was too late to grasp what was happening, too late to stop her. All he heard were Jocelyn's swelling growls as she ran up the stairs, her teeth bared.

And with a swing that hit it right out of the ballpark, she smashed the nice pot of chamomile tea into the witch's face.

The effect was astonishing. Splinters of glass and boiling-hot tea water splashed onto the wallpaper, and Grim had to jump aside to avoid them. The witch doubled over and instantly disappeared. Screaming, Jocelyn let go of the plastic handle and threw her arms around the body of her dead son.

-+-|-|-|-

THE POLICE CAME and asked questions. Thank God Mary VanderMeer had already taken Jocelyn to St. Luke's, because Grim didn't think she'd be capable of answering without shooting off her mouth. After he had Pete call 911, Grim sat down with Steve at the dining room table and asked him if he thought he was able to make a statement.

Steve slowly absorbed his question, as if he were coming back from a dark, faraway place. With infinitely sad eyes he asked, "Will they take Tyler down then?"

That did it; Grim felt all this was becoming too much, even for him, and he took Steve in his arms, holding the mourning father as close as he could. "Yes," Grim said, glad he didn't have to look him in the eye, "that's what they're gonna do, buddy." He managed to keep himself under control, partly because he had to make a professional diagnosis: Steve was lucid enough to realize what had happened, which meant that he would probably also know what he could and could not tell the police.

Grim let him go and sat upright. "Steve, I have to ask you this. Is there anything . . . anything that can explain this?"

Steve slowly shook his head.

"Something he may have said?" When Steve kept shaking his head no, Grim continued: "I'm asking you this in confidence, not for the Council. If anything happened, I need to know about it for the sake of security. I know Tyler was working on that website of his, but I don't believe this had anything to do with that or it would have happened much earlier. We tracked his laptop over the past month and haven't caught him working on anything new. Do you know if he had other stuff going on? Where in God's name did it go wrong?"

"I don't know, Robert," Steve said finally, sincere and composed.

Grim looked at him, met his gaze, and believed he was speaking the truth. Steve was as perplexed as he was shocked. He decided to leave it for now; Steve would have enough on his mind. He patted him on the shoulder. "Take it easy, buddy. I'll call you tonight."

Steve said thanks and Grim handed the car keys to Warren, who would stay behind as a friend of the family to handle the state police. Grim himself was relieved to get out of the house. He could feel the presence of death hanging over it like a heavy, contagious veil, creeping up on him from the every corner. It was superstition, of course, but in this house it seemed as if death had been obeying the laws of darkness, with disaster begetting more disaster and spreading like a sickness. With legs of rubber Robert Grim fled to the back door. He didn't stop until he got halfway across the backyard, inhaling the evening air in deep gulps, head bent and thighs trembling.

Baffled and more or less nonfunctional, he set out toward the former visitor center. In order to avoid bumping into the police he took the trail through the woods, which rose up sharply along a fallow field where the ground fog silently reflected the moonlight. The subzero temperatures of the previous week had been followed by a thaw, and the air was heavy with moisture. Grim watched his breath form little clouds in the dark.

After a few minutes, he was sorry he had taken the forest trail.

He used his cell phone to light the way and quickened his pace. The hemlocks formed a massive black wall to his left. Elsewhere in the hills, more to the north or farther to the west, people would exercise their dogs, go for evening walks, or make love on summer evenings. But not here, not in these bewitched parts. In Black Spring, no one went out after dark.

The eyes of that little kid.

How could anyone do that to himself? Had Katherine made him do it, or had she shown him something so deranged that he had wanted to blind himself, in an eerie imitation of the witch herself? How far did her influence extend?

The sight of Jocelyn smashing the pot of chamomile tea in the witch's face suddenly came back to him, but this time when the glass shattered, blood sprang from his own eyes and he staggered, falling backward down the stairs. . . .

Get a hold of yourself, idiot.

But he was badly shaken and he couldn't ease his mind. It was something about the way the wind rose just then, the way it made the trees flail in the sky. Robert Grim hurried along, trying not to let the darkness get to him. Alone out here, his incredulity and bewilderment were being shaped into something manageable, and the questions began to arise. How could this have happened? In the almost thirty years that Grim had been serving as HEX security chief, Katherine had never attacked in this way. She had claimed no suicide victims since the ones who cut the corner of her mouth open back in '67. Everyone knew what Katherine's whispering could make you do, and no one would ever take the risk and expose themselves to it. Tyler and his friends may have been playing on the edge with their pranks and clips, but Tyler had been a bright kid, and he never would have made such an enormous mistake, would he? Now, much too late, Grim began to get the gnawing feeling that he may have made the wrong choice in failing to let the Council know about Tyler's activities.

Hindsight is twenty-twenty, my friend. With all due respect, you didn't do him any favors by keeping mum.

He stopped and turned around. Something was moving on the trail behind him.

His feet began to slip on the frost-covered roots. He regained his balance, and whatever it was that had moved out there—the mist or his own mind playing tricks on him—was now gone. Driven by a sudden sense of urgency, Grim began to run. It hit him all at once, a sudden, irrational fear and a terrifying premonition of approaching horror.

Something dreadful was coming.

It was all part of the same downward spiral of cause and effect. The box cutter slicing into Katherine's breast. The death of the dog. The bewitched creek. The stoning and the subsequent madness in town. Jaydon, who had tottered on the brink of death at the hands of the executioner, but had come out on the right side. And now Tyler.

The children dug holes outside the walls of the settlement and carried fruit crates out to put in their graves, walking in procession. Their parents thought they were possessed, and the game was seen as a bad omen.

Wincing at the sharp stitch in his side, Grim took the gravel path that ran past the old Hopewell home and finally reached Deep Hollow Road. The street was well lit, and he continued with a stumbling gait to the former Popolopen Visitor Center.

Sitting on the edge of the roof, above the frieze, was a tawny owl. The bird stared at him with sinister, glistening predator's eyes. Grim couldn't understand why it filled him with such a sense of disaster and gloom, but he clapped his hands sharply to chase it away. Much to his dismay, the owl didn't move, didn't even blink its eyes. Only when Grim picked up a stone and viciously hurled it did it flap its strong wings and fly away.

Inside, Grim learned that Katherine had turned up in a kitchen in Lower South. He summoned Claire and Marty to go to the house, send the residents to The Point to Point, and not lose sight of the witch for a single second. There were no reports of any chamomile-induced casualties. Grim stayed behind in the control center and began working his way through the security cam footage. He played the images over and over again, winding back and forth between key moments. He saw Matt coming home from the bus stop. He saw the deceptive stillness behind the dark windows of the Grant home. In what twilight zone had Tyler lingered before his death? Between the time Matt came home from school and the time his parents drove into the driveway an hour and a half later there was nothing, literally nothing to be seen. Given what was unraveling inside, it was a picture of surreal, ghastly normality.

Warren called from St. Luke's. Steve Grant had stayed behind in Black Spring with Pete VanderMeer and the funeral director and would come later. Matt had suffered severe gastrointestinal poisoning from ingesting the toadstools, but at least he was out of danger. Now the doctors were working on his eyes, but there was no guarantee that they could be saved. Warren wanted to stay in Newburgh in case the boy woke up and started talking—highly unlikely, but not impossible.

Grim hung up. As he began considering various strategies to keep the public shock in town under wraps, he couldn't shake the feeling that he was overlooking something essential, something he would have to find out about fast before disaster struck. It rang through his head like funeral bells. He tried to shift his focus to practical matters: the questions he would have to ask the parents, what things he could make public, whether to have the funeral in or out of town. What if Katherine were to appear during the funeral in front of friends and relatives from outside, like a pyromaniac who comes to watch his own fires?

Maybe she had planned it all. Maybe Tyler's death was part of some dark, preconceived scheme.

Grim jumped as if someone had said these words out loud. With eyes wide open and the flesh on his body suddenly creeping over his bones, he stared at his cell phone, which was beside him on his desk. Two seconds later it began to ring. Claire.

"Hello?"

"Robert, she's gone. She left just a second ago."

At first he didn't understand where the heavy, stale stench of corpse was coming from. "Okay, just come . . ." he began, but then he heard the whispering. He looked around, straight into the tormented, nightmarish face of Katherine van Wyler. Her shredded lips were pressed together into a grin, pulling the stitches tight. The open corner on the left moved with great concentration, and the corrupted words entered his mind. Grim dropped the cell phone with a shriek and stumbled backward, rolled across his desk, knocked a pen box onto the floor, and landed next to it on the other side.

At a calm and wary pace Katherine walked around the desk and stood in front of him.

"Robert? Robert!" came the tinny sound from the phone.

Grim scrambled away on his ass as the Black Rock Witch came closer and closer on her bare, gray feet. Her nails were a morbid yellow, long and curved at the tips. The iron chains clanked around her gaunt body. In a state of pure panic, Grim bumped up against the big screen and slid backward into a corner—ah, it always ended in a corner.

Moments later Katherine was bending over him, her body rigid, her lips at his ear. It was impossible to flee from the dead woman without touching her, so Robert Grim froze on the spot, stuck his fingers in his ears, and began to sing for all he was worth. But this time it was not Katrina & the Waves, this time his pitiful wailing was not a song at all; the notes that came out were atonal sounds of survival, meant to protect him from the witch's whispers, and all the while he was compelled to look into her stitched-up eye sockets and to breathe in her sickly stench of mud and death.

TWENTY-FIVE

MATT WAS KEPT in an induced coma until Saturday afternoon. At four o'clock, when Steve, Jocelyn, Milford Hampton (Jocelyn's father who had flown in from Atlanta), and Mary VanderMeer returned from an almost untouched lunch in the hospital courtyard, Matt woke up. Soon it was clear that he was not responding to any external stimuli, however, and he was given the alarming diagnosis of catatonic stupor. They found him in his hospital bed, his skin bleak and translucent, bandages over his eyes like a morbid facial mask deluxe. The ghastly thing was that his head was hovering a couple of inches *above* the pillow, held aloft by stiffened muscles. The attending physician told them that when he changed the bandages, the pupil in his right eye had shown no reflex at all. His left eye wouldn't respond to anything without a cornea transplant. Steve knew from his own medical experience what it must look like under that bandage: grizzly white and cloudy, as if there were no eyeballs at all.

Neither Steve nor Jocelyn had slept. Jocelyn had not wanted to go back to Black Spring, so they checked in to the Ramada Inn at Stewart International Airport, where Mr. Hampton was staying. Steve wasn't in any condition to see how Jocelyn was doing. At the breakfast buffet she looked like she was suffering from a bad case of the flu. She spoke in disjointed sentences. In her shock, she had completely forgotten Black Spring protocol: The witch kept cropping up in her string of babble, and at one point she announced to her father, "Katherine did it." Mary, who dealt with Jocelyn's malleable confusion in a surprisingly professional way, tried to calm her without contradicting her, and finally took her to the ladies' room.

"God, what a dreadful mess," Mr. Hampton said. His eyes were red-rimmed and he hadn't shaved. Steve had always liked Jocelyn's father, but he and Jocelyn had never been able to make their extended families a full part of their life—and now their two worlds, which lay miles apart, were sliding over each other in ways that felt most unnatural. "Steve . . . who is this Katherine that Jocelyn keeps going on about?"

Steve had been unable to say anything to his wife. While his mind kept replaying the critical moments in an eternal loop, he was threatened by a pain of such terrible magnitude that he quickly slipped back into his safe state of semiconsciousness. But at least this last bit had registered.

"I don't know," he said. And even though he understood at that early stage just how unfair it was to have to lie about the death of his son, he heard himself twist the truth with disconcerting ease. "She's in shock. Her sense of time is all mixed up. I wondered whether she may have known someone named Katherine in the past?"

"I don't know." Suddenly the old man began to cry. He bent over the table and grabbed Steve's hands with trembling fists. "I can't believe it. Tyler, suicide? I mean, why? Did you and Jocelyn really not see . . . anything . . . coming?"

As he spoke these last words, he shook Steve's hands fiercely. *No, sir,* Steve wanted to say, suddenly enraged. *Our dog was hanged in a tree last month, higher than any normal man can climb, and we had a couple of boys tortured in the town square. It was a kind of town fair, actually. But golly, we sure didn't expect anything like this. Tyler was such a . . .*

Suddenly he knew what his father-in-law was about to say, and a terrible panic clutched at his throat because he didn't want to hear the words spoken out loud. Yet they were, and it was like salt being rubbed into his gaping wounds: "Tyler was such a lively boy."

Yeah, such a lively boy, that Tyler, what a terrific kid he was. Why are you speaking about him in the past tense, you moron, as if he were no longer here, as if he were something that had already happened, closed and gone? What a lively boy. "Help me, Dad," he asked, *and what did I do? What did I do?*

Slowly Steve shook his head. "I don't know, Milford."

"And he really didn't leave a note or anything? I don't need to know what's in it, but it would do me good to know it existed."

"No. I don't know." Where the hell were Jocelyn and Mary? Steve wanted, *needed* this moment to be over.

Mr. Hampton pulled his frail hands back and cast his eyes down. "Is it possible that Tyler did that to his little brother himself? That it was a kind of . . . fit of insanity?"

Steve had to bite down hard on his already battered lips in order to control himself. With a trembling voice he said, "I don't know, Milford."

-+-|-|-|-

THEY WERE TAKEN to a small room to speak with Matt's doctor and a hospital psychiatrist. Warren Castillo was with them, too, to offer the necessary support . . . and to keep an eye on the both of them. Jocelyn seemed to be a bit more present than she had been that morning, and she didn't disclose any confidential information. Instead, she started to sob, making abundant use of the box of Kleenex on the side table.

After the anticipated questions, most of which remained unanswered, the doctor said, "There's one other sensitive matter I would like to discuss with you. At the present time, there is no available donor cornea for Matt. The sooner we help him, the greater our chances of fully restoring his sight. Would you consider allowing us to use Tyler's cornea for his brother?"

Somehow Steve had expected this, but it shocked him nonetheless. The psychiatrist said, "You don't have to answer right away. Take your time and think about it. Perhaps this is a way of imparting some meaning to his death, as terrible as it is."

Oh, sure, he thought. *Let's take the best of both of them and turn it into one son. There must be some sort of logic hidden here, but if there is, it's beyond me.* Yet he immediately said yes because it was the obvious thing to do.

"And you, ma'am? What do you think?"

Jocelyn wiped her eyes. "If you're okay with it, Steve, then let's do it. Tyler would have given anything for Matt."

There was a disquieting moment in which both the doctor and the psychiatrist said nothing. Warren raised his eyebrows and observed them carefully. Jocelyn took no notice since she was crying again. But Steve understood: They didn't believe her. Like Jocelyn's father, they were convinced that Tyler had turned on his brother with the caulking gun before he killed himself. Warren saw it, too, and was satisfied. Steve felt his heart tear in half. His son, his Tyler, had been forced to take his own life against his will, bewitched by a power far too great to comprehend, a power that had gotten to Matt as well, and they all thought Tyler had been crazy. Just some sorry-ass, fucked-up teen with a lust for blood, like the ones who ended up in the papers.

It was that profound injustice that made Steve cry for the first time: long, swelling sobs from a deep, dismantling grief. And just as he had not been able to comfort Jocelyn earlier on, so was she unable to comfort him now. They sat side by side in their chairs, alone and lost in their sorrow, and Steve didn't know if he would have been able to receive her comfort even if she had offered it.

Warren ushered them away to the hospital's Hudson View Cafe. The large window overlooked the wooded parking lot with the river flowing lazily behind it. The enormous Christmas tree on the circular drive was waving back and forth as the daylight wound down to dark. The warm spell of the morning had been dispelled by a raw, cold December evening. Not so far away, in the mortuary in a different part of this building, was his son, naked and dissected, and by now the anatomical pathologist would be removing all his vital organs.

"I'm so terribly sorry," Warren said, "but there are a few practical matters that we have to deal with before Knocks & Cramer show up and start organizing the funeral. Do you want Tyler cremated or buried?"

"Buried," Steve said almost straight out, and Jocelyn stared at him, astounded.

"Steve . . ."

They didn't have funeral insurance, although money was not a problem. Steve had always believed that they were not the kind of people who attached any symbolic value to the grave. They had told each other in the past that they wanted to be cremated after their death—hypothetically speaking, of course, the way you'd say these things when death seemed far away. But now he suddenly saw their friends and family coming home with them after the cremation ceremony and digging into the salads and quiches they had brought, just as Tyler was being shoved into an oven. The heat would scorch and blacken his soft skin, singe his hair, and in a matter of minutes break down the muscles that had formed the body of his son for so many years. Nothing would be left of Tyler but a pile of ash and smoke that whirled out of a chimney and was carried away into the cold, until his molecules settled on the roofs of a thousand houses. That was more than Steve could bear, and he knew that he wanted to keep his son close to him no matter what.

"We're going to bury him," he said again.

"Oh, Steve, I don't know . . ." Jocelyn said. "Tyler always wanted to get away from Black Spring, to discover what's out there. Wouldn't it be better if we scattered his ashes, at some proper place . . . ?"

But Steve refused to give in. He wasn't sure why. Maybe it was a selfish choice, but it felt important, as if something from the outside was inspiring him and he was obeying that inner voice.

"I want to keep him with us, Jocelyn. I want to be able to visit him."

"Okay, I'll let you decide," she said. It was Tyler, after all; if Matt had died, she would have made the decision.

"Where do you want to bury him?" Warren asked.

Next to Fletcher in the backyard, Steven thought suddenly, and he felt his body turn to ice.

"In Black Spring."

"I was afraid of that," Warren sighed.

"That a problem?"

"No. Of course not. You'll get every opportunity to do it your way, you can count on it. We're just worried—to say the least. Katherine's patterns have changed and it's freaking out everyone in town. We don't know what to expect."

"Warren, Tyler must have heard her whispering somehow. That's the only reasonable explanation, right? It was a horrible accident."

Warren lowered his voice. "She attacked Robert last night."

Steve and Jocelyn stared at him in shock.

"Don't worry, he's fine. We've all been knocked for a loop, that's all. We just don't get it—it looked like a deliberate attack."

"Why would she do something like that?" Jocelyn asked, and her voice, already quavering, now broke. "Why did she kill Tyler, Steve? I try not to think about it, but I keep seeing it over and over again, him hanging there . . . and then I see Matt stuffing those mushrooms into his mouth . . . That wasn't him, you know; *she* made him do it, *she* wanted to take Matt away from us, too. . . . And every time I try to remember Tyler's face, I can't . . . all I can see is *her* face, and her eyes are open . . . and she's looking at me . . ." Tears were spilling down her cheeks. "Oh, Steve, help me please, hold me now, would you?"

Help me, Dad.

Steve did. He took her in his arms and held her as she cried inconsolably into his shirt, but it did nothing for him. It felt like he was hugging a hunk of dough. All the while he kept looking out the window at the people walking down the circular drive in the howling wind, possessed by their own ghosts and evil memories. But they were going home, and their reasons for being in the hospital would slip away from them; at home, their children would be waiting for them under the Christmas tree. Steve suddenly saw before him a gruesomely clear image of children floating in big jars of formaldehyde under pine boughs; naked, swollen children's corpses in yellowish water, and one of them was Tyler, his eyes bulging and reflecting the Christmas lights.

-+-|-|-|-+-

TYLER'S VIEWING WAS on Tuesday. Because the only funeral home in Black Spring was at the Roseburgh home for the elderly, they opted for the sun parlor at the back of the Quiet Man. Tyler had always enjoyed going there to have root beers with his friends, and the bartender told Steve with tears in his eyes that he had always been an exemplary and charming sight.

Jocelyn's confusion hit an all-time high on Monday afternoon. She started imagining that none of these terrible things had really happened and having panic attacks. Steve had found her in her Limbo where she was pulling the strands out of the carpet one by one. Dr. Stanton had given her an antipsychotic in the evening and she had slept for the first time since Friday, which was at least a slight bit of progress.

Pete urged Steve to divide his attention among the remaining members of his family. He knew in his mind that his friend was right. Jocelyn was in a state of total collapse and Matt wasn't getting any better. Although the cornea transplant had been a success, there was no real sign of awareness. Yet Steve was unable to give his youngest son or his wife the attention they needed and probably deserved; his mind was overwhelmed by thoughts of Tyler.

Earlier that morning, Tyler had been taken to the Quiet Man in a light-colored, modern, plywood coffin. Steve and Jocelyn were both there and had spent a moment alone with him before the closing of the coffin later in the day. Tyler was dressed just as they had wanted him to be, in jeans, a white V-neck T-shirt, and his favorite cardigan—the same clothes he would have worn in life. The mortician had really done a fine job on him. Even the bruises from the rope, which Steve knew ought to have been visible on his neck, were gone.

He was so beautiful. His son. His Tyler.

He looked as though he were sleeping. So peaceful. So alive. An uneasy feeling crept over him that Tyler was *really* asleep and just waiting to open his eyes, stretch, and step out of his coffin. But the gentle throbbing of the generator underneath the cooling bed shattered that illusion. Tyler was decomposing from the inside out, a process that could only be slowed down a little. If you were to pull up one of his eyelids, you'd see a Styrofoam ball staring back at you; the pathologist would have pushed it in to fill up the socket.

Laurie arrived. Her parents hadn't been able to get off work for the viewing, she said, but they'd be at the funeral. Steve cried with her and then accompanied her inside.

"Can I . . . touch him?" she asked after a while.

"Of course, sweetheart," Steve said. She carefully took Tyler's hand in hers but quickly let go, startled perhaps by how cold and stiff it felt.

Yes, that's how it is, Steve thought. *You can let him go. It will hurt for a while, but your life will go on. Next summer you may have a new boyfriend, and Tyler will be nothing but a painful memory that gradually fades.*

"I just don't understand it," Laurie sobbed, wiping the tears from her eyes with her sleeve.

Steve felt a sudden electrical charge in the room that seemed to be directed at him. Now was the time he was supposed to ask whether she had noticed anything strange about Tyler . . . something that could explain his unexpected suicide. He realized it was expected of him, and that perhaps Laurie was hurt that he didn't involve her. But Steve couldn't. That charade would have to come later, not in front of Tyler.

"Neither do I, Laurie," he finally said, trembling.

Then came all the others. Tyler's death had hit like a bomb, both within the community of Black Spring and beyond. A strange, detached tension ricocheted across the back room of the Quiet Man that morning. It was about more than just the sharing of grief: It was the head-on collision of so many people from Black Spring with so many people from the outside, the people who knew and the people who didn't. Even the upbeat Owl City tracks—Tyler's favorite—playing in the background did nothing to ease the tension. It was as if the town borders were running straight through the tavern that morning, and those who lived on one side shunned those on the other. The townsfolk were frozen to the marrow. Tyler had been touched by Katherine. The witch's curse was upon him. It was so subtle that Tyler's extended family members, O'Neill buddies, Raiders teammates, and teachers from the outside didn't even notice it, but the procession shuffling in from the main room and past his coffin moved with a certain haste and got no closer than three feet from the cooling bed. The townsfolk hardly dared to look at Tyler; they crossed themselves or made gestures to protect them from the evil eye. When they came out through the back room of the Quiet Man, they were greatly relieved. It was ludicrous; Steve was disgusted. If Tyler hadn't been so well liked in town, the vast majority of these people wouldn't even have worked up the courage to come and see him out.

Halfway through the viewing, he took Jocelyn aside. She was as pale as a sheet and looked as if she were about to have a nervous breakdown. Her cheeks hung slack and her hands were trembling. "Are you going to make it?" he asked softly.

"I don't know, Steve. If I hear one more fucking cliché, I think I'm going to scream." She had obviously been overwhelmed by all the condolences, each one cutting deeper and deeper wounds, from the meaningless "Time heals all wounds" and "Life isn't always fair" to the not-very-promising "Seven lean years will be followed by seven fat years," and the utterly incomprehensible "On the one end they come, on the other they go."

"I mean, what are they trying to tell me, for God's sake?" Jocelyn asked, profoundly upset. "Do they really think I'm going to jump up, all better, and say, 'Oh, thank you, ma'am, I really didn't know that. In that case, it's not so bad after all then, is it?'"

"Hush now," he said, taking her in his arms. She started crying again, and when Mary saw how uncomfortable he was, she hesitantly took over. Steve wanted to show his gratitude, but Mary turned her eyes down with slight reproach. No one was good at this, he decided. They could only try and do the best they could.

Griselda Holst had brought an impressive meat pie. Steve didn't know what to do with it, but he didn't have the heart to reject the gift. Until Pete took it from him, he stood there clumsily with the pie in his hands. "I feel so terrible for you all," Griselda said, briefly touching Steve's arm. She kept glancing up at him and then looking down, as if she felt guilty just being a resident of the place that had cost Tyler his life.

"Thank you for coming, Mrs. Holst," Steve said coolly.

"I pray every night for your other son." She looked around and said in a muted voice, "I can't understand why Katherine would do something like this. He just wanted to help her, right? We've all seen that he was on her side."

Steve didn't know what to say. Speaking of sides struck him as absurd at best. "Thank you, Mrs. Holst. How is Jaydon doing?"

Again, those nervous, downcast eyes. "Not so well. But he'll pull through."

"I'm sorry about what happened. I want you to know that I was against it—against the way the whole thing was handled."

"That's nice of you to say. I have never held anything against you."

Held anything against me? Steve wanted to ask, but suddenly he understood, and for one brief moment a terrible insight shot through his head with sharp, paralyzing fear . . . and disappeared just as quickly, like a tidal wave that had exposed something in the shoreline and then washed over it again. Steve tried to hang on to it, but it got the better of him. All those people. All those words. How much pain could a man bear in his heart? Why did it all feel so meaningless? Right there and then, his grief seized him more intensely than ever, and Steve would have given anything, literally anything in the world, to undo it all, to go back a week and stay with his son for those last few days to prevent what had happened to him.

Perhaps that could have been the end of it: that intense, personal sorrow that would cripple their lives for a long time to come but eventually evolve into something bearable, until it became a memory at last. And perhaps the day would come when they as a family would be able to resume life without Tyler. But Griselda Holst had to be the first to say the witch's name out loud, so he focused his sorrow on Katherine van Wyler. And all Steve could think was: Why? Why would someone bear so much malice and make innocent parents suffer so terribly? The butcher's wife may have been a little eccentric, but she was right: Tyler had been on *her* side, goddamn it. He had wanted to protect her from those sons of bitches who had set all this in motion with their sick plot to throw stones at her. Tyler had wanted to help her; couldn't she have shown any mercy? After all, Katherine herself had been forced to kill her own, resurrected son, so how could she—

It hit him like a landslide. Before Steve's very eyes, the town café began to topple, and the black-clad people dissolved from his field of vision. As if from a distance he heard Griselda Holst say, *He just wanted to help her, right? We've all seen that he was on her side.*

Pete VanderMeer, on the night they had apprised the Delarosas of the situation: *It's October 1664 when Katherine's nine-year-old son dies of smallpox. Witnesses testify that they've seen her, dressed in full mourning, burying his body up in the woods. But a few days later, the townsfolk see the boy walking around the streets of New Beeck as if Katherine had raised him from the dead, like Jesus did with Lazarus.*

He just wanted to help her, right?

If raising the dead isn't the ultimate proof that you're messing with stuff you shouldn't be messing with, I don't know what is.

After being tortured, she confessed, but they all did.

After being tortured, she confessed.

He just wanted to help her, right?

Raising the dead . . .

A shudder of primitive comprehension ran down Steve's spine, and in the distance he could hear the barking of a dog, on that cold night in November only a month and a half ago, a dog that had sounded so much like Fletcher.

TWENTY-SIX

TYLER WAS BURIED on Thursday morning in St. Mary's Cemetery behind the church, the larger of the two cemeteries in Black Spring. The weather was bleak, and a dull, flat December light welcomed the mourners, who had come in droves. Two people who attended only part of the ceremony, each for their own reasons, were Robert Grim and Griselda Holst.

Griselda had sat in the back of the church during the service. Now she walked over to a rise on the edge of the cemetery behind the crowd of mourners, who had gathered on the paths and between the graves all the way to the wrought-iron gate and beyond. She didn't dare mingle with them. Since Jaydon's trial and torture, they had made her an outcast. The townsfolk avoided her like the plague. Black Spring had never fully recovered from November 15. People simply didn't seem to know how to relate to each other anymore. For many, the excessive, appalling events at the crossroads had been so horrifying and inconsistent with their moral ideas that they had literally erased them from their memories. On the streets, people exchanged mere perfunctory greetings, and not a word was spoken about what had happened. Each wore the same shamefaced expression, for each bore the guilt for this infamy.

From the day in late November when Griselda had reopened her shop, the townsfolk had shunned Griselda's Butchery & Delicacies. The clientele was reduced to a sporadic dribble, far too few to cover expenses, and Griselda had started to worry about her future. Ironically enough, she understood more than ever how poor Katherine must feel. Katherine was an outcast, too, the vermin of society. Griselda felt intensely that they were kindred spirits, but since she had been ejected from the Council, she no longer dared to call on her. It was agony, but Griselda was terrified that she'd be caught by the security cams. And more than anything, she was terrified of Katherine's wrath.

Tyler Grant's mother, dressed in a black coat, looked to Griselda as if she had aged six years in six days. She was supported by her father, a hearty Outsider in his seventies, and kept glancing around in increasing disbelief, as if to confirm that her youngest son really was not present at his brother's funeral. It was so tragic: that poor kid lying in the hospital in Newburgh. Rumor had it that he had slipped into a psychosis from which he would never awaken. Steve Grant was standing next to his wife, but Griselda didn't fail to notice that he hadn't touched her once during the entire service. He looked lost and obsessed, like a man who was no longer capable of recognizing reality.

The Grant family was not religious, but because of the impact of the death on the community, the pastor had agreed to say a few words . . . discreet, as usual, when there were Outsiders present. Griselda's eyes passed over the crowd. She was shocked to see Colton Mathers hidden in the shadow of the crucifix over at the iron gates. His face was as emotionless as pale marble and his grasping, blue-veined man's hands were thrust deep into the pockets of his overcoat. Griselda felt a flash of cold-blooded hatred toward the councilman, who had dropped her like a ton of bricks, just as all the others had done.

She was a pariah. She, Griselda Holst, who had done all the dirty work in that Arthur Roth business and whose mediation with Katherine all those years had prevented something—something like *this*—from happening.

Griselda pressed her hankie against her nose and gave a wicked blow as she left the cemetery in a state of rage.

-+-l-l-l-

JUST OUTSIDE THE gate, mumbling some vicious profanity, she almost bumped into Robert Grim. It was no wonder that she didn't recognize him, for Robert Grim was a mere shadow of the man he had once been—until late Friday night, to be precise. He was bundled up in his parka, and there was no trace of that cynical sparkle in his eyes. His face was contorted, and with trembling fingers he kept jabbing the stub of a cigarette between his lips, a habit he had kicked twenty years before, but had resumed on Saturday morning.

He smoked mainly to erase the stench from his memory.

That evil, dark stench of the witch.

Grim had concealed it from his coworkers and had forced himself to do his job, but the truth was that he had had a nervous breakdown. Katherine's targeted attack had confirmed his premonition. The inner voice that had warned him of an approaching storm now sounded deeper, not just ominous but downright obsessive and malevolent. The townsfolk seemed to feel it, too. They kept looking up at the sky for no apparent reason, or peeking beyond the graves, wishing they could go back home and lock themselves away behind the deceptive security of bolted doors. They were sick with fear, and so was Robert Grim. If he had been able to run away from it, he would have done so. But there was no running away from Black Spring. Besides, he felt responsible. Maybe he could keep one step ahead of her.

Grim turned away from the ceremony and looked at the Outsiders' parked cars, forming an endless, melancholy row starting at the town square and running all the way along Lower Reservoir Road and up the hill. His right hand nervously fumbled with his cell phone, waiting for bad news. Katherine was up in the woods half a mile to the west and the entire HEX crew was on standby, ready to step in if the situation called for it. Volunteers had taken their positions all around the cemetery in case she decided to show herself here in an excess of bad taste. Grim half expected it to happen. *And what then?* he thought. *If she's planning to put on a show, we're going to dance to her tune like fucking puppets.*

His fingers froze in a cramp. Katherine had attacked him just when it had begun to dawn on him that this all was part of some pre-conceived plan. Could that be a coincidence?

Oh, come on.

But what did it mean if she really had calculated all this? Ah, if only he could see what lay within this ever-narrowing circle of related events, this chain that had been forged link by link . . . and if only he, by God, was strong enough to head it off at the pass.

-+-|-|-|-

A LITTLE FARTHER downhill, Griselda Holst was heading back to the shop, bent into the wind. She wanted to see how Jaydon was doing. Doodletown had broken him, and he had not wanted to attend the funeral of his former friend.

Since his release almost two weeks earlier, Griselda had become a little scared—not of Jaydon, but of herself. She remembered sitting on the couch with her son the evening he was brought home. Jaydon, who now moved like a frail old man, had curled up against her like a baby, his head in her lap. He fell asleep almost immediately. Griselda stroked his hair, humming softly. It was a moment of intense confusion and internal conflict: She cradled her son with love, something she hadn't been able to do since Jim left . . . but it was still her son who had stoned Katherine. Her Katherine. She hated him at the same time.

Cautiously, Griselda lifted the neckline of Jaydon's T-shirt. Jaydon didn't wake up. She winced when she noticed the revolting palette of badly healed wounds and mangled skin on his back. During his proba-tion, psychiatrists would help Jaydon deal with the symptoms of his trauma, but Griselda knew that these scars were for life. For three lonely weeks she had tried, for better or worse, to prepare herself for his release, but this was a reality she had completely overlooked: *Everyone knows he bears these scars. Everyone knows what Jaydon has done. This curse will be on him forever.*

Griselda picked up her embroidery and sung a slow lullaby for her son, alternating love with hatred: *"The wheels on the bus go round and round, round and round . . ."*

She pushed the needle through the fabric and snipped the thread with a pair of sewing scissors. Every time her hand was free, she stroked Jaydon's hair.

"The horn on the bus goes beep beep beep, beep beep beep . . ."

Suddenly Griselda stopped stitching and looked up, stunned, sewing scissors in one hand, the other casually stroking Jaydon's hair.

"The babies on the bus go wah wah wah, wah wah wah . . ."

Love and hate, love and hate.

"The mommies on the bus . . . go . . ."

All at once, Griselda had the idea of stabbing the sewing scissors into Jaydon's throat, below the rhythmic swelling and sinking of his Adam's apple. It was a purely rational thought, not born of hatred, but of love.

It would be like putting him out of his misery. Jaydon no longer had a life in this town, and there was no alternative. Didn't Griselda have the right to give his life meaning by making the ultimate sacrifice to Katherine?

Griselda Holst, whose poetic genius usually amounted to appreciating cutesy Hallmark cards, now thought, *My blood threw those terrible rocks at you. Now I give you my blood. The way they once forced you to kill your blood.*

With halting breath, she pressed the point of the scissors against the pale skin of Jaydon's throat.

The flesh yielded gently.

Jaydon didn't move.

In those few crucial seconds, she tried to imagine what life without Jaydon would be like, a life in which she would no longer have to hide him away like a shameful secret at the back of the butcher shop, a life without his tantrums and aggression, without him thwarting her efforts to obtain Katherine's grace. . . .

But then Jaydon moved in his sleep; laid his hand on her thigh—

and that gesture, the disarming gesture of a child instinctively searching for his mother's support, brought her back to her senses with a jolt. Her heart beat rapidly and painfully in her chest, and with a restrained sort of moan she threw the scissors into a corner of the room. Griselda pressed her lips together and wrestled to regain self-control.

"Hush, little baby," she said, and began stroking him again. "Hush now. You're safe with Mommy. Mommy is the only one you got. Nobody is ever going to hurt you anymore."

And it was almost as if she could hear Jaydon reply: *We'll make them all pay for what they did, Mom.*

Now it wasn't Jaydon who was being buried, but Tyler Grant. As if Katherine had given them a sign that she had forgiven them. And while Griselda Holst, cheeks stinging from the frost, stuck her key in the lock of the butcher shop, she thought, *Yes, son, I'll take you with me into Katherine's grace. I'll show you the right path. It's us and Katherine against the rest of them.*

The little bell jingled, and it was the stench that hit her first. Gagging, she recoiled and brought her hand up to her mouth. She grabbed the doorpost, harshly sucking in her breath and staring at the meat case in disbelief. At first she didn't understand what she was looking at, fooled into thinking that someone had taken all the meat away and replaced it with an odd, dusty blanket. Then she saw that everything was covered with a blue-gray layer of mold, like spongy tissue on an infected wound, dull but glaring in the striplight of the display case. All her meat, from left to right, was spoiled and flecked with fly eggs, as if she had been away for weeks instead of a little over forty minutes. The ground beef was crawling with pale worms. The steaks were discolored like tubercular lungs. The meatballs she had kneaded that morning stank as if they had been rotting in their gravy since October. A thick yellowish scum was caked onto the stew and infested with vermin.

It's an omen, Griselda thought with horror and dread. *Oh, good heavens, what the hell is happening?*

Outside, the funeral bells began to toll, and Griselda shrank with a scream, and ten miles north Matt's blind eyes suddenly shot open behind the bandages. And as the nurse rushed up to see what was wrong, he cried out, "Don't do it! Don't do it! Don't let him cut her eyes open! Mom! Dad! Don't let him cut her eyes open!"

TWENTY-SEVEN

AFTER THE FUNERAL, Jocelyn said she wanted to go with her father to St. Luke's to be with Matt. Tomorrow would mark his first week in Newburgh. After everyone had finally returned home that afternoon—the condolences seemed interminable—Jocelyn had told Steve that if there was no improvement by the next week, they would have to figure out a way to bring Matt back to Black Spring . . . before *her* hold on their youngest son became too strong.

Steve had nodded absently and said he still had a few odds and ends to wrap up with the funeral director, but he'd come to Newburgh later. All the while, he was thinking, *There it is again. Your youngest son. He's your only son now, and don't you forget it.*

In his black suit, but with his collar unbuttoned and his tie hanging loose, he walked to the end of the backyard, where Fletcher's grave was. The real reason he hadn't wanted to go was that he wanted to be alone with his grief. An insistent part of his brain refused to accept the fact that he had only one son left, refused to let Tyler go. It never let up; kept coming at him. The presence of so many familiar faces at the funeral had, in a sense, forced him to screen himself off from his despair, but afterward it returned in all its intensity. It tried to twist reality, and bounced back on his soul every time he was confronted with the facts. It caused a short-circuit that made him drift away not only from his family but also from himself. Despite his misery, he realized that by cutting himself off he was playing a dangerous game. On Tuesday, after the closing of the coffin, he had briefly—and in full possession of his senses—considered suicide as a logical conclusion of his pain. It had seemed stupid, an act of utter self-pity.

Steve Grant didn't believe in an afterlife, and it wouldn't bring him back to Tyler.

It was chilly. The light in the woods had a hostile quality. Years ago, before they had built the horse pen, little Tyler had spent summer after summer doing somersaults on the trampoline here with a lazy detachment and a blind faith, as if the future didn't exist at all. Steve remembered that Jocelyn had been a bit afraid of the dark pit under the trampoline. Someday one of the springs would snap and Tyler would end up with a twisted leg caught in that shadowy hole. Later they had removed the trampoline, but the hole remained: The hole was death, and it caught him in the end. He was in that hole now, a mile away in St. Mary's Cemetery, a hole in the dark, and that's where he'd stay.

Steve knelt down beside Fletcher's grave mound with the scrapwood marker Matt had fashioned, and he whispered, "Hey, boy. Take good care of Tyler, okay? I know you would have given your life for him. I'd do the same."

Suddenly he heard Tyler's voice: *Fletcher is dead, Matt. Did you ever hear Fletcher howl like that before?*

No, but he's never been dead before, either.

Steve felt a chill run through his whole body. He had dismissed it as bullshit that night, but it was also true, wasn't it? Fletcher had been dead . . . except that night, when they heard him howling in the woods, he wasn't. The night he was brought back to life by Katherine.

No. We don't think those kinds of things.

He shivered and thought, *Later I stopped believing in witches, so I did it as a balancing exercise.*

Someone cleared his throat, and he looked up with a start. It was Lawrence. He looked sad and worn-out in his funeral suit. "Sorry. I didn't mean to startle you."

"No problem, Lawrence. You okay?"

The boy shrugged, as if to say that whether *he* was okay was irrelevant. "I wanted to thank you for what you did. For not ratting on us, I mean. Tyler and me."

"That's all right."

Lawrence came around and stood next to him at the grave. "He was crazy about Fletcher, you know. Maybe . . . if Jaydon hadn't sicced that friggin dog on her . . . maybe none of this would have happened. He didn't deserve it, you know. . . ." His voice cracked and tears spilled down his cheeks. Steve felt something burst in his throat.

No, Tyler didn't deserve this—not Tyler. Don't let him slip away from you, because you'll never forgive yourself if you do. If there's pain, cherish it; if there's a flame, don't blow it out. Let it burn, keep it alive. Yes, keep him alive. . . .

Oh, Jesus. It was too much. This pain was too big; he wasn't able to bear it. Every cell in his body longed, *screamed* so intensely for Tyler— to hold him, to tell him he loved him. He would have given literally everything for the chance to undo what had happened. There was no journalistic breakthrough for Tyler, no pretty girlfriend from the city; he had died in a noose with his consciousness intact, fully aware of what was going on as the world spun away.

With all the restraint he could muster, Steve said, "Maybe you ought to go home now, Lawrence."

Lawrence wiped away his tears. "I got to tell you something. If I don't do it now, I'll never do it. It's about Tyler."

Steve squeezed his eyes shut and took a deep, shuddering breath. This boy next door had the idea that he owed him something, and now, in the darkest moment of his grief, he had come to unburden himself. Steve understood that he would have to drink this bitter medicine to the dregs.

"What is it?" he asked numbly.

"Tyler would never have done something like this on his own. He must have heard her whispering. There's no other way. But Tyler was never mean to her. The others were, but not Tyler. He always stood up for her. At first I didn't get why she'd want to take revenge on him, or whatever she did. But then I suddenly knew that *she* wasn't the one who did it."

Silence, time ticking out. "What do you mean?"

"We made a recording of her whispering. We had this guy from Highland Falls listen to it, to prove it wouldn't hurt him. I assumed that Tyler erased it when you both went to HEX. But, you know . . . we taped it with Jaydon's phone. I saw Jaydon erase it, but what if he was only pretending? I thought: No, they caught that fucker, right? They must have cleared out his phone right away. But it was an audio file. And that scared me. I mean, why would they take away his music?" Steve understood what Lawrence was getting at before he even said it. "What if Jaydon still has that recording?"

I have never held anything against you, he heard Griselda Holst say. No, maybe she hadn't. He got it now. In a flash of horror, it all fell into place. His mouth seemed to fall open by itself, and suddenly he thought about what had struck him that night on the bank of the Hudson, when they cleared out Tyler's MacBook: that maybe he wasn't doing Tyler any favors by sparing him.

Lawrence had just thanked him for what he'd done, but if what he suggested was true, then Steve, for all his good intentions, was responsible for the death of his son.

He clenched his fists uncontrollably, and for a moment the back-yard floated dangerously before his eyes, as if he were about to faint. His head pounded along with his heartbeat as the blood drained away. From a distance he could hear Lawrence's voice: "Maybe you can find something on his laptop. I know he blogged a lot about what he was doing, even if he didn't put it online. Maybe he wrote something . . . during the last days."

Steve heard himself say, "I don't know his password."

"Oh, but I do."

"What is it?"

"Your birthday."

-+-|-|-|-|-

HE REACHED THE toilet bowl just in time and threw up the half Danish and swallow of tasteless coffee from that morning in a nasty spurt. He fell to his knees, clamped his fingers over the john, and there he hung, eyes closed, head heavy with physical exhaustion and mental collapse until the nausea ebbed away. Most of what had come up was bile; he had hardly been able to get anything down his throat for days. When he felt able, he flushed and hoisted himself up to the sink. He rinsed his mouth and splashed water on his face. Then he glanced into the mirror to inspect the damage.

He froze abruptly. Behind the glass of the bathroom window was a tawny owl. The bird had a field mouse in its small, curved beak. It was carelessly torn apart and a string of intestines hung out of its mutilated little body. The owl's golden-brown full-moon eyes stared coldly at him until Steve gave the window a sudden, sharp rap.

With two rapid jerks the owl threw its head back and swallowed its prey whole. Then it flapped its wings and instantly disappeared.

Overcome by the longing to keep his son alive, Steve stumbled up the stairs to uncover the last facts about his death.

Tyler's bedroom was unchanged. Since last Friday Steve had only come back here to take the clothes they buried him in out of the closet. It immediately struck him how uncannily stale the atmosphere was, how much Tyler's smell was still present in the air. The blankets were rumpled, Tyler's desk chair pushed out. On the desk was his MacBook, waiting there since Tyler had closed the lid on Friday to get the rope from the stable. Steve tried to picture how Tyler must have experienced those last moments, but he was unable to do it, because there was something else, something much more alarming. The whole room felt highly charged, as if it were waiting for something . . . as if Tyler could walk in at any minute and pick up his life where he had left off, as if nothing had changed.

A few days later the townsfolk see the boy walking around the streets of New Beeck.

Heartsick, Steve sat down at Tyler's desk and opened the MacBook. Of course he knew the password wouldn't work. Tyler had gotten the laptop only nine days before his death as an early Christmas gift because the old one had most likely been bugged with spyware. Of course he would have come up with a new password. Still, Steve gave his birthday a try . . . and immediately Tyler's desktop popped up.

For a moment he felt uneasy . . . and much like a trespasser, as if Tyler were looking over his shoulder. He suddenly heard his voice crystal clear in his head: *You were supposed to help me, Dad.* Steve saw his son's face before him, but it looked shockingly different than the way he remembered it. He couldn't put his finger on it exactly how . . . but death had changed him. *You were supposed to help me,* he said, his voice sad and reproachful. *Nothing was supposed to happen to me, and now I'm dead. How could you have let that happen?*

It was too easy to shift all the responsibility onto Jaydon Holst. How strong were the seeds of hatred that Steve had sown in the heart of a boy who had been tortured before the whole town until he almost died—and all because Steve had tried to protect his son? How could he have been so stupid!

But it wasn't stupidity, Steve knew. He had done it out of love. But wasn't that almost the same thing?

I'm so sorry, Tyler. I'm so, so terribly sorry. . . .

Losing himself ever more deeply in that destructive web of guilt, Steve searched his son's computer. His hope soon diminished: There just wasn't that much there yet. He opened the Word documents and scanned through the browser's history. He looked at the latest vlogs on Tyler's YouTube channel and cried when he saw his son, TylerFlow95, as alive and cheerful as before. The GoPro memory card was empty except for a few old pics.

Harboring few illusions, Steve finally began browsing through the MP4 clips on Tyler's external hard drive. It wasn't until he was halfway through one of them that he found something he barely paid attention to at first . . . but that soon shocked him to the core.

-+-+-+-+-

IT'S A VIDEO. Of course it's a video, because that's how Tyler tells his story. First Steve doesn't understand what it is he's watching, because all he sees is green-black darkness, and all he hears are stumbling and whispers. But then someone calls Fletcher's name, and it's as if the temperature in Tyler's room has dropped ten degrees. It's Lawrence and Tyler, they're in the woods, the night is a subterranean black, and Steve suddenly knows what it is that's sneaking around them in the dark.

"That's not Fletcher down there," Lawrence whispers, "it's a deer or a fox or a fucking raccoon; it could be anything. I want to get the hell out of here." As Steve stares at the vague images, a sense of horror steals over him like a swarm of insects and makes the hairs on the back of his neck stand on end. "Oh, Jesus, it *is* him," Lawrence moans, and Tyler screams, "Fletcher!"

With growing dismay, barely connected to the here and now, Steve clings to the voices from the past. The only thing he's able to see is the shaft of light from Tyler's flashlight touching the shapes of tree trunks. What he doesn't realize is that his sanity is swaying like a tightrope walker over a dangerous sea of madness and his rationality is dissolving, just as an ominous thought emerges from the beyond and moves stealthily through his mind: *Nibble, nibble like a mouse; tomorrow everyone will die.*

"They say Katherine raised her son from the dead, right?" Tyler says. "Isn't that why they hanged her? Do you believe that? Do you believe she can raise the dead?"

Oh, Jesus Christ! Steve's thoughts take flight with a shriek. *Jesus Christ! He says it himself! Tyler says it himself! What's the point of denying it, you stupid coward? If Katherine was capable of resurrecting her son . . . can't she bring Tyler back, too?*

"I don't know," Lawrence says. "But I don't think it's Fletcher out there, man. If it *is* Fletcher, why doesn't he come?"

Now that it's finally come out—the idea that has been continuously

percolating in the back of his mind since the viewing on Tuesday—
Steve watches the rest of the video as if in a dream. He clutches the
edge of the desk with white knuckles. It's pure madness, it's un-
academic bullshit, but his days as an academic are gone forever. The
slowly dying flame by which he was keeping Tyler alive flares up like a
fiery spark of hope.

There's a scream from the MacBook's built-in speakers and the
image begins to shake. They're running down the hill in a panic.
Flashes of light and darkness alternate in a nightmarish escape scene.
And it is at some point during that flight through the darkness that the
jolting camera lunges backward and captures a few frames of something that completely wipes out Steve's notion of normality. Steve has
no way of knowing that he's staring at the same frames that haunted his
son's nightmares during the last month of his life. Nor does he know
that outside the window his son's murderer entered on that fateful night
to make him listen to Katherine's whispering, three owls have landed
on a branch and are staring into the room. The only thing Steve can
think is: *So it's true. Oh, dear God, it's true.*

Is it a dog? In all fairness, Steve wouldn't bet his life on that, not
even when he freezes the image. But it looks suspiciously like some sort
of animal form. A squat animal form. Black and white. Something is
glittering. Maybe it's an eye, or a gleaming tooth. The buckle of a dog
collar, perhaps. If you're willing to believe that this vague, blurry video
image is a dog, then it's a dog.

And Steve is willing . . . if it can bring Tyler back to him, he's *more*
than willing.

Then one of the owls crash-bangs against the window and Steve
jumps to his feet with a shout.

-+-|-|-|-

SPLINTERS OF GLASS scattered across the desk, and the sheer
curtain billowed out with a gust of cold December air. Lying amid the
jagged shards of glass was the owl, thrashing its broken wing about as it

kept hooting and trying to raise its head, staring at him maliciously. All at once, in a delayed shock reaction, Steve's eyes snapped open. He had become aware of the other owls. There were no longer three now, but eight or nine. The sight was so unnatural that it took a second for the truth to sink in: *It's her.*

Something was blocking his windpipe.

Steve clutched at his throat and tried to breathe, but he couldn't get any air in his lungs. The only sounds he could make were muffled squeaks. He broke out in a cold sweat. Stumbling backward into the hallway, he bumped into the door, turned around, and cupped his hands over his mouth in an effort to fight the hyperventilation.

Suddenly the sound of fluttering filled the house. It was everywhere. A powerful and malignant flapping, as if entire flocks of owls were swooping around the roof. Then a loud crunch, and the thumpety-thumping of something tumbling down overhead. Steve tried to scream but wasn't able; he couldn't get any air. His face turned a fiery red and tears sprang to his eyes.

He managed to get halfway down the stairs and then began to slide, painfully bouncing down the last few steps before slamming headlong onto the floor. Although he was able to break his fall, his elbows gave way and his cheek smashed against the cold tiles. A sharp pain shot through his jaw, followed by a dizzying wave of nausea that made his whole body writhe. Drenched with sweat, he suddenly realized that he wasn't hyperventilating at all . . . there really *was* something in his throat squeezing his windpipe shut.

I'm choking. . . .

As he dragged himself over the doorsill into the dining room, his stomach took a dive and his esophagus began contracting uncontrollably. His body went into convulsions. Steve felt like he was spinning around, turning somersaults. Whatever it was that was blocking his windpipe came up along with several stinking burps and stale stomach acid and the awful sensation that his mouth was full of hair. There was another stab of pain, excruciating this time, and Steve threw up slimy strands of bile and an undigested plug-shaped tangle of hair the size of a plum. It rolled across his tongue and dropped onto the floor with a wet plop. At long last, the oxygen rushed into his windpipe.

With a wildly racing heart, he hoisted himself onto one knee in front of the thing he had regurgitated. Steve had lived at the edge of Black Rock Forest for eighteen years, and he knew exactly what it was: an owl pellet. Except . . .

Except the hairs in it weren't gray, like the fur of a field mouse, but blond.

Flaxen hair, straggly, and of the same thickness as Tyler's.

If you throw up the remains of your son, he thought, so consciously that it made him giggle, *it's a good sign you ought to be losing your mind.* His giggle swelled to a high-pitched, hollow laugh that reverberated throughout the empty house, shrill and insane.

Far away, as in a dream, Pete VanderMeer's voice spoke up in his mind like a mantra: *Later I stopped believing in witches, so I did it as a balancing exercise.*

"Please," Steve whispered with a voice that was barely his own. "Bring back my Tyler. Bring back my Tyler and I'll do anything for you."

He looked up, straight into the mud-stained rags of Katherine van Wyler.

TWENTY-EIGHT

STEVE CLOSED THE curtains and maneuvered himself out of Jocelyn's Limbo. His thigh bumped into the arm of the sofa, and when he crossed to the middle of the room he stumbled against the coffee table. His whole body was trembling. Outside, the wind was shrieking around the house. The street had been empty . . . nobody there to have seen Steve peeking out the window at that critical moment, as if the stars had been favorably aligned for the execution of some obscure destiny.

Katherine van Wyler was standing beside the dining room table, her figure emaciated and drooping as if her spinal column had been horribly deformed. She came with a foul, low smell of age and corruption. Decay had taken the dignity from her face, but beneath that etched layer of dirt something seemed to be waiting. She followed Steve's every movement. Behind the stitched-up lids, her eyes were fixed on him—he felt her gaze in every cell of his body. He wondered if he was under some sort of a spell or hypnosis that dominated his will, but felt no indication that he was. If he chose to do so, he could flee the house that very moment, jump in the car, and drive to Newburgh to join Jocelyn and Matt. For a brief moment, he actually considered it—he felt the car keys in his pocket as a tempting way out.

But even now Steve knew that what was driving him was not hypnosis but something far more dangerous: it was love. Steve was following his heart, which bled with longing for his son.

He stopped in the open French doors, retching from the overwhelming smell of death. Katherine nodded. It was a forced, animal-like movement, barely human at all. Now she had finally come to his home . . . as if part of him had known this was coming, ever since he had found Tyler dead last Friday. The compulsion to go to her was powerful, but so was the fear, trickling with hesitation from the chambers of his heart. *My God, what are you contemplating, Steve? Do you really want to go through with this?*

Yes, he thought, he would go through with this . . . because Katherine was welcoming him. She wasn't whispering. She just nodded at the human hair that made up the owl pellet. And when she turned around and crossed to the kitchen, he followed submissively.

Her bare feet left tracks of mud on the tiles, and Steve thought, *If you had them examined in a lab, you'd find sediments and bacteria that haven't been seen in these parts for over three hundred years.*

When she got to the kitchen door, she stopped and looked up at him. Of course—he was expected to open the door. She was prevented from doing so by the iron chains that clung to her body. But getting so close to her inhuman presence made him feel giddy, as if he were standing on the edge of an abyss . . . a chasm to which *she* was seductively tempting him. Without taking a breath, he pressed himself against the doorpost, reached behind her past the cold window, twisted the key in the lock, and turned the knob. The door opened a crack and he gave it a gentle push. Heart pounding, he pulled his arm back . . .

. . . *and brushed her hand.*

Oh, Jesus! I touched her! I fucking touched her!

He felt as if he were going to lose it . . . but nothing happened, and he calmed down a bit. The witch walked placidly onto the patio and Steve followed. The hem of her dress fluttered in the chilly wind.

As they crossed the lawn, he did not look around to see if they were being observed. He knew they were walking in full view of the VanderMeers' upstairs windows, but Steve trusted that his neighbors wouldn't look outside. The circumstances were bewitched, as it were.

Halfway across the lawn on the way to the stable, he suddenly halted. The part of his crumbling mind that realized what road he was going down, and where it was leading, tried to guide him away from it, confronting him with a horror far beyond anything he could physically cope with. He felt something snap behind his eyeballs. His muscles tensed up. His hair was literally standing on end, and he jammed his clenched fists to his mouth. Everything he had feared for the past eighteen years was now manifesting itself in a climax of total terror. He was barely able to suppress a scream.

Turn around! Turn around! You can still go back! Do you really believe that anything good can come of this? That whatever forces you will arouse have your best interests at heart? This is madness!

Not madness, he thought. *Love.* Katherine had shown him what unspeakable suffering really was. Only if we have suffered can we make choices out of love.

The question was: Did he believe that Katherine was capable of raising Tyler from the dead? Steve had nothing to justify that hope, nothing but a three-hundred-fifty-year-old legend brought to life by Pete VanderMeer's flamboyant narrative style and a vague black-and-white smudge on a MacBook screen. It defied all logic; it was outright implausible.

And yet. All signs pointed in favor. Tyler had *said it out loud* when he and Lawrence were in the woods, fleeing from something that may have been Fletcher.

It had seemed like a message.

Help me, Dad.

Suddenly he was furious at every ounce of common sense that was trying to reason him out of his intention. Even if there was only one goddamn chance in a million, he'd take it.

Katherine had entered the stables and he rushed after her. Even before he went inside he could hear the horses going wild. Paladin kicked at the massive wooden door of his stall and almost knocked it out of true. Nuala snorted and sniffed as if she were rabid or possessed. After the animals had broken out in early November, Jocelyn had had new bolts installed. Steve hoped they could withstand such superhuman force. He tried to shush the animals, but Paladin reared up, eyes rolling, kicked dents in the walls with his powerful hooves, and Steve shrank back. *Get it over with and get the hell out of here, before the neighbors catch on.*

Katherine waited patiently at the workbench at the far end of the stable, paying no attention to the horses. When Steve approached her, she reached her arms as far from her body as they would go, tightening the chains. Then she nodded at the dusty workbench. At first Steve didn't understand what she was getting at. On the workbench he saw the feed bucket for the horses and the jigsaw, underneath it the metal toolbox . . .

Next to the toolbox was a pair of midsize bolt cutters.

Are you really willing to risk everything you have? begged the last slippery remains of Steve's reasoning brain. *You're putting everyone's life in the balance . . . not only the people of Black Spring, but your family. Your wife, your other son, yourself . . . and for what? For nothing more than a smudge on a screen. That's not love, that's selfishness. Think about Matt; think about Jocelyn! They're alive!*

But then he heard Tyler's voice: *If you had to let somebody die,* o padre mio, *who would it be: your own kid or the rest of our town?*

And with a sudden, cold savagery he thought about something Matt had said when he had offered his sports pennant at the Wicker Burning on All Hallows' Eve: *Besides, if you sacrifice something that isn't important to you, what's the point, right?*

Something audible clicked in his head: the collapse of his last resistance. The rest of his life—everything, except his most basic reflexes—seized up and retreated into the deepest holes of his memory.

Steve picked up the bolt cutters and felt the cold weight in his hands. In a confused image that meant little to him anymore he saw himself breaking the chain lock on Tyler's bike last spring—one of those occasions when Tyler had lost his keys. The blades were made to cut through modern stainless steel, and Steve assumed that brittle seventeenth-century iron, corroded by the elements, would present no problem.

Again, Katherine tried to stretch her arms.

With trembling hands, Steve placed the cutting blades around one of the links in the chain. In the distance, without recognizing it as the sound of his own screaming thoughts, he heard an anguished cry of madness: *What am I doing oh fuck what am I doing what am I doing WHAT AM I DOING?*

And then the lever closed.

With a loud *ZINNNNG!* the chain sprang open and both loose ends hit the stable floor.

Everywhere in Black Spring, people looked up from whatever they were doing, as if they heard distant thunder in the skies. People abruptly put down their work, stopped cooking or doing the dishes, and experienced a collective ripple of alarm that permeated into the core of their bones. No one could identify it, but everyone felt instinctively that something, *something* was dreadfully amiss.

The iron had to be cut in three more places; only then was Steve able to unwind the chains from the witch's gaunt body.

When it was done, she slowly raised her dead hands to her blind face. Then she beckoned at Steve to come.

She led him back to the house. Behind them, the horses, now crazed with fear, lashed into the stable doors, but Steve didn't hear them. Nor did he see his own reflection as they walked past the mirror in the dining room like a pair of ghosts, one after the other. That was a good thing, because if he had seen his face, he probably would have started screaming. It was the face of a decrepit old man, with eyes and a mouth so twisted that they looked as if they'd never close again.

Up in the bedroom, he found Jocelyn's fingernail scissors and a pair of tweezers.

Katherine waited downstairs, with all the patience in the world.

When he faced her again, she pointed to her mouth.

Steve tried to speak, but his voice cracked and he was barely able to produce sound. He cleared his throat and tried once more: "Bring back my Tyler."

The witch pointed to her mouth.

"Please. Bring him back to life, just like you did to your own son."

That finger: scrawny, commanding, unaffected.

Steve obeyed the order.

With trembling fingers, he snipped the stitches that held her lips together one by one.

With the tweezers he pulled the threads from her dead flesh.

As he took a step back, her mutilated mouth fell open with a limp plop. Katherine shuddered and drew a rasping, scraping breath. Once again, a shock ran through the townsfolk of Black Spring, even more severe this time. Eyes opened wide, cries rose in the streets, people looked at one another feverishly and thought, *For God's sake . . . what's happening?*

Oblivious to the scenes outside, Steve started on the stitches on her left eye.

The threads fell to the floor one by one.

The eyelid's flaking, bluish, inflamed skin quivered.

When he was done, Steve turned to the right eye.

And when that, too, was done, the witch turned away from him with her hand over her eyes in an effort to protect her liberator from herself. Her face became contorted as if she were suffering excruciating pain, and her body pitched forward unnaturally. She waved her free arm at Steve, gesturing at him to go away, away, away from here.

Just then, a new shock reverberated through Black Spring, but now it didn't strike the townsfolk from within; this time it seemed to come from the earth itself. For a moment, everything appeared to darken before their eyes. The streets were filled with a very real sound, a *low* sound, as if something gigantic had rolled over in the vaulted darkness beneath the town that made the asphalt and the woods quake. The bells of Crystal Meth Church resounded with a deep and sonorous hymn. At Ackerman's Corner, John Blanchard's sheep broke out and bolted. Jaydon Holst, lost in a fever dream about a faceless executioner who kept mutilating his tortured body over and over again, groaned restlessly in his sleep. In the HEX control center, Robert Grim and Claire Hammer came rushing down the aisle to the screen, which was flickering on and off with a humming electrical buzz. Then all the power in Black Spring went out. Emergency generators roared up but shut down immediately, and the Christmas lights in some of the windows sputtered in the dying daylight.

Black Spring wasn't the only place where darkness fell: All over the Highlands and the Hudson Valley—yes, even on the highways and in Manhattan office buildings—residents of Black Spring who happened to be outside the town limits when Katherine opened her eyes were struck by an unspeakable, morbid sadness and gloom that exceeded human comprehension. Immediately they began seeing images that were simply too much for their brittle spirits to bear and that awakened in them an irrepressible desire to seek death as the only way out of their existence. Those lucky enough to be relatively close to home understood that the force that had always bound them to Black Spring had intensified to the Nth degree, and they rushed to get back . . . but there were those for whom salvation came too late, and they hanged themselves in broom closets or ran their cars into trees with the pedal to the metal so their bodies were crushed in clouds of smoke and darkness.

In the house at the end of Deep Hollow Road, Steve gaped with horror at the inhuman, crooked figure who was still covering her evil eye with her hand. Again she waved for him to leave, a swastika of ashen flesh and bent limbs. For a moment, his legs seemed liquid, and he was unable to move his feet. Icy needles pricked his neck at the thought of her opening her eyes . . . and turning them on him.

Steve fled from his house, screaming. He ran into the woods, and he ran for his life.

TWENTY-NINE

TEN MILES AWAY in Newburgh, Jocelyn Grant did feel the initial shock, but she dismissed it as a jolt of unsettled biorhythms and put it out of her mind. When the second shock came, she looked up from the copy of *Esquire* she had been mindlessly leafing through and stared into the silent hospital room. And when the third shock followed shortly thereafter, more intense than the previous two put together, she rocketed out of her seat and the magazine slid to the floor.

Matt moaned and moved his head in his sleep. Startled, Jocelyn eased her way around his bed and put a hand on his shoulder. "Matt! Matt, can you hear me? Can you hear me, darling?"

But Matt didn't answer. His left eye was covered with a wad of cotton, held in place by a bandage wrapped around his head. The bandage over his right eye had been removed. The eye stayed shut, but this restlessness was a greater sign of life than he had shown in days. Would he finally wake up? Her excitement was no match, however, for her sudden rising panic: *Something's wrong. Something's very wrong.*

She felt it. This was not her imagination. It was all around her, but she couldn't get a handle on it. It was as untouchable as the static between two radio channels. The clock on the wall said it was a few minutes past five. The wind was having a field day in the parking lot, whipping a plastic bag against the grills of cars that glistened in the Christmas lighting. Everything looked normal, but it wasn't.

And it wasn't here that things were wrong; it was at home in Black Spring. She felt it pulling her, whatever it was.

She called Steve but got no answer, not even his voice mail. Only silence. And her mind responded uncompromisingly, as if that silence had everything to do with the hunch she was having: *We have to get home before it's too late.*

It took her by surprise: the dream, the same dream, and she recognized it immediately. It was the dream she had dreamt only once before, eighteen years ago in a bamboo bungalow in Thailand, but it had always been present in the back of her mind and had been responsible for much of the darkness of their life in Black Spring, despite the relative happiness they believed they had known.

The intensity was different, but the essence of the dream was the same. She saw herself hysterically pulling strands of her hair out. She saw herself tossing the papers from Matt's clipboard all around the room. They fluttered to the floor, and she saw them form a photo collage, pictures of the dead. All children, little children and big children. They had all sorts of cuts on their faces and bodies. In the next image, the dead children were actually lying in the hospital room, the children of Black Spring, and one of them was Matt. His face was cut off and stuffed with black coals. She saw herself naked and rolling in glittering pools of paint, her body red and black, while she was taken by a wild boar. The curved tusks of the animal gleamed as it thrust its member into her, snarling and grunting and stamping its hooves, and she screamed out in ecstasy.

Jocelyn hadn't the faintest idea how long she had been staring at Matt's bed in that numbed state of horror. Nor did all the images she saw register in her mind. The only thing that got through to her was the vague but urgent sense that she could end it all by taking her life. That prospect didn't frighten her; it only filled her with a dull sadness, nothing worse than what was tormenting her now. She crossed over to the window with leaden legs. She picked up the chair she had been sitting in by its back and heaved it over her head, about to smash the glass and remove the last obstacle from a four-story fall.

What saved her life was her phone, which began to ring at that very moment. Dazed, she looked up, not liberated from the immense sadness but at least conscious of herself, and she thought, *Oh my God. I really wanted to do it. I really wanted to jump out the window. What's happening to me?*

She groped for her phone, assuming she would see Steve's picture on the touch screen. But it wasn't Steve. It was her father.

"Dad!"

"You want to come down for dinner, maybe? It's not too crowded in—"

"Dad, I *have* to get home. Can you please take me there?"

"But I thought you—"

"There's something wrong with Steve," she said, the most obvious thing she could think of. And the truth: "I can't reach him." She couldn't explain to her father why she had to go back to Black Spring. The urgency had risen within her, as if a magnet had been put in place farther south that was pulling at her mind. She felt her home beckoning with gentle, swelling chants—compelling choir voices that she had to obey before something terrible happened.

"He's probably gone out for a breath of fresh air," Milford Hampton said calmly and charitably. "Jocelyn, you're at your wits' end. Tell you what, why don't you—"

"*Dad!* Please, I have to go home. Can you bring the car around? I'll see you at the entrance."

"Well, I suppose that's all right, if you really want to. . . ." her father said. Jocelyn hung up without answering. *Get a grip,* she thought. *Get a grip, keep focused . . .*

A noise behind her. Matt had torn out his IV tube and she saw him drawing the end to his lips. In a leap and a jump Jocelyn was at his bedside, snatching the tube from his hands with a shout. The needle flew from his arm, bandage and all, spattering a thin streak of blood on the sheet.

"Matt, calm down," she said feverishly. "I'm getting you out of here. Calm down. Everything's going to be all right."

But the gloom, that pull, that *swelling* inside her didn't go away, it only got stronger. It had taken hold of Matt as well. Cautiously but quickly, fighting the impulses that fired her mind with madness, she pulled the slippery feeding tube out of Matt's nose and dropped it on the blanket. Then she wrestled his rigid body into his hoodie. She had to start over again three times because her hands were trembling too much to disentangle the sleeves.

There was a wheelchair in the hall, and without hesitation, she rolled it through the doors. She dragged Matt into the chair, put his shoes on him, and set his feet up on the footrests. Matt didn't budge—didn't even seem to realize what was going on—but his fingers were now clutching the armrests and his one pearly white, wide-open eye stared into the room with blind intensity.

Suicide, she thought. *He tried to commit suicide, and so did you. . . . He's only been out of Black Spring for a week and you were there just this morning, and you know that's far too short a time to feel her power. What does that tell you? Oh, what was that shock a minute ago?*

Jocelyn wrapped Matt's legs in his sheet and blanket and snatched his eyedrops from the nightstand. Hoping the corridor was empty, she pushed her son out of the hospital room.

The corridor was not empty. At the far end near the beverage machine two nurses were drinking coffee. Jocelyn suppressed the urge to run and quickly headed for the elevators. She pushed the button. When the bell announced the elevator's arrival and the doors slid open, she heard voices behind her: "Ma'am?" And sharper: "Ma'am!"

With her jaws clenched, she gave the wheelchair a hard push as the footsteps hurried closer. She slapped the button for the ground floor and the elevator doors shut out the nurses' livid cries.

The reception area downstairs was humming with people, but nobody paid them any attention. Jocelyn worked her way through the crowd toward the exit. As she pushed the wheelchair through the revolving doors, she searched the pickup area for the Toyota—not there. The wind tugged at Matt's blanket. She felt that chasm opening up again, that strange, gloomy pull. To keep herself distracted she punched in Steve's number for the umpteenth time, but didn't get through.

"Damn!" she shouted, a cry of pure despair and frustration.

Finally her father came driving up. She yanked the back door open even before the car had come to a full stop. Mr. Hampton was aghast as she dragged Matt onto the backseat like a rag doll and kicked the wheelchair away so she could shut the car door behind her.

"Jocelyn, what the hell? What's Matt doing here?"

"Drive."

"But he hasn't been released from the hospital. Come on, Jocelyn, you're in a tailspin, and no wonder. Let's get him back now, I can't allow you to—"

"Don't you dare leave us here!" Jocelyn shouted, and Mr. Hampton shrank back. "Something very serious is wrong here and Matt *has* to go home, before it's too late."

"But what *is* it?" her father insisted. "Tell me what's going on!"

"I can't. It's got something to do with Steve. And with us. And . . ." She began to sob out of pure desperation, dropping her head in her hands. Mr. Hampton looked from his daughter to his grandson, a little unnerved. Through her tears, Jocelyn saw him for the first time as the tired old man he was. The tragic events of the past week had left irreversible traces on his face.

"All right. We'll drive to Black Spring, if we have to. We'll see how Steve's doing, and when we find him we'll take him with us and come straight back to the hospital. All this fuss can't be any good for Matt." He looked in the rearview mirror and drove out onto the circular drive. "But you owe me an explanation."

"Thanks, Dad," she sighed, sinking into the backseat, utterly exhausted.

-+-|-|-|-

BY THE TIME they left downtown Newburgh and started up 9W, which looped into the State Park, the digital clock on the dashboard said it was 5:43 p.m., and Jocelyn was beginning to feel the oppressive weight fermenting in her brain like a maddening poison. Back in Thailand it had been bad, but this was far worse. She was beside herself. Why didn't Steve pick up his goddamn phone? What kind of trouble was he in? And what kind of power had been unleashed that was capable of causing this despair? Her thoughts were adrift like loose clouds, creating an emptiness in her head. Her mind refused to bear the colossal pain; it simply wasn't up to it. Her world had drained into a big, stinking wound of misery. It broke her will to fight against it: Jocelyn wanted to die. And Matt, poor Matt: In his condition, he wasn't even able to free himself from this hopeless mess. . . .

"Jocelyn, for cryin' out loud!"

The Toyota was swerving all over the road, bouncing Jocelyn and Matt back and forth across the backseat. It snapped her out of her stupor momentarily, but she felt herself sinking right back down, like she was trying, and failing, to fight against anesthesia. With a jolt she came back to her senses, having caught herself winding Matt's seat belt around his neck in an attempt to strangle him with it—an act of maternal love, to set him free.

In a flash of intense, ineffable fear, she let go of the belt.

It's bewitching you. It's hypnotizing you. And once you're under, it will force you to commit suicide. That's how she must have gotten Tyler.

With a shrill whine, the Toyota came to a halt on the shoulder. "What the hell is wrong with you, goddamn it?" her father shouted, looking back from the driver's seat.

"Oh, Dad, I don't know." Mr. Hampton was startled by what he saw: Jocelyn really was downright terrified. Her eyes were wide and imploring. "Hurry, drive us home. And keep me talking—please . . ."

"But tell me what's going *on!*"

She couldn't, any more than she could tell her father the real reason for Tyler's death. She deeply regretted this, and she supposed she would tell him everything in due course. He had the right to know, even though it was against town rules, that Black Spring had cost him his oldest grandson. But first it was crucial that she get back to town, because she felt *her* influence dragging her down. . . .

"Please don't ask questions," she said, choking on her words. "I'll explain later. Just keep me talking; that's important."

There was something in those last words that finally struck Mr. Hampton as well. Whatever it was that had gotten into her, it was giving him the heebie-jeebies. So he steered the Toyota onto the exit off 9W and then onto Route 293 toward Black Spring. "I had a bad feeling about Steve staying home. You two should be together, 'specially right now. I'm worried about him. He's not coping well. Nobody is, goddamn it; it's all such a lousy, rotten business, but . . ."

With the very best of intentions, Mr. Hampton was making the fatal mistake of doing all the talking himself . . . so he didn't realize that Jocelyn's eyes had almost immediately lost their luster and were staring blankly into nothing. They hadn't gone halfway up to the single orange traffic light that marked the exit to Deep Hollow Road before Jocelyn and Matt, on opposite sides of the backseat, began bashing their heads against the car doors. Mr. Hampton let out a smothered curse. Glancing over his shoulder, he saw Jocelyn grope for the door handle, and he violently pounded on the brakes. The wheel spun in his hands, whirring so fast it burned his palms, and once again they jolted to a halt, all three of them thrown forward onto their seat belts.

"Dad, help me, please . . ." Jocelyn looked up at him, rigid with fear. There was a gash on the side of her head and blood was running down her face. She took Matt in her arms again and began to rock him.

Mr. Hampton stared at them blankly. He started feeling nauseated. It was beyond him, utterly beyond him, but he felt the urgency and it was eating at him. And suddenly he knew that the cause of all this was ahead of them, waiting . . . a secret at the end of this road, in the woods, in the night.

All at once, Mr. Hampton was convinced that if he never discovered what the secret was, he wouldn't be the least regretful.

With a trembling hand he shifted the car into gear and drove in the direction of Black Spring.

Jocelyn rolled down the window and felt her head clear in the cold airstream. The darkness of the Black Rock Forest lay in silence as they passed, suggesting a normality that wasn't there. She sensed how bad it was. A little farther down the road they would be safe, whatever that safety implied. There was no point in speculating, since she'd be seeing it with her own eyes in just a few moments . . . assuming there was something to see, of course.

With the sign WELCOME TO BLACK SPRING already in sight, she saw it—and her jaw dropped.

Mr. Hampton took his foot off the gas, then slammed on the brakes.

"I don't want to go to Black Spring," he muttered.

"Dad?"

"I . . . You know what? Let's go back. We still have . . . things to do . . . in Newburgh. Yeah. I ought to be somewhere else." He had already started to turn the car around, but he didn't take his eyes off what lay before them. It almost caused them to careen off the road and into the adjacent ditch.

"Dad—don't! We have to keep going!"

But her father wasn't listening. He muttered something unintelligible and the sound of his voice made Jocelyn turn stone cold. A dumbfounded expression appeared on her face that turned into full comprehension. This wasn't her father. The same influence that was driving her back to Black Spring was chasing him away from it.

Because he was an Outsider.

She yanked the car door open and pulled Matt out onto the street. They couldn't go back to Newburgh; that would be their grave. "Dad, please . . ." she begged.

"Sorry, hon." He looked around at her with eyes that were not her father's. "I got a lot to do. Back home, in Atlanta."

With the back door still open, the Toyota shot onto the road. It lurched forward, and, after a hundred feet, the door slammed shut. Jocelyn screamed after him, but he was soon gone.

At age thirteen, Matt was still a child waiting to hit his growth spurt, yet Jocelyn felt the heaviness of his slack weight in her arms. It would be a back buster carrying him home, but she had no choice. At the very least, they had to cross the town border. With her jaws set, she hoisted him up and began to walk.

Black Spring lay before them in total darkness.

On the Highland Falls side of the border the streetlights were on, reflecting dully in Long Pond at the side of the road. In Black Spring it was pitch-dark. The houses and the trees were monumental, barely distinguishable forms outlined against the night. She couldn't even make out the single traffic light farther down, apart from its creaking in the wind. The power was out. But it was more than just the absence of electric lights . . . it was as if the night *itself* had become more intense, a deeper shade of black, a darkness to which your eyes could never become accustomed. Here, at the edge of town, the contrast was undeniable. It felt to Jocelyn as if an ink blot had leaked into this remote corner of the world and would grow bigger and bigger until it had covered all of Black Spring and had blocked out every ray of light or hope. She moaned incoherently, knowing that the only salvation for Matt and herself lay in that darkness.

With her son in her arms, Jocelyn passed the welcome sign and was swallowed up by the gloom.

THIRTY

IN BLACK SPRING people were swarming through the streets. It was a little like New Year's Eve, when everyone would go outside to exchange happy greetings, except there were no fireworks. Instead the townsfolk were carrying flashlights, candles, or homemade torches that etched intensely dark, sharp-edged shadows on the frosty ground. There was nothing happy about it, either. Gradually the initial shock had ebbed away, only to be replaced by an abiding fear, fanned by the rumors that were spreading through town like wildfire.

"Did she claim another victim . . . ?"

"I tell you, it's just like back in '67 . . ."

"No . . . you don't think this is . . . tell me it's not true . . ."

Their eyes gleamed like mercury in the faint light, ghastly and afraid. Their bones ached from the cold, yet only a few turned back home; most wouldn't think of leaving until they got word of what was going on.

In the HEX control center, Robert Grim and Marty Keller were feverishly trying to start up the emergency generator. Not only had the power gone out in town—a grid-wide fucking failure; bye-bye wireless—but there was no more pressure in the water pipes and the entire telephone network was down, landlines included. The implications of this were beyond contemplation—*As is what caused it*, Grim thought with mounting trepidation—but right now his number-one priority was to get the control center up and running. If they couldn't even manage to do that, they'd be fried. The security cams, HEXApp, and the warning system wouldn't be worth shit. It meant that the general illusion of safety could not be maintained . . . and they sure as hell were heading that way.

The emergency generator didn't even budge. Not a fucking spark.

In the trembling ellipse of his headlight, Marty fiddled with the fuel line. His forehead was gleaming with sweat. They had tested the damn thing three weeks before and it had worked without a hitch. It was baffling, but no matter what they tried, it remained dark in the former Popolopen Visitor Center, and in that darkness Grim's thoughts ran rampant. *Oh, Christ, what was that shock? What was the shock we all felt?*

At the intersection farther down the road below Crystal Meth Church, the atmosphere was brewing. Warren Castillo had run all the way over at top speed to size things up. He had to clear a path through a tangle of worried residents who grabbed him, asking questions he couldn't answer and baring souls he couldn't enlighten. It was half past five, and at least two hundred people had flocked to The Point to Point Inn's plaza, where the hotel staff had lit a number of braziers. Warren heard rumors about people driving into town as if the Devil himself were on their heels and locking themselves into their houses without so much as a word. His first inclination was to dismiss it all as fear talking. But then he noticed Rey Darrel's Chevy with the words "Rush Painting" on the side diagonally parked across Deep Hollow Road with its headlights slicing through the dark. A blockade. Darrel's silhouette walked up to the crowd with his arms raised and shouted, "Do not leave town! It's not safe! Listen, people: Stay in town!"

Restless murmuring, hovering on the razor's edge. "What you talkin' about?" someone asked.

"You can't leave! You're gonna get yourself killed if you go out there!"

Warren pushed himself forward and grabbed Darrel by the collar. "Keep your ass down, dude. You're scaring the crap out of these people."

"They have every reason to be scared," Darrel said with plain sincerity, and Warren suddenly realized the painter was genuinely terrified.

"What happened?"

"I drove out of town. They seem to have normal power at the MWR at Round Pond. But as soon as I got out of Black Spring, something . . . something was stopping me. I don't know how else to describe it. It's like there's these big motherfucking suspenders strapped over the road that pull you back in as soon as you drive out of town. You can't see it, but you can feel it." His voice broke. "Even before I hit the golf course, I wanted to shoot myself. I wanted to get my Lancaster .410 out of the back and swallow a bullet. I have three kids and I've never wanted to commit suicide."

Deep silence.

"It's really, really bad," Darrel added—no shit, Sherlock.

That was the signal for the townsfolk to lose their wits. It had a domino effect: One began to whisper, another spoke up, a few tried to call their partners or family members who hadn't come home from work, all in a growing panic. It swept through the crowd like a wave. Warren looked around in dismay; he no longer recognized his fellow townspeople. His body was rigid, so rigid he couldn't get himself moving. He had been trained not to let himself be caught off guard by rumors and superstition. He tried to force himself to drag his emotions into the light, where they could be analyzed and swept aside because they made no sense whatsoever. But he couldn't. What if this time, this one time, the fear was legitimate? What if this time they really had been cut off from the outside world, forced to await the falling darkness and the following dawn and see what they held in store for Black Spring?

Farther east, in the direction he had come from, Warren heard screaming. There were no moon or stars to penetrate the night, and that end of Deep Hollow Road was a charcoal black. Nothing moved there. But what was that pressure in the atmosphere? And why was it so abnormally dark?

Warren couldn't keep from staring at it. The wind sank its teeth into him. It numbed him, blew through his hair, and made his eyeballs so cold they teared, but still he couldn't close them.

It's Katherine's night. The thought hit him out of nowhere . . . and then he understood. Then he understood everything.

The darkness spat out three shrieking men, running in a freak mirage cast by their own flashlights: *Now you see me, now you don't.* They kept looking over their shoulders at what was behind them until they stumbled into the glow of the braziers and met the glances of a good hundred townsfolk. Warren Castillo saw that one of them bore the face of a clown: He had scratched his nails like rays across his cheeks to draw a sunshine mask of blood.

"It's her eyes!" he screamed. "Her eyes are open! We've seen it, she was there! She *looked* at us! Run for your lives, people, the evil eye is upon all of us!"

And so doom came to Black Spring.

Its residents, a collective of bewitched souls who could find no escape from the panic that seized them, scattered in every direction. Imprisoned in a fate they all shared, not one of them raised their voice higher than that of their neighbor or suffered any less. These were the rules of chaos, and from that chaos a sort of deranged solidarity emerged: Within a few seconds, the illusion of individuality had been swept away and only one wish, one dying scream, prevailed over the collective consciousness of Black Spring. The people *were* Black Spring, and Black Spring had fallen. The primal scream that remained was *Away! Away! Away from her evil eye!*

The chaos was immeasurable. People let their bladders go, screamed their throats raw, trampled each other underfoot, and prayed to heaven for mercy. They pulled each other's limbs and hair. No app was necessary to spread the news, and within minutes even those living on the outskirts of town were aware of what had happened. But despite their fear, the witch didn't come. The witch's eyes were open, but no one except the doomsayers had seen it for themselves, and no one had any wish to see her coming. Many fled into their houses and barricaded their doors and windows with whatever was at hand. Quaking with fear, they said their prayers in the inky darkness. There were those who slit their wrists or swallowed the contents of their medicine cabinets. Although the possibility that this day might come had always been in the backs of the minds of even the most naïve among them, no one knew how it would reveal itself or what would happen afterward. Dying without finding out was better than living and having to wait for it. Those with a stronger survival instinct attempted to escape, but they turned around almost as soon as they passed the town limits, gripped by the terrifying realization that they were trapped. Rey Darrel was right. Only an unhappy few went on, and nothing was ever seen of them again.

By seven o'clock, only the wind and its shadow moved through the streets of Black Spring. Katherine's expected revenge failed to happen, and if people were dying it was under their own spell.

One of the first to succumb was Colton Mathers. All his life the old councilman had believed that suicides would go straight to hell, but God had sent him a vision. He had been in church praying when the panic broke out, and as he watched from the church steps a shaky image glimmered through his mind of colonial huts and rickety seventeenth-century farms. The buildings conveyed a sense of completely abandoned isolation, unholiness, and death, and Katherine van Wyler stood there motionless in the front yard of the church like a figurehead in the wind . . . *seeing*. This illusion, this Godly phantasm, was enough to convince Colton Mathers that the dear Lord had abandoned Black Spring for good. The fires of hell would be a soothing balm compared to what was in store for them here. And so the shepherd—as he was always wont to regard himself—abandoned his flock; he went home and threw himself from his balcony, broke every bone in his body, and bled to death later that night on the patio floor. When word spread at daybreak, many would call it an act of unprecedented cowardice.

And Katherine?

No one knew where she was.

No one knew what she wanted.

In their home in Upper Mineral Valley, Jackie and Clarence Hoffman had taken refuge in the kitchen along with their children, Joey and Naomi. It was a luxurious kitchen, usually bathed in the strong sunlight that fell through the double windows over the sink. But now the doors and windows were boarded up with wood from all the bookshelves in the house (they were passionate readers, the Hoffmans). Nevertheless, at 11:15 the lamp over the kitchen table began swaying back and forth as if the cold December air had found a way in, and all the candles blew out at once. An instant later, Katherine appeared in their midst. It so happened that the poor kids were at the other end of the kitchen at the time (they had overcome their exhaustion and were playing *Angry Birds* on their iPad while they still had battery left), and Katherine's appearance cut them off from their parents. She cast a grotesque shadow on the walls for the few seconds that little Joey was able to hold on to his iPad. Then he dropped it and the screen cracked on the kitchen floor, ushering in complete darkness.

No, not complete: There was a dim, lesser shade of black leaking from the cracks between the boards, just enough to distinguish the shapes of Joey and Naomi pressed rigidly against the barricaded door and the obscure shadow of the witch towering over them. Jackie screamed. Clarence Hoffman edged his way along the counter in order to reach his children, but suddenly the shadow twisted her body and hissed at him like a cat. There were no eyes to behold in the darkness, but Clarence felt them upon him nonetheless, inhuman and malevolent. He shrank back as if he had been hit by a brick and grabbed Jackie by the waist when she ran forward.

"Please don't hurt my children," she begged. "They're innocent, just like your children were, Katherine. . . . Oh, my God, what's she doing? Joey, tell Mommy what she's doing!"

"She's . . . I think she's giving us something, Mommy."

"Don't touch it!" their father shrieked.

"What is it?"

"I don't know . . . I think it's an onion."

"And mine's a carrot!" Naomi said.

"I told you not to touch it!"

But Jackie elbowed her husband in the side and whispered, "Don't get her worked up, Clarence . . . Maybe she means well. . . ."

The shadow didn't move; it seemed to persist. It began to dawn on Jackie Hoffman that if the vegetables came from her apron, they had been pulled out of the ground in 1665 and preserved by Katherine's death. Naomi didn't *like* carrots . . . but Jackie knew these wouldn't look even remotely like the prepackaged veggies from the cooler at Market & Deli. She understood what the witch was demanding.

"Go ahead, take a bite, darlings."

"But Mommy . . ."

"It's what she wants you to do, baby."

"But I don't want to, Mommy," Naomi whined in tears.

"Eat the fucking carrot!"

It must have been with enormous reluctance, but she heard the crunching of what must have been Joey's teeth in the onion's skin. Naomi soon followed the brave example of her big brother and took a bite of the carrot. Slowly they began to chew.

"It's sweet!" Naomi cried through her tears. Greedily, the little girl took another bite of her carrot, and then things rapidly got very strange. Later on, Clarence and Jackie Hoffman would never fully agree on exactly how it happened. Both remembered the terrifying moments when Katherine had each of the children by the hand, but neither had the courage to confess what they had seen after that. Or *thought* they had seen, because the scenes they had witnessed were so horrible and contradictory that they *must* have been imaginary. In one of them, Naomi and Joey chewed their way with bloody teeth through the boards that blocked the door, then looked around with eyes that gleamed, dull and obsessive, in a light that seemed to come from nowhere, their palates broken and full of splinters. Ludicrous: Of course it had to be imaginary, because Joey had been wearing a leather jerkin and Naomi a long, grubby smock. Whatever had happened, the fact remained that when Clarence and Jackie came to, the barrier and the door had rotted away as if infested by a plague of woodworms and the cold winter air was whirling through the kitchen. Jackie screamed her heart out for her missing children, but she didn't go out to look for them because she understood there were powers at work that a mere human being couldn't stand up against.

Many people saw the threesome walking the streets that night as they peered through the chinks between their curtains and windows. The witch was a mere shadow, eyes unseen—oh God, her eyes—but a few recognized the Hoffman children, although they couldn't make any sense of their strange, old-fashioned garments. As the wee hours advanced, more and more people saw the little boy in a doublet and breeches and the little girl in a thick cloak with a headscarf. Although their eyes looked glazed, they seemed to be walking with the witch willingly. There were those who believed they had seen the little girl carrying a toy windmill on a wooden stick that rattled around in the wind and made the child crow with laughter.

+I+I+I+I+

SHORTLY BEFORE DAWN, a shadow entered Griselda Holst's bedroom. The stench of rotten meat in the butcher shop had spread through the house like a sickly, sweet blanket, but Griselda hadn't felt up to going downstairs and throwing it out. Early in the evening, Jaydon had fallen asleep, stupefied by his high dose of lithium and barely—if at all—aware of what had happened. This in sheer contrast to his mother. God knows Griselda had prepared more thoroughly than anyone in town for the day when Katherine might eventually open her eyes . . . but now that it had happened, she found herself in a convulsive paralysis. It was too sudden. She hadn't even been warned! Did this imply that Katherine really *had* abandoned her?

Griselda needed time to think about what was ahead of her now. But the thoughts wouldn't come. With every unfamiliar sound, every creak of the baseboards, and every structural sigh, she got out of bed and haunted the silent upper floor of her house with the stub of a candle in her trembling hands, alert to every shadow that moved in the dark. But she was only chasing phantoms. Finally she fell asleep from exhaustion . . . and with every breath she took, the decay in the air whirled through her lungs and forced corruption into her pores.

She hadn't noticed the one shadow at her bedside. She merely muttered when her one and only friend finally gave her what she had desired so fervently all those years: a response. Suddenly those wide-open eyes were right in front of her, tethering her to the dream she was having. There was no face, no scenery, no mouth—only those eyes. Griselda tossed and turned, clammy with sweat, and buried her face in her pillow, for even in her dream she knew she was facing her worst nightmare. But then there was that voice. It wasn't really words, and it wasn't really language that Katherine used to tell her story. Griselda listened to it the way a rat in a cage listens to the jabbering of its tamer, unable to comprehend a thing. Katherine talked about the world and about being exiled from it, about deception and about the choices you made out of love, about being crushed by having to sacrifice the one you loved the most in order to save the *other* one you loved the most. Griselda couldn't tell exactly when the dream ended, but when she sat up in bed, gray morning light was slanting through the curtain. She had thrown off her quilt in her sleep, and now she looked down with disgust at her waxen, fleshy body, a body that had gone unloved for too long by others and by herself. Griselda had forgotten what it was like to make choices out of love; all she knew was tough self-preservation.

As a grim hubbub arose from a crowd of people who had apparently gathered on the town square outside her window, the oh-so-plausible idea began to dawn on Griselda that she could indeed save herself by sacrificing her son, Jaydon, to Katherine . . . thereby entirely misinterpreting what the witch had meant by her message.

THIRTY-ONE

"THIS IS IT, right?" Warren Castillo said after returning to the control center. "The end."

Grim nodded, hardly able to look him in the eyes. His coworker sounded like a frightened child begging his mother to tell him it was all just a nightmare, and Grim would have given his right kidney if he could have created that illusion for the both of them. His rectum, if he had to. "Warren, I appreciate that you came back, but if you want to be with your wife right now, I completely understand."

Warren had trouble restraining his emotions, but he pulled himself together. "No, I'm staying. The town needs us."

Then Grim did something totally out of character, something he had believed to be impossible under any circumstances: He took Warren in his arms and hugged him. It was a little awkward, but it strengthened both men at this moment of absolute darkness. All things considered, Warren had nailed it: Grim reckoned their chances of getting out of this alive to be about a zillion to one.

While he was feverishly trying to dream up a protocol, his thoughts kept on peppering him with shrapnel from the Delarosa talk: *What does the damn witch want from you, for crying out loud?*

Revenge.

We're assuming she wants revenge.

HEX didn't even have a calamity plan in place for the Day of Judgment, simply because no one had had the faintest idea how it would unfold. The only vaguely articulated scenario was to evacuate everyone as soon as possible, but if the rumors proved to be true, that road was a massive fucking no-go.

Grim had immediately sent Claire Hammer to find Eddie McConroy, the town's electrical engineer, to investigate the power glitch, but it soon became evident that what was cutting Black Spring off from the outside world was not a problem of the technical sort but a supernatural one. And it wasn't only the electricity. It was everything. The water supply system. The telephone lines. The gas connections. The whole goddamn shooting match. By nine o'clock that night, Robert Grim was convinced that Black Spring had been catapulted back into the seventeenth century, and his shock was so deep he could no longer clearly reflect on what that implied.

We have every reason to believe that if her eyes open and she starts uttering her spells, we will all die.

Focus! Think happy thoughts. Think babies. Blood!

He cracked his fingers behind his neck. "Okay. Right. We have to get help. There's no other way. The Point."

Claire stopped him in his tracks. "Robert, you know that without Colton Mathers we can't make that decision. . . ."

"Do you see Colton Mathers here?" He almost screamed these words. It was her forehead—it distracted him. He couldn't stand it. Claire had knotted her hair so tightly in the back of her head that it looked as if her face might tear loose from her skull at any moment and have to be secured with stitches. "No? Then I'm in charge!"

Claire recoiled. Grim suppressed the impulse to rip the elastic from her knot and release the pressure on her forehead, but instead he turned to the old CB. With sweat-soaked temples gleaming in the light of the Coleman lanterns, he tried to tune it in, but all he got was dead silence on all frequencies.

Lucy Everett came up with the satellite phone. "This won't connect, either, Robert. . . ."

"What the fuck!" He snatched it from her hands. "It's a fucking satellite. That doesn't have anything to do with our communication network!" He tapped the phone on the desk tentatively, looked at the screen, and hurled it into a corner. *Barbed wire, barbed wire,* he thought, attempting to calm himself, but his mind had a will of its own. *She doesn't want to be understood; she* must *not be understood. Katherine is a paranormal time bomb.*

"Robert, calm down," Claire's forehead implored, and it was all Grim could do to keep from screaming.

Marty Keller was in even worse shape. Not long after Warren had returned with the shocking news, the kid had snapped. He had thrown himself against the wall, flinging his hands and legs in every direction, while Lucy and Grim had tried to restrain him. His mouth was a wind tunnel of rage, revulsion, and fear. After finally managing to calm down, he hoarsely apologized. Said he was afraid of the dark, that it made him feel claustrophobic. But Grim knew what he didn't dare say out loud: it was the fear of death roaming the streets. Now he was slumped against the wall with a Maglite in his trembling hands, halfway through a bottle of lukewarm Smirnoff.

"We gotta kill her, before she wipes us all out," Marty now said from the floor. His voice sounded as if his tongue had turned to jelly.

"And how do you intend to do that?" Grim asked impatiently.

"The trick is to catch her unawares." Coming from someone who was up to his ass in a bottle of vodka, the logic sounded indisputable. "That's how those kids were able to stone her. She didn't see 'em coming. A quick bullet through the head is what I say. We might just stand a chance."

Grim managed to raise himself above Marty's hysteria, and that was good. It reinforced his self-confidence not to be the one without the backbone or even without common sense. "We've been trying to kill her for three fucking centuries," he said. "And, oh, by the way, her eyes were still shut then. You really don't get it, do you? The only reason they were able to stone her is because she let them do it. She *wanted* to be stoned. She wanted our morals to rot. It was all part of her plan. The

bleeding creek, the trial, that torture porn on the square, Tyler's suicide . . . it's all part of our ultimate collapse. Only then could she get
someone to cut her stitches away."

"Who do you think did it?" Claire asked.

"Jaydon Holst?" Warren said. "That wouldn't surprise me in the
least. Or his mother, that crazy butcher woman, as revenge for what
they did to her son."

Claire shook her head. "No way. She's as terrified with Katherine as
she was obsessed."

"I think it was Tyler Grant's father," Grim said.

"Steve? No . . . why?"

"I don't know." Grim frowned. His eyes strayed to the dark half of
the control center. The main screen was shrouded in gloom. Something was skittering around over there. Lucy had heard it, too, apparently, and she cocked her head. "Maybe because he's the last one you'd
expect."

"Makes no sense," Warren said, but there was a trace of doubt in
his voice.

Grim was staring into the darkness. Whatever had been moving
there now had friends. Failing to comprehend what his eyes were telling him, he saw a shadow flicker along the wall toward Marty: pitch-
black, wiry, fur teeming with fleas. Before Grim could utter a word,
Marty shouted and dropped the Maglite. Something shot away in the
rolling light beam: a humongous rat. About the size of a young cat,
Grim guessed.

"Son of a bitch! It bit me!" Marty moaned and scrambled to his
feet, holding his arm out in front of him. The skin on the back of his
hand was ripped and bleeding. Grim searched the area in front of the
screen with the beam of his own flashlight, then froze to the bone.
Five rats stared back at him with sly, beady eyes and wormtails curled
around their bloated bodies. One of the rodents was emaciated and had
a white film over its eyes; the animal was clearly sick.

Claire saw it, too, and said, "Let's get the hell out of here."

"Right," Grim said, unexpectedly resolute. "Lucy, help Marty with his hand. There's a first aid kit in the kitchen. Clean the wound thoroughly. It doesn't look deep, but I don't want him getting infected." *That's not what you're afraid of,* said a voice, but he suppressed it violently. "Claire, Warren, and I are taking the service car. We're driving up to West Point, and if we can't make that, for whatever reason, we'll stop at the first house in Upper Highland Falls and call whoever the fuck we can. You and Marty can take your car. I want you to look out for anything unusual—anything at all. If you find Katherine, stay away from her, but sound the alarm. Make sure the locals don't lose sight of her and report to Route 293 immediately—you'll find our car."

"We can't leave town, Robert . . ."

But Grim had to see for himself. The first summer houses down the road in Upper Highland Falls were less than three miles from the Black Spring border—for the first time in his life he was actually pleased by this fact—and the Army's MWR at Round Pond barely half a mile away. Katherine was a seventeenth-century witch, not an alien force field. Half a mile—how bad could it be?

-+-|-|-|-|-

BUT NO HELP would ever come.

None of them made it even halfway to the MWR lodge, where Christmas lights were still flickering. They almost lost Warren Castillo, and Grim had to pull a breakneck stunt to get him back that nearly cost him his own life. Earlier he had come close to killing all three of them, but Claire had had the presence of mind to call for a full stop just before the town limits so they could continue on foot . . . just in case.

Oh God. The images she showed them. Nothing in their everyday fantasies came even remotely close to such unutterable horror. Not in the darkest moments of their lives had they ever experienced such hostile melancholy, such destructive sorrow. As soon as they passed the back of the Black Spring welcome sign it was as if they had entered an invisible cloud of poisonous gas, leaden with pessimism, fear, and a craving for suicide. Grim had to keep Warren from smashing his skull against the road's pitted blacktop surface, but he himself yearned to crack his own head open and release the hideous thoughts that plagued it.

Somehow they managed to get back across the town limits of Black Spring. They stood like survivors of a shipwreck, hovering between two oceans of madness, gazing at the orange traffic light suspended in the distance at the MWR's safe haven. Before them was death, but Grim feared things far worse than death.

They shouted. They honked. They emptied the flare gun. They were joined by a couple of brave souls from nearby houses who were attracted by the noise, but no one came out of the MWR and no car came up the road. Claire suggested that the lodge might be abandoned (with all those Christmas lights?) or that their honking didn't carry more than a few hundred yards, but Grim didn't know who she was trying to convince. Sure, it was possible. Fifteen minutes later they returned with a shitload of fireworks from the back of Bob Tooky's pickup—Bobby was the local hotshot who always managed to fly under the radar during the holiday season. They put on a nonstop, phenomenal, red-and-green light show that lit up the contours of the hills and could be seen and heard for miles around, up to Highland Falls, West Point, and probably even across the Hudson.

But nothing happened.

No one came.

The only answer came a little before 11:30, after the air had cleared of the gunpowder smell: a shrill, maniacal cry that rose from the darkness *behind* them, a high-pitched, piercing shriek that seemed to freeze every joint in Grim's body. Yet he immediately recognized what it was—of course; what else could it be?

Farther back on the Black Spring side of the border, where the service car was parked, a peacock scurried across the road. It was followed by another . . . and another. From the undergrowth along the shoulder they jerked their heads toward Grim and his crew and began screeching their plaintive cries, first fragmented, then all together in unison. Grim had never thought that the sound of peacocks could fill him with such dizzying dread, but it did, and his vision began to go blindingly haywire. He forced down a lungful of cold air and managed not to faint. The air cleared his head a little—that was something, at least.

Warren turned toward him, and in the weak light Grim saw that all the fierce resolve he had mustered to rise up against whatever was happening had disappeared from his face, leaving only a bleak mask of resignation and fatalistic calm. "Peacocks. You know what that means, right?"

Grim didn't answer. He didn't have to. They were rats in a trap. With every passing hour that no one showed up, the chances of *anybody* showing up dwindled. Grim knew that. But what if the hours turned into days? What lay ahead of them then? As Grim thought about legends of freezing winters long ago, of starvation and epidemics and an empty town, the peacocks screeched their demented symphony, and after a while, Grim had the urge to screech along with them.

Maybe I ought to go for a walk, he thought. *Just walk a little ways down the road. What's there to lose?*

It was a tempting impulse and it felt like the inevitable thing to do . . . but Warren Castillo, grabbing his hand in a simple, grateful gesture and squeezing it gently, held him back. A captain was always the last to leave a sinking ship.

-|-|-|-|-

THE NEXT MORNING, Grim planned to go back to the town limits as soon as first light of day touched the Hudson sky. It was Friday morning and there were bound to be commuters on the road. Route 293 wasn't a major highway, but there were always cars. Always. They could wave them in when they got close.

And then—what next? What do you think the officials at The Point can do . . . Avada Kedavra and the witch is gone?

Grim pushed the thought aside. It was the least of his worries, as it turned out. For even from Old Miners Road he could hear it: the muted, restless clamor of a crowd that had gathered on the square and in the streets around Crystal Meth Church. Small groups of townsfolk hurried from every direction to see what was going on. Grim turned pale when he saw that many of them, fearful of the unknown that awaited them outside, had armed themselves with kitchen knives, hammers, baseball bats . . . and guns. Most held their weaponry limply at their sides, but their hands were clearly itching, and they were ready to draw blood if necessary. A neatly dressed woman whom he recognized as a nurse from Roseburgh had yanked the crucifix off the wall and was holding it grimly aloft as she followed the crowd, stumbling and wavering like a drunk.

"So here we go," Grim said. "Shit's gonna hit the fan."

Warren shook his head gloomily. "The shit hit the fan a long, long time ago."

He was struck with a strong sense of déjà vu: It was the town trauma all over again, the mass gathering of November 15 when the young convicts of the stoning were publicly tortured in the presence of all the citizenry . . . although not nearly as many people were out and about now as there were then. And the air was different, too, more oppressive. You could smell the stench of something bad about to happen. The townsfolk hadn't slept a wink and were chilled to the bone, but were surprised to find they had survived the first night. Now the dull light of day had given them fresh inspiration . . . in the form of rage that had replaced their fear like a changing of the guard. Incited by doomsayers like John Blanchard, they were beside themselves. They demanded to know what they were supposed to do.

And they demanded to know who was responsible.

As Grim made his way through the tangle of people at the intersection, Marty Keller suddenly burst through the crowd and clamped onto him. His eyes were wide open and red rimmed and there was a single teardrop of dried blood on his lip that had come from his nostril. "Robert! We've got to do something!"

"Marty, what the hell's going on?"

"There are riots everywhere. They trashed Market & Deli like a bunch of wild pigs. Someone threw a chair through the front window of Jim's Supply Store and they've emptied it, I tell you. People are hoarding—they're afraid no help is coming. But that's not true, is it? Help is coming, right?"

It's already happening, Grim thought, shocked. *This is all it takes for people to plunge into insanity: one night alone with themselves and what they fear the most.*

Marty was clinging to his arm now. He looked as though he was about to cry. "You don't think so, do you? I can see it in your face. They say fires have been lit at North and South 293, but they aren't attracting anybody. The electric companies must have known something's seriously wrong since fucking yesterday. And what about family members? They must have sounded the alarm, so close to Christmas. But why isn't anyone coming? I mean, what the fuck?"

"I don't know, Marty," Grim muttered. "Are you all right? You look like shit."

"I . . . I don't feel too well. Think I have a fever."

"Where the hell is Mathers?"

"Don't you know?"

"Know what?"

"Mathers committed suicide."

Under nearly any other circumstances, Grim would have sounded the alphorns with great pomp and ceremony and tooted his way across mountains and valleys to sing the happy news of Mathers's death, but now his only thought was: *Fuck me! So now that things are getting too hot, the weasel bails out on us.*

At least the councilman would have been able to calm the mob. Now the minister was trying to do the same from the paved square in front of the church, but his voice wasn't nearly strong enough to be heard above the prevailing turmoil. He looked grateful when Grim climbed the church steps and took over.

"Everyone, please!" he roared. "Calm down!"

"Stick it up your ass, Grim," a man in the crowd yelped—he was crying, which somehow upset Grim deeply. "Her eyes are open. What's the point of calming down now?"

Someone else piped up in agreement, and in no time at all the crowd became a wild tangle of furious eyes and shaking fists. They didn't chant slogans, and it was impossible to distinguish individual voices in that wall of sound, but the tone was one of rage and dissension. Church-goers, unbelievers, and those bereft of hope had all joined forces and whipped each other up with the same questions:

"Where is she?"

"What does she want?"

"What's she going to do?"

"What's going to happen to us?"

"It's our right as Americans to know!"

"Why hasn't anybody come to help us out?"

"Is it true that that coward Mathers did himself in?"

"What about our loved ones who were out of town—where are they?"

Soon the square was too small for so many lost souls, and the crowd began to push, shove, and squeeze, as if everyone needed to be where their neighbor was, and, once they got there, join in the surge to return to their original spot. Some lost their balance in the crush and some started fights. Grim saw a young woman get knocked over on the cobblestones, after which a fat man planted his heel on her face and broke her jaw.

This is madness, Grim thought. *Madness. Yesterday afternoon these folks were still ordinary, mild-mannered twenty-first-century Americans. . . .*

"A sacrifice!" John Blanchard screamed suddenly with the passion of the insane. "We must offer a blood sacrifice! Whoever it was that called this doom upon us! Bring him here! Stone him!"

Swelling cheers.

"Goddamn it, calm down!" Grim shouted, but only the few dozen people surrounding him paused to listen. "We're doing everything we can to get the situation under control, but there's no point in trying if we lose our composure! Since there's no communication, we're going to start giving updates on the town square every three hours. . . . Hey, listen to me!"

"Tell us somethin' we don't already know!" someone roared. "Who opened her eyes?"

"Yeah, who did it?!"

"Kill him!"

"Tear him to pieces!"

Grim began to panic: He was powerless before this mob. The rage that possessed them could not be exorcized by one man, and Grim sensed that something terrible was about to happen.

In the lower corner of the square, the crowd began to push back from Griselda's Butchery & Delicacies' shop window. Mother Holst and her son had just come outside, petrified in the presence of so many people. The expression on Jaydon's face was one of total bewilderment. Grim wondered if it was possible that he really didn't have a clue about what had taken place around him. Even the crowd fell silent, face-to-face with their heretic, their convict, their exile.

Griselda had offered sacrifices before: She knew the wordless vocabulary of such an act and made use of the moment by slipping back inside and pulling the door shut behind her.

"There he is!" someone roared, pointing with a desk lamp he'd brought from home.

"He did it!"

Yes, they all knew. They were all convinced. Who else could have opened Katherine's eyes but this piece of scum who had stoned her, who had been given his rightful punishment and been released at their merciful hands, only to turn around and take vengeance on all of Black Spring? This injustice ignited a maddening frenzy that no one could resist. Soon a semicircle of thirty or forty people closed in on the perpetrator, pushing forward with trembling hands and clenched fists.

In those last moments, Jaydon must have seen the dehumanization on their faces, and he turned toward the door of the butcher shop with his own face twisted in a primal grin of fear. What must he have thought when he realized the door was locked? What must have gone through his mind as he began to bang on the glass, his mother staring out with stony eyes, and saw the reflection of the ever-tightening circle closing around him?

Then, all at once, his attackers abandoned their last shred of restraint and the circle collapsed on top of him. In an instant they had him raised up above their heads like savages and carried him along over the undulating, roaring throng. Jaydon screamed his lungs out. From the church steps, Grim could see his eyes bulging as the townsfolk tore at his clothes, his limbs, his hair. It wasn't long before he fell, and the people attacked him like wolves. They sank their devouring claws and knives and hammers into his flesh, and Grim, all hope and resistance gone, went down on his knees and threw up on the concrete steps.

A deep loathing of his fellow men overtook him; he wanted to distance himself from it all, from being human in his core, for if this was humanity, he wanted nothing to do with it. He dropped onto the paving stones and sank into the cloudy depths in a bubble of his own consciousness, sweating and suffering for no one but himself, his throat choked by hot, sick tears and the sour taste of bile. He had no idea how long he lay there like that—until he heard the gunshot resonating against the surrounding houses. So he did have something in common with them after all: The noise made all of them flinch.

Grim looked up, wiped his face.

To the left of where the lynching had taken place was Marty Keller, lost in the rage of the populace. He was holding a black .38 Special over his head with both hands, still trembling from the force of the shot.

The haggard eyes of hundreds stared at him in disbelief, the blood still dripping down their fingers, their cheeks covered in sweat, their fires extinguished.

The kid had taken the goddamn service gun from the safe and had stuck it in his belt. Grim didn't know who had given him permission to do *that,* but he could have kissed him.

Then came the witch.

It ran through the crowd like a loveless prayer: *the witch, there's the witch, oh God, it's the witch* . . . All around him the people shrank back, exposing what was left of Jaydon Holst: a reduced pulp of luke-warm blood and convulsing muscle. But their eyes were not focused on him. All of them turned to face the same direction as their worst nightmare came to meet them, and Grim followed their gaze.

Katherine van Wyler came walking down Upper Reservoir Road with a costumed child in each hand, an absurd picture of calmness. Undaunted, without any impulse to hurry, she strode to meet her flock. For the first time, the townsfolk were greeted by the sight of her open eyes, and all their happy thoughts vanished at a stroke. Her pallid face bore the characteristic features they knew so well, but now the bloodless, needle-pitted flesh of her lips and eyelids had come to life and was gleaming like fresh tissue. Each and every soul on the square was struck by the fact that her eyes did not squint, nor did they possess the hideous, sickly luster they had expected in their darkest dreams. In fact, now that her ghastly mask of stitched-up eyes and mouth was gone, Katherine's face was strikingly *human.* Beneath the horror, its gentle lines and refined structure had become visible. She gazed at the streets, the houses, and the twenty-first-century people with a pent-up eagerness born of three hundred fifty years of dark-ness, smiling with amazement and delight. There was no trace of malice: just a mother and her children. Was that what she had wanted all along? The expression in her eyes could only be described as one of unparalleled bliss.

This was so out of keeping with the horrific images that Katherine had imprinted in their minds, and the fears they had lived with for all those years, that the residents of Black Spring naturally felt very ill at ease. Could this really be true? She wasn't an abomination—*they* had turned her into an abomination.

Robert Grim looked on in absolute terror as Katherine and her children reached the square. It had almost all the makings of a happy scene—but it wasn't happy; it wasn't the idyll it should have been. Because it was then that Katherine looked out over the terrified townsfolk and the sad remains of Jaydon Holst, and her eyes filled with sorrow.

And Grim thought, *We never learn.*

The crowd shrank back even farther. Some tried to make a run for it, but most understood that running away was pointless. As if at an invisible cue they all dropped to their knees, hundreds together, like Muslims turning toward Mecca. With lumps in their throats, they threw themselves at the witch's feet, entirely at her mercy, and begged her in a collective prayer, *We're sorry, Katherine. We accept you, Katherine. Spare us, Katherine.*

But there was still blood on their hands, and soon more blood would flow. From the corner of his eye, Robert Grim saw fate approaching in the form of Marty Keller, who held the gun in his trembling hands and stepped forward amid the kneeling throng.

Grim tried to stand up and scream at him to back off, but he stumbled and fell facefirst onto the paving stones. The air was knocked out of his lungs, and although he did scream, it came too late.

Marty shot, but Marty was a data specialist, not a marksman. Not only that, but never in his life had he been under such enormous pressure as the second he pulled that trigger. Little Joey Hoffman was struck in the neck and was thrown onto the pavement. A fan-shaped stipplework of blood sprayed Katherine's dress as she bent over in a shocked attempt to catch the child, but he was dead before he hit the ground.

Little Naomi screamed, stamped her feet, and threw her arms around the witch's neck. The next bullet, meant to blow away Katherine's curse once and for all, tore away the greater part of the girl's skull.

They heard the witch hoarsely gasp for breath as she lost the second child as well, staggering in a macabre waltz with the two little bodies.

This is a joke, Grim thought. *Some kind of terrible misunderstanding that I cannot get my head around.*

The witch looked up at Marty.

Marty began to scream. He tried to get away, but his feet wouldn't obey him. The witch came for him, crooked, calm, imprisoning his gaze in her attitude of contempt, grief, and merciless revenge.

She laid her hands on Marty's shoulders and looked up at him. For more than ten seconds she stared at the brand-new executioner, as the crowd backed farther and farther away. Then she coughed in his face.

Marty took one unsteady step backward and turned toward the crowd. He began to shiver and sweat as if he had suddenly been struck by a high fever, and blood spat furiously from his nose. He started hacking up blood, too, foaming on his lips.

"Help me . . ." he stammered, but his fellow townsfolk only shrank away, terrified of being contaminated by whatever it was that had seized him. Marty reached his hands toward them and fell to his knees. Grim saw dark, dimpled papules swelling up on his cheeks and neck to form a grotesque mask of flaky, depigmented scabs. His breathing faltered and he could no longer stop coughing, a hideous, rasping, croaking hiccup that sounded as if he were coughing up his lungs. Soon he fell to the street and started twitching, kicking his legs as his veins snapped beneath the skin and his gaping face turned a charred black. And while death took possession of him, he stared with blind, up-turned, accusatory eyes at the bewildered onlookers, one of whom was Dr. Walt Stanton, whose lips formed a single dreadful word: *Small-pox.* . . .

Katherine threw herself down and struck the pavement with both fists. The earth seemed to tremble. Cracks appeared beneath her hands, and Grim knew that on this morning of retribution, there would be no restraint, no reason. Only penance. The people of Black Spring had brought this on themselves: It was *they* who were evil, a human evil. *They* had created the evil that was Katherine by allowing the doom and gloom in themselves to gain the upper hand, by punishing the innocent and glorying in their own sense of righteousness. She had given them a *choice*. Now it was too late, and as everyone around Robert Grim started running in a vain attempt to flee Katherine's evil eye, this realization gave rise to a primordial horror that could only be matched by his earliest memories in the womb: that first loss, that first irreversible departure from a safe haven, that first longing to cling to what lay behind you.

The infant's only answer to the cruel hallucination of birth was to scream . . . so that's what Grim did.

THIRTY-TWO

LATE IN THE afternoon of Monday, December 24, Steve Grant woke up with water dripping on his face. He was lying on the frost-covered forest floor beneath an endless roof of skeletal branches. He tried to get up but fell back helplessly, rolled onto his side, and cracked through the paper-thin ice crust on the marshy undergrowth. Pain shot through his body, forcing his lips into a tight, white gash. Where the hell was he, and what was he doing there? His watch told him it was 4:30 on the twenty-fourth, but Steve couldn't grasp what that meant. Christ, he had been in the woods for four days and four nights.

He lay there apathetically for quite some time, listening to the unnatural silence of the woods. He was wet and numb from the cold and couldn't stop shivering. He was still wearing his funeral clothes. Stubble pricked his chin. His lips felt swollen and painful. His mouth was dry and sticky, coated with a layer of saliva that tasted like woodlands and pinecones. Steve tried to force his body back into the stupor from which he had awakened, but he stayed alert and clung . . . not to life, but to . . .

Tyler! Did she bring Tyler back?

That drove him to his feet. A sharp stab of pain in his back brought a grimace to his lips, and he leaned against a leaf-covered earthen wall. He looked around and saw groves of tall, ancient hemlocks on the slope, which he recognized without much emotion as the woods of Mount Misery behind his house. Apparently he had hidden himself in one of the overgrown trenches that the Military Academy had dug out when they used to drill in these parts—or maybe they dated back all the way to the Revolutionary War. Food for the minks and the rattle-snakes.

The events of the past days began to come back to him now, slow and fragmented, like pieces of driftwood washing ashore in the aftermath of a shipwreck. He remembered being home alone after Tyler's funeral, and that he . . .

Oh, God. The owl pellet. Tyler's hair. *She* had come to him and he had cut her eyes open. What in God's name had he done?

His memory of what had happened between fleeing into the woods and now was shaky. Was it possible that he had been in a state of delirium all that time? That his mind had been so paralyzed by the premonition of what he had brought upon himself that it had simply shut itself down? Apparently he had wandered around unawares and had slept for hours unawakened by his physical needs. Although you really couldn't call it sleep; more a state of semiconsciousness in which nightmares and reality merged like a double image in a stereopticon. And it *must* have been delirium. Why else would he seem to recall seeing a procession of chanting flagellants making their way through the woods and whipping their naked backs with knotted ropes as a cynical expiation? That must have been a delusion, right?

Somewhere a branch snapped, and Steve froze, his scalp crawling. Once again he noticed the unnatural stillness. No birds, no living things scurrying in the underbrush. Only the gentle whisper of the wind through the treetops and the occasional crunch of frosty leaves. But what had caused that branch to pop? Was it Katherine? *Had she been with him in the dark as he lay sleeping?* Or . . . could it be Tyler?

"Cut it out," he said hoarsely. The realization that, although in full possession of his faculties, he was considering the possibility that his dead son was trailing him in these woods caused the skin on his skull to tighten and sent shivers down his spine.

It has to happen one way or another, right? The promised resurrection—let's call it what it is.

But he didn't dare—he *couldn't*—invest his hope in . . . in what, really? Steve shuddered and tried to erase the possibility from his thoughts, but it refused to go away. Everything felt dreadfully wrong. The silence was wrong; the way the gathering twilight sank through the trees was wrong. What he had done pressed down on him like a dead-weight. He groped in his pockets for his cell phone, but apparently he had left it at home.

Steve didn't need a crystal ball to see what now lay ahead of him: He'd follow the trail back home and face the consequences of his actions. It was probably expected of him, and he felt the obligation. . . .

But the hell with it. The fact was that he didn't dare face it just yet. He prayed that Jocelyn, for whatever reason, had stayed at St. Luke's with Matt. Or that she had turned around at the first sign of . . . of whatever indication there was that Katherine's eyes were open, and had fled back to the safety of a Newburgh motel.

That's why the plan was so doggone perfect, right? Jocelyn had been in Newburgh with Matt . . . out of the way, safe and sound. Maybe it was Katherine herself who had waited for the right circumstances to be in place . . . so we could be kept out of harm's way.

He prayed this was true, but he didn't allow himself the luxury of believing it.

He would walk down the trail, but not the trail that zigzagged through Philosopher's Deep and back to his house. He would go farther south, across Ackerman's Corner where Spy Rock Valley switchbacked into town. And he would make a judgment. Size up the situation. If it could reasonably be assumed that everything was more or less all right, he would go home to see if Jocelyn was there. But not before. Because if the blood of Black Spring was on his hands, there was a terrible chance he was also responsible for the fate of his wife . . . and he didn't know if he was ready to face that.

Steve began to walk downhill in the last light of day. His body hurt all over and his stomach rose up in revolt, but after a little while he seemed to settle into a rhythm. Even if he hit Philosopher's Trail, he'd keep strictly to the right—he wouldn't even look down that way.

What were those sounds coming from town last night?

The thought came to him unbidden and he braced himself to withstand it—it had the power to almost knock him off his feet. Yes, there had been cold and pain, he now recalled. There had been hunger and cramps, and there had been uncontrolled shivering, but the physical suffering was nothing compared with the mental torture he had had to endure. The annihilating fear of the darkness he had unleashed had lent his stupor some seriously sick hallucinatory effects, probably boosted by a severe case of panic-induced oxygen deprivation. It had started with the noises. Along with the noises came the smells. And inspired by the noises and the smells came hideous images that should have robbed him of his sanity . . . and maybe they had. As he heard moaning, he saw people suffering, writhing and black-faced with swollen buboes in their armpits and necks. Not from smallpox, though: This was the disease of the Old World. As he smelled the stench of melting asphalt, he saw tar barrels being burned on the street corners in an effort to purify the miasmatic air; for some reason it was Pete VanderMeer who set them afire, with a homemade torch made from a pair of gasoline-soaked Levi's wrapped around a Rubbermaid mop, while bundles of straw hung from derelict façades to show which houses were infected. And as he smelled fire, he saw Crystal Meth Church ablaze. Behind the stained glass were the sick and the dead, and all of them were screaming. The faces in his vision were gaping masks of horror, and Steve turned away as if he didn't want to acknowledge the fact—not even in his dream—that his friends and fellow townsfolk were burning.

But always there was Katherine. Always she was standing there, motionless, looking on.

At a certain point, a totally surreal illusion had appeared before his eyes. In the middle of the town square, all the children of Black Spring were tightly swaddled in cocoons of white linen, some small, some a little bigger, and bound together in an enormous, upright network of tightly stretched sheets. The structure reached high in the sky and was shaped like a rounded cone, much like a female breast. You could see rosy-cheeked faces sticking out of the linen: the four hundred children of Black Spring, remarkably *alive,* dreamy luster in their glazy-dazed eyes. The true ordeal was for the parents, who were clamoring in the streets at the foot of the magnificent tower but collectively holding each other back, since it was clear that if one of them were unable to resist the temptation to take away their swaddled child the whole design would collapse, with all that would entail. On top of the breast was Katherine, like a gracious maternal nipple, pouring warm milk from a silver jug. It trickled down on all sides like a perfectly symmetrical fountain and was licked up by hundreds of eager children's tongues.

She's sparing the children, Steve thought, staring at the scene in his delirium. *Don't they get it? Don't let them ruin it; she's sparing the children. . . .*

Exactly where this grotesque image had come from, he did not know. In his most bizarre fantasies, he had never pictured such sinister madness combined with such a disconcerting, natural beauty. Steve had lain there, breathlessly staring, as if he were witnessing a miracle. But then the image had flickered, and it wasn't Katherine with her milk jug who crowned the nipple on the woven breast but Griselda Holst, the butcher's wife, naked as the day she was born. Fat and fleshy, she towered over the parents of Black Spring. Just as she had always offered them her meat, now she was feeding it to their children. She was giving birth to it. Streams of pâté gushed endlessly from her womb like after-birth and dripped down the sides of the fountain, staining the perfect linen and sticking in globs to the children's faces.

I'm not really seeing this, Steve thought. *No fucking way. I'm still in some kind of delirium. Must be. I'll wake up in a minute, just you wait and see.*

Again the image seemed to flutter—and now it was Katherine again, or maybe it had been her all along. And suddenly Steve understood that the townsfolk only saw what they *chose* to see: the obscene, the bad, the ugly. Whereas Katherine had created a vision of bliss, the parents knew only cruelty. And therefore they had to destroy it.

It was a well-thrown rock, and it hit Griselda-Katherine in the forehead, slicing the nipple like a box cutter. She flipped backward with flailing arms and tumbled into the web of swaddled children. A low *zinnng!* could be heard like the breaking string of a double bass, and suddenly children were being spewed from unwrapped cloths where the breast's flank had been destroyed. Soon the entire structure gave way and the masterpiece crumbled. Four hundred children flew into the air as if they had been shot from catapults. Steve's mouth fell open in a quaking hole of horror as he saw the sudden realization on their faces, heard their pitiful cries of fear and bewilderment. Their parents had failed their test, and now their children were crashing down on them in a rain of broken bones and clattering limbs. The lamentation that arose was not human and was far beyond the limits of madness, and even in his delirium, Steve knew that if he wasn't insane yet, it wouldn't be long before he was. Then the image faded from his mind and he sank again into darkness. The only thing it had left behind was the vague certainty that he held the outcome of this agony in his own hands.

As the woods opened before him, the sky was a blue-almost-black, the clouds a scalding shade of crimson. With a peculiar sense of homecoming, Steve realized where he was. Behind the barbed wire that ran along the path were the steep frozen pastures of Ackerman's Corner, where John Blanchard always put his sheep out to graze. The landscape had a strange dead look. He was surrounded by Highland Woods on three sides, and Black Spring lay below, invisible beyond the ridge. Farther southeast, the land fell away into the Hudson Valley and he could make out the glistening lights of Fort Montgomery and Peekskill. Families would be gathering for Christmas Eve dinners by now, the gifts already wrapped, the fireplace lit. The thought filled him with a strong sense of melancholy: The towns of the Valley seemed like exotic destinations, as tempting as they were unreachable.

Not unreachable. This is my Purgatory, Steve thought. *If you pass your test, Paradise awaits you, right?*

That brought him back to last night's vision, and a sour weight dropped onto him like a stone.

Sick fuck, he thought stupidly. Suppressing that, he began walking down the hillside toward Black Spring.

-+-|-|-|-

THERE WAS PROBABLY nothing in the world that could have prepared Steve Grant for his confrontation with the town in which he had raised his children.

Chaos had come to Black Spring. Only poetry or madness could do justice to the noises that rose in the radiant sky, even when he passed the historic waterwheel at the town hall and ran down Upper Reservoir Road. A thick, suffocating smoke issuing from the center of town pricked his eyes and made it difficult for Steve to breathe. But only when he came around the final curve and reached the top corner of Temple Hill did the spectacle fully reveal itself to him.

The town square was a surging horde of human abnormality. Now not hundreds but two or three thousand people were participating in the total pandemonium of bellowing, wailing, and brawling people. *Everyone* was there—all of Black Spring. And it was impossible to tell who was fighting what cause. Griselda's Butchery & Delicacies lay in ashes; other buildings were burning as well, billowing fires that lit the mob, grazed the treetops, colored the bronze statue of the washerwoman at the fountain with a reddish glare, and reflected in the odd-shaped windows of Crystal Meth Church, giving it the surreal appearance of rising even higher and looking out over the unholy throng with the eyes of the inferno. Steve tried to recognize his fellow townsfolk in the features of individuals, but realized it was impossible: Their faces seemed rubbed out, without eyes and without mouths, and not a single madman's face deviated from that of another. These were the faces of Black Spring, and Black Spring was at its darkest hour.

Something caused him to turn then, some force that seemed to come from outside him, and Steve could barely suppress a scream. It was Katherine van Wyler. She was standing on one of the hilltop driveways taking in the vista below, right in front of a twin chrome-tailpiped Grand Am that looked like it wasn't going anywhere anytime soon. Its hood and all its windows were smashed, and Katherine was standing barefoot amid a litter of broken glass. She didn't seem to mind, though: The witch observed the anarchy unfolding in front of her with a look of total impassivity.

"Stop it!" Steve screamed. He took a few reeling steps toward her on legs that had lost all feeling. When he was close enough, he lowered his voice, because that, too, seemed to have lost its power. "Please, make them stop. Don't do this anymore. It's enough. *Please.*"

But then Katherine slowly turned her head toward him. And as soon as he saw her face, he understood that what he had mistaken for impassivity was in fact a hollow shock closely mirroring his own. Then he knew. Of course; then he knew. *It wasn't the witch who was doing this.*

This was no penance, no retaliation. It was Black Spring itself.

Katherine raised her arm and pointed at the church.

Jocelyn and Matt, he thought . . . and suddenly he found himself staring at the crystal-clear image from his delirium, the image of the church burning. Inside it was teeming with ghosts, except now his wife and his youngest were among them. Matt's one eye patch was damp and ashen and Jocelyn's hair was tangled and dirty. Matt desperately clung to his mom, but Jocelyn screamed when an overhead arch exploded in sizzling cinders that whirled down on both of them.

It wasn't so much a recollection of last night's fever dream as an image being projected onto his mind. Katherine was showing it to him.

And Steve knew with a sudden sickening certainty that Jocelyn and Matt were indeed in the church, and that something terrible was about to happen, something he had to prevent.

"Matt's in the hospital," he muttered. All the color drained from his face. He seemed to lose control of his muscles. His mouth dropped open in a scream, *"Matt's in the hospital, he can't be there!"*

But Katherine's finger pointed mercilessly.

There were gunshots on the other side of the square and a woman started screaming, a harrowing scream that rose out over the rabble: *My baby, not my baby!* But Steve could hardly take it in.

Oh, Jesus. Matt's here; Jocelyn's here. Are you happy now with what you've brought about, you damn fucking fool? How's it even possible that Matt's here?

But was he really so stupid as to believe that they could have stayed in Newburgh, to escape a climax in a play as dark as *this*? That's not how tragedies were supposed to end, not even if you wished them to be untrue. So exactly who was he kidding?

He turned to the witch. "Where's Tyler?"

Katherine pointed unrelentingly toward the church.

That finger, that pointing, the full implication of what he had heard himself asking; those things frightened him even more than the hoarse, shaky quality of his voice.

"I have to know. Is Tyler in there?"

Nothing, only that finger.

Hurry up, you fuck; this is out of her control. It was never hers to begin with. The town's gone crazy and Jocelyn and Matt are probably in the middle of it. She's offering you a chance. . . .

Steve hesitated, torn at the sight of sadness, not evil, in the witch's eyes . . . and then he started running.

Steve plunged into the maelstrom.

—|-|-|-|—

HE STARTED OUT by making his way through the mob unseen. Once he got down to the middle of the slope, his view was entirely blocked by the confusion before him, and he soon lost his sense of direction. He was being jostled on all sides by filthy, sweaty bodies whose smell was sickening: a degenerated stench of fear, barely short of toxic.

Steve saw things he would never forget as long as he lived.

Eve Modjeski, the now former clerk at the Market & Deli, was staggering around, her face painted with blood from a huge gash on her forehead, droning a singsong jump-rope rhyme with eyes that seemed to have rolled back in her head. A man whose name he did not know but who used to work as a clerk at Marnell's Hardware was making his way through the hubbub with two naked toddlers in his arms whom he recognized as Claire Hammer's children. And there were dead bodies, too. Some had been shot—they were the lucky ones.

Struggling against the panic that seized him, Steve began screaming the names of his wife and son, but then he realized his mistake: His shrill voice inevitably drew the attention of those in his vicinity, who now *saw* him. People shrank from him on every side. Their eyes, in which he had until now only seen the dull luster of ignorance, gleamed with a sudden superstitious horror . . . and accusation.

"It's him!" a high-pitched voice shrieked, and Steve was shocked to see none other than Bammy Delarosa pointing her finger at him. "He's the one who brought the evil eye upon us!"

A frenzy of terror immediately seized hold of the crowd. While the woman who'd begun this furor shrieked the same accusation over and over—and that *couldn't* be Bammy, he *must* be mistaken, right?— others began to gabble prayers, giving him the sign of the horned hand or crossing themselves in a desperate attempt to protect themselves from their culprit. Incredulously, Steve stared back at them, recoiling slowly but bumping into others who reached out for him and clawed at his clothes.

They knew.

They knew he was the one who had opened the witch's eyes. He was like the scapegoat in a seventeenth-century trapper's colony . . . and you know how these stories went.

He yanked himself loose and started to run. The crowd parted before him and Steve took advantage of their terrified state, but the cry for his execution spread quicker than his ability to make his way through this impregnable lunacy. The only reason why he stopped when he recognized Warren Castillo was because he knew with an ir-rational clarity he wasn't *meant* to flee. Don't ask how, but it was true.

"Warren!" He hesitated, then touched the man's arm. "What the hell is going on here?"

Warren turned around and Steve saw that he was carrying the big-gest cleaver he had ever seen. "Steve," he said. "Haven't seen you in a while. How was the funeral?"

Steve took a step back. He could smell a foul odor in Warren's sweat. There was something about his voice that was off. He didn't like the tone of it. Not at all. Warren seemed heavily intoxicated, but Steve couldn't smell alcohol on his breath, only advanced decay.

"Have you seen Jocelyn?"

"Who's Jocelyn?"

Silence. "My wife."

"My wife?" Again that strange tone in Warren's voice. "My wife picked a bunch of juniper berries and ragwort in the woods this morn-ing. Says it purifies the air. Don't know who taught her that but . . ." He stopped mid-sentence and slid his thumb along the blade of his cleaver. "Why did you do it, Steve? Why did you have to open her eyes?"

He tried to reply, but when he opened his mouth he found his throat too constricted to force any air up. A second later, something exploded in his upper back and this time the air did come out; the blow literally pounded it out of his lungs. Steve was knocked down onto his chin. His teeth banged together and a blackness leaped up from the sneakers, boots, and slip-ons that were suddenly closing in on his vision. Groaning, he rolled over onto his back and stared straight into the upside-down face of Rey Darrel and the black-eyed barrels of the rifle he had been struck with.

"Well, look at you, boy," Darrel said. "Ain't you a sight to make a proud American weep?"

"Rey," he hissed. "Don't . . ."

"Fucking traitor."

And with that, Rey leaned back and booted him in the face. Steve heard a bony crunch and felt an excruciating flash shoot through his jaw. His head lolled loosely on his neck, his skull thudding on the cobblestones, and blood sprayed from his mouth in a vertical curtain.

Steve must have passed out for a minute then, maybe even for just a few seconds, because the next thing he knew he was being dragged, then lifted, as cries of incitement rose from the mob. He smelled pavement, smoke, madness. He choked on blood, coughed out a tooth. The world toppled over as he was raised over their heads, and Steve had the nauseating but intense sensation that he was flying and would never come back down. As the crowd carried him through the graveyard to his trial-less conviction, his face burned from the horrors, and his tightly stretched skin crawled over his skull as if it were preparing his mauled jaws for the scream that would herald the end of everything.

But then something peculiar happened.

The periphery of his vision swelled and wavered, and he had the sudden realization that he could see the faces of the townsfolk through the very eyes he had feared for so long . . . the eyes he had cut the stitches from. Maybe it was because, like Katherine, he now knew what it was like to be marked as a pariah. Maybe it was because, like Katherine, he was now the target of their anger. Or maybe it was just that only in the face of his impending death could he allow himself the freedom to embrace what had always seemed like his greatest fear in Black Spring but now felt strangely like coming home.

This revelation came as they got closer to the church and the nightmare around him grew darker. He felt intimately connected to Katherine, and there was an odd sense of relief in that, a sense of belonging. Steve relaxed into the hands of his inquisitors and felt their soothing touch on his body. He closed his eyes but still saw with Katherine's: Forced out of a merciful darkness, she was made to behold what three hundred fifty years of progressive civilization had done to her fellow townsfolk. Women being dragged along by their legs or their hair and thrown into the church. A chorus rising: *"Witch! Witch! Witch!"* Gasoline-drenched stacks of hay and rubber tires being piled up against the church walls. Theo Stackhouse, the now unmasked executioner of Temple Hill, raising a torch over his head. A woman with a baby in her arms trying to flee and being shot in the back of the head, after which her body was dragged into the church with the baby, alive, still clutched to her.

Then Steve, too, was thrown into Crystal Meth's narthex. He landed on a human pile and the church doors were slammed in his face.

He crawled away over limbs and skin and was nearly trampled underfoot himself, until he felt the cold ground beneath his hands. Steve pushed himself along on all fours, then hoisted himself to his feet. He took a few drunken steps, almost swaying back to the floor. The pain was a dull but dizzying pressure in his swollen face. His lower lip felt if it were hanging loose. His jaw was probably broken.

It wasn't long before the soft, gathering whisper of the fire outside became a roar that drowned out even the fury of howls and squeals from the townsfolk trapped in the church. And it wasn't long before one of the crystal-shaped glass panes blew in and a Molotov cocktail sailed through the dim arcade, exploding amid the pews halfway down the nave.

The blast of the heat was immediate and savage and illumined the desecrated church in a hellish glare. In that light he saw the church was full of people desperately throwing themselves at the barred doors, crashing into walls, trying to reach for the stained-glass windows, and ducking as the panes were blown in and flames boiled through the openings. He saw two people on fire—men, women, impossible to say. As he started down the center aisle to get away from the walls where the heat was building fastest, many reached out for him, begging him, asking him, why had he done it? He saw people he had once called his friends—Pete VanderMeer, who knelt with a dead child in his arms. When Pete looked up, their gazes met in a paralyzing moment, and the blank expression on his best friend's face turned into a mask of despair . . . and reproach.

Even here, he had been found guilty.

But was he? Was this really a hell of his making? His decision to cut open Katherine's eyes had only been a catalysis caused by his grief over the death of his son, and who was responsible for that? Jaydon Holst had made Tyler listen to Katherine's whispering. But could Jaydon himself be held responsible, after what the town had done to him? Could Katherine, after what they had done to *her*?

One evil spawned another, greater evil, and ultimately everything could be traced back to Black Spring.

Black Spring had brought this upon itself.

A chill overcame him of a nature so dark and primal that Steve began to shudder all over despite the terrifying heat. He loathed them. *Loathed* them. All of them. The ones inside the church and the ones out there. They were all the same. He saw that now.

His eyes had been stitched shut for all these years, but not anymore.

All those gaping mouths and bulbous eyes just shrieking at him with derision!

Let him be their pariah.

They couldn't blind him anymore—not him.

And as he reached the chancel, he cursed them all. His upturned face was blasted by scintillating gusts of embers that came down from the almost transparent membrane of fire devouring the roof, but he didn't mind: It was his fire. Damn those people. Damn their never-ending chain of selfish choices. Damn their refusal to seek reconciliation, damn their inability to love, damn their sick insistence to see the ugly, not the good. Tyler had been different; Tyler had had dreams. Damn, damn, *damn*; cursed be them who had taken his Tyler away from him!

"Dad?"

Steve had found the door that everyone else had forgotten, hidden in a recess behind the lectern. It was as if his feet had taken him there. But now he stopped abruptly. He was still trembling, not from the cold but from a feverish heat born of rage. He had already snatched the key ring from the peg, and clutching it tightly, he turned around.

It was them.

All the way across the church, through a haze of thickening smoke: Jocelyn shielding Matt from the flaming cascade with her body. Her naked back and buttocks were scorched and festering with blisters, but when she looked up, the face was undeniably hers. Steve saw her lips move and absently realized she was whispering his name, as if she were dreaming of seeing an angel. Soon her voice swelled to a husky screech: "Steve, is that you? Oh, God, Steve, help us!"

But it was Matt who had spotted him first: He had awakened from his catatonic state, and now he tore himself loose and started running toward him.

And Steve felt his face darken.

The sight of his youngest son, pale skinned from the hospital and still wearing one stained eye patch, finally brought home the full meaning of his family's eternal dichotomy and his grief over Tyler . . . Tyler, where all this had started. Those few paralyzing seconds robbed him of whatever defenses remained. He felt the eyes of the damned upon him. They had been drawn by Matt's ardor and came rushing down the nave in a frenzy, and he shrank back against the heavy door, opening it with trembling hands.

"Dad, wait!"

He looked down the spiral staircase. A deep, dark hole. Total darkness.

Some of the paths you set out on lead through such a darkness, and to walk them would be immoral or madness.

Not madness, Steve knew. *Love.*

Katherine had been forced to sacrifice her one child to save the other. What else could that be but love?

Steve drew back in the doorway and put the key in the lock. He closed the door behind him, twisted the key, and slammed the bolt shut, just before the first hands could reach him.

-+-|-|-|-|-

HE TUMBLED DOWN the steep flight of steps.

He hit rock bottom with a thud and lay there just as he had landed, curled up on the cooling stones and groaning with pain. The vault was a pitch-dark, the kind of dark your eyes would never become accustomed to. But what it lacked in sights, it made up for in sounds. He heard the door rumble, a ceaseless pounding on unyielding wood, rising over the roar of the fire. And he heard people screaming. They sounded just like ghosts. Once, he thought he heard his own name—a tormented cry of sorrow and pain. A thought threatened to surface, but he violently repressed it.

He rolled onto his back. Opened his eyes, closed them, opened them again.

It was rather comfortable here. This darkness suited him well.

It turned his thoughts to love. Somewhere, in another world, he could hear dying screams, and he imagined the damned were singing. Steve rolled himself up into a ball, making himself as small as he could, and stuck his fingers in his ears. He began to sing along.

Just before he had sung himself to sleep, he whispered, "I love you, Tyler."

But in that darkness, no one answered.

-+-|-|-|-

AND AT THE same time, Katherine van Wyler arose, and she arose looking just like every child of Black Spring had seen her in their worst nightmares. A misbegotten witch appealing to forces that were older than mankind itself, forces from parts of the universe that were old before the earth was born. She stood there on Temple Hill facing the burning church and made druidic arm gestures toward the heavens, murmuring corrupted words and sounds in a language that none of her flock could identify, but made their every hair stand on end. The few who saw her began to scream, but Katherine continued with her underworld incantation to the skies . . .

. . . and all the while, she was crying.

The people of Black Spring started walking eastward: an everlasting procession of broken souls, some of them naked, all with the same dazed, blank look on their faces. They all walked away from the burning church, as in a dream. When they reached Route 293, they didn't follow it, but simply disappeared into the forest on the other side. It was almost three hours before the first of them emerged on a sleepy town road south of Fort Montgomery. Behind the windows of clean-limned upstate colonials, parents stole downstairs from their attics with armfuls of colorfully wrapped gifts. They laid them out in the glow of dying hearth fires, while outside on the road the nightmarish parade passed endlessly by, unseen. The people of Black Spring faded away underneath the highway overpass and headed straight for the Hudson.

One by one they walked into the river, disappearing under the icy cold water where they were seized by the current.

Many hours later, the sky over the Highlands flushed a blood red.

And when daybreak finally arrived, hundreds of swollen bodies were seen floating languidly under the Tappan Zee Bridge on their way toward New York . . . giving the earliest risers a glimpse of somebody else's nightmare.

It was Christmas Day.

EPILOGUE

STEVE GRANT WOKE up with pale sunlight in his face and the foul taste of copper in his swollen mouth. His eyes were stinging, silty and inflamed, and he had to get them adjusted to the light before he could fully open them. He was lying on the slate tiles of his dining room floor.

So he had come home. He tried to piece together how or when he had left the burning church, but he couldn't. The time that had lapsed between shutting the chancel door behind him and now was one big, black hole. Like a vault in the earth.

He heaved himself up and clenched his teeth from the pain. What remained of his clothes were full of scorch marks and stank of smoke. The skin on his hands was glowing a fiery red. He had twisted something in his back and his knee throbbed like a bad tooth. But his face was the worst: The left side was puffed up like a balloon, as if there was a terrible deformation of the jaw under the skin. Yep, broken, no doubt about it. Probably gone septic by now. *If you had any hopes for running for* America's Next Top Model *this season,* he thought without emotion, *you probably need to reconsider.*

He hoisted himself to his feet and gazed dully around. Everything looked the same, but it wasn't; it felt disorientingly different. The silence in the house crept up on him. It was so oppressive that he could hear the blood ringing in his ears. Something felt wrong. Very wrong. The Christmas tree was still standing in Jocelyn's Limbo, undecorated. They had set it up so they could decorate it the afternoon they came back from the mall. But that's when they had found Tyler.

Now it had started to lose needles.

Something caught his eye under the dining room table: a frayed black piece of thread. A stitch cut from Katherine's eye.

But where was she now? And where was Tyler?

Steve lurched into the hallway. On the way, he glanced in the mirror and immediately wished he hadn't. The face staring back at him—with its deep grooves, sinister red glow, and haunted, bulging eyes—was an atrocity in which he recognized nothing of his old self. His left cheek and lower lip were a bulbous purple-going-black, and there was a dark beard of crusted blood all over his lower face. That jaw was going to need wiring. He had a suturing needle in the medicine cabinet, but that wouldn't do the job.

He limped to the front door and drew the panel curtain aside with his thumb, then peeked out. The lawn was wet with dew and glistened in the bleak sunlight. It was going to be a nice day. Yet the outside also felt wrong, and the air was heavy with that same oppressive silence. He gazed westward down Deep Hollow Road, but all he could see were the wooden and brick houses waiting in the morning sunshine for people to come out. But they never would, he realized. Even from here, he could sense that the houses were empty. Steve wondered what he would see if he were to walk farther into town. The air smelled clean; there was no trace of smoke. There was just . . . nothing. Only that eerie silence.

The authorities would probably come before too long. And then what? It would be just like in February 1665. When they came, they would find nothing but this silence. Three thousand people gone without a trace. A ghost town.

That's right, he thought. *And I'm the mayor.*

Steve started to laugh—in fact, he roared with laughter. His laughter came in odd, hollow bursts and resounded obsessively through the abandoned house, like the laughter of a dead man. It brought to mind the pendulum, that mighty, medieval torture machine that had hung over their lives the day he and Jocelyn came home and found Tyler dead: razor-sharp, swinging back and forth, back and forth, uttering its merciless sentence. Well, the judgment had been passed; the sentence had been executed. Now he was nothing but a pile of stinking body parts laughing in the corner of the hallway.

Soon his laughter turned to screaming.

Steve had no clear recollection of the next minutes, except that he was cold to the marrow of his bones, so cold that he knew he would never be warm again.

When he came to, he found himself sitting halfway down the hall, back slumped against the wall and legs splayed out. On the floor next to him was a selection of items from his suturing kit: catgut, a scalpel, tweezers, a curved needle. It vaguely alarmed him that he couldn't remember getting it from the cabinet, nor what his intention had been. His face needed metal, not cotton.

He lay there empty-headed until a thought finally erupted: *Jocelyn and Matt are dead. I hope you're aware of the fact that you let them burn last night? They're dead, just like Tyler.*

His arm slammed against the wall as if it had a life of its own, clawing in vain for something to hold on to, then sank back down. He was trembling all over—*so cold!*

Here, at the end of everything, the paralyzing, almost unbearable certainty dawned on him that he had made the wrong decision. Steve had escaped from the darkness, but it was the light, that damned light, that made him see it. Sacrificing one child to save the other hadn't been Katherine's choice, it had been the decision made by the judges. And was he so naïve as to think they would have let her daughter live after having flung Katherine's body into the witch's pool?

Now he was the judge. In his final ordeal he, too, hadn't shown any desire for reconciliation; had presumed only the worst of people, like all the townsfolk of Black Spring. Did he really believe that he deserved to welcome Tyler with hands that were filthy with the blood of his wife and second son? And even if Tyler *did* return, that he would be anything but a revolting abomination?

Oh, the darkness. If only he could enter back into it! If only he could undo his deeds! He didn't want to see what awaited him at the end of this unforgiving light. All he could do was cling to the dwindling hope that his obsession with Tyler's death had been based on reason.

Not reason, he thought. *Love.*

There was a knock at the door.

Steve gasped.

He looked up.

In the sunlight, behind the panel curtain, was a shadow. Only its silhouette was visible, waiting, motionless.

The silhouette . . . of a boy?

Steve sat in the hallway, paralyzed with fear.

And he wished it would go away. Oh, God, please—if only he could make it go away. What awaited him there was not his son, and what he felt was not love, but a fathomless abyss that was opening beneath him and was much, much deeper than love.

The knock came again.

A slow, loud thud—only one.

He saw the shadow of knuckles resting on the windowpane.

Steve Grant picked up the needle and the catgut, and as the thing at the door kept knocking and knocking, he started on his eyes, hoping the loneliness of the eternal darkness would offer him a bit of comfort from the cold.

ACKNOWLEDGMENTS

Sorry for that—I got a bit carried away.

When I think about the people that scared me when I was younger, I have to start with my babysitter. Her name was Margot, and each time she watched me and my sister, she used to tell us a bedtime story. I was seven years old when Margot told us the story of Roald Dahl's *The Witches* in a detailed episodic style, like the TV series you watch on Netflix today. After each cliff-hanger she turned off the lights, and there I was, lying paralyzed underneath the covers, bulging eyes staring into the dark, watching her words come to life in my mind's eye.

It must have been around the same time that my uncle Manus took me out for a hike in the woods and told me about the fairy rings we ran into on the trail. You *had* to walk past them with your eyes closed if you wanted to live to tell the tale.

That same year—1990—the film adaptation of Roald Dahl's book played in Dutch cinemas, starring Anjelica Huston as the Grand High Witch. Bless my innocent pre-CGI heart . . . but, damn, that movie is scary for a seven-year-old.

I found out the hard way.

Each night for the next six months, I screamed for my mom, seeing witches in every shadow on the landing outside my bedroom door. By day, I was terrified to walk the streets by myself . . . let alone cross the woods near my home. There could be witches anywhere. Every woman was a suspect. The book and movie had left me severely traumatized. The witches in Roald Dahl's tale wear gloves to hide their hideous claws, so you can imagine how slowly winter passed that year.

And each time I came across a fairy ring, I walked past it with my eyes closed.

Later I stopped believing in witches, so I did it as a balancing exercise.

Like most people, all great writers die at some point, but I bet if Roald Dahl could have been around to read what he did to me, he would have leaned back in his chair with a wide, contented grin on his face. He was the kind of writer who secretly rejoiced in traumatizing innocent little children . . . and their parents, for that matter.

Let me tell you a secret: I turned out the same way. When *HEX* first came out in the Netherlands, I started getting hundreds of messages from readers whose nightmares had been haunted by Katherine and who had to leave the lights on at night. Ah, that silly grin on my face! It's still there. And now this book is in your hands, wherever in the world you are. If you're one of the readers who this story managed to scare, drop me a note on Facebook or Twitter. I'd love to grin some more.

So thank you, Roald Dahl. Thank you, Margot and Manus. Thank you for my traumatized childhood. Without you, this book couldn't have been written.

The book you've just finished is different from the original novel *HEX*, which appeared in the Netherlands and Belgium in 2013. That book was set in a small Dutch village and ended on a rather different note. As an author, you rarely get the chance to rewrite a book *after* its publication. But when my agents sold the English language rights to publishers on both sides of the Atlantic, I was suddenly presented with the opportunity to make the original book work in a wholly new environment, with a fresh backstory.

Don't get me wrong: it's not that I didn't like the Dutch setting. I loved the Dutch setting, and I loved the utter *Dutchness* of the book. Not in the sense that the witch smoked pot or stood behind some Amsterdam red-framed window; I'm talking about the secular nature of small-town Dutch communities and the down-to-earthness of its people. If a sane person sees a disfigured seventeenth-century witch appear in a corner of the living room, he runs for his life. If a Dutch person sees a disfigured seventeenth-century witch appear in a corner of the living room, he hangs a dishcloth over her face, sits on the couch, and reads the paper. And maybe sacrifices a peacock.

But when I see a creative challenge, I take it. And what fun it would be! I had a book that I loved, featuring characters whom I loved, and here I had the opportunity to relive it all without having to face the horrors of a *sequel*.

Instead, I could create an enhanced version—a *HEX 2.0*, if you will—with new rich and layered details, culturally specific legends and superstitions, all without losing touch with the Dutch elements of the original. Katherine Van Wyler came to the new land on one of Peter Stuyvesant's early ships. The rural town of Beek became the Dutch trapper's colony of New Beeck, later renamed Black Spring. The Dutch characters became Americans, but with the down-to-earth quality of the Dutch. The dishcloth stayed. So did the peacock. And the public flogging of minors, a common and fun tradition we celebrate annually in many a small town all over the Netherlands.

The upshot of being Dutch—this is a cliché about us, but it's true—is that I speak several languages. English almost as fluently as Dutch. That allowed me to not only read but also edit Nancy Forest-Flier's fantastic translation of the book and find my own voice in English. Working on the book in a language that's not my mother tongue gave me strong new insights into the plot, the most important of which was about the ending. It had to go. It felt off. There was a much scarier and better way I could end this tale.

So that's what you've just read. The last several chapters, from the moment things pretty much start going downhill for Black Spring, are all new. I wrote them in English, and I had a blast while I was at it. In my opinion, it's become a better book.

Of course, I hear you wondering: how did the Dutch version end?

I'm not gonna tell.

Bribe a Dutch person—maybe they will.

I'd like to take the opportunity to thank Nancy, who is a truly remarkable translator, and a pleasure to work with. The importance of translators can never be stressed enough, as they create the opportunity for people around the world to discover new worlds and wonders in words. Nancy is terrific. And so is Liz Gorinsky, who edited this book. Even when Nancy and I thought we had tackled all the culturally specific issues that arise when you relocate a novel, Liz discovered so many interesting anomalies. Liz, you made this an even better book, and I learned a lot from you. So thank you.

Others on Team *HEX* are Oliver Johnson (the wonderful UK editor, and a wonderful guy), Rod Downey, Vincent Docherty, Jacques Post, Maarten Basjes, and all the fine people at Tor Books in the United States, Hodder &

Stoughton in the United Kingdom, and Luitingh-Sijthoff in the Netherlands. A special thanks goes out to Ann VanderMeer, who, apart from being a fantastic and kindhearted person, boosts the careers of so many young writers. Ann, I cannot thank you enough for what you've done for me. The same goes for Sally Harding, the most classy and witty literary agent I could wish for. Together with Ron Eckel, Sally has done the near-impossible for any writer that comes from a small, faraway country. Sally and Ron: you rock and you know it.

Anja, your help with practical issues has been invaluable. You hand me a pen before I even know I need to sign a book, and you have eyes where I do not. Wes, you're still the creative brain behind so many clever finds, and so often come up with the perfect solution when I'm stuck. You're also my best buddy in life. The Grant family: sorry for slaughtering your dog. My own family: ~~sorry for slaughtering~~ I love you. Francine: you especially. And David, thanks for standing tall beside me. Always you.

Now.

All that I said about the new setting doesn't make Black Spring any less real. You've just come from there, right? And when you were there, you experienced some pretty dark times. I can't say it ended too well for the town.

If you're in New York some day, you can take a car and drive up north along the Hudson. It's a beautiful ride. Cross the Bear Mountain Bridge and take 9W past Highland Falls and into the realm of the Black Rock Forest. The officials at West Point have sealed off everything to the left and right of route 293, where the town of Black Spring used to be. You can see it for yourself, although the fences and barracks are not particularly interesting. At some point, someone will come and tell you to go away—the kind of someone you are inclined to take orders from.

Instead, I'd suggest you go for a hike in the woods up north. It's rugged land, but there are a few trails, and most lead somewhere. Listen to the silence. It might be a little eerie, out there on your own, but I assure you the sound you heard was only the wind in the trees. No birds. No beasties.

None whatsoever.

If you come across a fairy ring, make sure to walk past it with your eyes closed.

But don't keep them shut for too long.

You never know what you might bump into.